KIDS SHOULDN'T KNOW

a novel by

STANLEY G. MIDDLETON

Kids Shouldn't Know
Published: December 2018
Printed in the United States of America
ISBN: 978-0-692-17993-2

Cover design by Self-Publishing Relief

This book was published with the assistance of Self-Publishing Relief, a division
of Writer's Relief.

CONTENTS

Dedicated to:
Jan, who ignited the fire,
Brandon, my son,
Brandon Xavier and Logan James, my grandsons

ACKNOWLEDGEMENTS

Every new writer must go through some of the same things I have gone through—no one is going to read this book, this book is terrible, it will never be published, why am wasting my time? But for a cohort of close friends and professional colleagues, I might have abandoned the effort long ago. They not only told me it's good, they said they get the message. They know what I am saying and it's important and needs to be said.

How can I ever thank them? My lifelong friends, Tony Tarntino, Todd Kane, August Dorsett and Sharon Iden have been my soul mates throughout this effort. August Dorsett was a member of the faculty of the Theater Arts Department of Towson University in Maryland. His sharp criticisms kept me on focus. Jonny Pine, an absolute computer wizard, taught me everything electrical about getting my work online and was the youngest person to read my work and urge me to get it printed. Imagine the reassurance of a youngster like Jonny letting you know that your book could appeal to a wide range of audiences. Warm thanks to my young friend, Tony Villa, for telling me my writing is best seller quality. No matter how the book fares, that is certainly a kind and encouraging thing to say to a first-time author.

Special thanks to Dr. Douglas Butler and John Bowland, both authors of numerous books, who encouraged me to keep working at the book. Thanks to a cast of other folks who have critiqued my work: Jan Huber, Barbara Dean, Pam Bell, Dr. Stephen Gumeiner, Tommy Washburn, Dr. Jeremy Roth, Lois Carpenter, Dr. Jon Oletsky and my good buddy, Tom Riddle. My sister, Rosemary Baum, did a lot of typing for me and has been my confidant. My good friend, Scott Moses, himself a struggling first-time writer just like me, has brought humor and hope to many a night of work and worry, both of us fantasizing on a day when we will publish.

I thank Paulette Kinnes my editor from Platinum Editing Group and all my friends at Writer's Relief, Jen, Michael, Catherine, Carol and the entire staff.

I thank my son, Brandon, and my grandsons, Brandon and Logan, for their tolerance and support of their father and grandfather being cooped up in his room pounding away at the keys.

CHAPTER 1
HOW SERIOUS COULD SOMETHING BE

Mrs. Wilcamp frowned with worry as she watched her youngest son troop down the front steps of their row home with his older brother. Something weighed heavily on his mind. She was certain of it. A part of her wanted to reach out to her son and ask him what was troubling him. But another part of her was angry with him and refused to allow that maternal instinct to control her. Why, she asked herself mournfully, did Jeremy have to be a boy?

Her heart had been so set on having a daughter, and certainly, she wanted to have more children, but after Jeremy, she could never have either. Jeremy's difficult birth had ended all hope of having the daughter she dreamed of. The obstetrician's explanation for what went wrong had not mattered to Mrs. Wilcamp. Jeremy mattered.

There would be no fancy clothes, no cute hair-dos, no dolls and dances, no magnificent wedding with all the trimmings that she and her husband had not had, none of it, because of Jeremy. If it had been the daughter she had wanted instead of Jeremy, the obstetric catastrophe would not have happened. At some level of her mind, a level which could never be put into words, she blamed Jeremy.

Be all that as it may, Mrs. Wilcamp sensed her son's uneasiness. Everything about her son, his mood, the anxious expression on his face, the caution in his footsteps, told her that her son's mind was distracted. She was not accustomed to seeing Jeremy so pensive this early in the day. But as her sons hopped into the car her husband was warming up against the unusually cool early October day, she reminded herself that Jeremy was only fourteen years old. How serious could something be that a fourteen-year-old, eighth-grade schoolboy was worrying about, and she shrugged, relaxed the muscles of her face, closed the front door, and headed toward the kitchen where breakfast dishes waited.

The morning news, weather reports, advertisements, and an occasional country song filled the car with idle chatter from the radio. Jeremy stared at his brother, who sat in the front seat, cramming for a history quiz. Neither son spoke because their father did not like talking while he drove. Brian got out of the car at Saint Michael's High School, and half a mile farther, Jeremy hopped out at Saint Michael's Monastery Church.

"Bye, Dad."

"See you tonight." His father gunned his old Chevy up from first to second gear and drove off down Patterson Parkway to work.

As his dad shifted the gears of his 1951 Chevrolet, Jeremy noticed puffs of black smoke spewing from the exhaust.

Hmm, Dad's going to be getting a new company car soon. He should. It's seven years old. That'll be nice. Man, what if he got that new 1958 Cadillac Eldorado? What a dream-boat that thing is. Fat chance of that, Wilcamp. It'll be another Chevy or a Ford. But, so what? It'll be new.

Jeremy smiled as he entered the altar boys' room and saw his best friend, Stevie Stockton, rummaging through the cabinets searching for a cassock and surplice that fit him.

"Hey, Steve."

"Hey, dude. You've got to get a move on. We'll be late."

Jeremy tossed his blue duffel bookbag and lunch onto one of the church pews in the back of the altar boys' room, took off his jacket, and hustled to the clothes closets.

Jeremy and Stevie wore the same sizes. At five feet eight inches, both were taller than most of their classmates. They were lean and fit, because they were always outside doing something, playing, riding bikes, or making money cutting lawns and doing yard work.

But they were also a year older than their classmates. Maybe coincidence or blind fate had put Jeremy and Stevie into the first grade at the same time, and in the same school, but whatever it was, it had created two inseparable friends. Both the Wilcamps and the Stocktons had been forced to move to Baltimore in late 1951 because of job re-locations. Jeremy and Stevie had not been able to start the first grade until they were seven years old, a year later than most of their classmates.

"Must have been lousy high school kids in here for the 7:00," Steve said. "Look at the mess. Father Francis is going to be mad when he sees this place all junked up. Bet he blows his mind over it at the altar boys' meeting tonight."

Jeremy stopped and glanced at Steve, pawing his way through the cassocks. Jeremy's heart pounded, and the color faded from his face as Steve had made him remember the altar boys' meeting.

Steve did not notice the transformation and poked him gently in the stomach. "Come on, you've got to get ready."

Jeremy came to life and resumed digging through the cassocks.

"You're coming to the meeting, aren't you, Steve?" Jeremy posed his question nonchalantly without looking up from the long black cassocks.

"Are you kidding? My Mom would never believe that I'd even think of not going to an altar boys' meeting."

3

"Mine too."

"Can I meet you outside before the meeting starts, Steve?"

"Sure. I'll keep an eye out for you, but you know I'll be here. We can meet at Abington Road and Dennis Street if you want."

"Yeah, Stevie, that'll be fine." *Boy, that's a relief. At least Stevie will be here.*

They zipped up the cassocks which completely covered their street clothes, and pulled the white surplices, which covered their upper bodies except for their forearms, over their heads, making two handsome altar boys.

They scurried up the stone steps with Jeremy hoping that Steve had not realized how desperately he needed his companion to be with him that night.

"You get the wine and the water." "I'll go light the candles," and Steve sped off for the sanctuary.

Jeremy prepared the wine and the water, pouring them into glass cruets. The red wine, to be imbibed by the priest during the service, symbolized the blood of Christ. The blessed water was used by the priest to rinse his fingers after serving communion to the parishioners. The white wafers of communion symbolized the body of Christ.

Catholic dogma taught that the white wafers are the body of Christ, and the wine is the blood of Christ. Stevie did not believe either tenet. He believed that he was eating a piece of bread when he went to communion and not the body of Christ. And the wine is wine, not Christ's blood. He was smart enough, however, to not make an issue over it in school, in church, or at home. Jeremy didn't think about it at all.

As he wiped a few drops of the wine off the cruets, Jeremy wondered how he had gotten into this mess. He hadn't wanted to join the altar boys, but his mother had forced him. Brian had done it. He had to do it too.

His whimpering appeal to his father had earned him nothing more than an indifferent glance from behind the newspaper. Arguing with his mother only made her mad, and he never won. He hadn't bothered. She had forced to him join this past summer. His parents had never encouraged Jeremy to join the altar boys until Brian decided that he didn't fit in with altar boys anymore when he reached sixteen. Then his mother had demanded that Jeremy join. She wanted to maintain her membership in the altar boys' mothers club.

Jeremy had impressed Father Francis, the moderator of the altar boys, with how quickly he had learned the Latin and understood the role of the altar boy at mass. He rewarded Jeremy by allowing him to serve the 8:00 mass with his best friend. Every altar boy coveted serving the 8:00. It was the daily mass for the school children. If an altar boy served the 8:00 mass, he didn't have to get to school until 9:15, maybe even later, plenty of time to goof off after mass.

Jeremy whiffed the scent of the rich wine.

"You pretty sharp on your Latin?" Steve's question brought Jeremy back to reality. "We've got Father Brendan. He doesn't miss much. You want to go over anything?"

"No, I've got it all down okay."

"If we had any priest other than Father Brendan, you could mumble through the Confiteor. I know the words and can carry us. But Father Brendan will be listening to you because you're new, and he'll be on your case afterwards if you aren't perfect and go blabbing about it to Father Francis. I've seen him do it to lots of beginners."

"Okay," Jeremy yielded. "Let's run through the Confiteor."

With its long sentences and complicated Latin, the Confiteor challenged the memory skills of every altar boy.

"Confiteor Dei Omnipotente." I confess to Almighty God…Jeremy got no further, as Father Brendan entered the sacristy.

"You fellows ready?"

"Yes, Father," Steve answered, and went to help Father Brendan into the vestments worn by the priest for mass.

Jeremy watched Father Brendan don the vestments, whispering prayers for each one and kissing them before putting them on. The oak flooring beneath Father Brendan squeaked to his movements before the vestry stand. It seemed spooky to Jeremy, like something out of a horror movie where Father Brendan transformed into a vampire or a werewolf and attacked Stevie.

The purple-colored vestments brought memories of Bob Campbell to Jeremy. After finishing grammar school, Bob had gone to a high school in Upstate New York that prepared kids to go to a seminary when they graduated. *Why would he want to go to a high school like that where you spend half the day praying? Maybe his parents pressured him, like mine pressured me to be an altar boy.*

Jeremy hid a giggle. *No way will anyone ever talk me into going to some dumb seminary prep school, or an even dumber seminary. Not me.* But then, for the second time that morning, he froze, his heart pounding in his chest.

Blood surged into his head, and his face flushed red as Father Brendan faced him.

"Well, Jeremy, is this not my first mass with you? I'll be listening to your Latin, but I am sure you know it." The priest gave Jeremy a wry smile and returned to vesting.

A numbing feeling of guilt swept over Jeremy. *Father Brendan caught that giggle. He read my mind. He knows what I think about going into a seminary and being a priest.*

"You want to help me with the chasuble, Jeremy?"

The chasuble is the outer vestment worn by the priest at mass. It's an ornate gown that fits over the priest's head and covers him front, side, and back.

Jeremy gasped. *He must even know what I think about being an altar boy. He's already on my case.*

"Gee, Father, maybe Steve better do it. I haven't seen it done too many times yet."

"All right, but how about tomorrow, you try it."

"Yes, Father."

Jeremy fastened his eyes diligently on priest and altar boy as Steve helped Father Brendan pick up the garment and hoist it over the tall priest's head.

What am I going to do? I'll hit him in the head with that thing tomorrow for sure.

Jeremy and Steve's eyes met as Father Brendan whispered the final prayer. *Oh, man, I hope Steve is planning on going to Saint Michael's High School next year and doesn't pull some last-minute seminary prep school stunt. He's been in the altar boys for a long time. What if one of the priests have gotten to him and convinced him to be a priest?*

The bottom seemed to drop out of Jeremy's chest as he stared at Steve. What would he do if Steve did go to a seminary prep school? *No, no way. Stevie isn't going to do that. He would have said something to me about it.*

Father Brendan picked up the gold chalice draped in its veil, put on his biretta, and bowed before the crucifix overhanging the sacristy. Steve and Jeremy took the holy hint and joined each other in front of Father Brendan. The mute, solemn ceremony began.

Steve yanked the sanctuary bell cord announcing the beginning of mass. A chill passed across Jeremy's neck as the bell rang through his body, and he and Steve entered the sanctuary for Jeremy's first

8:00 mass as an altar boy. His testicles practically jumped back into their embryonic origins as he rounded the huge marble pillars supporting the altar's massive canopy, decorated in bright paints and brilliant colors, and swirls and frills of handmade carpentry.

What a sight he beheld. All sixteen classes of Saint Michael's Monastery Grammar School were rising to their feet for the 8:00 mass, brought there by Steve's ring of the sanctuary bell. To Jeremy, they looked like an army getting in position to charge.

Jeremy had never seen the church filled with people from the altar side of the railing before. He had always been on the other side with the rest of the kids. Now, the kids faced him, watching him.

What am I doing here? Why did this have to happen?

None of Jeremy's Gestalt boom seemed to have captivated Steve, and Jeremy followed along feeling like a puppy being led by its master.

The sound of Father Brendan's rosary jangling beneath his vestments, and the slap of his sandals on the marble floor set up a focus in Jeremy's brain, reminding him that he was serving mass and that he had to remember what to do. As the trio arrived at the steps before the altar, that focus broke through Jeremy's dazzlement. It made his body take one knee in unison with Steve, and then go to his side of the altar as Steve went to his side, and Father Brendan advanced up the stairs covered in thick red carpet.

Jeremy watched Father Brendan place the gold chalice, from which he would drink the wine, on the altar, take a knee before the altar, and then return to the foot of the steps to say the opening prayers of the mass. Father Brendan stood before the altar steps with his altar boys, one on each side of him, kneeling on the first step.

A few beads of sweat appeared on Jeremy's forehead, and his armpits felt hot and scratchy. *I guess having hair makes your armpits itch when you're nervous. I don't care. I'm just glad my body is doing what it is supposed to do.*

He heard the first prayer, but it did not register in his mind. Stevie's voice answering the prayer broke the trance, and Jeremy peeked across Father Brendan at Steve. He was surprised to see Steve staring at him with sharp but encouraging eyes. Steve flicked his right eyebrow as Father Brendan rattled along with the next prayer.

Jeremy responded, speaking clearly in his best Latin. When they got to the Confiteor with its drawn-out sentences about how sorry he was before Almighty God, Jeremy bowed down with Steve, and they chanted a fine recitation. When they raised their heads at the end of the prayer, Jeremy glanced at Steve, who had his right hand in his left armpit at that moment.

Jeremy knew that he had gotten over the first hurdle without any mistakes as Father Brendan spoke the last amen and strode up the steps to the altar. Shades of doubt pestered him nevertheless. *He's going to be upset because he saw Steve passing me cues across the altar. Father Brandan will be all over both of us after mass. Steve didn't deserve that.*

In the next moment, Jeremy almost jumped up from his place on the altar where he was kneeling. An explosion of sound shocked his ears as eight grades of grammar school children shouted Kyrie Eleison, Lord Have Mercy, the first prayer in the mass recited by those in attendance.

The clamor started in the front of the church where grade 8B sat. Jeremy heard the booming voice of Tom Mulnick trigger it. Jeremy had never liked the way in which the school kids recited the prayers during mass. To him, the excitement in the kids' voices smacked of irreverence and didn't belong in church.

The two eighth grades, 8A and 8B, sat in the front of the church on opposite sides of the center aisle like two gunslingers ready to shoot it out, trying to see who could get the prayer off first. It had nothing to do with God or religion or anything, other than flat-out competition. It was a game with the whole school for an audience.

Why, Jeremy had asked himself over and over through all his years at Saint Michael's, did the nuns and priests allow it to go on? Some fanatic leader in each of the eighth-grade classes was fixated on every move the priest made so that he caught the first sign of the next prayer and shouted it out before the other grade could. This year, Tom Mulnick summoned 8B, and Joe Miller returned fire in 8A.

It was ludicrous when one of them launched the wrong prayer. Steve and Jeremy had chuckled away many times when one of the eighth grades had miscued in the race to be first.

As the sounds of Saint Michael's children reverberated throughout the church, Jeremy wondered if attending a public school where the kids didn't go to daily mass would be better, and he didn't have to be an altar boy. *Ah, I'd rather be here.*

* * *

Jeremy's suspicions proved to be correct. Father Brendan had noticed the exchanges across the altar, and he confronted Steve and Jeremy about it when they were in the sacristy after mass.

"You joined the altar boys late in your grammar school career, Jeremy, and I understand that you might need some help, but it seemed to me that you and Steven were having a private conversation during the mass. I hope that that's not true fellows, because church is the most holy of all places. As altar boys, you must always remember that. You too Steven. No matter how much you might have wanted to help Jeremy, God comes first in church. You do realize that, don't you?"

"Oh, yes Father," Steve said contritely as he rolled his eyes and muffled a laugh.

"But you two did very well with the Latin. Sometimes, the altar boys are not in harmony. They seem to be competing. You made a good team. Kneel now, and I will give you my blessing."

Jeremy and Steve rose from their knees after Father Brendan's blessing, thanked him, and retreated to the heavy metal door that led downstairs to the altar boys' room. Steve shook Jeremy's shoulder as the door closed behind them.

"Bless your ass, Jeremy."

"Yeah," Jeremy sighed with relief as his footsteps carried him away from Father Brendan.

"What an unholy, bastard altar boy you are, Wilcamp, even getting me into trouble."

The boys shed their surplices and cassocks in a flash.

"Shouldn't we clean this mess up, Steve?"

"No. Father Francis has probably already seen it. Let's put our things away and get out of here. Besides, I've got a surprise for you. I'm taking you through the grove on the way to school."

"What? We can't go there, Steve. You know we can't go there."

"Sure, we can. Nobody's going to stop us. I've done it before, and it's a terrific way for you to break into serving the 8:00. Mulnick let it rip this morning, didn't he?"

"Stevie, I don't care about Tom Mulnick right now. We can't do this."

"Jeremy, take it easy. We can. You're going to love it."

"You know what," Steve asserted, "we can blow thirty or forty minutes in the grove before we show up in class. We can tell Sister Verona that we had to clean up an awful mess in the altar boys' room. She'll eat it right up, especially when I tell her how scared your balls were of Father Brendan because he told us to clean up before we left. We can lay it all on those high school dudes who served the 7:00, and she'd never be able to check up even if she wanted to."

"You're going to get us into all kinds of trouble, Stevie. Suppose we run into one of those old priests out there reading his prayer book or something? You know what Jimmy Waite said the priests did to him when they caught him in there last year, don't you?"

"That's a lie, Jeremy. Jimmy made that story up."

"Now, come on, Jeremy, time's wasting. This is a fantastic day to go into the grove with this wind. You won't believe what it sounds like in there when the wind blows through those pine trees. We can eat our breakfast in there. What'd your mom give you for breakfast?"

Steve's trying to change the topic.

A pit was forming in Jeremy's stomach. He wanted to scream at Stevie, but he stood there speechless. He couldn't think about what his mother had put in his lunch bag for breakfast before Steve pulled him into the stone-walled corridor that led outdoors. Jeremy tripped on a crack in the stone floor of the dungeon-like hallway.

Steve helped him up. "Come on. Father Brendan would probably say it's the second most holy place in the world."

Steve had overwhelmed Jeremy with too many things at once. Leave the altar boys' room a mess, go through the grove, be late for school, tell Sister Verona a pack of lies. Jeremy grew exasperated, his sense of fear increasing.

"Steve, if we get caught at this, my father will beat me to death. Let's not do this, okay?"

His pleading seemed to go unheard. Steve pulled the heavy metal door open. The dampness of the underground corridor made the hinges squeak. Outside, a blast of October wind hit them as they hustled up the stone steps.

"Nothing is going to happen, Jeremy. Will you stop being such a scaredy-cat. The grove is magical right now with all this wind. It's a different world in there."

The halves of some imaginary vice closed in on Jeremy's head as he walked dumbly next to Steve in disbelief at a loss for anything to say. *We're going to get caught.*

Steve stopped. "Hold on a minute. There's Sister Mary Elizabeth leading the last of the first-graders out. We've got plenty of time. The first-graders are just starting down Montclair Street. We can spend forty minutes in the grove, no sweat."

This comment stunned Jeremy out of his speechless amazement. "Stevie, it took a lot to get it up for this altar boys' thing today, you know, the Latin, 8:00 mass for the first time, Father Brendan trying to catch me making a mistake. How about we do this tomorrow?"

"No, Jeremy, putting things off gets you nowhere. Sister Verona knows that we have our altar boys' meetings on the first Monday of every month, and she'll believe that we didn't want to leave the altar boys' room a mess. She knows the 8:00 is the last mass, and we were the last altar boys, and it makes perfect sense for us to not leave it a pig sty. Tomorrow, we won't have such a believable excuse for being late. We can get away with it today."

Oh, man, the altar boys' meeting. Stevie, stop doing this to me.

Jeremy felt like he would tear in two. His heart seemed to be rising into his throat, and he feared he would fall to his knees and cry like some lunatic.

What is wrong with Stevie?

Steve felt his friend's fear. He stopped and faced Jeremy. "Jeremy, it's me, Stevie Stockton, your best friend. I would never take you anywhere if I thought something bad would happen to you. Don't tell me that you're afraid to go into the grove."

Jeremy knew that he had to go into the grove with Steve. Steve would never understand if he didn't. *Maybe I'll lose my best friend if I don't cool this.* Jeremy shrugged and smiled.

"No, I'm not scared of the grove. It's just that if my father ever found out, he would beat the daylights out of me, and I don't want any more beatings."

Jeremy's comment puzzled Steve. "Jeremy, come on, is your father still beating you? Didn't he stop doing that? You're too old for him to be beating you."

Jeremy stood frozen and said nothing.

"Listen, everything will be all right. We aren't going to get caught. Your father will never know. Trust me. Come on, we can make it now."

Their footsteps quickened as the flagstones of the entrance to Saint Michael's Monastery Church sped beneath them. To their right, the three, separate, double-doored entrances to the Monastery passed them by. To their left the four large pillars of cement, with Gothic carving at their tops and bottoms, maintained their sentry, holding up the outer roof, covering the entrance to the Monastery.

As the two boys stole across the front of the Monastery, Jeremy glanced up at the faces of saints and apostles that stood above the church doors sculpted into a frozen panel of stone across the entire entrance. Every one of those stone physiognomies glared at Jeremy Wilcamp with a fierce warning from God. This is the holiest of places, they shouted in unison. Get out of this sanctuary of the Almighty Lord before you are forever condemned to hell. Jeremy could feel the message, and it made his feet move faster.

Jeremy was relieved to make it by the Monastery entrance, but when they got to the grove, the eerie sound of the wind, wildly wrapping itself around the huge stone church, with all its heights and towers, iced his spine. They stopped for a moment in the carefully manicured gardens surrounding the church.

From here the new Monastery church and the older Monastery church to the south could be seen together, the newer almost three times the size of the older. The new Monastery church had to be constructed to accommodate the rapid growth of the parish following the end of World War II. Like so many other parishes throughout the country in the 1950s, Saint Michaels housed an older, smaller church that stood in near disuse. The postwar baby boom had required a newer, larger facility.

Jeremy fixed his eyes on the immense stained-glass windows of the church. An army of heavenly characters were encased in them. In that moment, a crack in the October clouds opened, and a brilliant flash of sunlight exploded from the gray sky and splashed onto the windows. What colors! Jeremy took a deep breath. His bowels rose in his abdomen. That army of heavenly hosts bore down on Jeremy Wilcamp, warning him to stay out of the grove.

Stevie, why are you making me do this?

The clouds closed, and the windows were again dark. A pain buffeted through his chest as Jeremy breathed the fresh, fast-moving October wind.

"Come on," Steve yelled over the wind, "here's where I get into the grove."

Before Jeremy stood the chain link fence that surrounded the grove. *How am I going to get over the fence?*

"I'm not too good at fence climbing, Steve."

"You puss. Why do I have to work so hard to get you into things?"

No shit, Jeremy wanted to say, but didn't.

"Let's throw our bookbags and lunches over. Don't worry. I'll give you a boost."

Steve knelt and cupped his hands. "Here, put a foot in my hands and up you go."

Jeremy grabbed the top of the fence and swung his left leg over. He then raised his right foot out of Steve's cupped hands, but as he swung his leg over the top, he felt something latch onto his thigh.

Nothing could stop the downward motion of his leg even though he tried to thrust his body off the fence without tearing his pants. Pain stung his inner thigh as he plummeted into the grove.

Jeremy raised his head and saw Steve scamper up and over the fence as if he was an Olympic trainee in fence climbing.

"Man, I'm sorry, Jeremy. Let me see it."

Steve noted a two-inch tear in Jeremy's blue uniform school pants. Blood oozed from a small cut in Jeremy's thigh.

Jeremy peeked through the tear at his leg. Visions of his mother scolding him for another disaster for her to repair filled his mind. He put pressure on the cut.

"Your mom is going to be mad, isn't she?"

Jeremy made no comment.

"How's this sound, Jeremy? Tell your mother there was a nail sticking up in one of the church pews in the back of the altar boys' room, and you tore your pants on it. She goes for all that religious stuff, doesn't she?

"Before she jumps all over you, tell her how glad you are that your pants got torn and not your cassock. Tell her that you banged the nail into the pew with your shoe, so the same thing wouldn't happen to some other goodly altar boy. Your mother will think you are a saint if you can get all that out before she blows her top."

"You don't know my mom well enough, Steve. She'd make me take my shoe off and show her a mark from where I hit the nail."

"Give me your shoe, and I'll put a mark on it for her. If you really want to win her over, get some big tears in your eyes and show her your leg and tell her how you offered up all the pain and suffering from the cut for the poor souls in purgatory, and she should offer up the grief of sewing up your pants for them too."

"Yeah, Steve, then I can go to school without a head on my shoulders. Mom gets so mad over everything. How am I supposed to get big tears in my eyes?"

"It's simple. When she's all garbled up with anger examining your pants, bash yourself in the nose. Do it right, and your eyes will get teary."

"You're kidding? Have you done that before?"

"Of course. I'm not making it up.

"What do you think, Jeremy? Would your mom make a big deal over it if you made up a story like that?"

Come on, Wilcamp, don't ruin this. Stevie wants you to go into the grove. He's begging you.

"No. I'll hide the pants in the back of my closet for a while. My parents are going to have to buy me new ones soon anyway because I am outgrowing the ones I have."

He struggled to appear cheery. "You know what else. I don't care if my father does find out. It's worth it to get out of class for a while."

"Ah, great, Jeremy. Your father will never find out. This place is fantastic. Come on, I've got my own hideaway. Your leg stop bleeding?"

"Yeah, it's okay." Jeremy refused to show Steve the near panic raging in his mind. He felt like a criminal, and the tear in his pants proved his guilt. His heart raced as he pictured his father coming after him with that thick leather belt he wore, but Jeremy shrugged and strode alongside Steve.

The wind ferociously thrashed the mighty pine trees about, but as the boys progressed deeper into the grove, the pine trees formed a warming blanket of protection around them.

The grove, the Monastery, and its parking lot took up one square city block, and the grammar school occupied half of the next city block adjacent to the Monastery. The grove was bordered by Saint Michael's Street and the grammar school to the east, Patterson Parkway to the south, and Montclair Street to the north. On the west side of the grove, where Steve and Jeremy stood, the Monastery buildings with their spacious lawns and the parking lot bounded the grove. Plans to use some of the grove to build a retreat center and expand the parking lot were still nascent.

Until those plans came to fruition, the grove was the exclusive domain of the priests and novices who ran the Monastery. No one else had access to the grove.

The only entrance was through the rectory, the residence where the priests and novices lived. Fences barred outsiders from entry.

Jeremy's fears subsided as he realized that no one was in the grove and, even if there were, he and Stevie were well hidden. Jeremy perceived that Steve had violated the privacy of this place some time ago. He led Jeremy down one hill and up into a thick grouping of tall pines. They sat on a soft bed of pine needles. The scent of the pine trees and the howling wind excited Jeremy. The sense of being outdoors and inundated by nature thrilled him. The grove was truly an enticing escape from the regimen of school, and now he wondered why he had not joined Steve in this adventure sooner.

Steve grinned at Jeremy with wildly excited eyes as if he had been waiting a long time to bring him there. "What did I tell you, you fence climbing turkey?"

Jeremy leaned back against the hillside where he sat. His muscles relaxed, and the crescendo tension in his body faded.

"There's such a feeling of power and forces in here with all this wind, but I feel okay. It's as if we were in the eye of a hurricane, but we belong here. You've got your own private nest in here, don't you, Stevie?"

Steve liked what Jeremy was saying. "No wonder those priests don't want to let anybody in here, huh, Jeremy? It's a chunk of heaven in the middle of the city."

"This place is more like a jungle than a grove," Jeremy remarked. "It surprises me that the priests would let it get so overgrown."

"Jeremy, I think the priests have let that happen on purpose. They want it private. The area of the grove around the churches and the rectory is well maintained with lawns and some statues and benches, and pathways run throughout the grove. The novices can go to those places and pray, or read, or do whatever they do. But the rest of it is overgrown.

"That's why, Mr. Wilcamp, nobody will ever find us in here."

Jeremy's curiosity could no longer be contained. "Okay, Mr. Stockton, come on. Truth time. When did you get balls enough to come into this place, and how come you never told me? We've never kept secrets from each other."

"I've told you dozens of times, Jeremy, but you've never heard me. How many times have we come up Montclair Street after school, and I poke you in the ribs and say, let's go in. You always clam up, and then you laugh it off. You get so frightened that I drop it because I figure you don't want to hear it."

"Steve, the grove belongs to the priests and novices. It's a holy and sacred place. We can't be playing around in here. We've got to be committing a sacrilege barging into the grove."

"No way," Steve declared. "This place is like stepping into the neatest state of grace you'll ever find."

"And I thought I'm the only one being sacrilegious. Out with it, Stockton. When did you first come in here?"

"It's almost one year ago, exactly to this day. It was windy then, but nothing like today. Still, it played with your mind if you were coming in here for the first time, especially at night. It was a Monday night, after the altar boys' meeting."

Steve stopped and stared straight at Jeremy. Jeremy's eyes had flashed. His heart had jumped within his chest, and his body had tensed as if some cold hand had reached out of the October clouds and clasped him. Steve's words had shocked him. Jeremy knew that Steve had done it deliberately.

But Steve lifted his eyes from Jeremy and gazed up the length of one of the pine trees. Maybe, he hoped, if they could be calm about what lay before them, Jeremy would believe they could master the situation.

"It was during the initiation."

Steve had astonished Jeremy. How could Steve have known how much the coming initiation worried him? Jeremy presumed that he had been hiding his fears. He hadn't wanted Steve to think that he couldn't defend himself or was afraid of a Nancy-pants altar boys' initiation, and he had avoided talking to Steve about it. But he had not come up with a plan for how to deal with the initiation or dodge it.

Jeremy and Stevie could not get together until well after the altar boys' meeting because Steve was scheduled to serve the Monday night benediction, which followed the altar boys' meeting. Jeremy would be stuck in the initiation by himself when it was at its hottest and didn't know what he would do until Stevie joined him.

"Most of the time the initiations are fun and playtime, Jeremy. Everybody goes, and it is more the older, bigger guys playing with the younger, shorter guys, and nobody singles out the beginners that much. As soon as the youngest kid's parents have picked them up and gone, the older guys herd the younger kids toward the hill outside the altar boys' room, and the older ones spread themselves along the top and bottom of the hill. They sort of play King of the Mountain. They grab the younger kids and roll them down the hill. The guys at the bottom chase them back up the hill, and they keep doing that until everybody is exhausted with it and laughed themselves silly.

"Then, they rip the shoes off the younger kids and the beginners, and everybody runs around on the lawn, throwing shoes back and forth through the air, chasing and tackling each other, and screaming and yelling. It's pretty much of a hoot. One or two of the beginners get their pants pulled down. But that's it. They pull their pants back up and everybody laughs.

"Finally, they throw all the shoes in one big pile, and the kids have to find their shoes. That's when it gets neat, because the older guys pitch in and help the younger ones. When it's all over, the new kids feel like they're members of something and that the older guys are their friends, and they'll help them whenever they need it."

Jeremy sat in silence listening to Steve describe the initiations.

"But sometimes, a kid joins whom everybody hates. He's a teacher's pet or maybe a couple of guys have a grudge against him, and the kid gets shoved around and slapped up. The guys pull his pants down and sometimes take his pants off. They hide his shoes where he can't find them and break the kid down, so he cries and begs and all that."

"You know Mark Bimonte in the seventh grade, right?"

"Yeah, sure," Jeremy answered.

21

"Mark joined the altar boys last year. He's got all that teacher's pet stuff with him because his father and he go to the convent every Sunday and drive old Sister Carissima, Sister Irene and Sister Mary Judith to church for Sunday mass and bring them back to the convent after mass. No teacher ever hits Mark, beats his hands with a ruler, stands him in a corner, or sends him to the principal's office, or even yells at him. Some of the guys in Mark's class don't like it that they get all that stuff, and Mark gets nothing."

Jeremy nodded his head. "Yeah, I've heard about that. We get the same thing sometimes, but nobody has balls enough to mess with us."

"Hmm, that's true, Wilcamp.

"Being a teacher's pet wasn't half of Mark's problem, though. You remember when we had a fire drill during the noon recess a week or so after school started last year?"

"Yeah, probably everybody remembers that. What a circus, Stevie. The sisters were in such a dither expecting the school to go up in flames."

"Oh, God, yeah, Jeremy. How about when the fire engines showed up. Unreal.

"I found out later that some eighth-graders had gone up on the third floor of the school and set off a fire alarm. I'm pretty sure Tommy Fletcher, Tim Clayton and Justin Finnerty were the dunces stupid enough to do that.

"Somehow, Mark knew who had set the alarm off, and he told Sister Sullpicia. I don't know how he found out, but my guess is that he overheard Jenny Tolister mouthing off to her girl-friends about it. Tommy probably told Jenny, and she couldn't keep it a secret."

"Don't those two make you sick, Stevie? Always playing the hot teenage lovers, hugging and kissing on the playground?"

"They're disgusting. They've got some touchy-feely stuff too, Jeremy. Tommy paid the price for having a girl-friend, and he blamed Mark for that too.

"Word slipped out that Mark had blown the whistle. Apparently, Sister Sullpicia made it clear that nobody had better touch Mark. And nobody is going to dare incur the wrath of our monster principal. Mark never got payback.

"That incident happened about one week after Mark joined the altar boys, just before the initiation."

"Oh, man, Stevie, you got involved, didn't you?"

"Couldn't help it, Jeremy. I kept seeing Tommy Fletcher pick on Mark during recesses. That's what made me think Tommy had been involved with the fire alarm and had plans to get even with Mark during the initiation.

"Mark needed protection and had nobody."

"Yeah, Stevie. If Jenny got in trouble as well because of Mark, Tommy would want to kill him."

"I was determined to do something to help him. I went to Mark during the noon recess on the day of the initiation and told him I would look out for him after the altar boys' meeting. When he discovered that I had a plan, he was like ecstatic. We became instant best friends. I told him that we'd sit next to the door and bust out of the altar boys' meeting while the altar boys were saying the closing prayer, and we'd run our asses out of there before anybody could catch him.

"Jeremy, I'll never forget how he looked at me, so much surprise and relief on his face."

Jeremy fixed his eyes on Steve. His amazement grew as he listened.

"When Father Francis had everybody stand up to say the closing prayer of the meeting, I nudged Mark, and we beat it out of the church while the altar boys were still praying. We started running across the lawn toward the old church and, boom! I got a punch in my belly, and somebody else grabbed Mark and took him to the ground. Two guys from the high school had us trapped. They had to have known that Mark and I would be the first ones tearing out of that meeting. I supposed that Tommy Fletcher had to have seen me talking to Mark during the noon recess and put two and two together."

"Stevie, Tommy Fletcher plays basketball with some of the high school kids. Chris Scharlan, who's on the high school basketball team, lives down the street from me and has a hoop in his back yard. I've seen Tommy and Tim Clayton playing there."

"I didn't recognize them, Jeremy. But I knew they were from the high school.

"The guy who had grabbed Mark was pulling Mark's pants down. Mark was crying and screaming bloody murder. Whoever had hit me told me to not move an inch. I don't remember what I yelled at him, but I got up and made a mad dash at him. He reared his fist back getting ready to hit me again. But I beat him to it. I planted my foot straight into his balls. It couldn't have been a better kick. He fell down moaning and curled up, grabbing his high school hot rocks."

Jeremy clapped his hands, rolled over in the pine needles and came up saying, "Stevie Stockton, God bless you!" "That's so perfect. You clocked him in the right place. What are high school kids doing taking Mark's pants down? That's crap."

"Something took me over, Jeremy, because I about went crazy. I tore after the guy who had Mark. He let go of Mark and started to get up to face me, but I dove into his thighs and sank my teeth into his ass. He screamed and tried to throw me off, but I let go and bit him again. The second time, I got him in the fat of his ass. The first bite got too much muscle, and it didn't hurt that much. Man, he howled with the second bite. His ass hurt so bad he didn't know what to grab. I bit in as hard as I could."

A flash of lightning and a violent clap of thunder interrupted them. The sky was getting grayer and the winds stronger.

"Man, Jeremy, bet we're going to have one heck of a storm soon."

"Shouldn't we be getting off to school, Steve?"

"No, we've still got some time. The church bell hasn't rung for 9:00 yet."

"So that's how you time it, Stevie. I was wondering how we were going to know when to get out of here. What happened next?"

"I let go of that guy's ass and went to help Mark pull his pants up. Tears were streaming out of the kid's eyes. I told him that he was safe, and he had to stop crying, and we had to move. We ran across the lawn toward the old church. Kids started pouring out the altar boys' room, and I heard Tommy Fetcher yelling. 'Markie, Markie baby, where are you?' I knew that Tommy Fletcher had friends, and those two high school pricks would want to maul us if they caught us after what I did to them.

"We got all the way across the lawn and onto the driveway in front of the old church. Tommy was ganging up with four guys on the lawn by the altar boys' room. The grove stood before us, all fenced in, our only escape. Mark could never outrun them. 'Mark,' I said, 'we're going over the fence.'

"He didn't say a word. He raised his arms for me to lift him up onto the fence. I had him sit on the top while I got myself there. When I got to the top, I took Mark by the shoulders, lowered him into the grove, and let him go. I dropped down into the grove beside him. Tommy and his buddies arrived at the fence as we bounced to our feet.

"Mark started yelling, 'What are we going to do?' The guy whom I had kicked in the balls, leaped onto the fence. A broken tree branch laid on the ground, and I grabbed it just in time to swing it up and whack him on his head. He held onto the fence with one hand and rubbed his head with the other. That guy was a dumb ass. I had already smashed his balls, cracked his head, and now, his hand holding onto the fence begged me to strike. I whacked his hand harder than I got his head."

Jeremy jumped up and waved his hands in the air. "Stevie, you're a one-man army. How did you do all that? Can you imagine what that high school dude must have felt like to get so much shit from a measly seventh-grader?"

"He was a pretty ugly guy, Jeremy. Must've had a cold or something, because his nose kept running, and he snorted that gunk back into his nose and spit it out."

"Gross."

"I climbed up to the top of the fence with the branch, held myself there with one hand, and threw the branch straight at Tommy Fletcher. I missed, but I came close enough to make them stop. They backed off across the church driveway. There were three eighth-graders. Tommy Fletcher, Tim Clayton and Justin Finnerty, and the two high school guys. I didn't recognize them.

"They shouted filthy names at us, telling us we were in big trouble for going into the grove. The guy whom I had kicked grabbed himself and acted like he was going to piss on us. It made me laugh."

"Did Mark see that?" Jeremy asked, as he sat down.

"Yeah. It made him laugh too. Mark's not a dumb kid, Jeremy. He's got some ideas about what's going on.

"Anyway, Tim Clayton yelled at us that we were going to have to come out of the grove, and they were waiting for us. That got me thinking. It was dark, and Mark had to get home. We had to find a way out without Tommy and his nitwit friends catching us. Mark and I plodded deeper into the grove until we were out of sight, and then we set off toward the old church.

"All kinds of strange things happened. An owl hooted, and we heard what sounded like small animals rustling around. The noises terrified Mark. I tried to convince him that rabbits made noises like that and that he shouldn't be so scared.

"We were almost to the back of the old church when a gust of wind blew an opening through the trees, and the street light shined on something in front of us. Jeremy, no shit, I thought it was a monster. Our very own Big Foot. We both froze. Mark grabbed me around the waist and screamed for help. I picked him up and shouted in his ear that he had to be quiet, or he'd give our position away, and I bolted toward the fence.

"The fence stood a couple of feet in front of us when I tripped on something. I grabbed Mark by the face and growled at him to shut up. I said that whatever we had seen had to have been a shadow. It couldn't have been anything else.

"Mark calmed down and said to me, 'Stevie, please, I wanna go home.' 'Look,' I said to him, 'there isn't any monster coming for us now, so let's go.' Mark asked me if I was sure that shadow wasn't a man or something."

"What'd you tell him?"

"It had scared me too, Jeremy, but, I guess, I told him what actually happened. I said, the wind was blowing so hard, letting light in and cutting it off so fast, that we got the impression that something was moving toward us, and that scared us. It made sense to me, and Mark liked it, but when it happened, I didn't figure that out. I wanted to get out of there."

"That sounds like a good explanation to me, Steve."

"Nothing else made sense, Jeremy.

"When we got past the old church, I considered climbing the fence and going home, but I knew that it would be safer if we found a way into the rectory. Those guys, especially the one I kicked in the nuts, were plenty pissed. Running into them would be a big mistake. It was a quick run to get to the rectory once we passed the old church. Mark spotted the ground level door to the rectory.

"The only entrance to the grove is through the rectory. Of course, the door was locked. We slinked along the back of the rectory and came to this small, hinged window that swings out. It was open a crack. I opened it, squirmed through and then helped Mark in. I found a light switch and turned it on. I figured nobody would see it. You couldn't picture a tinier bathroom than what we were in. How we got in without putting a foot in the toilet is a miracle to me. Nothing could have been better. Both of us needed to take a leak."

"Oh, no, Stevie, bet you flushed the toilet and set off all kinds of noises."

"Nope, not that dumb, but I just did grab Mark's hand as he reached for the handle. When we got done pissing, Mark said that his right hip hurt. We checked it. The guy who had taken Mark's pants down had slashed an eight-inch-long fingernail gash in Mark's hip. It had bled earlier, but then it just looked raw. I told him to take some hot baths for a few days, and it would heal."

"What is it with these guys and their initiations?" Jeremy shouted. "What's the big thrill in ripping a kid's pants off and chasing him around in his underwear, or even getting him naked. It's such bullshit."

"Jeremy, I swear, that's the only time I ever saw anything like that at an initiation. You know what I thought? Tommy Fletcher had some friends in the high school who had never been altar boys and had never attended Saint Michael's grammar school, and he got them do the dirty work. If those high school pricks had been in the altar boys, I would have recognized them. Nobody knows who the mystery guys were that attacked Mark, and everybody gets away with it. Unfortunately, one of the mystery guys got kicked in the nuts, smashed on his head, and whacked on his hand. And the other guy got bit on his ass."

Jeremy and Steve both burst out laughing.

"Steve, that's perfect poetic justice. No lie. Those guys got what they deserved. What'd you do when you were in the rectory?"

"I opened the bathroom door and let the light out. The bathroom was in a conference room. Folding tables and chairs were arranged in the room, and pads of paper and pencils were stacked on the tables. We saw the door on the other side of the room. I turned the bathroom light off, and we worked our way around the conference room, feeling the walls with our hands until we got to the door. Light coming from outside the conference room outlined the door for us.

"We slipped through the door and found ourselves in a hallway at the bottom of a flight of stairs. An exit sign lit the hallway. I said to Mark, 'If we run into a priest or somebody, we are going to tell them the truth. Some kids chased us into the grove after the altar boys' meeting, and we're lost. Could they guide us to the altar boys' room so that we can go home?'

"Mark agreed. He might have been hoping that we would be found. We started up the stairs. After two steps, a bell rang. Unbelievable. Next, we heard men singing. Vespers, I guessed. I grabbed Mark's shoulder and said, 'they'll never hear us now.' We scooted up the rest of the stairs.

"At the top of the stairs, we were in a hallway that connected the old church, the rectory, and the corridor leading to the sacristy of the new church. The rectory, where the singing came from, was to our right, and the doors were closed. To our left was the sacristy of the old church, and the doors to the corridor faced us. On the right side of the corridor, there was another door. I had no idea of where that led.

"'We're good, Mark,' I said. 'We'd race our asses through the corridor to the new church and be out of there and home in no time.' Mark was about to pull the door open when I stopped him. 'Look,' I said, 'suppose somebody is coming.' 'Let's peek first.'

"Jeremy, it must have been my guardian angel that made me do that. I opened the door the slightest bit, and Father Andrew, the pastor of the Monastery of all people, was strolling through the corridor. The moonlight coming through the windows lit up his face making him look like a bloodthirsty Dracula swooping down on us.

"'Man,' I said, 'why is this happening to us.' We had to hide, and fast. I opened the only remaining door in the hall to the right of the corridor. It led to the basement of the new church. I took Mark behind the door and said, 'Don't panic. It's Father Andrew, and he'll pass by us and never know we're here. Be perfectly still.' Father Andrew came out of the corridor and went into the rectory.

"I stared into that basement. We were at the top of a curved staircase that led down to a walkway. I couldn't see much more. Those priests are chintzy with electricity. I've never been in so many places where there are so few lights.

"We checked out the corridor to the new church again. Nobody. We tore ass through the corridor and pounced into the sacristy of the new church. God was the only person hanging out in the sacristy. If he saw us, he didn't say anything."

"Oh, man, Stevie," Jeremy giggled. "What if you and Mark had come flying into the sacristy, and this feeling came over you and Mark that God knew you had invaded his sacred home, and he decided to sling your asses into hell forever?"

"No, Jeremy. If God allowed us to burst into his sacred home, he wanted us there. The loneliness of being there by himself bored him, and Mark and I had made him laugh. Maybe he'd offer us milk and cookies."

"Stevie, I know God didn't offer you milk and cookies. What did he do?"

"He saved us. Mark asked me if we were safe. I pulled my Swiss army knife out of my pocket and showed it to him. I told Mark that if anybody messed with us, they were in for a surprise."

"Wow! Do you think you would have used the knife, Stevie?"

"As soon as I blurted that out, I wished I hadn't. I wouldn't have hesitated to pull the knife out if those jerks had been waiting for us. But I would only use it to scare them. I don't know if I have it in me to stab someone. Here's the thing, though. Mark felt more confident. Nothing else happened. I put the knife away and didn't have to take it out again.

"We went downstairs to the bathroom, and I cleaned Mark's face and brushed his clothes off. I told him that Tommy Fletcher and his goofball friends would be too afraid of me to bother him again, and those high school kids were never coming back to the grammar school to pick on a student. Then, I took him straight to his front door."

"Stevie, what a story. Is that kind of crap going to happen to me tonight?"

"Whoa, there's more. And, no. You're not going through any of that."

CHAPTER 2
AND NOW IT'S YOU, MY BEST FRIEND

"Do we have time for this, Stevie?"

"We still have time. It won't matter if we're a little late. Sister Verona is easygoing, you know that."

"Yeah, Stevie, and she likes you."

"That does help, but she likes you too, Jeremy. She sees you and me together, and she wouldn't want to hurt either one of us. We won't have any problem.

"Anyway, guess what Mark did when we got to his front porch? He burst out into tears."

"What was he crying about, Steve? He should have been as happy as a lark to get home?"

"He was scared for me. He didn't want me to go home alone. Everything broke loose in him. He kept saying his father could take me home, and no sooner did those words tumble out of his mouth, then his mother rushed out onto the porch.

"I felt sick as if I was going to pass out. My knees got weak and I thought I might vomit. His mother grabbed Mark up into her arms, hugging him, and she shouted at me what happened? I didn't know what to say.

"Then Mr. Bimonte blasted out of the house. He seemed to think that I had done something bad to Mark. And suddenly, I don't know why, I felt guilty about the whole thing. Like somehow, the altar boys, the initiation, the grove, everything, I had made it all happen. I almost cried. Mr. Bimonte stomped across the porch, stood over me like a gorilla with his arms on his hips, and asked me in a calm, but very angry voice, did I do something to Mark? He's a huge man.

"Mark shouted, 'No, Dad, no, he saved me. Please, Dad, don't hurt Stevie.'"

"Oh, Stevie, you must have been petrified."

"It's a good thing Mark spoke up, because, you're right, Mr. Bimonte scared me.

"Mark had confused his father. He had gotten out of his mother's grasp and grabbed his father's arm yelling all this Stevie saved me stuff. I had to say something.

"I focused my eyes onto Mark's with a pleading look on my face and said, 'Yeah, Mr. Bimonte, we were coming home from the altar boys' meeting, and the wind was blowing so hard that a branch broke and fell out of a tree, and I just managed to pull Mark out of the way.' I winked at Mark as I said it. Mark stood there dumbfounded. I gave him that pleading look again and told his parents that it had been close and that Mark might have gotten a few scratches, but the main thing was that it had been so scary.

"'Oh, dear God,' Mrs. Bimonte wailed, and she hugged Mark again. Mark kept looking at me strangely, wondering why I hadn't told his parents the truth."

Steve paused and stared at the angry gray clouds in the sky. "I don't know why I didn't tell them what happened. It wasn't good, man. It wasn't the right thing to do."

"Stevie, nobody would want to tell all that stuff to Mark's parents. It would be like waving a red flag in front of a bull to inform Mr. Bimonte that some kid ripped his son's pants down after an altar boys' meeting. And mention that scratch on Mark's hip. Never."

"Umm...Mr. Wilcamp, that does make sense. Perfect sense. Maybe that's why I didn't do it."

"I think so, Stevie. I wouldn't have wanted to tell him what happened."

"Well, Mr. Bimonte told me to wait on the porch, and he went to get his car keys and take me home. On the way home, he wanted to give me a dollar for saving Mark.

"Jeremy, I felt like the lowest thing on earth. I still can't put it into words today why I felt so bad. I was trying to do what seemed like a good thing, but how can anything good come out of something so bad? Such an innocent kid as Mark Bimonte being dragged through that entire affair and me being part of it. It should never have happened. And here's his father giving me a dollar when he has no idea of what his son went through."

"But, Steve, you tried to help him, and you did."

"That sounds good, Jeremy, but it didn't help how I felt then, and it never has ever since."

"Stevie, think of what might have happened to Mark if you hadn't been there. That high school punk had already taken Mark's pants down and put a scratch on his hip when you got to him. What do you think he would have done next?"

Steve crossed his legs and propped his elbows on his thighs and his head in his hands. "I had to do it their way, Jeremy. I wanted to hurt them like they wanted to hurt Mark. It wasn't only about getting Mark out of it. I wanted Tommy and whoever he brought along to know what it's like to be afraid and get beaten up. Don't you see? That's why I'm part of it. I had to do it in their terms, so they knew I had beaten them at their own stupid game."

"No, Steve," Jeremy retorted, as he hopped to his feet. "You're blaming yourself for something that you got stuck in. Come on, you didn't plan any of it. It happened, and, once it got rolling, none of you were in control of it."

Silence fell over them as Steve rose to his feet. Jeremy could see that Steve was drained. He had never known Steve to take something so hard, especially after such a long time.

Stevie faced Jeremy. "And now it's you, my best friend. You've got to go through it tonight."

Jeremy felt his heart pounding at what Steve had said.

The sound of the church bell tolling nine times for 9:00 began. They both listened to the sounds of the brisk October day, the wind, the trees, the church bell, birds chirping, squirrels scurrying through the grove. The roar of a bus driving up Montclair Street brought their eyes together.

"We'd better get on to school now, don't you think, Steve?"

"No, we've got fifteen minutes and besides, I need to talk to you. Come on, sit down."

"Jeremy, we've known each other forever, and I know you don't go for this violent stuff. It's not you, but you're no chicken. I know that you're worried about this initiation tonight. If a gang of altar boys which includes some kids from the high school, whom you don't know and who are bigger than you, want to mess with you, you're going to fight. You're going to kick as many guys in the nuts as you can, just like I did. I can see you going at those guys with everything you've got. You're proud and brave, and you don't want those guys to break you down."

Jeremy started to say something.

"No," Steve raised his hand. "I know you, Jeremy. You'd put up a fight. But if three or four older altar boys decide they want to smack you around, it's only going to get worse when you resist. It isn't often that an eighth-grader joins, and those high school guys can play a lot harder with you than the younger kids.

"But that's only part of the reason for why you'll be targeted tonight. Some people don't like our friendship. We get along with teachers because we're respectful and do our homework. But some guys never have the right answer and get into trouble all the time. They don't like us. And, to be honest with you, Jeremy, there's a couple of high school altar boys that I don't like, and they don't like me. You're not going through it. We're not taking a chance on you getting into a fight you can't win. No way. I've got it all worked out. They will never get near you. Wait until you hear how I've got it all planned.

"The first thing we're going to do is switch places for benediction tonight."

"What!" Jeremy sat straight up. "We can't do that."

"Oh, yes we can, and we're going to."

"Stevie, that would be a disaster. Father Francis might throw both of us out of the altar boys. I haven't been in the altar boys for two months, and I get booted out after my brother's been in them for almost his whole life. How's that going to fly in my home?

"Steve, you don't understand how my parents are always telling me what a smart son Brian is and what a nothing I am. My father would beat the daylights out of me. My mother would be so bent out of shape. She'd be up there at church, begging Father Francis to take me back. I can't take all that, Steve. I won't."

"Whoa, hold on, I've got it all planned. I've already talked to Father Francis about it, and he said you could fill in for me."

Total frustration appeared on Jeremy's face. "You already talked to him. What about my parents?"

"Give me a minute to explain it. You've got to stop yelling and listen up. We're running out of time. Come on, you won't believe what a manipulator Stevie boy is." "You see," Steve's eyes sparkled, "I know that Father Francis makes out the schedule before the altar boys' meeting every month. So, last month I came early to the meeting and went up to his office where he was working on the October schedule."

"Is that why you wanted to meet me at church last month instead of us coming together? I was sure you were up to something."

"You know me too well, Wilcamp. How am I ever supposed to sneak anything by you?"

Jeremy was glum. Steve pressed on, trying to get Jeremy out of the doldrums. "I told Father Francis that I came to his office to tell him that I couldn't serve anything during the first weekend in November and the first Monday because my dad is taking me and my mom to New York. Which is true. Dad has to attend a combined work-vacation convention for his company. We aren't going to get back until late Monday night. I told Father Francis that I could serve benediction on the first Monday in October to make up for it.

"Father Francis said it wasn't necessary for me to do that, but then he thought it over, and said it would be good if I could, because a lot of kids can't make Monday night benediction. Whammy, I'm scheduled to serve benediction after the altar boys' meeting. Perfect. You've got to admit Wilcamp, that's cunning."

"Yeah, Stevie, I remember you telling me about that convention. The company is paying for everything, right?"

"Yep."

"Your dad works for a good company, Steve. My dad's company never does anything like that."

"Your dad's smart, Jeremy, maybe he'll move on someday and get a better job."

"Yeah, maybe."

"Well, anyway, I thought we were golden, but Father Francis got this worried expression on his face and mentioned that he usually put high school kids on for benediction because it was dark in October after benediction."

"Uh, oh. That's a tough one, Stevie. How'd you get out of that?"

"Trust me. I had thought of that and had a solution. I told him that if he put Donny Rohr on with me, we would have a ride home because his father takes him everywhere. How's that for being prepared, Wilcamp?

"You know what a flake Donny Rohr is. The guy thinks he knows everything, but he usually doesn't know anything, and his father never lets him go anywhere by himself. Father Francis said that was a good idea, because Donny likes serving benedictions, and he put me and Donny Rohr on for benediction on initiation night.

"Step one, my name appears on the October schedule for benediction on the first Monday of the month. Presto, anybody who wants to go after you or has a grudge against you, thinks I'm at benediction, and your sorry ass is out there in the initiation without your best friend. All by your sweet self. A sitting duck.

"Step two, last Friday, I went to the rectory and made a personal call to see Father Francis. Can you believe that, Wilcamp? When's the last time you think an altar boy went all by himself to see the giant in the rectory? Huh? Never! That's when."

Jeremy sat on the ground grinning.

"He was a little upset when he found out that after the altar boys' meeting, I had to help my father pick up these new cabinets that he had ordered and couldn't serve benediction. I said that my father had been having a lot of back pain from an injury at work, and I didn't want to tell him I couldn't help him. Then I said that I would have told him sooner, but we just found out that the cabinets are arriving Monday.

"Father Francis made a comment about how I didn't have to come to the rectory, and all my father had to do was call, and it would have been taken care of.

"That made me nervous. What if Father Francis decided to call my father? I figured I had to say something. Imagine what my father would think if Father Francis called him up and told him he was praying for him at mass so that his back gets better."

"Holy, cow, Stockton," and Jeremy burst out laughing. "Man, you do think of everything."

"Hey, we're talking about Father Francis here. He'd do something like that. So, I told him that if my father knew I had to serve benediction, he would never allow me to miss it for any reason. He would insist that benediction was more important and not let me help him.

"That all seemed to win Father Francis over. He said that in some ways my father might have been correct, but he understood how important it was for me to help him."

"Stockton, you're a genius. It's crucial for Father Francis to think that your father doesn't know about the benediction. It means that he will never call your father to check up on your story. That's sneaky."

"Don't give me too much credit. It just popped into my head. But, you're right, and I'm glad it did. But then, I threw him my real curve ball. I told him I had asked you to do it for me, and you said that was fine. Isn't that marvelous? I had solved the problem I had created for him, and he doesn't have to do anything. Wouldn't you think he would love that?

"Guess what he said? He wasn't sure that you knew enough about benediction to serve it. I told him that you're a bright guy, and I had asked you if you were sure that you could do it, and you had said it was no problem.

39

"I told Father Francis that Donny would want to be the censor bearer. That's the only difficult part for the altar boys at benediction. Donny would have a seizure if you even thought about being the censor bearer. That dingbat will be in his glory swinging the thing, making the sign of the cross with incense smoke. For the most part, all you do is kneel there at benediction. You don't say any Latin. The worst part about benediction is listening to those old ladies screeching singing. Wait until you hear them doing *Mother Dearest, Pray for Me.*"

Jeremy chuckled at Steve.

"No kidding. There's this one old biddy who shows up for every benediction. Her name is Mrs. Nussblow or Noseblow, something like that."

"Now, I know you're kidding, Stockton."

"No, she's incredible. She thinks she's a prima donna. Mother is a simple word, right? She's got to dress it up. She puts about fifty o's and a bunch of u's in it. She sounds about like this." Steve contorted his face, inflated his cheeks, and sang out in his loudest girlish voice,

"Mmmoooooouuuuuuuthhhheeeerrrr Deeeaaaarrrrreeessssttt..."

Before he could finish, he burst out laughing, blew the rest of the wind out of his lungs, and rolled over. Jeremy and Steve were now almost in tears laughing.

"Holy shit," Jeremy giggled along with Steve. "Stockton, if you don't go to hell for talking about that dear lady like that, nobody will. You should burn forever, making fun of that lady, and I'll get dragged along for listening."

"Shucks, Jeremy, those burning souls in hell need somebody like us to liven things up. Here's the good part. Father Francis said okay with the switch, and that's it. You're good to go for benediction.

"And there you have step three. Anybody who wants to gang up on you after the meeting, won't be able to find you because they won't know where you are."

"Well, it sounds like a plan that might work as far as it goes, but the older kids are liable to still be fooling around after benediction. Benediction only takes about half an hour or so. Still, it's not bad, Steve. At least there should be fewer of them by that time."

"Jeremy, that's only part of my plan. Believe me, I've got it all worked out. It might be worse later because the meanest ones will be hanging around then, itching to do something bad. The ones whose parents don't care what time they get home. They would love to run into you then.

"Nope, we've got to go a few steps further. I am counting on being back in church with those nice ladies singing away to Mother Mary before benediction is over. I would never desert you at a time like this, but I have one thing to do while you're at benediction."

"What's that?"

"I promised Carl Easler and Mickey Quinn that I would get them out of the initiation. Just because those two are top A students, they're labeled as teacher's pets. Mickey wears glasses. About two weeks ago, I caught Joe Delaney holding Mickey's glasses up in the air in the boy's bathroom, refusing to give them to Mickey. I almost broke Joe's arm, and I don't think he'll be messing with Mickey again, but Mickey asked me if I thought Joe would be after him at the initiation because of what I had done to him.

"What was I going to do? Mickey and Carl hang together all the time, and I told them I would get them out of the initiation. If Joe Delaney or anybody goes after Mickey at the initiation, they'll take his glasses and tease him. I can't let that happen. It shouldn't take me more than twenty minutes to get them home and be back to church before benediction is over.

41

"But if I am late, here's what you're going to do."

Steve is taking so much on himself.

"You know that door in the back of the altar boys' room? The blackboard is usually sitting in front of it."

"Yeah, sure, I know it."

"That door opens up into the basement of the Monastery."

"Stevie, come on," Jeremy snarled, "you don't think I'm going down there, do you?'

"Nothing to it. When you and Donny leave the altar boys' room, make believe that you need to use the bathroom. As soon as Donny is gone, hightail it back into the altar boys' room and go behind that door."

"Steve, suppose somebody is in the basement?"

"Nobody will be there, Jeremy, and that's how I am planning for us to duck out of the initiation anyway. But I plan on being with you when it's time to go into the basement, and we can do anything together.

"If I don't get back into church before benediction is over, and you do have to go into the basement alone, you need to know what it's like down there. There's only a couple of lights that are ever lit. Must be lots more, but I have never found any light switches. One light is at the top of the stairs by the altar boys' room entrance, and one is on the other side at the top of the stairs leading to the old church where Mark and I hid from Father Andrew. If you stand on your tip toes, you can unscrew that lightbulb by the altar boys' room.

"Look the stairs over before you do, so that you know where you're going. You'll be standing on a platform at the top of a curved staircase that goes down about fifteen steps to a cement walkway. The walkway goes across the top of the basement over to the staircase that leads to the old church. That's how we are going to escape. We'll go across that walkway to the old church, out the old church, and off to home.

"If you hear anyone but me come into the altar boys' room, unscrew that light bulb. Put your hands on the wall and work your way down the steps to the walkway and stay there. Jeremy, if some of the guys from the initiation are after you, they won't go down those stairs in the dark. Even football players aren't going to want to tackle that darkness."

"Whew," Jeremy squirmed uncomfortably, "I'm liable to freak out listening to this."

"It's a piece of cake. I've already done it several times. It's nothing more than walking down a flight of steps. That's it. What if it is dark? Keep your hands on the wall. It's a beautiful plan, but you should never be there by yourself. I've got to be back before then. But if I do show up after you, I'll screw the bulb in and call you first thing. Just wait on the walkway."

"It sounds spooky, Steve. The church basement?"

"You want to know how I know? Somebody did it before. I was in the third grade when they pulled it off. But nobody has done it since, and I doubt anybody knows that you can get out through the basement anymore.

"It's insane down there even with the lights on. In the winter time, the furnaces are roaring on and off, and, in the summer, it's those fan motors. The hot water heaters are down there, and the sewage and water pipes are always making strange noises. It would scare anybody the way those things blast on and off.

"But you've got to be careful. I don't know how far of a drop it is into the basement. There's a single rung iron railing that runs down the stairs and across the walkway. In the middle of the walkway is another staircase that goes down into the basement, but there's a tall chain link gate at the top, and it's locked. Do you have a flashlight at home?"

"I don't know, Stevie, maybe, but I doubt it. I can look, but, even if I found one, how would I hide it? My mom would catch me with it, and then, all hell would break loose."

"Hmm," Steve mumbled. "Your mother doesn't trust you, does she?"

"She'd think I was going out to steal something."

"That's ridiculous. When have you ever stolen anything? I've already searched my house looking for one, but we don't have one. Can you get some matches? Your mother must have some laying around in a drawer somewhere."

"Yeah, maybe," Jeremy ran his hands through his hair, "Mom usually keeps some in the kitchen. I ought to be able to sneak matches out."

"Bring them along. That will give you some light in case you have to hide on that walkway, and I know we must have some at home too. I'll bring whatever I can find to the meeting."

Jeremy took a deep breath and raised his shoulders. "Stevie, how did you think of all this?"

"Like I told you. I heard about someone doing it once before, and I've checked it out. You and I can do it again."

Jeremy made a feeble attempt at a laugh.

A few drops of rain fell.

"What do you think, Jeremy? Can we do it?"

Jeremy felt a lump in his throat and his chin crimped. "You know what, Stevie. You know why I was so afraid of the initiation? I thought that you weren't going to be with me. I saw your name on the schedule for benediction tonight when Father Francis posted it on the bulletin board last month, and I knew I was going to be alone.

I didn't know how to handle it. And here you are, planning this the whole time. Steve, I swear, I think I am going to cry."

"No, Jeremy, don't. We've got them beat."

Jeremy's shoulders shook, and tears made their way into his eyes. He looked through blurred eyes at Steve. "Stevie, I wish I could do something for you." He wiped the tears away.

Steve put a hand on Jeremy's shoulder. "Jeremy, we're best friends. It's nothing you do. It's what we are, best friends. We always will be."

Steve dropped his hand from Jeremy's shoulder. The rain was getting harder. Jeremy jumped up, wiped his face again, let out a soft growl, and held his hand out to Steve. They shook a firm handshake.

"Last one to the fence is a rotten egg," Jeremy shouted. He grabbed his bookbag and lunch and sprinted toward the east side of the grove and the grammar school.

"And I bet I get over the fence before you do."

CHAPTER 3
PAROCHIAL SCHOOL

The rain whipped around him, and the wind blew through his hair as Jeremy raced toward the east side fence of the grove on Saint Michael's Street. Another clap of thunder brought chills to his skin. He leaped up in the air and twirled around to see how big of a lead he had on Steve. His feet landed on the soft earth in full stride. He resisted an impulse to laugh. Steve's plan had eased his fears, and, with the head start he had, Steve could not beat him to the fence. He felt relieved and happy.

Jeremy heaved his bookbag and lunch onto the lawn next to the grove, dug his fingers and feet into the diamond shaped holes of the fence, and forced himself up.

"You'll never do it Wilcamp."

Jeremy felt Steve grab the fence beneath him. They vaulted over the fence, Jeremy ahead of Steve, and toppled to the ground, falling onto each other.

"I had to have beaten you, Stockton, since you landed on top of me. Didn't think I could learn how to climb a fence so fast, did you?"

"It was my good training." Steve grinned, as he got up and brushed the leaves and dirt off his pants.

"What are we going to tell Sister Verona?" Jeremy joined Steve in brushing off his clothes. "She'll never believe we took this long to clean the altar boys' room. We could have painted it by now."

46

"We're not that late. Don't worry, I'll come up with something appropriate for altar boys to have been doing."

They hurried across Saint Michael's Street and entered the middle entrance on the lower level of the large three-story red brick schoolhouse, Saint Michael's Monastery Grammar School. The third through fifth grades occupied the first level of the school, the sixth through eighth grades and the administrative offices composed the second level, and the auditorium and storage areas filled the third level. The first and second grades were in a separate building, affectionately named, the Small School. The Small School and the convent were just south of the grammar school.

Steve leaned against the wall at the bottom of the steel staircase leading to the second level. "Let me do all the talking, okay, Jeremy. We're later that we ought to be, but we'll get out of it without a lick of punishment. Watch and see."

"Okay, Stevie, if you say so."

Steve led the way up the stairs. He knocked on the door to 8B and entered. Jeremy tagged along behind Steve too closely, wishing that he was invisible. His right foot bumped Steve's left heel, but, in an amazing piece of good luck, he didn't trip Steve.

Oh, man, suppose I had made Steve stumble into Sister Verona, and he ripped her hood off or something like that. What a scene that would make. Jeremy glanced around the classroom with fearful eyes as he realized how narrowly he had missed making a laughing stock out of Steve and himself.

Sister Verona was diagramming a compound sentence on the blackboard for the class.

Steve ambled up to her before she could speak. "Sister, I know we're late, but Jeremy and I ran into a situation after mass that we had to help out with. You know that stooped-over old lady who dresses in rags and walks so slowly and funny with her cane? We saw her creeping down Monastery Avenue when we left the altar boys' room after mass. She was carrying two shopping bags full of soda bottles down to Montclair Market to get the deposit money on them. When she stepped off the curb at Dennis Street, two of the bottles fell and broke. We couldn't ignore her and not help her because she needs that money."

"Steve," Sister Verona swiped her chalky hands across a gray apron, "what are you talking about?"

"Well, you know how you get two cents deposit money back for every soda bottle you return to the store?" Steve kept talking without giving Sister Verona a chance to speak. "That's how that old lady makes extra money. She goes around looking for soda bottles that people throw away, and she takes them to Montclair Market and gets the deposit money for them."

"Steve, I know about deposit money, but what has that got to do with an altar boy who is supposed to eat his breakfast in the altar boys' room after mass and then come straight to school."

"That lady was carrying more than she could handle and when she dropped the bottles, Jeremy and I felt like we had to help her. Jeremy took one bag and I took the other, and we walked her down to Montclair Market."

"I know it's important to do good-deeds, Steve, but why did it take this long? It's almost 10:00."

"Sister, she can barely walk even with that cane, and she seemed so happy to have someone to talk to. She kept repeating herself about how her husband was dead, how she has no family, how she only gets one small pension check every month, and how nobody ever talks to her. She was almost crying, but me and Jeremy told her that she was performing a great service for the community by collecting all the bottles people leave lying around.

"She didn't want to let us go, Sister, but that's what took so long."

Jeremy struggled to keep a straight face as he listened to Steve. He was already contorting the hell out of himself trying to keep from laughing when he peeked at Steve.

Jeremy bowed his head to hide his face and bit into his lower lip. Tears had formed in Steve's eyes.

How can he do stuff like this? I didn't see him bash himself in the nose. Jeremy dug his right thumbnail into his palm until it hurt, telling himself that if he lost control, they were going to be in deep trouble.

"Well, Steve, sometimes the needs of other people are so great that it would be wrong to not help them, and I understand that. You two did a good thing, but if something like this happens again, you must be much quicker about it."

Curiosity tickled Jeremy, and he stole another peek at Steve. This time Jeremy giggled, but he brought his hand up to his mouth and faked a cough. Steve had gotten a tear to trickle down his face.

Stevie. If you do anything else, I'm going to burst.

Sister Verona's heart melted when she saw the tear. "Okay, Steve, it's all right. Go to the coatroom, hang your coats up, and then take your seats. We are diagraming sentences."

"Thank you, Sister," Steve murmured.

Sister Verona called the class to attention. She felt guilty that she had forced Steve to such a drastic point when she knew that he was one of the best students she had ever taught, and she didn't want the class to see him like this. She had to reprimand Steve and Jeremy, but now she felt that she should have believed Steve in the first place and not pushed it so far.

Once they were in the coatroom, Jeremy sat on the floor, buried his mouth in his jacket and tried to hold back his mirth. Steve was as staid as if he was a parent admonishing a child.

He gave Jeremy a soft kick. "Come on, now, be serious."

But then Steve doubled over too. They composed themselves and walked to their desks and sat down.

Jeremy sat in the sixth seat in the third row and Steve sat across the aisle from him in the fourth row. It was so close to the morning recess that Sister Verona diagramed only two more sentences before the recess bell rang.

At 10:15, the eighth-grade classes had a fifteen-minute break in which students could go to the bathroom and have a drink at the water fountain if they wanted. The sixth and seventh grades had a similar break before the eighth-graders. Sister Sullpicia and the respective teachers monitored the hallways making sure that the kids got back to class promptly.

Jeremy and Steve walked sheepishly up the aisles to go to the bathroom, avoiding Sister Verona's eyes.

But Sister Verona called Steve to her desk.

"Steve, it's I and Jeremy or Jeremy and I but not me and Jeremy."

"Oh, yeah, Sister, guess I slipped up there, didn't I? Thanks, Sister. I am sorry about being late. I didn't realize how long we had taken."

"It's okay, Steve. You better be getting on or you'll be late again."

"Yes, Sister."

After they left the classroom, Steve said, "Jeremy, don't laugh. Everybody will know we're lying. You've got to play being serious."

Jeremy's entire torso shook as he tried to muffle his laugher. "Steve, you are something else, man."

"I bet you Sister Verona and everybody else in the class thinks that old lady is evil. Evil enough to be a witch. She would throw a bottle at us before she would let us help her.

"And, Steve, how can you possibly tell that story and cry. That's phenomenal. You should be an actor. I couldn't do any of what you did."

"Come on, Jeremy, don't talk about it so much. One of those frivolous girls will be up there telling Sister Verona, and she might think about checking up. But, believe me, she isn't going to do anything more than think about it."

Steve and Jeremy stood next to each other at the urinals pissing and giggling. Before Jeremy could finish, someone grabbed his arms around his elbows and pulled him away from the urinal so that he was pissing on the floor.

"Well, Jeremy, sweetie pie," he heard the voice of Brad Maddox say, "let's see what we'll be checking out at the initiation tonight."

Jeremy kicked Brad's shin with his right heel. Brad tightened his grip on Jeremy's arms, but then, Jeremy saw Steve's fist moving like a rocket behind him, and he felt Steve's punch on Brad's face through his entire body. Brad reeled backwards, and blood poured from his nose.

Jeremy and Steve zipped up and faced Brad. Brad stood a head taller than Steve and Jeremy. He leaned against the wall holding his nose. The gushing of blood stopped everyone in the bathroom.

"You dickheads. Wait until you see what we do to you tonight." Brad headed for the door.

Steve pounced on him in a second. He snagged Brad's shoulders, propped his left foot behind Brad's right ankle, and spun him around, thrusting him to the floor.

"How about right now, shit face," Steve yelled, towering over Brad. "What's your bad ass going to do right now, big boy?"

Steve was livid with anger.

Blood streamed down Brad's face running onto his white school shirt and blue tie.

From outside the bathroom, all the boys heard Sister Verona's voice, "Come out of there, every one of you."

Brad stood with his fists clenched and fury in his eyes. "You can't protect his queer ass forever, and a few guys will be fixing you too tonight."

He shoved Steve as he blew past him moving toward the door.

Sister Verona called again.

Steve planted his foot in Brad's ass, and Brad flew forward, slamming into the wall. Fear replaced fury in Brad's eyes, and he scrammed out of the bathroom.

Jeremy was in a state of shock. "Oh, Stevie, maybe you shouldn't have done all that. You're going to be in all kinds of trouble because of me."

The bathroom door opened and Sister Sullpicia poked her head in. "Out, every one of you, right now."

"Jeremy," Steve whispered, "when you've got somebody who deserves to be gotten, you give it to them." "You pound your point into their head, so they don't ever forget."

"Out of there, you two!" Sister Sullpicia shrilled.

Steve and Jeremy stepped around a fuming Sister Sullpicia. Her strong hands clasped Jeremy and Steve by the back of their necks with a power that surprised them. She shook them and smacked their heads together.

"Nobody ever fights in this school." She smacked their heads together again. "Nobody," she shouted even louder, "ever fights in my school." She shook them more violently. "Do you understand that?"

"Yes, Sister," they responded in unison.

"Up to my office, all three of you."

On the way up the stairs, even though neither Steve nor Jeremy had ever had any but the slightest encounters with her, both were thinking that they knew why this nun was the principal of Saint Michael's Monastery grammar school.

At the top of the stairs, Sister Sullpicia instructed Sister Verona to take Brad to the school nurse and to have the nurse send him to her office after he was attended to. She ordered the students of 8B to get into their classroom, sit in their seats, and study something until she got there. She dared them to let her catch one of them talking.

She then clasped Steve and Jeremy each by an upper arm and led them to her office. She was putting a good hurt on them by the time they arrived there. She sat them down in two wooden armchairs next to each other along a wall in her office.

"Stay in those chairs, and don't move an inch until I get back." Then, she went back to 8B.

Steve grinned as he gazed into his best friend's eyes. It was seldom that Steve did not think he had control over most situations in which he either found himself or had gotten himself into by whatever senseless means. But now, he resigned himself to take whatever came from what appeared to be an impossible battleax.

Jeremy placed his hand on Steve's forearm. He could feel and see Steve's dejection. "Thanks, Steve."

Jeremy felt like crying. He wasn't sure why. A strong feeling for Steve gripped his entire being. He didn't understand it, but whatever it was, it made him feel like crying.

Sister Sullpicia returned to her office and closed the oak door behind her. She was a tall woman and rather robust, who could move a lot of things with a lot of force, if she so chose.

She sat down in the chair behind her large desk and eyed Steve and Jeremy coldly for a moment. She then rocked her chair back and rotated it toward the wall opposite her captives.

The picture of Jesus Christ crucified hanging on the wall with a crown of thorns on his head and blood streaming down his face, drew her attention, as it had many times in the past, encouraging her to find the best way to deal with these two students.

She grasped the rosary hanging at her side. So many of the wonderful and holy things that she wanted for all her school children passed through her mind. She let the silence stand. It was an old and effective tactic.

Her mind wrestled with that mixture of feelings that such a position as being a nun, a principal, a teacher, a friend, and even a mother figure to so many children over so many years brings to a person with such responsibilities. How to do the right thing all the time. How to do the right thing now, in this situation, with these boys so bent on fighting. It was so important to this grammar school principal. How to punish with meaning and not purely for punishment's sake.

She called the school nurse on the phone for a report on Brad.

"It doesn't matter," Sister Sullpicia spoke into the phone, "have Sister Martha take him to the hospital and get the nose x-rayed. We must be certain that it isn't broken."

She hung the phone up and allowed the silence to persist, wanting these boys to think about what they had done and to wonder with some trepidation about their fate. Steve fixed his eyes on the floor. Jeremy contemplated the school principal.

She can't be the principal just because she's a bully and can beat the crap out of any kid, can she? She must be more than that.

Jeremy rose from his seat and stepped toward her desk. Sister Sullpicia had turned her swivel chair toward the window behind her desk, from which she could see the statue of the Blessed Virgin Mary in the middle of the school children's playground. Her back now faced Steve and Jeremy, and she could not detect Jeremy's advance.

Jeremy had no idea of what to do. *I can't let Stevie take the blame for this. I've got to do something. He's always protected me. I've got to try.*

Even though it was a spacious office with a high ceiling and large, bright windows, Jeremy felt the walls closing in on him. The atmosphere seemed suffocating, and his chest rose and fell deeply as he tried to take in more air.

"Sister," Jeremy wrung his hands together.

She whirled her chair around, stunned that Jeremy had dared to approach her desk.

"Sister," Jeremy shuffled his feet on the floor, "maybe sometimes, things happen that are bad enough for everyone to realize that they shouldn't have done them. The result is so wrong and so many people are hurt that no one needs to be hurt any more by it.

"Sister, my parents would never understand a thing like this. They can't. They would be convinced that I am responsible and did something in a bathroom that humiliated and shamed our family. No matter what happened or how anybody tries to explain it, I will have disgraced my family in this school, which means so much to them. I would never be forgiven, Sister. My parents might never trust me again.

"And maybe, I have a friend like Stevie who takes care of me and watches out for me all the time. He knows what my parents would think of me if they found out about this. We do everything together." Jeremy paused and took a long, deep breath.

"Stevie tried to protect me, Sister. He didn't want to fight Brad. But Brad wouldn't let go of me. And maybe, a tough guy like Brad only meant to play a prank on me and didn't mean too much by it. And then, it all happened. Nobody meant any of it to happen the way it did.

"Stevie stepped in to try to keep me from being involved so that my parents don't have to know. Maybe now, everybody knows that we did a wrong thing. Everybody is sorry. None of us will ever do it again.

"It wasn't Stevie's fault, Sister." Jeremy struggled to maintain composure, but his eyes were tearing.

"Can't it stop here, Sister? Can't this, please, be enough punishment for everybody?"

Jeremy had astonished Sister Sullpicia. She had not anticipated anything that he had said and did not know how to interpret his words. She had expected a typical teenage boys' brawl. Not this. Steven protecting Jeremy seemed a far cry from a bathroom brawl.

She had had few contacts with the adolescent standing before her, but it was easy for her to conclude that he had lived in the shadow of his older brother, because she had known Brian very well. The words this boy spoke, his intensity, his presentation before her, all worried her.

Control, order, security, knowledge of everything around her were the workings of Sister Sullpicia's mind. God, country, school, parents, peace and security. Jeremy hinted of chaos. *What is happening to him right here in this school.* His insecurity, his fear within his own family, which he suffered with such bravery, disturbed her. She had seldom seen this in her years of teaching, and it usually presaged ominous happenings.

She suddenly realized that her silence must be cutting deeply into this already terrified child. "Maybe you are right, Jeremy. Maybe the lesson has been learned. Jeremy, I want you to go to the bathroom and freshen yourself up. You are a fine young man, and I am proud of you for defending your friend no matter what happened. We will not discuss it any further. Steven will meet you in the bathroom in a few minutes, and then the two of you may return to class together."

Jeremy wiped his face. "Thanks, Sister."

She rose from her chair. "Jeremy, God is your friend also. He will guide and help you even when everything seems as bad as it can be. And I am here to help every student in this school. Come here any time you want, even if it is nothing special."

"Thank you, Sister."

Jeremy had known in the silence after he had spoken, that he had affected Sister Sullpicia. She had seen something in him, something that had shocked her. As he turned from Sister Sullpicia to leave her office, he saw the same shocked expression on Stevie's face.

As soon as the door to her office closed, Stevie popped up from his chair. "Sister..."

"Sit down, Steven."

"But, Sister..."

"Be quiet and listen to me. Sit down."

Steve reluctantly sat down in the uncomfortable chair.

"I want you to go to Jeremy and stay with him until you think he is composed and ready to return to class. You are the most important person in his life right now, the only one who knows what's going on. I want you to tell him that I am not going to call his parents. Make it clear to him that I understand that Brad instigated the entire confrontation. Brad has caused problems here before. Jeremy has never caused any problem. Do you understand me?"

"Yes, Sister."

Sister Sullpicia put her hands on her desk and rocked her chair forward. "I would never ask or expect a student to do this, but Jeremy is not able to deal with an authority figure at this moment. He needs friendship. Reassure him as much as you can. I want you to come to my office after the noon recess. Now, go to him, and if you think you need help or if you think that Jeremy should not go to class, you come here and get me. I'll wait here in my office."

"Yes, Sister."

Steve left her office and raced after Jeremy.

Sister Sullpicia called Mrs. Morgan, the school secretary, into her office. "Mrs. Morgan, please take this note to Sister Verona in 8B."

In her impeccable, flowing penmanship, she wrote that Jeremy and Steven were to be allowed into class without questions. She closed the brief note, telling Sister Verona that they would talk in her office during the lunch break.

"Mrs. Morgan, as soon as you get back, bring me the records of both of the Wilcamp boys, Stephen Stockton, and Brad Maddox, will you?"

"Certainly, Sister."

The principal reached for her rosary as she sat at her desk. She was shaken. In her career as a principal, she had dealt with eight families in which a child had run away from home, three children who had been blatantly abused, coming to school with bruises on their bodies, and one suicide. An eighth-grade boy, like Jeremy.

Jeremy had unearthed all the bitter and heartrending memories of that suicide. Sister Sullpicia wondered what could be happening to Jeremy in his own home to make him so fearful of his parents.

She was certain that Jeremy's plight was not like that of the child who had commit suicide. Jeremy had Stevie. The other child had had nobody. Sister Sullpicia had recognized that Jeremy was on the brink of hysteria. She believed that Steve might be able to lead Jeremy out of his excited state and avoid a distressful, uncontrollable outburst of emotion in Jeremy.

Her decision on how to handle the matter posed the most imminent threat to Jeremy. She had elected to defuse the threat as soon as she understood it, abandoning all thought of punishing him further as he requested, allaying Jeremy's fears, and allowing him contact with his best friend. As the beads of her rosary slipped through her fingers, she hoped that she had done the right thing to relinquish her control of the situation.

Jeremy and Steven are best friends. Steven's help will be much better than mine right now. My turn will come later.

* * *

Steve flew down the stairs two at a time and darted into the bathroom. Jeremy sat on the floor at the far wall with his back against the radiator underneath the window, his arms crossed over his flexed knees, his head resting on his forearms. He raised his head as Steve entered the bathroom.

Steve knelt next to Jeremy. "Jeremy are you okay?"

Jeremy's face was drawn and pale. "I think so, but I feel weak. I wish I could go to sleep for a while."

"Jeremy, you were great. You must've made her remember what a principal is supposed to be, or maybe she's an okay person. I don't know, but she believed you. We're off the hook. She knows Brad caused the whole problem. She doesn't even know what happened yet, but she is certain that Brad is responsible. She said that he has caused problems here before."

"She's going to call my mother, Steve. She's going to call my mother." He dropped his head onto his forearms and cried.

"No, no, Jeremy, she isn't going to do that."

"Stevie, you don't know what it's like. I don't have anybody at home. My parents don't love me or something. I can never do anything right." Jeremy's voice cracked as he spoke. "They're always telling me how fabulous Brian is and how worthless I am. They go to everything he's involved in if they can. They always go to his parents-teacher conferences.

"You think that my mom would come here to see Sister Verona? No way. She knows I am doing better with Sister Verona than I have done with any other teacher. But when I had such a rough time in Sister Vincentia's class last year, she didn't miss a conference, gabbing with Sister Vincentia about what a lousy student I am.

"Steve, my parents don't do anything with me. They don't care if I get into activities, because they aren't coming to see me. All they want me to do is stay out of trouble, come home bright and early, and keep my face hidden. Steve, you know what my mother said to me once. She told me she wished I had never been born."

All control was gone, and Jeremy Wilcamp sobbed desperately.

Steve wrapped his arm around Jeremy's shoulders.

"What am I going to do, Steve. My father is going to beat me again. You don't believe me because your parents love you so much. They would do anything for you. Your Dad probably never beat you once in your life."

"Jeremy, I believe you. I want to make it different somehow. Please, listen to me. She's not going to call your mother. She told me to tell you that. I would never lie to you. You've got to believe me."

"Steve, no matter what she told you, you know she's going to call. She saw something in me. I was like an open book. She thinks I'm cracking up. Don't you know how these religious people are by now? Anything they can't handle, they shove into somebody else's lap and say God loves you and God will help you. Keep those prayers flowing, and it will all get better and now get out of my life."

Steve knelt on the floor in front of Jeremy. "Jeremy, suppose Sister Sullpicia isn't like that. Suppose she doesn't want you to get hurt, and she realizes that only grief awaits you if your parents get involved. Suppose she saw so much hurt in you that every good thing in her went out to you. What if she's you're friend? You've got to give her a chance."

Tears creeped into Steve's eyes. "If you don't give her a chance, it might turn out that you're being your own worst enemy."

Jeremy stared at the bathroom door. "Steve, I've got to run away. I can't go through it anymore. My father is going to be so mad...and my mother...she hates me, Steve. If she finds out about this, our whole house will explode. Everybody will be yelling at each other and at me, accusing me of everything. Maybe I could hide in the grove, and you could bring me some food and stuff."

Steve's best friend frightened him. What if he couldn't bring Jeremy out of this. His heart beat fast and hard as Sister Sullpicia's words slammed through his brain. If you think that Jeremy should not go back to class, you come here and get me. Steve now understood what she meant. Jeremy was so terrified of what his parents might do that he was losing it.

"Jeremy, please, don't think that. You don't have to run away. You didn't do anything but go to the bathroom and take a leak.

You're not any part of this. You're the victim. Should you be punished? Sister Sullpicia knows you didn't do anything.

"Do you really think she's going to call your mother and tell her that you broke down in her office and cried because somebody dragged your body out into the middle of the bathroom so that half the boys in the class could see your dick? No way, Jeremy. If she calls your mother, she would have to tell her what happened. Can you picture Sister Sullpicia broadcasting the news that it's not safe for a boy to go to the bathroom in this school because he might get molested by some other student?

"Man, sisters don't have it in them to talk to an eighth-grade boy's parents about something that involves their son's dick. They won't do that. I tell you, Jeremy, these nuns don't believe any apple caused the problem in the Garden of Eden. They think it was Adam's big dick. That apple is nothing but a symbol. What's the first thing Adam does after the big sin? He hides his nuts with a fig leaf. You don't have to be a genius to know what that means. Even a nun can figure that out.

"What if your mother asked Sister Sullpicia something like this, 'Oh, my God, Sister Sullpicia, how many boys saw my son's penis?' Sister Sullpicia would shit her pants. That is, if she has any under that outfit they wear. She has probably never had to answer a question like that in her life, and I don't think she wants to start now.

"She doesn't know what happened yet, Jeremy. When she finds out what happened, she's not gonna want to talk your mother about it."

Jeremy had stopped crying while listening to Steve. He smiled, and then he burst out laughing.

"Stevie Stockton, that's the most amazing thing I ever heard."

Jeremy's sides now hurt so much from laughing and crying that he thought he might burst. "Steve, Adam's big dick! Sister

Sullpicia's underpants! Are you for real? How do you ever think of stuff like that?"

Steve wrapped his arms around Jeremy and hugged him. "Welcome back to earth, man. You were scaring me. I have a hunch that Sister Sullpicia isn't so bad. Maybe she gets mad fast and acts violently. That's what a principal must do sometimes, I guess, if things get out of control. But she figured out what's going on.

"She realized that you were telling her the truth, and she got you out of her office because she didn't want you to keep hurting. She recognized that Brad was the problem, and she sent me down here because she could see that we're the best friends ever. What you said, stopped her cold, Jeremy.

"Let me tell you something else. I'm going to be over your house all the time from now on, and your parents are going to find out what a great kid they have because I'm going to show them."

"You might be right about Sister Sullpicia, but you'll never show may parents anything, especially my mother."

"Oh, yeah, your big, smart brother doesn't have any friends like you and me."

Jeremy dried his face on his shirt sleeve. "You think she won't call my mom?"

"I know she's not going to call. That's what she told me."

Steve ran some warm water and ripped a handful of paper towels from the dispenser. "Come on, we have to get you fixed up." Steve reached out a hand. Jeremy took it, and Steve gave him a pull up.

Steve helped Jeremy get himself together. "Now listen, don't panic, but I've got to tell you one more thing. Sister Sullpicia wants me to go to her office after the noon recess and talk about what happened in the bathroom. For good and sure, what she really wants to do is pick my brains about you, but don't worry. It'll be easy enough for me to handle her. I'll play it dumb and tell her what I told you, you know, how embarrassed you were by what Brad did and how you never wanted to tell your mom about that, okay?"

"Steve, please, don't tell her anything more about me. I gave away enough in there. Tell her…I don't know what to tell her. Why's she got to do that? Why can't she leave me alone?" Jeremy fussed with his tie.

"It's her nature. She's driven by God to save even your poor soul. She's committed to helping you with your parents. She's a nun. She's the principal. Those kinds of people think they are ordained to fix everything, and they believe God is going to help them do it. You can't let it get you down. Eight more months, and we're out of here. Trust me, Jeremy, will you? I can talk my way around anything."

"Steve, don't mention the initiation tonight. If you do, she's liable to try to do something about it. It's better that we get that thing over with."

"You know what I'll do? I'll tell her you had a big hardon when Brad pulled you back, and you were stroking it."

"Steve, come on."

"Yeah, and when she gets that real cold, how-could-you look on her face, I can say, Sister, you wouldn't believe how big it was."

"Oh, God," Jeremy's tone hinted of exasperation, "or maybe you could lay some more Adam and Eve stories on her. Your new edition of the bible would be a big hit.

"Steve, your mind is firing ten times faster than anyone else's. You dream up some outrageous things. But, get serious, okay. If she pulls some strings to get me out of that initiation, Brad and his buddies will be after me all through high school. They'll be calling me Sister Sullpicia's pet or something like that."

"You've got to stop worrying so much, Jeremy. You'll go through your whole life without having any fun."

Jeremy ran his hands through his brown hair and evaluated his reflection in the mirror. "Will I pass for being on the team that beat the shit out of Brad Maddox and broke his nose?"

"Yes. If the class cheers when we walk in," Steve clapped jubilantly, "we're going to take a bow."

"Tell you one thing, Steve, there's a lot of kids in our class who would like to see Brad taken down a peg or two."

"He's an incredible asshole," Steve muttered as they left the bathroom. "Always picking on somebody."

Outside the bathroom, Steve hesitated at the bottom of the stairs. "Jeremy, it's my turn to thank you."

"For what?"

"For how you handled Sister Sullpicia. I expected her to take us over her lap and tan our hides good. Then suspend us. Even expel us, or at least me. I couldn't believe my eyes when I saw you standing in front of her desk."

"It wasn't that much."

"What do you mean, it wasn't that much, Jeremy? Most kids would have spilled the beans about the initiation and gotten Brad into one heck of a mess. But you didn't do that. Instead, you opened up something very private to her so that she'd know I had a real reason for going after Brad."

"Thanks, Steve, but if I had brought up the initiation, Brad would have denied it. Then we would be stuck proving it. Come on, man, let's not worry about it anymore. We better get back to class before Sister Sullpicia comes looking for us."

* * *

The rain had stopped, and the sun was shining. The nuns had huddled together and decided to let the kids go outside for recess after their lunch. Winter was on the way, and they would be spending their recess time in class. Most of the teachers preferred that the kids got out on the playground whenever possible. Saint Michael's Street was blocked off every school day from 12 noon to 1:00 and became the playground for the fifth through eighth grades. A smaller playground bordering the school was designated for the first through fourth grades.

Jeremy and Steve traipsed across Saint Michael's Street and sat down under a large maple tree still clinging to its golden, yellow leaves of autumn. They sat close to where they had scrambled over the fence that morning.

"Guess what," Steve boasted, "my mom put a pack of Hostess Twinkies in my lunch bag, and I saved them for now." "You want one?"

"Yes. I was so hungry at lunch. We never did eat our breakfast this morning."

"I feel like I could eat another lunch, Jeremy. What's your mother been giving her new altar boy for breakfast now that he is serving mass and going to communion on schooldays?"

Catholics were restricted from eating food for three hours before receiving communion. An altar boy had to bring breakfast with him and eat it after mass.

"So far, she's been giving me the same thing she gave Brian. She puts a scrambled egg on two pieces of toast and wraps it up in aluminum foil. She thinks the foil keeps it warm, but it doesn't. It gets soggy, but it tastes good. This is all new stuff for me, Steve, going to communion on weekdays in front of the whole school. Do you ever not go to communion when you're serving mass?"

"Jeremy, it all comes with serving the good Lord. You can't be on the altar serving mass and not go to communion. Your priest expects every altar boy to go to communion, or they better not be on the altar. If they don't go, it means one thing. The altar boy has mortal sin on his soul and is forbidden to take the body of Christ into his body at communion. Everybody would know that you're a sinner. You've got to go.

"If you don't, your mother will hear about it. And, you know what that means." Steve gave Jeremy a shove.

"I knew you were going to say something like that. Well, what do you do if you commit a mortal sin the night before you're supposed to serve mass, and you can't go to communion?"

"What kind of mortal sin is an innocent guy like you committing that is so bad that he can't go to communion?"

Jeremy blurted out with a smile, "I beat off in the bathtub."

Steve had a mouthful of Hostess Twinkie which he promptly gagged on and spat out as he burst out laughing. He rolled over onto his back and yelled, "You pervert, Wilcamp. A pervert and an infidel."

Jeremy babbled on among shrieks of laughter, "Do you run in the next morning and say, 'Father Brendan, can we slip in a confession before mass. Bless me, Father, for I have sinned. I jerked off in the bathtub while I was trying out this new soap sample that I found in the mail box when I got home from school. It would never have happened, Father, except for this brand-new bar of soap, and I solemnly promise to never offend God again.'"

"Jeremy, you'll never catch me going to Father Brendan for confession."

"But what if he's the only priest available. Just asking, because I would never go to him, either. I couldn't look at him if I admitted to beating off."

"Jeremy, I stopped torturing myself about it. Once it started happening, I knelt on the altar one day and made my confession to God. 'God, I can't stop it. I am not hurting anyone when I do it, and if I don't go to communion, I'll be setting a bad example for all those people out there, and your priest will be mad at me, and so, I am going to serve mass and go to communion, Amen.' God has forgiven me for it for all time."

"You shit, Steve," and Jeremy gave Steve a return shove.

"Jeremy, that's all there is to it, and I haven't worried about it since."

"You really did that?"

"Yes."

"Wow. Maybe that's what I'll do. This concept of mortal sin is so overdone. It's wrong sometimes. I'm sick of being afraid of committing a sin and feeling guilty all the time and thinking that I'm going to hell. Mom is always telling me what a sinner I am, and then I come to school and am told that it's a sin to even look at my body or touch it. Once you find out what your dick does, why wouldn't you do it? Why would it be a mortal sin? Why are you going straight to hell for doing it, when it seems so natural? How am I supposed to serve mass thinking all that?"

Steve leaned back and propped himself up on his elbows. "I wish we had something else to eat. I'm still hungry."

"Jeremy, do you really believe you're going to hell because you went to communion with a mortal sin on your soul?"

"Well, yeah, Steve, that's what they teach us in religion class. Don't you believe it?"

"No, Jeremy. I might be Catholic, but I'm not stupid. That white wafer is not the body of Christ. It's a piece of bread. How can anybody in their right mind believe that because a priest bends over a piece of bread on an altar and whispers some Latin mumbo jumbo over it, the bread becomes the body of Christ. That's ridiculous. And, at the same time, the priest's words change all the wafers he's going to pass out at communion into Christ's body as well. How convenient that the mumbo jumbo travels so far. It's nonsense. God is not going to condemn you to hell because somebody else believes the impossible."

"Man, when did you start thinking that?"

Steve paused. "Do you have to know?"

"If you don't want to tell me, it's okay. You seem so sure about it. I'm wondering why."

"If you must know, I asked my father one day why he never goes to communion. He told me what I told you. I think he's right. But if he isn't, I don't care. If Dad goes to hell because he doesn't go to communion, I want to go to hell too."

Stevie moaned. "I don't believe what the church says about how not going to Sunday mass is a mortal sin, either. My Dad only goes to Sunday mass when I am one of the altar boys. Otherwise, he doesn't go. I don't worry about it. My dad never does anything bad. And he does so much good. He's not going to hell because he misses Sunday mass or doesn't go to communion.

"Think of it like this, Jeremy. All the people in the world who aren't Catholic, don't go to Sunday mass or take communion every Sunday. All those people are not going to hell because of that. What kind of God would let that happen? Why would God let all those people be born, if he's going to send them all to hell?"

Jeremy didn't know what to say and said nothing. The Catholic Church taught that it was a mortal sin to not go to mass on Sundays. Mortal sin meant condemnation to hell if the sin was not forgiven by a priest. Steve's dad was piling up mortal sin after mortal sin.

Stevie yawned. "Religion has a way of sneaking up on you, Jeremy. If I had been beating off in the second grade when I joined the altar boys and known what a big sin it's supposed to be, I would never have allowed my parents to sucker me into joining. Then, later, I find out what it's all about and discover that I am not supposed to do it, so I can be a good altar boy. That's not fair."

"How long was it before you found out?"

"Maybe it was in the third grade." Steve chuckled, and hit Jeremy on his head with his lunch bag.

"I'm glad it stopped raining," Steve said happily, "I hate it when we have to stay inside for recess."

"Wonder what Sister Sullpicia is going to ask you."

"I am not too concerned about her," Steve stated confidently, even though he was concerned. "I am more worried about what's going to happen tonight."

"Yeah. I was thinking about that too."

"Brad's a stupid bully, Jeremy, but he's going to play football in high school next year, and he's got friends on the football team. No doubt, Brad can get some of them to join him to gang up on us tonight.

"If Brad's nose is broken, we'll be in the clear. He'll be in too much pain to show up. But I doubt it's broken. The biggest impact of the punch was on his cheek. Chances are he didn't get anything worse than a nasty nosebleed. But, you know what I'm thinking?"

"What?" Jeremy sat up straighter.

"We should go into the grove when we get over to the old church. Bully Brad and his bully friends will never know where we are. We can follow the fence up to Montclair Street, and then we will be at the opposite end of where they should be. And even if they aren't, we can see them from the grove, but they can't see us. I'm gambling that they'll be too afraid to go into the grove. It's a dangerous place in the dark.

"Fear is an amazing thing isn't it, Jeremy. It makes some people cowards. They can't do anything but give up, beg and lose. Other people do impossible things. Makes them champions and heroes."

"I don't know, Steve, maybe you get stuck in something that's dangerous, and you do what you can at that moment, and then you go on. Maybe you feel fear, or you feel brave, but it doesn't make you a coward or a hero. You're you, and you do what you are at that moment."

Jeremy's comment gave Steve pause. Steve regarded being a hero or a coward as a black and white matter. Either, or. Jeremy had grayed the matter. Maybe, maybe not.

"A philosopher too. Shake my hand, Mr. Wilcamp, glad to know you." They shook hands.

"It's nothing, Stevie. People make too big a deal about every minute thing. That's all I'm saying."

"You know, Brad's a real piece of work, Jeremy. He got kicked out of the altar boys last year, and Father Francis just let him come back this year."

"What!" Jeremy hooted. "You're kidding?"

"Sorry, I'm not. Father Francis booted him out last year after he ran away to Ocean City. Remember that?"

"Yeah, sure. If he wanted to come back into the altar boys, why would he take a chance on doing something so dumb as attacking other altar boys? If he gets caught, he'll be thrown out again."

"He's still mad over being ousted last year and wants to let off some steam. He loves bullying people. He's bigger than you and me, Jeremy, and almost everybody else in our class, and he's an asshole."

"Man, Stevie, and now he's creating this headache for us. That's so messed up."

"Yeah," Steve fingered a few whiskers growing on his chin, "but it must be more than that." "Why did he do what he did to you this morning? He's after you for some reason. Maybe it's our friendship. You notice, he never bothers us the way he gets into most other people's faces. We're together all the time, and he can't get either one of us alone to hassle us. We are too protective of each other."

"Well, he obviously thinks we're a couple of queers, Stevie. But we aren't. Why did he call me a queer ass in the bathroom? He doesn't have any reason to think something like that."

"For the same reason that anybody calls someone else queer, Jeremy. They're queers themselves. After all, he did go after you when your dick was hanging out, and he grabbed you by your arms so that you couldn't put it away. He said he wanted to see your dick, and he called you sweetie pie. I'd say that qualifies him as being queer."

"Jeez, I hadn't thought about all that. Maybe he is queer."

Steve snapped his fingers. "I know what it is, Jeremy. He must've just figured out from the schedule that I'll be at benediction tonight and you'll be alone at the initiation, and he thinks he's got you. Attacking you this morning was his bonehead way of letting us know. But it backfired on him, didn't it?"

"Yeah, Stevie, I would say so."

"Let's not think about it anymore. He might not show tonight because of his nose." Steve lay back and closed his eyes.

Jeremy noticed Sister Margaret encouraging the fourth-grade girls to play HORSE on a basketball court at the north end of the playground. Not one girl made a basket, but they had a lot of fun trying as Sister Margaret cheered them on.

Jeremy listened to the voices of the school children yelling and screaming their way through the noon recess as the gray clouds above flitted through the sky. A sparkle of excitement sprang from Jeremy. "I love days like this, Steve. Think of how far we could string our kites out in this wind."

"Yeah, Jeremy, too bad we can't be doing that now. That beats going to school anytime."

* * *

The ringing of the bell announcing the end of the noon recess brought groans from both Steve and Jeremy. They trudged for the 8B location on the school playground. With a few demanding looks and some sharp commands from the nuns who taught at Saint Michael's, all sixteen classes came to silence and stood at attention, each in its allocated place on the playground.

Sister Sullpicia rang the school bell, and all sixteen classes shouted out the Pledge of Allegiance to the United States of America. With a second ring, the Our Father followed. Then, everyone trooped back to their classrooms in silence.

Steve winked at Jeremy. "I'll pass you a note as soon as I get back to class."

But Jeremy clutched Steve's wrist. "Maybe you ought to go to class first, and when everybody is sitting, you can tell Sister Verona that you have to go to Sister Sullpicia's office."

Steve felt the electricity radiating from Jeremy. It was like a circuit straight into his terrified mind.

Even though Steve had no doubt that Sister Verona knew he was supposed to go to the principal's office, Steve nodded in agreement. "Yeah, your right."

Steve followed Jeremy down the third isle. They sat in their seats and faced each other. "Jeremy, hang in, okay. I won't let Sister Sullpicia think anything bad."

Jeremy eyes wandered around the room. Then, he focused on Steve. Time had run out.

"Stevie, I wish you didn't have to deal with Sister Sullpicia alone. I..." He didn't know what to say, but the fear was so real.

"It's my fault, Stevie. You shouldn't have to do this. I'm the one who opened my mouth. It should be me talking to her."

"Hey, man, it's not your fault. Trust me, I won't let you down. And listen, believe in good things and think of good luck. We've got it, man, you and me, together. We've got good luck. Try to keep thinking of that until I get back. I'll bring you her scalp if she's got one under that hood they wear."

A smile passed between them. Steve got up, grasped Jeremy's shoulder for a moment and left the room.

He ambled up the corridor toward the principal's office, but then he decided to go down to the bathroom first. He halted at the radiator where Jeremy had sat that morning.

He saw the reflection of his own face in the window above the radiator. His heart felt heavy. He had no recollection of the last time his eyes had filled with tears before that morning, but tears welled up again. *Jeremy shouldn't have to feel like this.*

First-grade had been a long time ago, and Steve could not recall any one thing that had caused he and Jeremy to be such close friends, but they had always been, right from the start.

He wiped the moisture from his eyes and stepped to a urinal. As he stood there, he wondered what Sister Sullpicia wanted from him. *Brad is not a big concern to her. Her worst problem with him is keeping him from tormenting other kids. I did her a big favor when it comes to that. Brad's punk-ass got put down. But Jeremy is a different story. She's worried about him.*

Steve sidled up to a sink. *This altar boy thing has forced Jeremy out of all his hiding places and thrown him into a mess of problems. His father beating him, his mother mad at him, whatever Sister Sullpicia is going to do, and the initiation waiting for him tonight, not to mention all the mortal sins he thinks he's committing and suspecting that he might get kicked out of the altar boys.*

What's with Jeremy's father? Jeremy hasn't mentioned getting beat in a long time. I thought that was over.

Steve grappled with pangs of guilt because he had wanted Jeremy to join the altar boy's years ago. Performing altar boys' duties with kids who seemed so dumb and immature, bored Stevie. He knew the tasks would be fun if Jeremy joined him. Steve threw some cold-water on his face and blinked at himself in the mirror.

His light brown hair had gotten darker. It had been blond until he turned eight, and then it started to get darker. But it still turned shades lighter in the summer. The tears caused his blue eyes to sparkle. "Don't you fail me eyes, okay? No crying."

You've got to outsmart this nun somehow, Stockton. She's going to decide what to do based on what you say. I know that's what she wants to do. She wants me to give her the excuse to break her word and confront Jeremy's parents. Maybe not right now over this issue, but she'll be going after them soon enough. She knows something is wrong. She's had time to think it over, and she's made her mind up about what she needs to do.

He exited the bathroom. *You can't blow this. It's going to be almost impossible to fool her about anything. If I am forced to lie, I've got to be perfect at it. I can't make any mistakes. She'll know.* He entered Mrs. Morgan's office feeling as tense as a drum.

"Hello, Steven, Sister Sullpicia is on the phone. She'll be with you in a few minutes. Have a seat." Mrs. Morgan's pleasant demeanor did not relax Steve.

More of her waiting games. She's already trying to psych me out, and I'm not even in her office yet. Sit and wait. How nice. He bobbed his legs up and down. It seemed like an eternity before he heard a buzz over the counter top.

"Okay, Steven, you may go in now."

He stood with his hands in his pockets, thanked Mrs. Morgan, and opened the door to Sister Sullpicia's office.

Sister Sullpicia looked up from her desk, where she sat with a pen in her hand. "Come in, Steven. Close the door."

He aimed for the same chair in which he had sat that morning, but she beckoned him to sit in the chair next to her desk.

Sister Sullpicia moved the pen across a piece of paper on her desk, but Steve felt her eyes on him and all her senses perceiving every motion he made as he approached the chair. It was the strangest feeling, but he felt as though he was naked in front of her.

As he lowered himself into the chair, he checked his zipper. Then his face flashed red. *What if she saw me do that? Oh, God, this fight happened in the boys' bathroom, and I'm fooling with my zipper. What do I do now?*

Sister Sullpicia gave no indication that she had noticed anything untoward, and words still flowed from her jet-black Schaeffer fountain pen.

When Steve had settled into the chair, she put the top on her pen, laid it on the desk and leaned forward. "Steven, a school principal doesn't always get to know every child as well as she might like to, even though most of them are here for eight years. Children change as they grow up. One summer vacation may change a child a great deal. But I know you quite well."

What does she know about me? Today was the first time I have ever been in her office. Steve squirmed in the chair.

"I have heard stories about you from every one of your teachers, and those stories have always been unusual for a student. Something clicks in your mind when you see someone unjustly hurt or when someone who is overwhelmed needs help. You do more than recognize the problem and feel sorry about it. While others stand and gawk, you take action. That is what has impressed your teachers. And last year, I saw you myself.

"I was standing here at my window, watching your class play dodgeball. You were in the seventh grade. You remember what it was, don't you?"

She resumed talking as if she neither expected nor wanted an answer. "I was worried about how the boys were playing dodgeball. Some of the bigger boys were hitting the smaller boys so hard with the ball. Little Timmy Butler is exceptional at playing dodgeball, isn't he? It fascinates me to see Timmy standing in front of the bigger boys, and then he ducks when they throw the ball, and they miss him. He waits until the last instant and then ducks as they release the ball. Timmy's timing is perfect.

"That day, when I was watching your class, Johnny Compton, who was at least a foot taller than the rest of you, got the ball, and Timmy stood in front of him. Johnny reared back as though he were going to throw the ball, and he started his forward motion. Timmy ducked, but Johnny held onto the ball. Johnny raised that ball up in the air and slammed it down on Timmy with all his might.

"Everyone in the game stopped. Timmy curled up on the ground crying. None of Johnny's classmates dared retaliate for what Johnny had done. They knew that they were no match for Johnny.

"Even though I realized that Johnny wanted to vent his frustration with having missed Timmy so many times, he had infuriated me with the way he hit Timmy. But I could only watch to see if Timmy had been hurt. What I saw next, was one of the bravest things I have ever seen a child do at this school."

Steve blushed and again his face got red hot.

"You charged full speed at Johnny. You hadn't even been playing the game, but you had seen what had happened, and you refused to let Johnny get away with it, didn't you?"

Sister Sullpicia smiled. "I will never approve of fighting, but I had to admire you when you dove headlong into Johnny. I suppose that you think a nun and, certainly, a principal, would never want to see such a thing as a fight. Believe me, that is correct. It hurts me deeply when I see children fight in my school.

"But bravery doesn't have an on and off switch, does it Steven. Seeing Timmy lying on the ground, crying, enraged you, didn't it? You reacted to what Johnny had done when no one else in your class dared. You had to have known that all of them were too afraid of Johnny Compton to help you.

"As determined as you might have been, you couldn't handle him. Thankfully, Sister Amata stopped the fight before Johnny got the upper hand on you. Do you know why you never got punished for that fight, Steven? Sister Amata assumed it had been your fault, didn't she?"

"Yes, Sister, she knew I had started it. I expected to be punished, but nothing ever happened."

"I stopped her, Steven. I told her that you were not to be punished, and I had her send Johnny Compton to me. I made him sit in that chair where you sit now, except that a dodgeball waited there for him."

Why is she telling me this? If I'm supposed to be relieved, I'm not.

"I made Johnny take the dodgeball and kneel down here on the floor next to my chair." She pointed to a spot on the floor. "I gave him a tablespoon, and I told him to tear the dodgeball apart with the tablespoon."

Steve's eyes widened, and he made tight fists around the arm rests of the chair as he listened.

"Johnny worked for about five minutes and then stopped in frustration. I smacked him so hard against his head that he fell on his side against the wall." She pointed to a spot on the wall.

Steve gasped. Although his mind raced with empathy for Johnny Compton and with an urgent fear for himself, Sister Sullpicia narrated her story in an expressionless, matter-of-fact manner that frightened him more than the story itself. *She's not going to get away with doing that to me, but how am I going to stop her?*

"Johnny cried," Sister Sullpicia continued, "but I told him to stop crying and to get back on his knees and to work on the ball until I said he could stop. I sat with him for fifteen minutes while he tried to tear the ball apart. He kept digging the spoon into the air hole where you fill the ball with air."

Steve had a tough time believing what Sister Sullpicia was telling him. *How could she do all that to Johnny. After all, even though he had grown faster than the other kids, he was only in the seventh grade. She shouldn't be hitting him.*

"I asked him why he wasn't able to take the ball apart. He said it was the tablespoon. It wasn't the right tool. Then I asked him why he kept trying to dig the spoon into the air hole. He said it might be a weak spot in the ball.

"I squeezed his wrist. I said what did you say? He repeated himself, he thought the air hole was a weak spot. Then I said, are you sure? And he was sure."

God, yes. I bet he would have been sure of anything you wanted.

"I squeezed harder, and I asked him why he hit Timmy Butler so hard with the dodge ball. It took a few rounds of the same question before he admitted that he had hit Timmy because he was smaller and weaker. Then he really cried, telling me that he was sorry and would never do it again."

Steve was nervous. His palms were sweating. *I'm going to be kneeling on the floor trying to do something with something, and, whatever it is, it's going to be impossible. At least I know to not to stop trying.*

"I explained to him that weak spots, like the air hole, can deceive. Yes, I said, Timmy's size might make him weak when it came to fighting Johnny Compton, but it made him excellent at playing dodgeball. I told him that Stephen Stockton's size might also make him a lesser combatant when it came to fighting Johnny Compton, but his bravery and sense of right and wrong had more than compensated.

"I allowed him to stand, and I told him that I wanted him to play dodgeball with the excellence of Timmy Butler and the good spiritedness of Stephen Stockton, so that I could be proud of him instead of ashamed of him, and his classmates could have fun with him instead of being afraid of him. But I also told him that he had to learn one more thing. Can you guess what that was?"

"No, Sister."

"He had to learn that if I ever caught him doing something like he had done to Timmy Butler again, or if he went after you in any way, he would be very much sorrier about it than he was this time."

Steve took a deep breath. *What is she going to do to me?*

"Now, Steven, sometime later this week, probably tomorrow, but not until I am sure that Brad's nose is not broken, I am going to supervise him as he cleans the boys' bathroom with a toothbrush, and I can guarantee you that he will never again hurt either you or Jeremy. In fact, when I get done with him, he is going to know to never bully another student in this school.

"Do you understand why I have told you about Johnny Compton, Steven?"

Steve ran the palms of his hands over the thighs of his pants legs to dry the sweat. He wanted to get out of there.

"Yes, Sister, I think I understand okay."

"Brad is going to learn to respect his classmates, the same way that Johnny learned. Steven, I know that neither you nor Jeremy are responsible for what happened in the bathroom. I know that Brad chose to pick on someone who could not defend himself, and you intervened. Sister Verona and I have talked, and she pieced the information together from the other boys.

"But, Steven, even before I spoke to Sister Verona, I had no doubt that you had to have been protecting Jeremy. I was convinced of that when I saw you and Jeremy here this morning. I would rather not have smacked your heads together, but you did not come when both Sister Verona and I called you, and you needed to know that you must obey commands and that fighting is not tolerated in this school. This does make sense to you, doesn't it?"

"Yes, Sister."

"What happened in my office this morning only scratched the surface, didn't it, Steven? Jeremy is troubled. I have been in teaching for many years, and children with as much fear in their minds as Jeremy often cannot deal with whatever is frightening them, and they think about and even do tragic things.

"You are Jeremy's friend. You may be the only one who knows what Jeremy is feeling, and you may have to decide to help him in ways that he may not understand. You may think that you are hurting Jeremy to discuss the problems within his family. But you will be helping him. If Jeremy can get the help he needs, he will realize that you had no intention to hurt him.

"I am not trying to ruin or challenge your friendship with Jeremy. But he is living in fear, and you know that. Something is tearing away at his spirit, and you know what it is, don't you, Steven?"

"Jeremy's okay, Sister. Nothing is bothering him that much. He and I don't have any trouble having fun. He just didn't want you to come down on me this morning. He knew the fight was Brad's fault, and I had gotten into it to help Jeremy. He didn't want me to get blamed."

"Stop it, Stephen. You are not hearing what I am telling you. You are telling me what you came to say. Now, listen again."

What does that mean?

"Your friend needs more help than you can give him alone. Whatever is wrong with him and with his family requires very careful handling. If I have some knowledge of what is wrong, I can avoid making mistakes and hurting feelings by taking a wrong approach."

Think, Stevie. You've got to say something.

"He doesn't have any big problem at home, Sister. He wanted to let you know how close we are as friends, so you would believe him and understand that I didn't start a fight with Brad. He tries not to show how much he feels, but Jeremy is a deep person inside. When you smashed our heads together this morning, he believed that was only the beginning of what we were going to get. And it was such an embarrassing thing that Brad did.

"Jeremy figured that he was going to have to tell you what happened, and then maybe his parents if you called them, and maybe my parents if they got involved. What happened is something no kid wants to tell his mother or discuss with the school principal. It was too embarrassing. Brad should have to admit what he did. Jeremy shouldn't have to tell anyone what happened."

Steve splayed his hands out in front of him. "It all blew up into one huge complicated mess, which he had nothing to do with. Sister, Jeremy made his mind up to try and stop this thing without anybody getting hurt anymore over it, and him being forced to talk about something that he didn't do, and he got emotional. That's all. He should grow out of it, shouldn't he? He won't be so emotional when he gets into high school."

Yeah. I'm saying the right things now. She ought to relate to the growing out of it idea.

"Steven, do Jeremy's parents beat him?"

The question stung Steve like the bite of a snake. He sat back in the chair with a bewildered expression on his face, perplexed by the question. *It's as if I am talking to myself.*

Steve paused before he spoke. "Not that I know of. I don't think so. Jeremy has never talked about anything like that."

"Does he ever talk to you about his parents and his brother?"

Steve breathed deeply, certain that his anxiety over these questions was evident. *I can't give anything away. I've got to protect Jeremy.* "Well, yes, he talks about his family sometimes."

"Does he think his parents care more for his brother than they do for him? Does he think his parents love Brian more than they love him? Does Jeremy think his parents don't love him at all, Steven?"

What right does she have to ask me this stuff? What right does she have to even think it?

"No. No, Sister, nothing like that."

"These are painful questions for you to answer, aren't they? Do you know why? It's because you are trying to protect him again, when you know that you should be helping him. You think a friend shouldn't tell such things on his friend. But think of this. If I asked Jeremy the same questions, what would he do? Would he fall to pieces here in front of me because he needs help? Is he falling to pieces at home because he lives those questions every day? Do you think I want that to happen to him? I don't, and I must try to help him, as you also know that you must.

"I know the Wilcamp family well and what convinced me that something is wrong was Jeremy's sincerity and, as you have said, his intensity. No one could have told me that such a problem existed in his family until I saw him his morning."

"Please, Sister, it's not that way." Steve had no doubt that Sister Sullpicia was going to create upheaval in Jeremy's family. "Sister, I've been to Jeremy's home lots of times. It's not like that there. You're making way too much out of this."

"Has Jeremy ever talked about running away from home, Steven?"

"No, Sister, never." *God, please, let her believe me.*

Sister Sullpicia stared into Steve's eyes with an almost burning fervency. "Steven, has Jeremy ever talked about hurting himself to get attention from his parents or to get even with them? Listen to me, Steven. Has Jeremy ever talked about suicide?"

A cold determination replaced the bewilderment on Steve's face. He had to stop her. If she went to Jeremy's parents with those kinds of ideas and asked questions like these, life would become a nightmare for Jeremy Wilcamp. And his parents would blame Jeremy for making Sister Sullpicia think those things.

Every muscle in Steve's body tightened. "You know what I think, Sister Sullpicia, if Jeremy was sitting here and I was sitting back in the classroom and you were interrogating Jeremy like this, I would be mad. I don't want this kind of help from anyone."

He took a deep breath. "It's easy to say you've got to hurt your friends to help them, and it sounds religious too, like Jesus Christ dying on the cross for all of us, but I don't believe it. And I'm not going to do it, even if Jesus would."

Steve's voice broke, and his eyes were tearing, but he was going to finish. "I'm not Jesus Christ, Sister. I'm Stevie Stockton. I know what it means to be Jeremy's friend, and you don't. Regardless of whether you believe it, Jeremy is a happy person who was trying to return a favor to his friend.

"Jeremy and I have fun all the time doing things. He doesn't go around moping, threatening to kill himself. So, before you drop some bombshell into Jeremy's life that blows his family to pieces, maybe you ought to think that you aren't Jesus Christ, either, and that you're not hanging from any cross suffering for Jeremy. You're not going to suffer the way that Jeremy will suffer if you say these things to his family, when he did nothing…nothing wrong in your school."

He was unable to say another word, but Steve stared through tears straight at Sister Sullpicia.

Her face showed no emotion. She sat in her seat with her eyes fixed on Stevie, letting the silence thicken. He expected her to slap him to death at any moment. But he refused to flinch, daring her to do it.

"You may go back to your class, Steven."

He was shocked, as if she had slapped him. He sat speechless, not comprehending what she had said. *Wow.*

"Yes, Sister," he said softly, and got up and left her office.

He felt so subdued. *How did I say all that? Where did it come from?*

She wants to help Jeremy. But here's a kid who has been coming here every day since school started and for seven years before that, with no problem that she's ever had to deal with. He has one problem that's about as embarrassing as any could be, he cries over it, and she thinks that he wants to commit suicide. That's so wrong. Jeremy is just under a lot of pressure that she doesn't know about. If she hits the Wilcamps with any of those questions that she asked me, she'll ruin Jeremy's life. What family anywhere could deal with a school principal telling them all that?

He sat down on the stair steps outside of 8B and took the pen out of his shirt pocket and the piece of paper out of his pants pocket that he had put there before recess. His bloodshot eyes searched the steel staircase. His shoulders slumped, and his head felt heavy.

Jeremy, please, don't be thinking about suicide. If she's right about that, what would I do? No, she's wrong. Jeremy might be unhappy sometimes, but he's not like that. He's too well put together to even think of that. He loves life. He loves doing things. Why is she thinking stuff like that? Why would she tell me? Why would she want to tell that to Jeremy's parents?

Despite all his rationalizations, he felt miserable. He wrote a brief note to Jeremy. Then he wiped his face, ran his hands through his hair, moaned, and stepped to the door of 8B. He knocked on the door, entered, nodded to Sister Verona, and took his seat.

Jeremy sensed Steve's oppression as soon as he entered the classroom. *What did she do to him?*

As Steve slipped into his seat, he placed his note on Jeremy's desk. Somewhere in the background, both he and Jeremy were aware of Sister Verona saying something about paying attention, but it didn't faze either one of them. Jeremy opened the note and read:

> I don't think she is going
> to call your parents, but
> she may call mine.
> Stevie

Even though it was well after 1:30 when Steve returned to class, the afternoon dragged on. Jeremy and Steve glanced across the aisle at each other occasionally as Sister Verona taught the class something about a civil war battle until 2:00 and then made them read about Australia in their geography books.

At 2:45, fifteen minutes before the school bell would ring announcing the end of the school day, Mrs. Morgan knocked at the

8B classroom door. She gave Sister Verona a white envelope, and they spoke for a few moments.

After the 3:00 bell rang, Sister Verona allowed the class to go to the coatroom row by row, get their jackets and leave the classroom in single file. Jeremy stood outside the door waiting for Steve. Sister Verona had stopped Steve at her desk. When the class emptied, she returned to her desk.

"Steve, Sister Sullpicia sent this envelope for you. Mrs. Morgan told me that you should open it up later after school." She gave him the envelope with a truly compassionate expression on her face.

"Steve, you are one of the happiest, brightest students we have here. Sister Sullpicia is handling this matter, but I want you to know that I am not angry with you. You did what you needed to do to stop Brad. I know that. Sister Sullpicia is not going to punish you over this, so, come on, Steve, smile, will you.

"Mrs. Morgan told me that Brad's nose is not broken, but he has been sent home. The matter is over. So, Steve, stop worrying. Everything is going to be all right."

Steve smiled. "Thanks, Sister. May I go now?"

Stevie why did you say that? So rude.

Steve's abrupt request to go was not what Sister Verona expected. Her face showed her disappointment. But Steve's heart wasn't into saying anything, and all he could do was stand there speechless.

"Yes, of course, Steve, and may God bless you."

He put the envelope in his pants pocket and walked to the door. He faced Sister Verona whose eyes were still fixed on him.

"You, too, Sister."

CHAPTER 4
DON'T EVER THINK ABOUT SUICIDE

Steve closed the door to 8B, leaned on it, and felt helpless as he saw the anxiety in Jeremy's eyes and on his face.

"Let's get out of here and talk about it later, okay?"

"Yeah, sure, Steve."

On the other side of Saint Michael's Street, Steve said, "What do you say, let's go into the grove for a while."

This time, the suggestion did not arouse an avalanche of fear in Jeremy as it had that morning. He wanted to go into the grove. It presented a perfect escape from everybody and everything.

"I can go for that right now, Steve."

"Come on, I'll show you where I get in from Montclair Street."

"I bet I know where it is. It's that section of pines next to the fire hydrant on Montclair Street."

"How did you know that, Wilcamp?"

"Easy, if you're going to go into the grove after school, do it from the same place every time, and you'll know what to expect and where you are. The hydrant is a perfect marker."

"Wilcamp, are you becoming a detective? That's pretty shrewd thinking."

"I wish, Stevie. It seems obvious to me."

"Whoa, ho, Wilcamp, no being a smarty-pants about it."

"Well, Stevie, it is a fire hydrant standing there as big as life."

"Come on, dude." Steve and Jeremy jogged toward the fire hydrant.

The lead came out of the shoes of these two fourteen-year-old adolescents, and that happy feeling which the end of a school day brought to a kid's mind sank its way into Steve and Jeremy. The wind had about worn itself out along with the rest of the day, but an occasional gust made the grove hum. The thinning clouds made their way across the sky to some unknown eastern destination.

The property lines of the Monastery ended eight feet behind the sidewalks on Montclair Street and Saint Michael's Street. That was because when the Catholic Church purchased the property years before, Patterson Parkway was the only road that existed abutting the property. On the northern border of the grove along Montclair Street, the pine trees extended all the way to the sidewalk. Some of the trees had to be removed when the fence had been constructed years earlier. Over time, the barren spots had filled in with new growth except for the spot alongside the fire hydrant. Two very large trees had been removed there, leaving a barren space alongside the fence. It was a perfect place for Steve to duck behind the new growth and have space to climb the fence without being seen.

When they arrived at the fire hydrant, Steve asked, "Do you want to try it again, or do you want a boost?"

"Give me a boost, I still have one good pants leg left."

Steve's mood lightened as he boosted Jeremy up the fence and then climbed over himself. Steve took the lead and made his way to the same cluster of pine trees where they had been that morning.

"Are you starting to like it in here?"

"Yeah, and I am going to like it more and more. You know what I'm thinking, Steve, maybe we can sneak in here for the noon recess. If we're smart about it, no one will ever catch us."

"Jeremy, are you sure?"

"Yeah, I am. Aren't you sick of everyone telling you what to do all day? I'm getting fed up with Saint Michael's Monastery."

"We'll do it tomorrow, dude." Steve had not expected Jeremy to take to the grove so quickly, and his suggestion surpassed anything Steve had dreamed possible.

They sat down in the same soft bed of pine needles. Jeremy had no doubt that Steve had taken him to the thickest and tallest grouping of pines in the entire grove.

"You've been all over this place, haven't you, Steve?"

"I know most of it. There's a neat place that I've got to show you sometime, Jeremy. Almost dead center in the grove is a white stone statue of Jesus Christ crucified. A French sculptor must have carved it because the name etched into the statue is Pierre somebody. The novices go there to do their penance or pray or whatever they do in their spare time.

"Every now and then, I've come across one or two of them at that statue lying on the ground with their faces smack on the dirt praying or meditating. They stretch their arms out over their heads with their hands folded, like this."

Steve laid on the ground stretching his arms out above his head, folding his hands and interlocking his fingers. He placed the right side of his face on the ground.

"Steve, you spied on them. What if they caught you?"

"They'd never catch me. They're in a different world. I'd say they're about as lost as a soul could be, out here lying on the ground in front of a statue. Ridiculous. Seems like a waste of time to me. They don't seem to be aware of anything else that's going on around them when they pray.

"You won't believe this, but, I swear, Jeremy, it's the truth. You remember last year when we had that hurricane? I had to come in here when the wind was blowing so wildly. I couldn't resist. It was incredible. If I hadn't been able to hold onto the pine branches, I might have been blown away.

"I made it to that statue and what do you think? One of the novices had stretched his body out on the ground in front of the statue, probably saying his prayers and all, but he was deep into it. Instead of having his arms up over his head, he had them extended out as if he was crucified, and, no joking, he had his face buried right in the dirt. No turning your face to the side. Not this novice. Let me show you."

Steve laid on the ground with his arms extended out and planted his face on the pine needles. Then he sat up and blew the pine needles and dirt from his lips, shook his head and ran his hands though his hair.

"Steve, you're making this up," Jeremy chuckled.

"No, listen, man, this guy was serious. He must have either had some bad, bad sins on his soul, or he was trying to save the entire planet with one prayer."

"Steve, novices don't commit sins, do they?"

"Jeremy, everybody commits sins. I bet some of them commit more sins than you, dude."

"Steve, that's not nice."

"Maybe that novice was fantasizing, thinking he was in heaven or going to heaven or something like that. Anyway, the next thing you know, a violent bolt of lightning exploded in the sky, and I heard the worst blast of thunder ever.

"But there was another sound too. I wasn't standing any more than fifty feet or so from where that lightning had hit this huge pine tree, and it was cracking and falling. You could probably hear that tree falling for a mile around. And the smell, man. The smell of that burnt wood was something else.

"That novice kept lying there with his arms stretched out and his face buried in the earth as if he was an ignoramus ostrich. He didn't budge, and that tree was headed straight for him. I jumped up and down and yelled and waved my arms, but that sucker refused to hear anything. I couldn't believe what I was seeing."

"What happened then?"

"The tree fell right on him. One branch went through his right hand, and another branch went through his left, just like nails in Christ's hands, and another branch went through his heart. The rest of the tree mashed him like a pancake, and then the whole tree was blown up into the heavens with that novice tattooed on it as if he was Jesus Christ himself."

"You son-of-a-gun. I'll tattoo you."

Jeremy leaped across the few feet that separated him from Stevie, and they rolled down a hill holding onto each other, laughing and throwing handfuls of pine needles at each other. They came to a stop when they landed next to a pine tree. They sat up smiling at each other with pine needles in their hair and covering their clothes.

"You look like a porcupine, Wilcamp."

"You smell like a skunk, Stockton. How can you tell a story like that in here? This is about the fifth time today you've said something that should take us straight to hell."

"Come on, Wilcamp, the good Lord understands a joke." Steve threw another handful of pine needles at Jeremy. Jeremy lowered his head but got plastered anyway. He got up with a grin on his face, extended a hand to Steve, and pulled him up.

"Let's go back up there for a while." Jeremy took the lead.

They made their way through the pine branches and sat down. They said nothing as minutes passed. Steve wanted to keep clowning around and go roaming through the grove and maybe sneak up on a novice doing his penance or praying, but he knew that

Jeremy wanted to know what had happened in Sister Sullpicia's office.

Steve decided that Jeremy didn't need to know what Sister Sullpicia had done to Johnny Compton, or what she had planned for Brad. If she ever did get Jeremy into her office by himself and he knew the things that she did to teach a kid a lesson, Jeremy would be petrified. *No, it's a mistake to tell him all of that.*

"Jeremy, I'll never understand why adults won't let kids be kids, so they can enjoy their lives. Why can't kids be grownups when they are grownups instead of having adults spoil all the good times by expecting kids to be something they aren't?"

Jeremy didn't understand what Steve meant, but he remained silent, letting Steve collect his thoughts.

Steve took in a huge gulp of the fresh October air. "It was tough in there, Jeremy. It isn't in me to hurt anyone, especially when they intend to help, but before it was all over, I pretty much let Sister Sullpicia have it. At least, I guess I did. But she was trying to trick me the whole time. She had to hear it from me. She had to hear me say that your parents love Brian more than they love you and that you think your parents don't love you at all. I couldn't figure out where she was getting that stuff from. Why would she ask that? You didn't say a word about Brian."

"Did she really want to know that?"

"She was all over it, Jeremy, and she wouldn't let go of it."

"You didn't tell her that, did you, Stevie?"

"No, of course, not. But she kept at it. I couldn't stop her. I told her things that should have stopped her. I told her sensible things like how much you feel inside and that sometimes you are so intense. That she had scared you when she bashed our heads together outside the bathroom and that you were sure that that was only the beginning of what we were going to get. I told her how you were taking all the blame on yourself and that you wanted to protect me the way I had protected you in the bathroom.

"I might as well have been talking to the walls. She claimed that I was saying what I wanted to say and not listening to what she was telling me. Now, tell me, what does that mean and why would she say that? Did she think I wrote a script before I came to her office? What makes her think that I know what she's going to ask me?

"I couldn't reason with her. She kept laying this guilt trip on me about how if I was your friend, I would hurt you to help you. I even told her that you are going to grow out of being so emotional as you go into high school and get older.

"Doesn't that sound sensible? It's the kind of thing she should understand if she's so smart. Give you some time. She said that one summer vacation could change a child so much. She knows that you'll be in high school next year, getting older, growing up and maturing. Why does she have to make a crisis out of this?

"Man, when I said you would grow out of it once you were in high school, I was proud of myself. I thought that was her language. She's an educator. She's been watching kids grow up for years. But no. She kept pouncing on me with how no one would be able to help you because I, your best friend, refused to help you."

"Steve, she must have made you feel terrible."

"No, she made me mad. Even if she had tortured me, I wasn't going to say what she wanted to hear.

"The worst part about this situation with Sister Sullpicia is what does she think she's going to do with it once she hears it? What kind of power does she think she has? Is she going to tell your parents, God isn't going to like it if you don't start loving Jeremy? Big deal. All she can do is make your situation at home worse. That isn't going to help you. She can't understand that she might hurt you by messing with your family. There's a balance in your family that lets all of you live together, even if your parents are mad at you. She was setting out to destroy that."

"I'm so sorry this ever happened, Stevie."

"No, Jeremy, you can't be sorry for what happened. You and I didn't make it happen, but we've got to deal with it because it did."

"Steve, that's not what I mean. I mean that you had to protect me like this, lying for me and covering up for me. I wish I hadn't had to ask you to do that."

"You never had to ask me anything. I would have done it no matter what, the same way you would do it for me. The same way you did it for me in her office this morning, man! What you did took a lot more balls than what I did.

"Jeremy, I told her the obvious. I asked her to imagine how crazy and mixed up you were feeling because you had all these things going on in your mind at the same time. Her punishing us, maybe even suspending us, calling your parents, calling my parents, and you trying to explain the whole stupid thing to all those people and protect me at the same time. And you didn't do a single thing wrong. Nothing. None of it is your fault. Like I told you, you're the victim. Who wouldn't cry over that?

"You were standing there minding your own business when this incredible pile of shit drops out of nowhere all over your life. That's what happened. She said she knows your mother well. If she knows your mother that well, then she should know that your mother would go nuts if she found out that something obscene happened in the boys' bathroom, and you were at the center of it.

"If your mother is convinced that you are up to hanky-panky because you're serving benediction for me, what's she supposed to think if she finds out that you were standing out in the middle of the boys' bathroom exposed. She would never believe someone yanked you away from the urinal. She'd believe you staged the whole thing because she thinks her own son is some weirdo kid. What's any parent supposed to think if they were told their child was in the middle of something like that?

"Nothing I said fazed Sister Sullpicia. She was on a mission to find something wrong with your family. You know what she asked me after I said all these things that seem perfectly reasonable? She asked me if your parents beat you. That did it. I had no doubt that she intended to confront your parents. I had to do something."

"She actually asked you that?"

"Yes."

"Man, how could she know something like that?"

"She was fishing, Jeremy, trying to trick me into spilling the beans. I let her have it. I told her I am Stevie Stockton and not Jesus Christ, and Stevie Stockton doesn't believe in hurting his friends to help them, and Stevie Stockton isn't going to do it, even if Jesus Christ would. And then, I told her she isn't Jesus Christ either, and before she destroys your family, she ought to realize that she isn't hanging on any cross suffering for you, and you're the one, who didn't do a single thing wrong in her school, who is going to suffer if she goes after your family. And then I cried. I don't know why. The tears just came out of me."

"Oh, my God, Stevie. You told her all that?"

"Yep. I wanted her to stop laying into me because she seemed like she was going to do it forever. She doesn't know you at all, Jeremy. I had no plan to say any of that, but that's what came to me.

"Not a single thing about what happened, not one word of the truth mattered to her. Not what Brad did and how you and I reacted. It was nothing to her. So, I hit her in her world of God and heaven and angels and saints where she lives."

"What an unreal spot to be in, Stevie. That's about what happened to me in her office this morning. I kept saying what came to me. I didn't know what else to do. I didn't have anything planned, and I couldn't think about the consequences of what I was saying. But I was so thankful that I kept coming up with things to say and that it worked."

Steve pointed through the tree tops into the sky.

"Jeremy, there's a flock of birds heading south." They got to their feet and reveled in the beauty of nature granting them a reprieve from Sister Sullpicia and her plotting. Several hundred birds flew southward in V formations. "That's beautiful how birds do things like that. Get up and fly south for the winter. And they're so organized in how they do it. It's so fascinating. It's like every bird has its own place and knows exactly where that is."

"Yeah, Steve, it's something to see, isn't it? I'm glad you spotted them. I'd rather do anything than sit here talking about Sister Sullpicia."

As the birds grew fainter in the southern sky, Steve and Jeremy sat down.

"I couldn't stop crying, but I refused to flinch, and I fixed my eyes on her face. I expected her to slap the daylights out of me. She stared back at me without a sign on her face about what she was thinking or how she felt. After a minute or two, she told me that I could go back to my class."

"What, Stevie! You mean she told you to go after saying what you said?"

"That's what she did. I probably shocked her. She's thinking that she has one huge problem with you that she's got to solve, and she finds out a brat heretic is sitting in front of her. Maybe it dawned on her that people might think she's the one who needs help if she went after both our families."

"Hey, was that envelope for you, Steve?"

"Oh, yeah, I forgot about that. Bet it's my walking papers." Steve opened the envelope and found a note. He and Jeremy read it together.

> Steven,
>
> Now I have seen the second bravest thing
> a child ever did in this school. If Brad
> bothers either Jeremy or you again, you are
> to come to me, and I will take care of him.
>
> Sister Sullpicia

"What do you think it means, Steve?"

"It means that we won the battle. Let's hope we don't get home and find out that we lost the war. Man, we are lying low until we get out of here."

"Come on, Steve, who could lie any lower than we do? We never cause trouble. How did we get into this mess? It's like everybody is after us."

"I don't know, but we are up to our knees in it. I wouldn't be surprised to find out that Sister Sullpicia is having a conference with Sister Verona right now, telling her that they have to work to save our souls before June."

They both fell silent. Minutes passed.

"You know what, Jeremy, we ought to stop worrying about it altogether and act like nothing happened. This is a mixed-up situation for the school. It's the kind of happening that can damage the school's reputation and upset parents. Letting this cat out of the bag could have messy consequences.

"Now that Sister Sullpicia knows how determined you and I are to keep our parents out of this, she probably thinks it's wisest to let it blow over. Brad will get punished, but it will be for picking on another student. Sister Sullpicia will never tell his parents what he did or write it in some report unless she absolutely must. And, she will never call your mother for the same reasons, unless you force her to by doing something dumb, like running away. What do you think?"

"Hmm, Stevie. Why didn't you say that in the first place this morning? That makes sense."

"It only occurred to me now, and you're right. It makes very good sense for Sister Sullpicia to not press this issue any further."

"Stevie did anything about the altar boys' meeting come up?"

"Not a word."

Steve flexed his legs and crossed his arms over his knees. "You know what I am thinking? We ought to go by the altar boys' room and check things out, so that you know exactly what it's going to be like tonight."

"That's a great idea, Steve. Let's do it."

Steve and Jeremy scampered through the grove. When they got to the west side fence, Steve stopped and stared at Jeremy.

"What's wrong, Stevie?"

Steve leaned into the fence. "Sister Sullpicia brought up something else, and I was wondering about it."

"What?"

"She seemed to think that you might try to hurt yourself or do something bad to yourself to get your parents to care about you and love you. Did you ever do anything like that?"

"No. No. No way."

"Yeah, Sister Sullpicia has this thing so blown out of proportion."

Steve knelt on the ground, cupped his hands and boosted Jeremy over the fence. As Jeremy went over the top, Steve wondered if Jeremy had ever thought about committing suicide. It was on the tip of his tongue to ask, but he held back.

If he never did think about it, why make him think about it now. Please, Jeremy, don't ever think about suicide.

"You'll get the hang of fence climbing, Jeremy."

"I guess so, but it's easier if you give me a boost."

CHAPTER 5
MAN, THAT'S TOO MUCH

Steve led Jeremy boldly to the altar boys' room, knowing that nothing should be going on in the church at that time of day.

"Come on, Jeremy, let's check out the basement."

They opened the door to the basement. A single, bare light bulb illuminated the staircase exactly as Steve had described.

"You see this railing? It's this one top bar with a post about every six feet all the way down the stairs and across the walkway over to the old church. The only break is that gate that I told you about, blocking the staircase that goes down into the basement. You can unscrew the light bulb, can't you?"

"Yeah, I can do it. It's hot." He screwed the bulb back in.

"Now watch, Jeremy, stand with your back to the wall, place your hands on the wall like this, and here we go." They made their way down the stairs feeling the wall behind them with the palms of their hands.

"If you stay against the wall like this, you'll never be close enough to the railing to fall off."

Daylight coming through the few, small windows at the top of the basement walls enabled the boys to see the furnaces and what seemed to be miles of piping and electrical lines that coursed along the ceiling and walls of the basement.

"This place is creepy, Steve. Do you suppose that rats and mice can get in here?"

"Don't even think about that," Steve grimaced.

"I wonder why they made the basement so big and deep, Steve. It seems like it would be a waste and expensive."

"It's a principle of architecture, Jeremy. If you're going to build a place as big and high as the Monastery, you've got to have a foundation that goes this deep. My dad told me once, when we were on vacation in New York city, that the Empire State building goes fifty-five feet into the ground. That's a deep foundation."

"Tell you what, Stockton, I'd rather be above ground than down in the foundation."

"Come on, Wilcamp, you can make this. You shouldn't have to go any farther than this walkway but remember what I told you before. The walkway goes straight over to that staircase going up to the hallway between the old church and the rectory where Mark and I were. There's a light at the top of that staircase."

"Now, comes the big test, Jeremy. Let's go back up and do it with the light out."

"No, Steve. Come on. Do we have to?"

"Not only do we have to, but you're going to do it by yourself."

"Man, that's too much."

"You can do it, Jeremy. You might have to do it tonight, and it's going to be better for you if you know you can do it, and you've already done it. If anybody from the initiation is after you, they won't have that advantage. You will. I'm going to give you about two minutes, and you've got to get down the steps and onto the walkway. Okay?"

"You're making this tough on me, Stockton."

"Nah, Wilcamp, come on, let's do it."

They tramped back up the stairs and into the altar boys' room. "You're on, Jeremy. Lay some skin on me."

They slapped palms and Jeremy trudged into the basement solo. He unscrewed the light bulb and stood there trying to adjust to the darkness.

He heard Steve yell from the altar boys' room, "Go for it, Jeremy, you've got to get down those steps fast."

Jeremy felt the wall with his hands and worked his way down the steps. *How did Steve know I was standing there trying to see in the dark?* The bright flash the bulb had left in his eyes when he unscrewed it, still glared in his eyes when he reached the walkway. *If Steve hadn't said something, I'd still be standing at the top of the stairs.* In less than a minute, he saw light from the stairway and heard Steve calling him. Steve skipped down the steps in what seemed a second.

"Beautiful, Wilcamp, I'll make a bandit out of you yet. Now, see, you don't want to wait at the top of the stairs after you unscrew the light bulb. You've got to hop to it. If anybody else but me comes into the altar boys' room, you might not have any more than a couple of minutes before they open closed doors. You can't be standing there like a dumb bell. If you don't make it snappy, you could blow the whole plan. Once you're down here, you ought to be safe."

"Steve, how do you come up with all these things? I can't believe it."

"God helps me, Jeremy."

"Yeah, sure, right here in his own house."

"Especially in his own house. God knows I mean well."

"Stevie, I swear. Let's get out of here."

At the top of the stairs, Jeremy peered into the basement one more time. "Whew, how many times have you been in this place?"

"A few."

"Steve, why would you ever come to a place like this all by yourself? You're making me feel guilty for not joining the altar boys sooner now that I know you were doing this."

"Why not? After Mark and I found it, I had to know what the priests are hiding in the basement. You know what? I've been checking out that staircase that goes down into the basement. We can get down it in no time. I figure I can climb over the gate and then reach around the side and grab onto your arm and hold you while you come around the side. It's a bit of a stretch, but your legs are long enough to do it."

"You sure you haven't already tried it?"

"No, I haven't tried it yet, but it's been on my list of things to do for a long time. I've been waiting for you to show up. If we do it together, we won't have any trouble. It's a bad place to get stuck by yourself."

"No fooling, so get me stuck in here with you."

"It's better than being alone. We can do it, Jeremy. Those novices must have all kinds of neat stuff tucked away. Maybe even a few skeletons. I'm saving up money from my allowance to buy a flashlight, so we can investigate."

"Yeah, Steve, or maybe we can end up being skeletons ourselves. What are we supposed to do if somebody comes along while you and I are hunting for skeletons?"

"We would hide. Nothing to it, Jeremy. Must be a million places to hide. We could stand out in the open, and no one would ever see us. Some old statues are stored down there, and the nativity set that is put out in front of the church at Christmas is there too. We'd make great statues. I can curl up in the Virgin Mary's lap and make believe I'm the baby Jesus, and you can drop your pants and make believe that you're one of those naked boy angels."

"Oooohhhh, Stockton."

Steve grabbed Jeremy by his jacket while he opened the door to the basement and yanked Jeremy into the altar boys' room.

"That's nasty, Steve."

"What do you mean? It's a perfect disguise for you."

"Thanks a lot. Some fine baby Jesus you would make."

"Do you think you've got it now? If you have any question about what's happening in the altar boys' room, get down onto the walkway. Keep knowing that you'll be much safer hiding on that walkway. And, if you had to, you could go across the walkway over to the old church and rectory, and even leave through the old church. You've got an escape. But I plan on being back in church before benediction is over, so you won't be by yourself. Speaking of which, let's do one more thing. Let's pick out a cassock and surplice for you."

Steve rummaged through the cabinets until he found the right sizes for Jeremy, which were the same sizes Steve wore. "We're going to take these upstairs and hide them in the candle closet. As soon as the altar boys' meeting is over, you'll go into the hall and make a nice, smart move up the stairs to the sacristy. No one except Donny Rohr will ever know where you are. Come on, let's go put these in the closet."

They opened the door to the sacristy. No one was there. The candle closet was next to the door, and Steve put the garments in an obscure place on the bottom shelf.

"See how easy it's all going to be, Jeremy. Donny Rohr will be downstairs thinking that he is way ahead of me, and then he'll get up here and find you. He likes to be first everywhere, doesn't he?"

Jeremy grinned. *It might work.* "Steve, you're a genius."

"No, it's more like I'm a deviant."

"You know what would be neat, Steve? Trap Brad and his gang of bullies in the basement."

Steve raised an eyebrow. "Kiddo, you might be more of an evil genius than you know. That would be a surprise twist. But it would require a lot of manipulating to pull that off."

They went back downstairs and outside. As they crossed Monastery Avenue and started up Dennis Street, Jeremy asked Steve how he was going to handle Carl and Mickey.

"That's a good question. Now that I punched out Brad, I'm not sure of how I am going to handle them. I was thinking that if I see Brad before the meeting gets started, I'll go straight up to him and ask him if he wants to pick things up where we left off, you know, give him the tough-guy routine. I might even kick him in the nuts. That would cool him off. Or maybe get another jab in at his nose."

"Steve, I can't do stuff like that. I'm glad we're friends and not enemies."

"Listen, I'm not so fearless as you think. I'm afraid of things sometimes, and you're not the scaredy-cat you think you are. Didn't I see you kick Brad in the shin this morning. You're the only one I want on my side."

"What a great trick it will be to fake Brad out tonight." Jeremy clapped his hands.

"That's what we're going to do."

"Hey, I didn't mean that I won't help you if you want to take it to Brad right away tonight, Steve. I'm ready for him. He needs to be taken down."

"Brad's afraid of me, Jeremy. I know he is. I saw it in his face this morning. He'll back off if I leave him some space, and he'll get the message that I'll be coming after him when his punk friends aren't around if he makes any trouble for us tonight. Maybe that will be enough."

"I know what you mean, Steve, but when somebody has built themselves up to be such a bad ass the way Brad has, they can't back down when they're being seen by so many people. All the altar boys will be there watching. You bested him this morning, but he's a big kid. Tell you what, though, I hope he does try something. The both of us together can take him down."

"Jeremy, Brad thinks he's some big, tough guy who can beat anybody. Let me tell you something, I can tear that son-of-a-bitch apart. And if I have to, I will."

"But, Steve, he won't be alone tonight."

They walked along in silence for a few moments with Jeremy wondering about Steve. He had never heard Steve say anything like he had just said. He didn't know what to think about it, and it worried him. *Steve is too overconfident. But he did take Brad down in one move in the bathroom.* That was also the first time Jeremy had ever seen Steve do something like that.

Jeremy's eyes brightened, and he raised his hand up in the air. "I know what you can do about Carl and Mickey. Take them up into the sacristy with me after the altar boys' meeting, and then go out through the front of the church. Go up Montclair Street to Monastery Avenue. Dash across the top of Monastery Avenue and then continue up Montclair to Caroline Street which is the next block over from Monastery Avenue. Then haul ass down Caroline to Patterson Parkway. You would have to hold up here at Dennis Street, but if you wait for a car to go by, the car lights will blind everybody from spotting you.

"The only place where you might be seen is running across Monastery Avenue. But that is so unlikely. Everybody will be down by the altar boys' room. It's more time consuming, but there's almost no chance of being seen. Smart ass Brad will be cocksure that we've got to leave by the altar boys' room exit and that's where he'll be waiting.

"It must be a mortal sin for an altar boy to go through the sanctuary in street clothes, don't you think? Brad would think pathetic do-gooders like us would never be brazen enough to do that. He would be convinced that the altar boys' room is our only way out. I'm sure of it."

Steve stopped walking, and Jeremy halted one step in front of him.

"Jeremy, that's the perfect way out of this. All I have to do is convince Carl and Mickey that they can go through the sanctuary in their street clothes without getting caught."

"If you convinced Mark Bimonte to go through the grove, Steve, you can get Carl and Mickey to go through the sanctuary. If they think it's a sin, tell them how the ushers go through there every Sunday with the collection baskets. Ushers don't go to hell for walking through the sanctuary in their street clothes, do they?"

"Jeremy, listen to yourself. And you're telling me I've got things all figured out. I like it. That's what we'll do. Now, I do have to say this. Going through the sanctuary in street clothes is only a venial sin, unless you are carrying a collection basket. In that case, it's no sin at all unless you are planning on stealing the collection basket. Then, it's a mortal sin."

"Steve, maybe we better not say anything at all about sin to Carl and Mickey."

"That's another good idea Jeremy," and they both giggled away walking up Dennis Street.

Dennis Street came to Abington Road, and Steve and Jeremy had to go separate ways. They stopped at Abington.

"We'll kick butt tonight, Jeremy."

"You've got it."

Jeremy was about to go his way, but Stevie didn't budge.

"What's wrong, Stevie?"

"Jeremy, can I ask you something? It's sort of personal."

"Yeah, of course."

"Let's sit here on the curb for a couple of minutes."

"Is your father still beating you? You haven't said anything about that in such a long time. I had no idea he was still doing that."

The question brought sadness to Jeremy's face. His shoulders slumped.

"Stevie, I didn't want to talk about it. I don't want you or anybody to know about it. I hate it so much. But you're right. He hasn't beaten me with his belt in a long time.

"He's been grabbing my ear and shaking my head, or squeezing the hell out of my arm, telling me that I better not do whatever I did. But I keep remembering what he used to do to me, and picturing it, and worrying that he is going to do it again. It's always on my mind anytime something goes wrong. Going into the grove this morning seemed like such a hugely wrong thing to do that it made me think my father would do what he used to do to me if he found out.

"Steve, he used to take me into their bedroom, put his left hand on my back and hold me down on their bed, rip my pants down and beat my ass with that leather belt he wears. I don't want him to ever do that to me again. I feel like I've got to fight him, but my Dad is so strong that he would kill me. I don't know what I am going to do if he does that again. I'm to the point where I would rather take a fist whipping than have him take my pants down."

"How could he do that to you, Jeremy? He must know that if he did that to you now, you would never forgive him. You're fourteen years old. He can't be ripping your clothes off you."

They both paused, neither saying anything.

"Jeremy, maybe the reason he hasn't done that in such a long time is that he knows it's wrong. He knows that you would hate him forever, and your dad doesn't want that. He beats you because that's probably how he was raised. I doubt he is ever going to do that again. Not at your age."

"Steve, I hope you're right, because I don't want to go through it again. Listen, man, we should go home."

"Yeah, you're right. I'm sorry, Jeremy. I was just so surprised to hear you say that this morning."

They stood up. "Me, too, Steve. I hope it's over."

Steve set off up Abington Road, and Jeremy ambled down Abington Road toward Patterson Parkway.

As soon as Steve saves up enough money for a flashlight, we'll be going into the basement. He laughed out loud as he envisioned Steve and himself roaming around in the basement of the Monastery with a flashlight searching for skeletons.

Stevie, what won't you get us into?

CHAPTER 6
STOP THIS SOMEHOW

An empty house greeted Jeremy. His mother's car was gone. *Mom must be out food shopping. Brian's still at football practice.*

Jeremy knew he had some time. He went upstairs to his bedroom, dropped his bookbag on the floor next to his desk and stopped in front of the mirror on his dresser. He opened the middle drawer and took out a sock, tossed it onto his bed, and took his school clothes off.

Fifteen minutes later, he was shoving the sock into one of his tennis shoes when he heard the phone ring. He tossed the shoe into the back of the closet, hustled to his parent's bedroom and picked up the receiver.

"What're you doing, dude?"

Jeremy laughed and rolled back onto his parents' bed. "Oh, nothing, Stevie. What're you doing?"

"Hmm. He who answers a question with a question, is guilty of something. Listen, before you get into doing something, you better see if you can find some matches. I've only found one pack so far."

"Oh, yeah, it's a good thing you called. I almost forgot about it. Nobody is home, so I can search now."

"Go for it. I'll meet you at Abington and Dennis at about 6:45, okay. That'll give me time to talk to Carl and Mickey, and we can all show up to the meeting together."

"Sounds good to me Steve."

"Okay, bye."

Jeremy hung the phone up and rushed downstairs to the kitchen. He first inspected the knife and fork drawer where his mother kept matches to light the stove. He found two packs, but one of them was half empty. *It will arouse less suspicion if I take the full pack. Mom would remember the half empty pack and might forget the full one. I can hope.* His mother had the most amazing ability to find out anything that he didn't want her to know.

Then he scooted into the dining room and rummaged through every drawer in the buffet. No matches. He checked the street in front of the house through the dining room window to make sure that his mother had not returned and then dashed upstairs to his parent's bedroom. His hands sweated, and his heart pounded as he surveyed their bedroom.

What a terrific way to top everything off today, if I get caught in here doing this.

There were no matches in his father's dresser. He hesitated and wondered if he should go to the closet and hunt through his father's pants pockets or if he should check the street once more. *Jeremy, you just checked. You would have heard her.*

The Wilcamp family car was a 1954 Mercury Monterey and it came equipped with a louder exhaust system than most four door sedans. It wasn't hot rod volume, but it was close.

Despite realizing that he would surely hear her car arrive, Jeremy procrastinated. *It's going to take a while to go through all of Dad's clothes pockets. I better check.*

Satisfied that his mother was still shopping, Jeremy rifled through every pocket in his father's clothes. Nothing. He also found no matches in the night tables next to the bed. Despite his disappointment, he was elated to get out of their bedroom.

He darted down the stairs to the living room and then took the basement stairs two at a time. A vain check of the laundry room and the storage room, where his father kept his tools, completed his search. He pulled the only pack of matches that he could take with him to the initiation out of his pocket.

Steve, this is it. I hope you find some more.

Jeremy jaunted back upstairs to his bedroom, sat on his bed, took off his shoes and tossed his jacket around his shoulders. He curled up on his bed, snuggling his head into the pillow, and fell into a dreamless sleep.

Forty-five minutes later, a loud thump in the bedroom adjacent to his awakened him. Brian had thrown his bookbag into a corner of his room and was banging around.

Brian is mad about something. What else is new?

The house felt cool and Jeremy kept his jacket around his shoulders. He trudged to his desk and yanked his math book out of his bookbag. *Maybe I can get my math homework done before dinner.*

Jeremy sat back and frowned. Dinner. He smelled it cooking. That meant only one thing. Sister Sullpicia had not done anything. If Sister Sullpicia had called his mother, she would not be cooking dinner. She would be all over him by now.

Jeremy sat in his usual place at the dinner table. Brian talked during most of the dinner about his football practice. Brian wanted to be the starting quarterback for the junior varsity football team and was telling his father how hard he was working to get the position.

"I can throw the ball farther, and I'm more accurate than Ron Alworth, but I know the coaches are going to pick him to start."

"How can you be so sure?" his father asked.

"He's a teacher's pet, and the coaches like him. That's all I can see. They think he's some great guy because he looks so good with his prissy blond hair and blue eyes."

"Brian, you know you have a bad temper, and you show it too much. Maybe the coach thinks this other guy can run the team better. Distance and accuracy are important, but these coaches are into leadership also. Strong leaders can sometimes make an average team play like a championship team."

"No, Dad, I've been careful on the field controlling my temper, but I can't stand to see the coaches play favorites, and they do it all the time. You know what I think? They're going to cut me from the team."

"Oh, come on," his father placed his fork on the table. "It's a Catholic school. They're not supposed to play favorites."

"They do, Dad, and I don't want to sit on the bench while somebody else who's not as good as I am plays. If I'm not going to play, I'm going to quit the team."

Brian's comment alarmed Jeremy. *If he quits the team, he'll be unbearable to live with. He'll be home here picking on me every day after school. I've got to talk him out of quitting.*

Jeremy inhaled a deep breath, screwed up his courage, and spoke. "Maybe the other quarterback will get injured, and then you'll have a chance to show them what you can do."

"Jeremy," his mother shouted, "what a terrible thing to say."

His mother glared at him from her place at the table with an expression of disbelief, disgust, and anger all in one. "Those Brothers are supposed to referee the games so that the boys don't get hurt. It's only high school football. And your brother is not the type of boy who wants a chance to play because another boy suffers an injury. That's not a Christian way to think."

Sensing his danger, Jeremy concentrated on his plate.

"You don't know anything about it anyway, so why you gotta pipe in, little brother?"

Jeremy's face blazed scarlet, and the walls of the kitchen seemed to be closing in on him, taking his breath away as he sat there idly pushing the fork through his food.

Jeremy dared to lift his head when his father came to his defense. "Well, it does happen, you know, Brothers or no Brothers, quarterbacks can get hurt no matter how well the referees control the game. If they don't pick you to start, you'll get a chance to play at some point. Maybe the other quarterback will lose a few games and then you'll get a chance. If you think about it, Brian, instead being mad and giving up, you'll find all kinds of reasons to stick it out, especially if you are better with the ball. Coaches can be into leadership, but if things don't go right, the guy who can throw a touchdown is the guy who matters."

"Savvy?"

"Yes, sir. I get you."

"You love football, Brian. You'd be one sad sack puttering around here instead of being on the playing field."

Dad, don't stop. Get me out of this. I only said one thing.

"That's all well and good, but that's not what we're talking about. No decent Christian boy would think what Jeremy thinks." Jeremy's mother glared at him disapprovingly. "What kind of boy wants to get ahead because some other boy gets hurt?"

It's smarter to keep your mouth shut, Wilcamp.

Mrs. Wilcamp's anger had killed anyone else's desire to chat about anything, and the rest of the dinner passed without conversation. She went to the stove to turn the coffee pot on. It sat on a back burner that never lit on its own, but she always turned it on anyway to see if it might light. When it didn't, she turned the gas off and went to the knife and fork drawer.

Jeremy's eyes were fixed on his mother. She picked up the pack of matches and then hunted around in the drawer.

"Ken," she queried her husband, "did you take a pack of matches out of the drawer?"

"No."

His mother confronted him immediately. "Jeremy, did you take that pack of matches out of the drawer?"

If he didn't confess, he knew he would next be emptying his pockets. "Yes, ma'am, here it is." He took the pack out of his pants pocket.

His father's hand shot across the table with lighting speed. He clasped Jeremy's wrist and squeezed it so hard that it turned blue. Jeremy feared his wrist was going to break.

"Young man, what are you doing taking matches?"

"Dad, I need them to light the candles in church. I'm serving benediction tonight for Stevie Stockton, and I've got to light the candles."

"Why didn't you ask for them?" His mother's anger had not abated.

"Dad," Brian interjected, "the altar boys don't use matches to light the candles. They use strikers to light the candle torches and then light the candles with the torches. No matches. You can't reach the candles with matches."

Jeremy's father let go of his wrist, and he smacked Jeremy across his mouth with the back of his hand. "Don't you lie to me, boy. Have you been smoking cigarettes?"

Jeremy burst into tears.

"I couldn't get the striker to work, he blubbered between sobs. There was a pack of matches on the shelf in the closet and when I tried to light the wick on the candle torch with a match this morning at mass, I set the whole book on fire. Now there's no matches for tonight. Dad, I don't even know how to light a match right. I never smoked any cigarettes."

Jeremy's lip was swollen, and he tasted blood in his mouth.

"Stop that crying." Mr. Wilcamp grabbed Jeremy's wrist again. "Stop it."

Jeremy struggled to control himself.

"Don't you ever take matches out of this house without asking me and telling me what you want them for. Do you understand that?"

"Yes, sir?"

"Now go upstairs to your room."

"Wait a minute," his mother commanded. "Since when do you have to serve benediction tonight?"

"Let him go upstairs," Mr. Stockton repeated himself. "We'll talk about the benediction later."

Jeremy left the table and went to his bedroom. He fell onto his bed, buried his head in the pillow and cried desperately.

Jeremy's rapid response to his question about smoking cigarettes and the apparent sincerity on his son's face, baffled Mr. Wilcamp. He suspected that Jeremy might be telling the truth, despite what Brian had said. "Did you ever see matches in there where they light the candle torches, Brian?"

"I don't think so, Dad. I always used the striker."

"Yes, but Jeremy just started serving mass, and maybe he didn't know how to use it. Now, can you say you never saw matches in that closet?"

"No, there might have been some, and there probably are kids so dumb that they can't get the striker to work."

Brian rocked back in his chair. "Oh, what am I thinking? Dad, the altar boys use matches to light the charcoals for benedictions and high masses. I'm sorry. I was only thinking about the candles. Everybody uses the striker for that. I forgot about the charcoals."

"Well, he knows better than to take matches out of the house without asking," Mrs. Wilcamp moderated her tone.

"It's only a pack of matches, and it seems as though he had good reason. Jeremy is probably telling the truth about the whole thing, and we've got to stop coming down so hard on him all the time. He's at a delicate age, and we've got to let him develop. I'll talk to him after dinner, and I don't want any more discussion about it."

"I sure hope you know what you're doing, and you don't find your son hanging around on street corners smoking and doing all the dreadful things that kids are doing today. Most kids who need matches for what Jeremy says he needs them, know to ask their parents. If Jeremy is telling the truth, why didn't he tell us?"

"If he thought we wouldn't believe him and didn't let him have the matches, what would he do at benediction tonight?"

"That's another thing." Mrs. Wilcamp ignored her husband's question. "Why didn't he tell us about that? How are we supposed to believe anything he says? There's too many smart aleck teenagers around today, lying to their parents all the time and causing them nothing but trouble."

Mr. Wilcamp had learned long ago to let his wife have her say, but he felt that he had hit Jeremy too quickly because of Brian's comment.

When they finished dinner, Mr. Wilcamp picked up the pack of matches, went into the living room, and called Jeremy to come downstairs.

Jeremy knelt on the floor of his bedroom, his chest pressed against the bed, his head buried in the pillow. His father's call startled him. He sighed and tried to stop crying.

He beseeched the crucifix hanging on the wall above his bed to help him. *God, Oh God, you know I try to be good. Please, help me. I never meant anything bad. Please, stop this somehow.*

He sobbed as he heard his father call him a second time.

"Yes, sir." Jeremy got up, wiped his eyes, and made his way down the stairs. His father sat in his easy chair in the living room.

"Why does Steve want you to serve benediction tonight, Jeremy?"

"I don't know why, Dad." He struggled mightily to talk without crying. "Steve said that he isn't able to do it and that he cleared it with Father Francis for me to do it for him. He told me about it at school today, and I didn't think that there was any reason for why I couldn't do it. I was going to tell you and Mom, but I hadn't gotten to it yet."

Mrs. Wilcamp stormed into the living room. "Why didn't he tell you why he couldn't do it?"

"It's best that I take care of this," Mr. Wilcamp stated.

"Sure, you take care of it, but I'll find out the real reason soon enough." Mrs. Wilcamp allowed the kitchen door to slam behind her.

Mr. Wilcamp was moved by what he saw. His fourteen-year-old son was maturing, and he hadn't noticed. Yet, he was standing before his father holding back tears as if he were an eight-year-old kid who had gotten caught stealing a cookie. *I shouldn't have hit him. Brian spoke up too soon, and I didn't give Jeremy a chance to explain himself.*

"Jeremy, you're old enough now to be doing things on your own and having more responsibility. I'm going to see that you get that. You're a good boy, and I want you to do things that make you happy and make your family proud of you. Now, come here."

Jeremy stepped across the living room to his father's chair. His father took the pack of matches out of his pocket.

"If you need to light a match, here's how you do it. You take the match out by pulling it back like this. Then you grab it at the bottom and pull it out. If you pull it from the middle or top, you can tear it in two, and sometimes you tear the whole pack apart. It's only held together by one staple.

"Close the book. That's how you set the pack on fire this morning. You didn't close the book before you lit the match. Hold the match like this, strike it across the bottom, and keep your motion going so that you come up with the match lit away from the book. That way, you can't set it on fire." Mr. Wilcamp lit one of the matches. "Now you try it."

Jeremy wiped his eyes and tried to light a match. When it didn't light, his father told him to strike a little harder. Both Mr. Wilcamp and Jeremy heard Mrs. Wilcamp huffing from the kitchen. Jeremy lit the match on the second try.

"Alright, try one more."

Jeremy tried another match and lit it the first time.

Mr. Wilcamp stood. "Now take this pack of matches with you, and I want you to bring it home with you tonight." He ran his hand through Jeremy's hair. "Now go upstairs and get ready for the altar boys' meeting. You should to be home between 9:00 and 9:30, right?"

"Yes, sir. I think so."

Jeremy put the pack of matches in his pocket and took the stairs two at a time. He dried his eyes in a towel and peered into his green eyes in the mirror. *Green eyes aren't anything special, but I like my eyes because they have so many diamond shapes of different shades of green and splotches of brown around my pupils.*

A fair-sized swelling bulged under his upper lip, but it appeared worse inside than outside. He ran some hot water in the basin, took his shirt off, and washed his face and armpits. The hot water felt soothing. He wished that he could sprawl out in the bathtub and soak forever. He hastened to his bedroom and donned a clean shirt and his jacket. The crucifix on the wall caught his eye as he was about to leave the room.

Jeremy knelt by his bed. "Thanks, God. Thank you so much."

If only I can get out of here without Mom yelling at me again. Jeremy tread lightly down the steps and entered the living room. The clock on the mantle indicated 6:25. *I've got to get a move on.* His mother and father sat in the living room reading parts of the newspaper.

"Bye, Mom and Dad."

"All right, Jeremy," his father said, but his mother maintained a cold silence.

Jeremy strode briskly for Patterson Parkway. Fifteen minutes later, he broke into a trot when he saw Stevie waiting for him under the street light at the corner of Abington Road and Dennis Street.

CHAPTER 7
I LOVE MY PARENTS

"What happened to your lip?" Steve squinted and contorted his face, as if he felt the pain in Jeremy's swollen upper lip.

Jeremy grimaced, and he and Steve proceeded up Dennis Street toward the Monastery. "It's a long story, Stevie, and if I get into it, I'll get jumbled up, and I don't want to."

"Tell me something, man. What happened?"

"If you must know, my mother caught me with the matches, and I ended up getting a good smack from my father."

"Oh, no. What'd they think you were going to do that deserved that, burn the church down with a pack of matches?"

"Stevie, please, it's so much."

"Ah, Jeremy, your father made you cry right front of Brian, didn't he?"

"It was more like, because of Brian."

"Boy, you really put in rough days sometimes."

Jeremy kicked a small stone on the sidewalk. He moaned and decided that he had to tell Stevie what had happened. "Believe it or not, it's the first time my father ever felt sorry for hitting me. And he looked at me real funny later, as if I was someone different from who I usually am. I didn't understand it.

"You know what else? It's the first time I ever told my parents such a pack of lies. I must be hanging around you too much,

Stockton. You would've been proud of me for thinking so fast. I told my father that I needed the matches to light the candles in church tonight because I set the only pack of matches that was there on fire this morning trying to light a match. Smart-mouth Brian blurts out that the altar boys don't use matches to light the candles. They use the striker to light the candle torches, and they use the candle torch to light the candles, not matches. That set my parents off."

"Your brother is such a girly tattletale, always getting you into trouble. Does he ever back you up on anything?"

"Never. He tries to make things worse."

"Jeremy, I swear. Talk about Brad Maddox being a bully, your whole family sounds like a bunch of bullies, always beating up on you for something."

"No, Stevie," Jeremy said with a sorrowful face, "my family isn't like Brad Maddox."

"Sorry, Jeremy. I shouldn't have said that."

"It's okay, Stevie. It might seem that way sometimes, but they aren't. Brad is evil. My family isn't evil.

"Anyway, my father believed me when I said I don't know how to use the striker, and I had to use the matches. My mom didn't believe a word of it. She thinks I'm smoking cigarettes and standing on street corners making trouble with a gang of wild teenagers."

"Jeremy, she can't really think something like that, can she?"

"Yes, she can, and she got all huffy and announced that she's going to find out why you wanted me to serve benediction for you tonight. So, please, tell your mother something when you get home because my mom will be calling her first thing in the morning."

"Don't worry, I will. I'll make sure Mom understands. Do you really think your mother doesn't believe that you're going to serve benediction tonight?"

"It doesn't matter, Stevie. She has it in her mind that I'm a bad kid who can't be trusted, and she's got to check up on me. This might sound absurd, but I think she believes that if she can find reasons to check up on me and discover something I did wrong, it proves what she has always thought about me. I am a bad kid. That's the way she sees me. Do you get what I mean? It doesn't matter what I do. She finds some way to make it wrong in her mind."

"Jeremy, that's deep stuff."

"Even when she finds out that I did serve benediction, I'll still be on her shit list because she was so sure she had to check up on me. She'll be mad because we pulled the switch off. I don't have any right to do something like that on my own."

"Not even if she finds out that I asked you today, and you couldn't possibly have let her know any sooner?"

"You can't fool my mom, Steve. She'll know we were up to something. Even if we weren't, she'd have it in her mind that we were. She'll be after me for weeks any time I am scheduled to serve something, asking me if I am making a switch with somebody who's doing something they aren't supposed to be doing."

Jeremy wore a sad and bewildered expression. "Steve, what can I say? How can I be better friends with your parents than I am with my own? It doesn't make any sense. And I don't know how to change it. I'm never able to get on their good side, no matter what I do.

"You know what I think, Steve. My Mom wanted a girl. She didn't want me. Have you ever noticed all the pictures and statues of little girls my mom has in the house? She has a picture of Aunt Catherine and Uncle Eddie and their family on the buffet. They have three girls. Mom will sit in the dining room and hold that picture in her hands. Sometimes she gets tears in her eyes over it. When Aunt Catherine and Uncle Eddie bring the kids over for a visit, my mom is thrilled.

"When we were younger, she used to pick the girls up, hug and kiss them and play with them. Steve, I swear, she gives more to those girls at Christmas than she ever gives to me."

"Jeremy, if that's true, you'll never fix that problem."

"I know. I love my parents, Steve. I want to be a good son, but I am always screwing things up. Like this matchbook thing tonight. Thank God my father believed what I said, because it would take my mother forever to get over it if he hadn't come to my rescue."

Jeremy stopped cold on the sidewalk. "Steve, suppose she calls Father Francis. What would he say?"

"Jeremy, come on, relax. That's not a problem. I did clear it with him. I'll tell my mother the story about the cabinets, so she has it straight in case your mother calls her. You're not going to be in any trouble. You are going to serve benediction tonight. All she can find out is the truth.

"I can ask my mother to call your mother tonight when I get home, Jeremy. She can thank her for letting you serve benediction for me. That should do the trick. It'll get you off the hook in case we're late getting home. Besides, it's unlikely that even your mother is suspicious enough to call Father Francis. That's too drastic. What's the moderator of the altar boys supposed to think if he finds out that an altar boy's own mother doesn't trust him? Your mother won't want him to think that."

Jeremy's shoulders relaxed as color came back into his face. "Yeah, if your Mom calls, it might be enough to convince my mother that everything is on the up and up. You think things out better than I do, Steve."

"No, Jeremy, it's more than that. It's that when we put our heads together, things come out all right. Come on, cheer up, will you."

Jeremy massaged his upper lip. "Is everybody going to notice my lip?"

"No. I saw it right away, but I see you so much. If anybody notices your lip, tell them you banged into a door. It's the classic excuse. No big deal. Hey, you didn't tell me whether they let you have the matches."

"Oh, yeah. My father must have done some thinking about it. He gave me a talk about how he thinks I am a good boy, and he showed me how to light a match without setting the whole book on fire. Then he gave me the pack of matches. Let's hope nothing happens, because I'm supposed to bring it back home tonight."

"I'm glad he let you have them because I only found one pack too. Here, put my pack in your right pants pocket and use that first. Put yours in your left pocket and maybe you won't have to use it. You want to practice lighting a couple?"

"No, I can light a match, Steve. My father surprised me when he believed what I said. But I have seen people set a whole book on fire trying to light one match, haven't you?"

"I don't remember that ever happening, Jeremy."

"You will if you ever see it. It's like a firecracker going off in your fingertips. Get this, my next-door neighbor did it to himself trying to light a cigarette for his wife. It shocked me, and it really pissed off my neighbor because his wife laughed her ass off over it."

"What a sweetheart. I guess I haven't seen it happen, Jeremy. Maybe that's what made you think of telling your dad that you set the whole pack on fire."

"Yeah, that makes sense. You ought to keep one of these packs, Steve."

"No, I can handle that basement."

Jeremy made a soft, howling noise. He felt better.

As the daylight faded into twilight, Saint Michael's Monastery Church loomed like a huge, shadowy, dark mountain on Monastery Avenue.

"I'm supposed to meet Carl and Mickey under the street light at Monastery and Dennis. Looks like them, doesn't it?"

"Yeah, I see two critters shuffling around there."

CHAPTER 8
PLEASE GOD, HE'S MY BEST FRIEND

Both Carl and Mickey broke out into smiles when they saw Steve. "Oh, Steve, are we glad to see you."

"What'd you think, Carl? I would abandon you. Never."

"Well, it's almost time for the meeting," Mickey replied, "and we were getting nervous."

"Don't fret, guys. Let me tell you how we are going to skip out of the jolly initiation. We'll sit in the end chairs of the rows closest to the hallway and be the first ones to dash out of the altar boys' room as soon as Father Francis finishes the meeting. Then we'll make a smart move up the stairs to the sacristy before anyone knows we even left."

"You mean we're going through the front of the church, Steve?"

"Exactly, Mickey. No one will ever expect us to do that."

"Yeah, but what if we get caught?"

"Who's going to catch us? The priest will not be there yet for the benediction, and the altar boys will still be in the altar boys' room."

"That makes sense, Mickey," Carl concurred. "That's the perfect way to sneak out. In fact, it's the only way. Even if someone saw us going upstairs to the sacristy, no one would follow us."

"Nice, Carl. Good thinking. We'll leave through the front of the church, go up to Montclair Street, take that up to Monastery Avenue, cross Monastery Avenue, continue along Montclair to Caroline Street, and then tear down Caroline Street to Patterson Parkway. From there, you guys can scoot home."

With the concerned expression he had on his face, and wearing his horned rim glasses, Mickey appeared professorial. After some hefty deliberation, he cracked a smile and said, "Yep, that does sound pretty good."

Two top-notch A students scared to death by an altar boys' initiation. Jeremy clenched his fists. *Just because Carl and Mickey are bookworms getting A's in everything, somebody's got to single them out at this dumb initiation and humiliate them.*

"Steve, how many guys do you think Brad might have with him tonight?"

Steve frowned, "Hard to say, Jeremy, maybe five, maybe six, maybe three. Maybe no one."

"Do you think we could take them? I mean if we had a baseball bat or something like that."

"Too big for us, and they're probably aggressive guys who are going to have a lot of attitude because we beat the crap out of Brad, who was supposed to be invincible. If Brad catches you by yourself, Jeremy, he and his gang of bullies are going to slap you all over the place, push you around, and straighten your ass out like it's never been straightened out before, and do God knows what else to you. No, we've got to outsmart them. It's the only way. We can sneak out of this thing without running into them, and then it's done.

"Brad might be able to get some of his high school bozos together for some fun time tonight, but they aren't going to want to come back to the grammar school they attended and pick on you and me because Brad didn't get his way. They might find themselves kicked off the football team, suspended, even expelled for beating up on grammar school kids. What if the police got involved?

"The way I see it, this is Brad's only chance. If he doesn't get us tonight, it's over. And you and I, Jeremy, and, of course, Carl and Mickey here, are going to make laughing stocks out of anyone trying to fool with us because we're going to escape right under their noses."

Mickey Quinn had been listening to every word Steve and Jeremy said. He spoke up. "Brad sucks. The initiation sucks, and all of Brad's friends suck." All four boys laughed, and Steve reached a palm out to Mickey for a swipe. "Mickey, you're becoming our comic relief. We need one."

"Come on," Steve skipped ahead, "it's almost time for the meeting to start."

The four boys filed into the altar boys' room and took seats close to the entrance. Mickey and Carl sat in the two seats in front of Steve and Jeremy. A nervous pulse rippled through Steve's body. Neither Brad nor any of his friends had shown up.

Jeremy noticed the same thing. "Well, Steve, it looks like our plan to put it to Brad right away is shot."

"Yeah, I'm a little surprised that he's not here with a bunch of bruisers from the high school messing with us."

"Steve, here comes Scott." Scott had frequently been an altar boy partner with Steve at mass, and they were friends.

Scott was a year older than Steve and Jeremy and a freshman in Saint Michael's High School, but he was shorter than they were. He took the seat beside Steve.

Scott peered around the room. "Steve, I don't know what happened between you and Brad Maddox today, but he's out to get you tonight. And you too, Jeremy. He's got five or six high school punks from Saint Michael's with him."

"Where are they?"

"They're not coming to the meeting. Brad doesn't want Father Francis to have any idea of who's involved because they're planning to work you two over good tonight. They don't care about initiating anybody else. They want you two.

"Steve, they've got fireworks. Big stuff. M-80 firecrackers and cherry bombs. Joey Lardner's father buys that stuff when he goes down south on business trips, and Joey stole a couple of boxes."

Scott leaned toward Steve and whispered, "They've got this idea that you'll be going into the grove to protect Jeremy. Brad is swearing that they'll blow your asses out of there."

"How did you find all this out?" Steve's jaw tightened.

"That isn't all I know. They know you're serving benediction tonight, so, for God's sake, watch out. You want to know how I know? I was walking up Patterson Parkway with them. All I said was that maybe we're getting too old for this initiation stuff, and we should forget it. Brad kicked me in the ass, pushed me down on the sidewalk and told me to get fucking lost."

Scott rolled up his pants leg and showed them his knee. The entire surface was abraded and oozing blood.

"Oh, no," Steve said. "What would make Brad do something like that to you?" Steve reached into his pocket and clasped his Swiss army knife as he stared at Scott's knee.

"Scott, I'm so sorry Brad did that to you." "It's me he hates," Jeremy alleged. "What a brave guy to kick somebody a foot shorter than he is. Thanks for coming here and telling us."

"Yeah Scott," Steve echoed Jeremy's words, "you took a big chance coming here. Thanks, man."

"Let me tell you where I'm going. As soon as Father Francis comes through that door, I'm leaving before he sees me, and it's good-bye altar boys forever. I'm going up the stairs, through the church and out the front door. I don't want to run into them. I'm too small to get mixed up with the gang Brad hangs with, and they're into such a God-awful lot of malicious things. They vandalize kid's cars from other schools who come here for football games. Let the air out of a tire or scratch their cars. I'm finished with them."

"Shit." Steve made a strong fist around his Swiss Army knife.

Father Francis strolled into the altar boys' room.

Scott rose from his chair. "Good luck, you guys."

Steve grabbed Scott's hand. "Scott, if there's any way I can get to Brad tonight, I'll make him sorry for what he did to your knee."

Scott hesitated. He wanted to tell Steve to get out of there as fast as he could. Forget the meeting and go. But he knew that Steve was not one for backing down.

"Steve, some of those guys are big. Three of them are on the football team. Don't try to take them all on. Get out of here somehow. Can't you see what they did to me? And I'm a member of the gang. They're all wound up with their fireworks and ready to have a big bully's party at your guys expense. I'm not kidding you, Steve. They're talking nasty shit."

Steve, Jeremy, Carl and Mickey all fixed their eyes on Scott. Before anyone said another word, Father Francis called to Scott.

"I have to go to the bathroom, Father. Be right back." And Scott set off.

Jeremy's heart pounded, and he felt weak and sick in the stomach as Scott disappeared into the stairwell leading to the sacristy. Carl and Mickey still faced Steve.

"Hang in, guys," Steve attempted to reassure them. "Remember, Brad and his buddies are stupid, and we aren't. We've got something planned and they don't, and they'll be wanting to play around with everybody at the initiation to show off their fancy fireworks. Scott's going out the same way that we're leaving, and he'll be fine. No one will be there, and we'll get out too. Come on, now, don't panic." Carl and Mickey turned toward the front of the room.

Jeremy wondered if Father Francis knew of the altar boys' initiations. Father Francis was the tallest man Jeremy had ever seen, and he believed that if Father Francis knew an initiation was going on, he would quash it. But if he knew, he wasn't doing anything about it. *Maybe, if he suspects anything, he thinks it's harmless playing, and the kids should be allowed to do that.*

This was the third altar boys' meeting that Jeremy had attended. Every meeting had been a drag. Father Francis would have four boys say the Confiteor and then make a couple of other guys say the Suscipiat. After reviewing those two prayers with their complicated Latin, Father Francis chose two of the older boys to come up to the front of the room, kneel next to him and go through the entire sequence of prayers at the foot of the altar. The older boys were supposed to be showing the younger ones how to do it. It was hilarious when the high school kids goofed up their Latin. Father Francis would tease them about it. After doing the Latin check, Father Francis went over the rubrics for special services like baptisms or funerals, benedictions or weddings. Sometimes, he told them stories about things that had happened to altar boys.

At the previous meeting, Father Francis had taken the altar boys up to the altar and acted out a benediction with Jeremy being one of the altar boys. As Tom Mickel was saying the Suscipiat, Jeremy got the idea that Father Francis might call on him and Stevie to go through the prayers at the foot of the altar.

"Man," he murmured, and tried to sink lower into the seat. Carl and Mickey were not big enough to conceal Steve and Jeremy sitting behind them.

"Steve, pray that Father Francis doesn't call on us to do the prayers at the foot of the altar."

Jeremy's words brought Steve's mind back to the altar boys' meeting. That was a miserable possibility.

Steve rested his elbow on his thigh and his head in his hand and frowned at Jeremy. "If he does that, I'm going to puke."

Father Francis called on two of the high school kids. Both Steve and Jeremy sighed in relief.

Father Francis finally got around to the most important thing that he wanted to discuss and that was how messy the boys had been leaving the altar boys' room. He gave a stern message that everyone, especially the high school altar boys, had better be cleaning up behind themselves. Then Father Francis closed the meeting with a prayer.

Steve, Jeremy, Carl and Mickey trooped upstairs into the sacristy after the meeting. Steve grabbed the cassock and surplice that he had hidden earlier and said, "Let's go."

He stopped them at the entrance to a side room next to the sacristy where the wine for mass was stored and told Carl and Mickey to wait for a few minutes. Steve led Jeremy into the poorly-lit room and handed him the cassock and surplice.

When Jeremy was dressed, Steve faced his best friend. "Jeremy, listen to me. If Brad and his goons have fireworks, this thing might blow up into something ugly."

Steve pulled his Swiss Army knife out of his pants pocket. He opened the longest blade and showed it to Jeremy and then closed the knife and put it back into his pocket.

"I've got it with me. You're going to have to do something that's unbelievably tough tonight, Jeremy. Even if you hear fireworks going off, you've got to follow through with our plan. No matter what you think is going on, you've got to go down onto the walkway and wait until I get there.

"You're going to think that the worst things are happening to me, and you're going to want to come and help me. You won't care what happens to yourself. Your whole heart and mind will tell you that you need to be with me. But you've got to believe me. I can take care of myself. Brad and his punk hoodlums are no match for me in the grove. I know that grove even in the dark. And believe this, I can throw as big a scare into them with my knife as they can throw into me with their fireworks. No one is getting any closer to me than my knife blade."

Jeremy looked glum. His face drooped, and his chin crimped as he fought for control.

"We're going to be okay. Try not to worry so much. I know what you're thinking, Jeremy. If only you could do something for me. I do want you to do something for me. I want you to promise me that you won't try to come and help me. I want you to promise me you'll go into the basement, turn the light off, and stay on that walkway until I get there.

"Scott told me that Brad thinks I'm going into the grove. If I am forced, that is exactly where I will go. And if I do, they'll never catch me. I can hurt them in that grove. I can lead them to where they will get lost and find a lot of things that will slow them down and make them wish they had never gone in there. They'll be blowing their fireworks up on each other.

"It all starts at the fence, Jeremy. None of them can climb that fence as fast as I can. And when they do, I'll be hiding there waiting for them, and somebody is going to get a crack on their head they won't forget. Or, I climb the fence, move about ten or twenty feet down in the grove alongside the fence and wait for the beefcake football players to get themselves over the fence. While they're searching for me, I'll climb over the fence and run back to church for the finish of benediction, and they'll have no idea of where I am.

"If I can't do that, I'll lose them in the grove and come into the Monastery from the old church side, the way Mark Bimonte and I did. I'll call out to you from the old church side when I get into the basement. I've got three options and I'll choose the best one when I get there. In the meantime, you'll be safe in the basement, and I will get to you."

"You make it sound so easy, Stevie." He wrapped his arms around Stevie, and they stood hugging each other in the room off the sacristy. "Stevie, be careful."

Jeremy breathed deeply, hardened his face and stared at his best friend. "I promise you, Stevie. I promise. Don't worry about me. I'll be waiting for you." Jeremy forced a smile.

"We've got to go, Jeremy. Hang tough. We will find each other. I give you my word."

They went back into the sacristy. Steve put a hand on Carl and Mickey's backs. "Come on, altar boys, we're going home."

He led them through the sacristy, into the sanctuary and then up a side aisle to the front of the church. Twenty elderly women and a few old men were assembled in the church, waiting for benediction. They looked at this unlikely threesome of boys with a combination of indignation and surprise, as if wondering what these imps were doing at their benediction.

When they got to the inner front doors of the church leading into the vestibule, Steve stopped them. He waved at Jeremy. Jeremy returned the wave, but he felt as if he was going to collapse as he watched Steve lead Carl and Mickey into the vestibule. Every fiber in his body wanted to run after Steve. *Oh, God, we should do this together. I know we should do this together.*

Jeremy walked back into the sacristy trying to pull himself together.

"What are you doing here?" Donny Rohr was getting things ready for benediction.

Jeremy lingered in the shadows so that Donny wouldn't see his face. "Steve had a problem at home, and he isn't able to be here, so he arranged it with Father Francis that I could serve benediction in his place."

"Gee, have you done a benediction before?"

"Once, but if you see me doing something wrong, give me a high sign, will you?"

"I'll try, but I don't want to get in trouble because you don't know what to do."

Anger flashed in Jeremy's green eyes. His fists closed, and, for a moment, he indulged in the daydream of giving self-centered Donny Rohr a punch in the face.

But he sighed. "Okay, Donny, don't worry about it. I'll be fine."

Donny got a self-righteous expression on his face and stomped off to light the altar candles.

Jeremy heard sandals slapping the floor and rosary beads rattling. Father Salvatore entered the sacristy. Jeremy's shoulder muscles relaxed, and he sighed in relief when Father Salvatore entered the sacristy. Father Salvatore was a pleasant, plump, good-natured, elderly priest.

"Hello, young man, and what's your name?"

"Jeremy Wilcamp, Father."

"You must be new. Did you transfer in from another school?"

"No, Father, but I did join the altar boys recently."

"Really! It's unusual for boys to join when they're older. Father Francis does his best to get them when they're younger."

"A friend of mine wanted me to join, and he sort of dragged me into it, I guess." "Father," Jeremy fidgeted, "this is only the second time I have ever served a benediction, and the first time was a practice run that Father Francis had the altar boys do, so I might make a mistake."

"Don't you worry, Jeremy. It's easy. I'll point to you where to go if I see you having any trouble, and I'll keep an eye out for you."

"Thanks, Father."

Donny returned from lighting the candles. He couldn't believe that Jeremy was not helping Father Salvatore vest, and he shoved the candle torch into Jeremy's side and went to help the priest. Jeremy grabbed the torch before it fell on the floor. Red blasted through Jeremy's mind. He wanted to club Donny with the candle torch. But he took it to the closet. *How much can go wrong in one day?*

Jeremy stared at the place where Steve had hidden the cassock and surplice that he wore. His heart fluttered. *Stevie, I hope you're okay.* He closed the closet door and trudged back into the sacristy. Donny was telling Father Salvatore how much more experienced an altar boy he is than Jeremy, even though he wasn't exactly saying that.

"Ready, boys?

"Yes, Father, I sure am," Donny answered, with too much emphasis on the I.

Jeremy glanced at Father Salvatore, who now held the sacred golden monstrance studded with dozens of precious jewels. He winked at Jeremy and gave him a reassuring nod.

After the service had started, the three of them knelt at the foot of the altar, and Father Salvatore called out the litany of the saints. The elderly people in the church were answering pray-for-us after the name of each saint.

Jeremy's eyes fell upon the golden monstrance containing a large white wafer locked in a glass oval at its center, the Catholic Church's symbolic representation of the body of Christ. Then his eyes wandered up to the marble crucifix above the Monastery's altar. Jeremy's eyes peered into the eyes of Jesus Christ crucified.

God, I don't know how you helped me today, and I know it must be an awful lot for me to ask you to help me again, but Stevie is my best friend. He really is my only friend. Please God, take care of him. I promise you, I'll never do it again. I'll do everything I am supposed to do. Please, God, he's my best friend.

Jeremy had stopped hearing the litany as he implored his God to protect his friend. The touch of Father Salvatore's hand on his shoulder surprised him. The litany had ended, and Father Salvatore and Donny and all the people in the church had risen to their feet, except Jeremy.

Father Salvatore presumed that he was giving Jeremy a reminder as he had assured him he would. But the bloodshot eyes filled with tears and the trembling chin of the altar boy kneeling next to him on the altar of Saint Michael's Monastery Church, stunned him.

The instantaneous change in Father Salvatore's face raised red flags in Jeremy's mind. *I shouldn't have let him see me like this.* Jeremy rose to his feet, averting his face from Father Salvatore.

Father Salvatore was profoundly shaken. This youngster had brought his mind out of some happy, holy, lofty place where angels and saints praised God, to this forlorn lad, who was a picture of unrelenting anguish.

The priest wanted to comfort Jeremy and ask him what was wrong. But Jeremy's rigid stance with his face pointed at the altar reminded Father Salvatore of the benediction. Father Salvatore climbed the steps of the altar, but he had to struggle to remember where he was in the service.

Chapter 9
8:00

Steve led Carl and Mickey into the vestibule of the church where the three of them exchanged nervous glances among themselves.

"I've got to see what's going on outside, guys," Steve warned Carl and Mickey, "otherwise, we might walk straight into them."

But, at that moment, the center door of the church opened, and two ladies made their way into the vestibule. Steve stood on his tiptoes trying to see outside, but the opening only revealed one of the cement pillars in front of the church.

"Hello, sonny," the taller of the two ladies greeted Steve.

"Hi," Steve scooted to the inner door of the vestibule leading to the church and held it open for them.

"Thank you, young man. Are you boys coming to benediction?"

"No ma'am, we were leaving."

"That's too bad. It's a beautiful thing to do, but you must get home and study your lessons, I guess."

"Yes ma'am," Steve agreed, "we all three have tests tomorrow."

"Oh, my goodness! If you say a prayer before you do your lessons, it will help you with those tests. God bless you, boys."

"Thank, you," Steve groaned as the ladies waddled by. *Man, I'll never get out of here at this rate.*

"Okay, guys, I'm going outside to see what's happening. Stay here, and I'll be back in a few minutes." Carl and Mickey nodded.

"Steve," Mickey exhorted as Steve opened the church door, "don't get caught. Please."

"Don't worry. I'm just going to make sure nobody is out front, and then I'll be back."

Steve stepped onto the front entrance to the church. No kids were in sight, and he could hear sounds of the altar boys playing outside the altar boys' room.

What the heck, let me stop wasting time and get out of here.

Mickey was delighted to see Steve return so quickly.

"We're good here," Steve said, "but I want to make one change. Instead of taking Montclair Street up to Caroline Street, let's go through the alley behind Montclair and take that up to Caroline Street. It should be clear sailing."

"Does that sound okay to you guys?"

Carl was okay with it, but Mickey frowned at the idea. "The alley is going to be darker, Steve. The alleys only have one or two street lights."

"That's a good reason for taking the alley, Mick. Come on."

Steve led them up the wide front walkway of the church. Their shadows blended into the night as the light from the church entrance faded behind them. A chill passed through Steve as he surveyed the fence that separated the grove adjacent to the front lawn of the church from the world around it. *That's my world, Brad. Meet me in there tonight, and we'll see who's braver.*

The boys bolted up Montclair Street to its intersection with Monastery avenue. They crossed Monastery Avenue and dashed into the alley behind Montclair Street. Steve stopped them when they were in the alley. He searched the darkness looking for anyone or anything suspicious.

"So far, so good, guys. Nobody is in sight. Do you think we can run all the way to Caroline Street? We'll take a breather when we get there."

Mickey, lean and speedy, concurred, "Yeah, Steve."

Carl, husky and slow, entreated Steve to not go too fast.

"Okay, Carl, we'll take it in a steady jog."

About halfway up the alley, Steve halted them. Somebody had entered the alley from the north side of Caroline Street.

"Carl get on that side of me and stay next to each other." Steve reached into his pants pocket, pulled out his Swiss Army knife, and opened the longest blade. "If this is trouble, get behind me."

Carl and Mickey eyed each other, but they did what Steve told them.

"Steve," Mickey whispered, "maybe we should go back."

Carl whined, "Yeah, Steve, I think Mickey's right." They both stopped in their tracks.

"No, no, Carl. It's only one person, and he came into the alley from the north side. That is not someone from the initiation. Besides, everybody should still be playing around outside the altar boys' room. It's probably somebody out for some exercise. Now, come on. This person will suspect us of being up to something if we keep fooling around."

Mickey stumbled over his own feet, as he and Carl fell into step with Steve. Steve fixed his eyes on the approaching figure as the boys edged forward.

All three of them realized that the person approaching them was taller than any of them. He was strolling toward them, but he wasn't casing out the houses as if he wanted to break in or steal something, so Steve put his hand holding his knife into his jacket pocket.

"Hi, boys, where are you coming from?"

"Oh, we just got out of the altar boys' meeting at the Monastery," Steve answered, "and we're heading home."

"Altar boys. You kids are brave. Isn't it safer to stay on Montclair Street? That's lit much better than the alley."

"We're okay. This is a short cut for us, and we get home faster."

"Be careful, kids. Stay together."

"Yes, sir, we will. Thanks," Steve replied.

They resumed walking as if they weren't the least bit intimidated by anything, but then, all three of them turned around, wanting to be sure that the tall figure had moved on.

"My God," Steve grumbled, and he closed his knife and put it into his pants pocket.

Stevie, you're overreacting. Not everybody is toting a fist full of M80s and cherry bombs. And you shouldn't be brandishing your knife about. Stop scaring the shit out of Carl and Mickey. We're in no danger here.

"Come on, guys, let's vamoose."

They ran the rest of the way up the alley to Caroline Street, and then gamboled down Caroline to Montclair, relieved to be out of the alley.

"Okay, now we're going to cross Montclair Street like lightning because if we're going to be seen, it'll be there. You too, Carl. You've got to move fast. Then we're going into the alley behind Caroline instead of down the street. If we are forced to hide, we can find a lot more places in the alley than in the street. You guys ready?"

"Yeah," Mickey zipped his jacket up tight around his neck. Carl gave Steve a V with his fingers.

"Let's go."

They raced across the street and into the alley behind Caroline Street. Steve glanced in the direction of the Monastery, but he was moving so fast that he couldn't make out any detail. Steve supposed that Carl and Micky were thinking that it wasn't smart to go into another alley, but the encounter with the man had made him think it was safer than the street. None of the altar boys would want to venture into the alleys. They were too dark and creepy.

Steve stopped them in the alley. "All right," he said, as the three of them panted for breath. "We're halfway there. Nobody is going to find us now."

"You think we're safe?" The tension he was feeling, distorted Mickey's voice.

"Yeah, the alley is clear all the way to Patterson Parkway. Get your wind. We're going to run top speed down the alley to Dennis Street. We'll stop there and catch our breath. Come on."

They hadn't gone past two houses when a huge dog barked and charged through its backyard and slammed into the gate that was the only thing keeping it from clamping its teeth into somebody's arm, or worse. The infuriated dog leapt into the air trying to find a way to get out. Mickey, who was closest to the enraged animal, screamed and jumped back, bumping into Carl, knocking them both to the ground. Steve ran up to the gate and kicked it, which made the dog bare its teeth and slam into the gate again trying to bite Steve's foot.

"You bitch," Steve cursed under his breath.

Steve extended a hand to Mickey and helped him up. "You okay?" Terror shined in Mickey's eyes as the dog grew more agitated, barking furiously and drooling saliva.

"Come on, Mickey, you've got to get yourself together." Steve saw lights come on in the house with the dog and the house to its left.

"Let's get away from this stupid dog." Steve contemplated throwing something at the dog. But someone had opened the door of the house where the dog lived.

"Run," he whisper-shouted as he beckoned to Carl and Mickey. They raced to Dennis Street.

"Okay, guys, this is the trickiest part," Steve challenged them. "The entrance to the altar boys' room is a clear view from Dennis Street. We're going to wait for a car, like Jeremy said, and run like hell across Dennis Street when the car goes by.

"We're in luck. Here comes a car. As soon as the car passes us, we're taking off. The headlights will be shining toward the church, so no one will be able to see us."

After the car passed, the three of them sped off and didn't stop until they were on Patterson Parkway.

"Please, Steve," Mickey pleaded, "go up to Wendon with us." Carl and Mickey lived on Wendon Street which was one block west from where they stood.

"Okay, let's do it." They crossed Patterson Parkway and trotted briskly toward Wendon Street. They kept peeking backwards, expecting to see a gang of wild altar boys chasing them. Carl and Mickey saw their homes with the front porch lights on.

"Listen up, guys," Steve said. "If anyone says anything about tonight, you tell them you were at the initiation along with everybody else. Nobody will know the difference. Everybody usually comes out of there running in a hundred different directions anyway. Fake it out, and no one will be the wiser. Most likely, nobody will say anything."

"Steve, thanks for everything."

"It's okay, Mickey. I like beating them at their own game."

"Yeah, but don't be too daring, Steve," Carl warned, "Scott was really strung out about you."

"Let me tell you something. If I get my hands on some of these big-time altar boys, Carl, I'll be the one initiating them. Now run for it. I'll watch from here until I see you on your porches."

Steve fingered with his knife. Mickey reached his home first, then Carl. Steve dashed onto Patterson Parkway without looking to see if anything was coming. When he got to the other side, he stopped and gazed back across the four-lane parkway.

Stockton, what are you doing? That's a sure way to get killed. A lot of good you'll be to Jeremy if you get run over by a car. Keep your cool.

Steve raced up Patterson Parkway into the alley behind Caroline Street and re-traced his way back to Montclair Street. When he got to the top of the alley, he had to stop. His lungs burned as he took in deep breaths of the night air. *Wow, I bet that's as fast as I have ever run in my whole life.*

He smiled, guessing that the owner had either taken the dog in, or he had run by so fast that the dog hadn't noticed him. *How could anybody leave a monster like that out at night to scare somebody to death?*

Steve leaned against a telephone pole, catching his breath. The moonlight lit up Montclair Street and its intersection with Monastery Avenue. An elderly couple of ladies were coming from the church. Steve debated whether to go back through the alley the way he and Carl and Mickey had come, or chance it, and go straight for the church. The debate was short-lived.

Old ladies coming from the church. Benediction is over. I've got to get to you now, Jeremy, before Brad does.

Steve grabbed his knife, opened the longest blade and tore off down Montclair Street toward the church. *Hang in there, Jeremy. We'll be out of there in no time.*

In full stride, he raced toward the row of neatly trimmed hedges that was planted around the periphery of the Monastery lawns, protected by a knee-high fence running along the street side of the hedges. The hedge and fence were about one third of Steve's height, and, without hesitation, he cleared them.

As his feet landed on the thick grass, already moist with dew, he heard laughing in the distance, and then he saw a dim flickering light from near the front of the church, followed by a sparkling thing sailing through the air toward him. He stopped so abruptly that his feet flew out from under him. He ducked down and covered his head as he slid forward on the lawn.

The M-80 firecracker exploded a few feet in front of him. The explosion vibrated through him, and he was afraid that his eardrums had burst. *Don't those idiots know what that thing can do if it hit someone?*

Steve jumped up, changed his direction, and headed toward the grove. He sailed over the hedge onto the wide sidewalk that led up to the church entrance and, without breaking stride, cleared the next hedge that lined the other side of the sidewalk.

Almost immediately in front of him, another flash of light spooked him. An M-80 flying directly for him. He halted in midair and twirled around. The firecracker missed him by at least a foot and landed off to his right.

He was caught between two guys in front of him blocking his way to the grove, and two guys by the Monastery entrance blocking his way into the church, all throwing fireworks at him.

They must have seen Jeremy at benediction and guessed that I escaped them by going through the front of the church when they couldn't find me after the altar boys' meeting. They're set up perfectly, expecting me, and I'm trapped in the middle of it. Wonder if they got to Scott.

As Steve searched the darkness in front of him, it crossed his mind that there had to be more guys. *Must be a couple of them by the altar boys' room entrance waiting for me in case I went that way.*

They'll be here in a few minutes now that they've heard the firecrackers. I've got to get to the grove fast.

He heard someone say something, but his ears were still ringing from the first explosions. Steve charged the two assailants in front of him. One of them was lighting another firecracker. Steve darted toward that flash of light, hoping that the guy might realize that the closer Steve got to him, the closer the firecracker was going to explode near him also. Maybe detonate in his own hand.

Whoever it was could see that Steve was going to get to him before the firecracker was lit. He had lost his chance when he took his eyes off the match and saw gusty Stevie Stockton rushing him with a knife in his hand.

He threw the matches out of his hand and yelled, "He's got a knife."

Steve's assailant backed away after he saw the knife.

There's my chance. I can get by them.

But someone tackled Steve from the right and took him to the ground.

"Got your ass." Brad Maddox whooped in triumph.

Steve rotated the knife in his hands, raised it up, and cracked Brad on the head with the butt end of the knife. Brad had a hand around Stevie's throat. Steve raised the knife up and smashed Brad in the head a second time.

Brad screamed, "You bastard." He threw himself off Steve and kicked him in the right leg as he did.

Steve hopped up and swung his knife around wildly in the air, but the others stood back watching him and Brad fight.

"Get the son-of-a-bitch," Brad thundered.

Another flash of light coming from the front of the Monastery made Steve growl. He knew what it was.

Brad sprang to his feet rubbing his head. "You going to give up, Stockton, or do we have to blow the shit out of you?"

Steve bolted for the grove again. The M-80 came flying over his head. He tried to stop himself with a slide, and he raised his arms up over his head. His knife slipped out of his hand as his feet came to a stop close to the exploding firecracker. His knife had fallen to his left, and he rolled over to his left side as he came to the ground.

Brad was running for him. *Brad's going to kick me.* He saw his knife blade shining in the light of the nearly full October moon. He catapulted himself forward, clasped the knife and continued to roll so that Brad's foot barely grazed the side of Steve's head.

Steve was on his feet in a second and now Brad saw Stevie Stockton surging at him with his knife in his hand and with a kind of crazed madness in his eyes.

Steve lunged for Brad when another firecracker exploded in midair to his right. The explosion immobilized him. He stopped, frozen. The flash blinded him, and he couldn't hear anything.

Steve knew where the grove was, and he raced for it. He almost ran headlong into the fence when his vision cleared, and he stopped at the last second. He stuck his knife between his teeth and hurled himself onto the fence.

Come on, Stevie. Get over this fence. He had his right leg and shoulder above the fence and was about to hoist himself over when someone latched onto his left foot.

"Got you," the guy clutching Steve's ankle yelled. Steve did not recognize the voice, but he seemed awfully strong. He was trying to pull Steve off the fence and was about to do so. Steve snatched the knife out of his mouth and slashed it through the air close enough to the guy's face for Steve to let him know what was going to happen next. He stepped back when he saw the knife coming.

"Bring him down," Brad yelled, but Steve yanked his foot out of the guy's grasp and went over the fence. He dropped into the grove off balance and came down awkwardly on his left ankle. He felt it twist under his weight.

"Oh, God," Steve moaned.

Brad and two others scowled at Stevie from the other side of the fence, and two more approached from farther back.

"Come on," Brad bellowed, "we've got him." "He hurt his leg."

"Got a mind to drop a cherry bomb on him," someone else said, and he and Brad leaped onto the fence.

Steve grimaced with pain, but his mind was working at warp speed. He had seen dozens of movies where some character had been wounded or hurt but kept on fighting and won. It had always seemed phony, and he had usually sneered at it, but Steve was determined to do that now.

He gripped the fence with his left hand. He held his knife in his right hand and watched Brad climbing the fence. When Brad's shoulders were level with the top of the fence, Steve pushed with his right leg and pulled with his left hand and propelled himself up onto the fence and thrust the longest blade of the knife into Brad's shoulder.

Brad screamed, "He stabbed me," and both he and the other attacker dropped back off the fence.

Steve fell to the ground, got to his feet and hobbled deeper into the grove. *Dumb ass, what did you think I was going to do?*

Brad removed his coat and shirt to examine his shoulder, losing precious time in his quest to capture Steve. Steve reckoned that he hadn't done much more than break Brad's skin because he was wearing a leather jacket. But Steve knew that he had scared Brad and his gang with the knife.

Fear. You've got your fireworks and I've got my knife and the balls to use it. It's one thing to throw a firecracker. But it's another to wield a knife, you chicken shit. I scared your asses, and that's my escape. How many did you need to help you do it, Brad?

"We've got to find him and beat the shit out of him." Brad egged his comrades on.

"We'll never find him in there now," someone else shouted.

"And he's got a knife, douche bag," another, who obviously did not want to come after Stevie, jeered.

"Yeah, well let's see how he likes this." Yet another voice that Steve did not recognize.

They threw more firecrackers into the grove, calling Steve foul names and telling him what they were going to do to him when they caught him. The firecrackers lit the way for Steve, and he made his way deeper into the grove leaving Brad and his gang behind.

When the barrage of explosives ceased, Steve slumped to the ground with sweat dripping off his forehead. An urge to cry gripped him. He sniffed back tears and peered up through the pines into the black, starlit sky.

"Oh, God," he sighed.

He listened to the sounds of the night. A soft breeze hummed through the tops of the pine trees, crickets chirped, and frogs croaked, but he heard nothing else. *They must be gone, cleared out before somebody catches up with all that noise they made.*

A burning sensation stung Steve's face, but it didn't seem to be too bad. *That last M80 was too close.* He closed his knife, put it in his pants pocket, and massaged his left ankle. The swollen ankle throbbed with pain, but he could move it in all directions, and he didn't feel anything that seemed like broken bone.

"It's only a bad sprain, Jeremy."

If they knew that I would go into the grove, I wonder if they know about the basement too. Steve pushed himself up from the ground. *I've got to get to you, Jeremy. Even if they don't know about the basement, they'll be hot on your trail. Brad's play was to beat the crap out of me, so I wouldn't come looking for him later. If he couldn't do that, he'll want to hurt you, Jeremy. He must think I'll be afraid of him if he beats you up.*

That fool has no idea of what I will do to him if he does anything to you, Jeremy. Got to be the big, bad ass all the time, beating up somebody. He's got to save face because I punched him out today.

Anger raged inside him, but it was Jeremy that tore at Stevie's spirit. "I can't let them do that to you, Jeremy. I can't."

He plunged forward. As he did, his right foot slipped in the loose, damp earth, and he crashed to the ground. The pine branch he was holding onto escaped his grasp and slapped him across the face as he fell. Steve curled up on the ground hurting everywhere.

"Look, grove, you and I go back a long way. We're supposed to be friends. Don't do this now. Help me, you mother pine trees. Help me. You hear that?" Steve latched onto another pine branch and pulled himself up. "Come on, Stockton, you've got to get there." *Brad must be counting on you being around the altar boys' room, Jeremy, waiting for me. He knows that we switched places for benediction and that we're in this together.*

Steve limped through the grove clutching pine branches to support himself. All the while, he tormented himself with one question. *What are these bullies capable of doing to Jeremy, who has nothing to defend himself with, if they were willing to play with me the way they did?*

CHAPTER 10
OCTOBER 2ND
BOY, YOU REALLY PUT IN
ROUGH DAYS SOMETIMES

Jeremy tried to focus his attention on the benediction, but it became more and more difficult as the minutes passed. *It's a simple ceremony. I've got to remember what to do.*

But Father Salvatore had coaxed Jeremy into the right place and into doing the right thing several times. It had not bothered the priest in the least. He fancied that the priests were guardians of the altar boys. In fact, the altar boys were the greatest resource of new priests. To him every altar boy was potentially a future priest.

Father Salvatore had dedicated his life to bringing the message of the passion of Jesus Christ to the world. He strived to make what he believed was the greatest story of love in the history of mankind real and alive for all his parishioners.

Father Salvatore had known in one glimpse that this lad kneeling at his side was in a passion of his own. He hurt deeply for someone. Father Salvatore had no doubt that Jeremy had called upon his God with the purest humility from the very same altar on which the priest had preached dozens and dozens of sermons. Jeremy had incited in Father Salvatore emotions and feelings that the priest had tried to evoke from his parishioners over all his years as a priest with every sermon. Yet, the boy had not spoken a word. He had prayed.

The priest lifted his eyes to the crucifix above the altar. *Let not, Lord, this passion be for naught. Let whomever it is that this lad suffers for be protected and receive whatever grace he requests. Lord, make right whatever it is that he needs.*

Father Salvatore faced the handful of elderly women and men, holding the monstrance in his hands. He made the sign of the cross with the monstrance and spoke the words of benediction in Latin.

Jeremy had detected no change in Father Salvatore, but he had seen three older kids in the front of the church. Jeremy guessed that they were kids from the high school whom Brad had recruited to help him. They were too tall and well-built to be grammar school kids. They were gone now. *They're hunting for Steve. They know that Steve and I switched places.* His fear for Steve had brought near panic to his brain. He couldn't concentrate enough to pray anymore. He wanted to get off the altar and decide what to do.

Jeremy had stopped seeing Donny's dirty looks which had intensified as the service had moved along, and Jeremy seemed less and less aware of what was going on. Donny's words stung Jeremy back to reality as they paraded off the altar at the end of the service.

"You wait until I tell Father Francis on you." Donny wagged a finger at Jeremy.

The muscles in Jeremy's face tightened, and his eyes blazed with anger. Thoughts categorizing everything about Donny Rohr and his being on the altar ripped through Jeremy's mind. *Hypocrite. What is someone like you doing on this altar?*

"You know what else you can tell Father Francis, Donny? Tell him I told you to go fuck yourself."

Donny was shocked. He peeked at Father Salvatore as if to ask him if he had heard what Jeremy had said.

But Father Salvatore was oblivious to whatever was transpiring between Donny and Jeremy at that moment. It seemed to him that the sanctuary lights cast a dim, golden glitter off the sacred monstrance onto Jeremy's back as he walked in front of him, and he wanted to believe that it meant something.

The priest's mind was in turmoil as he debated how to approach this troubled lad. He knew that he had to. *Can I possibly relate to this young fellow, whom I have never seen before? He surely needs someone to talk to. He must feel very alone. There must be something more that I can do than just pray for him.*

The priest tightened his grip on the monstrance. *Of course, there is. That boy and I were put together on this altar for a reason. If I talk to him, something will come to me. I'll find a way to ease his burden, whatever it is.* First, he had to dismiss Donny. He placed the monstrance on the vestry stand and covered it with its silk hood.

"Well, Donny, young man, since you lit the candles and helped me vest before the service, perhaps we can let you off early, and Jeremy and I will tidy up."

"Oh, no, Father. I'm glad to help, and besides, I'm not sure Jeremy's got it all down yet."

"That's what I was thinking, Donny, and I plan to take a few moments to show Jeremy what to do. Now, both of you kneel, and I will give you my blessing."

Jeremy wanted to scream. His insides were rebelling. He had to get out of there. It was so difficult to restrain his impatience as he knelt before Father Salvatore. Donny now gloated with pride as he inferred that Father Salvatore must have seen the complete botch that Jeremy had made of the benediction and intended to scold him for it.

"Come now, Jeremy," Father Salvatore said, after his blessing. "Let me show you the fast way to put the candles out. Forget about the candle extinguisher." Father Salvatore picked up a pall from the vestry table.

I've got get out of here. Jeremy followed Father Salvatore into the sanctuary. *Why did I let him see me like that on the altar? He'll never let me go. Come on, Father Salvatore, you're supposed to be a nice guy. Don't do this to me.*

The sanctuary air was filled with the smell of burning incense from the benediction and felt oppressively heavy to Jeremy, making him think that he might suffocate. Beads of sweat made their way onto his forehead, and his knees felt weak. *Why won't he leave me alone?* Father Salvatore strode up the altar steps.

"Here's a good trick, Jeremy." Father Salvatore fanned the tall candles placed on the altar with the pall, and, that fast, they were all out. With a smile, the priest commented, "Beats the candle extinguisher, doesn't it?"

"Yes, Father."

But now the sanctuary air was filled with both the smell of incense and burning candle wax. Jeremy was afraid he wouldn't be able to breathe.

The priest bowed before the altar, took a knee and turned his back to the altar. The smile vanished from his face when he saw Jeremy staring dejectedly at the floor with beads of sweat across his forehead.

"Come with me, Jeremy. Let's sit over here for a few moments." He put a hand on Jeremy's shoulder and walked him to the three ornately carved sanctuary chairs.

"Do you feel okay, Jeremy? You look like you might faint. Here, sit down. Let me bring you some water. I'll be right back."

My, God. What is he thinking about?

Father Salvatore had sat Jeremy in the middle sanctuary chair. Jeremy jumped up as soon as Father Salvatore disappeared behind the altar. He folded his arms over his chest. *What made him put me there?* Bishops and Cardinals and every celebrant of every solemn high mass in the history of the Monastery had sat in that chair.

If the Pope came here, he would sit there. How could he place a lowly altar boy like me in that seat? Jeremy stared at the chair in disbelief.

With his arms folded and his eyes fixed on the floor, Jeremy stepped toward the sacristy. *Maybe I can make a run for it and get out of here before he comes back.* But the sound of sandals slapping the floor chased that idea away.

The graying priest looked at Jeremy with concern. "Are you sure you feel okay, fella?"

Father Salvatore fell into step with Jeremy, and they progressed toward the sacristy. Jeremy sighed in relief. At least he was off the altar and pointed in the right direction.

"Yes, Father, I feel fine."

Father Salvatore felt less worried as he saw color returning to Jeremy's face. "Please, Jeremy, young man, come here and sit with me for a few minutes. I'd like to talk to you," and he led Jeremy to a church bench in the back of the sacristy. "Now, drink this water. It might make you feel better."

Jeremy wondered where Father Salvatore had found the glass. The cool water was refreshing. Father Salvatore watched as Jeremy drank about half of the water in the glass.

"Thanks, Father."

"You don't want to talk, do you, fella?"

Jeremy swished the water around in the glass. "No, Father."

"It is so often difficult to talk about the things that are most important to us. Don't be frightened or worried, Jeremy. I won't keep you more than a few minutes." "Sometimes," Father Salvatore spoke slowly and deliberately, "you can look at someone and see something in them that brings many feelings to your heart, and many wonderful, but perhaps sad, ideas to your mind. You have done that to me tonight. You have inspired me because I see many fine qualities in you. And you have saddened me because something of immense importance weights so heavily on such young shoulders as yours.

"I wish that I could help you, and I was going to try. I have been thinking about what to say and how to help you throughout the benediction. But as I look at you now, I have a strong feeling that you want to be gone from here as quickly as you can. Am I right?"

"Sort of, Father. I do have to get home. My parents will worry."

"Yes, of course."

Let me go. Stop this. Get me out of here. Inwardly, his young body was about to explode, but he sat quietly on the wooden church bench glowering at the floor.

Father Salvatore placed a gnarled old hand on the top of Jeremy's head and patted him, and then he dropped his hand onto Jeremy's shoulder. The touch of the priest's hand startled Jeremy, and he glanced at the priest out of the corner of his eye. He did not move, and he returned his eyes to the patterns in the marble floor. In that moment, Jeremy's mind was off everything else, and every sense of his body focused on the man sitting next to him.

Whatever is bothering this lad will not be revealed. Father Salvatore knew that he had failed to connect with Jeremy, and he sensed that his attempt at friendship had made the youth uneasy. He removed his hand from Jeremy's shoulder. *Can such terrible things have happened to this boy that he will not confide in anyone?* The priest racked his brain searching for words of encouragement.

"Jeremy," the priest sighed, "I'm a friend to you at any time. Maybe, some other time, you might want to talk to someone, and I am here for you whenever you want. When you leave here, I am going into the sanctuary and praying one of the most holy and fervent prayers I have ever prayed so that whatever or whomever you feel so much for tonight, might be protected and loved by God."

Father Salvatore paused. Jeremy felt the priest's intensity. *He's trying to make me cry. I've got to get out of here before he does.* But the mention of leaving captured his attention. *He'll let me go if I hang in a little longer.*

"Thanks, Father."

"Go now. Do whatever you must, and may God be with you."

Jeremy was astounded. *Wow! I didn't think he would let me go that quickly.* He bolted up from the bench. The water splashed in the glass, but Jeremy manipulated the glass so that the water didn't spill.

"Thanks a lot, Father." Jeremy put the glass on the bench and headed for the door that led downstairs to the altar boys' room.

"Jeremy," Father Salvatore called, and he rose from the bench and came to Jeremy.

Please, don't bless me again.

"You did a fine thing on the altar tonight. You prayed to God. The simplest and most beautiful of prayers, I am sure. There is no task that an altar boy or anyone on the altar has that transcends the entire purpose of being there. Prayer. I am proud of you as an altar boy tonight, and I know that God is also. May he answer your prayer in a way that you can understand and accept."

Father Salvatore's comments bewildered Jeremy. "Thank you, Father Salvatore."

Jeremy could barely constrain himself from running to the door. *Is there anything about me that Father Salvatore doesn't know? How could he see so much in so little time?*

* * *

His footsteps slowed as he neared the bottom of the staircase, and he stopped on the last step. He listened and then poked his head into the hallway. No one. Jeremy tiptoed down the hall toward the altar boys' room. He put his hand on the door jamb and peeked inside. Donny was gone, and no one was there.

He faced the hallway that led to the outside. For a moment, he stood frozen. No reason came to his mind to explain to him what he was doing, but his feet seemed to be making him walk up the hallway toward the door. He leaned his ear against it and listened for anything going on outside. Nothing.

Still unguided by any reason, he grasped the doorknob. But then he remembered that he wore a cassock and surplice. *Great, Jeremy, you're going outside dressed like this?* He let go of the doorknob.

"Who cares?" Jeremy yanked the door open.

He heard no sounds of kids playing or fooling around.

"Man, where are they? What's going on?" He stepped out onto the stone staircase and listened. A car zoomed down Monastery Avenue, but that was all. Jeremy leaned against the cold stone wall and raised his head toward the clear October night.

"I promised you, Steve, so here goes. Good luck." He re-traced his steps down the hallway. Jeremy removed the cassock and surplice, grabbed his jacket, and scurried to the basement door. At the door, he paused. *No, I can't leave a mess.*

He dropped his jacket on the floor and went back to put the cassock and surplice away. As he put the garments in the clothes closets, his eyes fell onto the two chairs in which he and Stevie had sat during the meeting. *Steve, I wish we were sitting there now. Father Salvatore, I could never have as much pull with God as you do, so please, say the good prayer that you were talking about.*

Jeremy opened the basement door and stepped onto the platform at the top of the stairs. *Maybe I'll unscrew the lightbulb now and go down onto the walkway while I can take my time and do it carefully. But then, I'll have to sit in the dark and wait.* Jeremy stood rooted to the spot, debating what to do. *Stevie wouldn't waste a minute if he was here. He always knows what to do.*

Jeremy sighed as the options buzzed through his mind. He reached his hand up close to the light bulb, closed his eyes and unscrewed it.

It's dark down here. I don't think I have ever been anywhere where it was this dark. How am I going to do this? You've got no choice, Wilcamp. Come on. He placed the palms of his hands against the wall and stepped down the stairs feeling the wall with each step.

On the fifth step a swooshing sound broke through the silence of the basement.

"What was that?" After listening for a few minutes, he guessed that it had to be the hot water heaters igniting. *It's not cold enough to be the furnaces. Maybe it is.*

"Steve, you were so smart to bring me down here after school today. I don't know what I would be thinking now if you hadn't warned me about all the noises down here."

His eyes had not yet adjusted to the darkness. *Maybe those hot water heaters are giving off some light that I can see.* He quickened his pace, thinking that the heaters might go off before he had a chance to find them if he kept moving so slowly.

Yeah, Stevie, it's the right move to come down here while I've got time. It would be much harder to do if Brad and whoever he's got with him came into the altar boys' room, and I was planted on the platform at the top of the stairs.

His hands felt their way along the wall and his feet took the steps faster. When he reached the walkway, he raised his leg and contacted the railing.

It's about three feet in front of me. I can deal with that.

He peered into the basement, but it was too dark to discern anything. The hot water heaters were still humming, and he made his way across the walkway with his palms on the wall exactly as he and Steve had done that afternoon. He took about twenty steps and then eased himself down the wall and sat on the walkway.

A red light deep in the basement welcomed him. *How about that.* Jeremy glued his eyes to the light, but it was too deep in the basement to illuminate anything. Nevertheless, it made Jeremy feel less alone. He knew from what direction the noise of the hot water heaters came, but they could not be seen.

Must be behind a fire wall or something like that. As that conclusion passed through his mind, the heaters shut off. The sudden silence was almost as scary as the noise they had made when they first fired up.

Should have realized that they were going off at some point. Whew. Got to be aware of what's going on in here, Wilcamp.

Other noises eroded the silence and played games with Jeremy's ears and mind. He heard what seemed to be water running through pipes intermittently, and he was aware of occasional cracking noises that pipes make as they expand and contract. Jeremy heard other sounds as well, for which he had no explanation.

Please, don't let there be any rats or mice down here. He shuddered. *What about spiders and whatever other kinds of bugs?* He flexed his shoulders. "I've got to stop this."

"Steve, you should be here by now." He rested his elbows on his flexed knees.

You wanted to talk to me, didn't you, Father Salvatore? But I couldn't. I don't know who told me that you were a nice guy. It wasn't Stevie. Maybe I knew somehow. Maybe I was so desperate for something to go right that I made my mind up that you are okay. But I had to get out of there. Steve could have been coming. He might have needed me.

I'm glad you let me go when you did. You can't expect people to tell you everything about themselves because you are a priest. Especially because you're a priest. You're God's friend a lot more than you're my friend. And you make too much out of it. You see some poor kid in your church with tears in his eyes saying a prayer, and you act like it's the messiah or something, when it's only me.

Maybe I was praying for my sick goldfish. Why is it such a big deal? Why do you have to know what it's about? That's what you're supposed to do in church, isn't it? Pray and get all emotional. You think you can get anything out of me because I'm a kid. Bet you think I'm a louse now. Maybe I can make it up to you some other time like you said. Jeremy stretched out his legs and leaned his head against the wall. *Who would ever think a priest would touch you so much. I thought they never touched anybody.*

"Stevie, please, get here."

Jeremy took the two packs of matches out of his pants pockets. He held them tightly in his hands and sniffed them. Then he put them back into his pockets. Jeremy rose to his feet and extended a leg out until he felt the railing. He stepped forward and grasped the railing.

"Something's gone wrong. I've got to face it. If they've gotten to you, Steve... God, you better have protected Stevie. If you didn't...I will never forgive you. I...." Jeremy felt angry, but his lips and chin quivered, and all the muscles of his face tingled as he fought to keep from crying.

What am I thinking? I've got to defend myself. Why didn't I bring a weapon down here with me? I should be able to find something that can serve as a weapon. Maybe one of those candle torches. As narrow as this walkway is and as dark as it is, I might be able to hold Brad and his gang off with something like that and even scare them. They must be smart enough to recognize the danger of falling into the basement trying to fight someone here in the dark.

Is it too risky to go all the way back up to the sacristy now and get one of the candle torches? It's getting late. They've got to be hunting for me by now. Suppose I go up there and run into them? The options raced through Jeremy's mind.

Jeremy snapped his fingers. *The clothes tree. Sure. The clothes tree in the altar boys' room. That's a great weapon. I'll open the door a crack, make sure no one is there, and then run in and grab it. Yeah. But, Wilcamp, if you're going to do it, you better do it fast.*

The feel of the stone wall behind him, and the cement walkway beneath him gave him confidence as he moved toward the staircase. But after a few steps, he halted.

Wonder if I can carry that thing down here and still feel my way without falling. It's probably heavy. It's got to be awkward too, and I might make a lot of noise if I bang it into the railing. Man, what if I dropped the thing. God, what am I supposed to do? Steve, why don't you get here? Maybe I'll sit here and wait a while longer.

He moved back to where he had seen the red light and sat down. The red light had become a friend to him now. *Steve's right, nobody in their right mind would come down here in the dark. He's probably gotten into the grove and is waiting for Brad and his bully friends to get lost.*

I wonder if I can hear the church bell in here. Of course, you can hear that thing for miles around. I'll wait until it rings 10:00, and then I'll go to the old church if Steve hasn't gotten here. Dad's going to be so mad over this.

Mom is probably busting on Dad right now. It's got to be close to 9:30. It's certainly after 9:00. As soon as she sees 9:30 on the clock, she'll be yelling at Dad about how he should never have let me go out with matches. What a great night this'll be. All this initiation nonsense now and maybe a beating waiting for me when I get home. Please, Dad, don't do that to me. I can't take it.

Maybe Steve's Mom can get me out of this if she calls my mom. Hey, maybe I can go home with Steve, and his dad will take me home in his car and tell my parents some story about why we're late, and I'll get out of the whole mess. We can tell Mom that Steve lost his keys or his wallet on the lawn, and we spent so much time looking for them that we lost track of time. That should work. Steve will talk his parents into covering for me if they know I am going to get beat for being late. Mrs. Stockton can call my mom as soon as we get to Steve's home and tell Mom what happened. That gives Mom time to get over being mad before I get home. That's a perfect plan. I know Steve will do that.

Come on, Steve, get here.

The minutes seemed like hours. Jeremy put his hands into his jacket pockets. His muscles relaxed now that he had come up with an excuse for being late. *Maybe I can take a nap for a few minutes and when I wake up, Steve will be here.* He stretched out his legs and closed his eyes. He felt his feet dangling in the air over the basement.

"Steve, everything is so much fun when we're together. I wish you would hurry up. Please, get here."

A lot of kids in our class are good friends, but none of them are like you and me. My parents have a lot of friends, but they aren't close to any of them. You know what, Steve, I don't think my parents are too close to each other. Does that make any sense? They're married, but they don't seem happy to me. Are your parents happy?

I didn't know that your dad only goes to Sunday mass when you're serving. So, what if he doesn't go to mass every Sunday? God is not going to send your father to hell. He's such a great father. Maybe my father could be too if he wanted. God would never condemn your dad to hell. That's not what religion is about. That's how I know that God took care of you tonight, Stevie. Jeremy fought back tears. "Stevie, please be all right."

CHAPTER 11
JEREMY WILCAMP AND STEVIE STOCKTON

Minutes passed as a whirlwind of emotions engulfed Jeremy. The dark basement was forgotten. The strange noises of the hidden underworld of the Monastery no longer registered in his ears. He longed for the unbearable suspense of the unknown to end. All he wanted was to see his friend, tell him how happy he was that he had arrived, and that the plan had worked. He could see Stevie talking and laughing. Dozens of happy things that he and Steve had done ran through his mind. Why wasn't his friend there? Jeremy paced back and forth on the walkway.

"It's not right, Stevie. I know you're not afraid of Brad and anybody else he has with him and that you know how to take care of yourself, but how much can you do with one Swiss Army knife? Why didn't we stay together? Come on, Steve, get here, will you. This is driving me crazy."

Jeremy threw his hands up in the air and spoke with trembling lips, "God, please, stop this. Let him get here."

He stared into the basement and clenched the railing. He broke out into a chill as he peered into the darkness below. *Stevie wouldn't lose it like this. I've got to get control.*

Why am I safe in here and you're out there? You're trapped in this thing because of me. You weren't being initiated. You could have gone home, and that would be that. Steve, where would I ever find a friend like you? Think of it. Brad and his gang of bullies think they're big deal friends because they're out there ganging up on a bunch of younger kids, and they're doing it together and having a fun time blowing up fireworks.

Do you think Brad or any of his punk buddies care enough about anyone to do what you're doing for me? They don't know what a friend is. Imagine Brad kicking Scott, and they're supposed to be friends. What's wrong with them? Why do they have to be this way? Why do they want to hurt you or me...or anyone? Throw firecrackers and cherry bombs at us. That's crazy.

Jeremy stopped pacing and focused his eyes on the red light. "Stevie, I'm thinking of you. I can feel you. I didn't want any of this to happen. If only I could take it all away. Man, I can't even help you from here. Do you know how much I want to be there with you?"

"Shit." Jeremy kicked his foot along the walkway. *If I can't feel any vibes from him, why should he be able to feel any from me?* He grasped the railing. *Maybe I am getting a vibe from you, Steve. Maybe you are all right, because I'd know or feel something if you weren't.*

Do you believe that you can feel things from other people, even when they are far apart? The brain is strong. We don't know how it works. Our minds can connect, Steve. I know they can. Please, hear me. Connect with me. I never wanted anyone to be safe and okay in my whole life more than I want you to be now.

Come on, Wilcamp, you've got to keep it together. You can't panic. Jeremy backed away from the railing until he felt the stone wall behind him. He eased his body down the wall and sat on the walkway. He crossed his arms over his flexed knees and gazed at the red light.

I'm going to be strong, Stevie, and if you don't get here soon, I'm coming for you, and we'll show them what friendship is. I'll go over to the rectory and out that same window you went through with Mark Bimonte, and I'll find you. You'll be in the grove somewhere. If Brad hurt you, Stevie, I swear, I'll tear the son-of-a-bitch apart myself, just like you said. I swear to you, Stevie, I'll do it. Jeremy rested his head on his forearms and closed his eyes.

Jeremy was deep in thought when a noise startled him. His head shot up, and he listened intently. He wiped his eyes and rose to his feet. Jeremy's heart pounded in his chest. *Somebody's up there. Steve would never make noise like that. He'd screw the lightbulb in and call me exactly as he said he would. Someone is hitting the railing with a stick or something.* Jeremy felt the railing resounding in front of him.

"Jeremy, cutie pie, are you in there waiting for Stevie boy?"

Someone else sang out in a girly voice, "Jeremy, we're going to get you, baby doll."

The voices were still distant, but the dark basement air carried them clearly to his ears. Jeremy did not recognize either voice. Every muscle in Jeremy's body tightened, and an intense fear seared through his entire body.

"Oh, my God."

He moved toward the staircase that led to the old church and the rectory, but he had hardly taken a step before he heard the same banging of the railing coming from that side as well. He stopped.

One of Brad's high school goons must have known about the basement. Steve, I hope you're okay.

"What are you going to do without your precious boyfriend, Jeremy?" Another voice Jeremy did not recognize.

He heard laughter coming from the altar boys' room side of the walkway. It was Brad Maddox. Jeremy faced the wall behind him and ran his hands along the wall as high as he could reach, seeking anything that he could latch onto and climb. There was nothing.

He pulled Stevie's pack of matches out of his pocket, got on his knees and moved his hands along the walkway until he felt the edge. He lay on his stomach and leaned his upper body out over the side. Jeremy reached his arms out, opened the pack of matches, and pulled one out. When he struck the match, it didn't light. It didn't light the second time either. He threw it away and tried another.

"Come on." He struck harder and the match lit but he caught the whole book on fire. It burned his fingertips, and he dropped the pack into the basement. Jeremy held back a scream of pain and shoved his fingers into his mouth. Then he remembered what he had been trying to do and focused his attention on the basement, but the pack of matches had vanished, and the depths of the basement remained hidden.

He retrieved the other pack from his pocket and took out another match. This time he closed the match book as his father had instructed, and he struck the match. It lit promptly. He dropped the match into the basement. It went out before it had fallen three feet, and Jeremy could still not see how far the drop would be or what was on the basement floor.

Do it right, will you? He lit another match and kept his motion going forward as his father had shone him. He held his arms out over the basement and ignited the whole pack. But just as he dropped it into the basement, a scraping noise coming along the walkway distracted him. The noise attracted his attention for a split second. In that split second, the matchbook melted into the darkness.

Must be some water on the floor or the matches blew out on the way down. God, can't you give me any kind of a break?

"There you are, Jeremy. We slid a live weapon to you, so you can fight like Steve. Let's see if you can come out swinging and find us like your faggot boyfriend you little prick," Brad scoffed.

Jeremy didn't move. *Hmm, you are a queer aren't you, Brad? Faggoty stuff seems to be all you think about. You'll never lay a hand on me. They're having their own problems with the darkness, and they want me to do their work for them. Give myself up. No way I'm doing that.*

Someone else whom Jeremy didn't recognize taunted, "Yeah, be a big, brave boy like Steve. We'll show you what happens to big, brave shitheads."

Jeremy knew that they had made their way down the stairs and were on the walkway.

Brad broke the dark silence. "Did Steve tell you we would be afraid of the basement, Jeremy, sweetie? We weren't supposed to come into Steve's secret hiding places, were we? You're going to find out who's afraid soon enough." Brad followed that with some ugly snickering and more banging on the railing.

"How do you like Stevie's hiding places now, Jeremy? Soon, you might be running around in your skivvies in Steve's private grove all by yourself if you don't smarten up." Laughter now came from both sides of the walkway. Jeremy did not recognize the voice, but it was not the voice of a grammar school kid.

You incredible sons-of-bitches. Brad Maddox, if you did that to Steve, he'll make you wish you'd never been born. They're taking their time, enjoying this. Well, morons, catch me. Let's see if you've got the balls to do it. They were getting close and Jeremy knew he had to act.

"This is it, Wilcamp," he prodded himself, "you've got to do it now." Jeremy lowered his legs over the edge of the walkway and inched himself over the side up to his waist. He planned to lower himself over the edge of the walkway and hold onto the walkway with his hands. If he held on for a few minutes, they would never see him in the darkness and move on. If he couldn't hold on, he would let himself drop into the basement. *Maybe it won't be too bad if I can stay close to the wall. Maybe the basement isn't that deep, and it won't be such a long drop.*

His would-be captors were nearing. Jeremy lowered himself over the edge of the walkway, scraping his feet on the wall trying to find something to support himself. And there he was, holding onto the edge of the walkway with his fingers. The surface of the wall was smooth, and he found nothing to support himself.

He heard someone say, "He's not here." The pain in his burnt fingers was unbelievable. There was grit under his right hand, and he felt it giving. He shifted his weight to the left and tried to get a better grip. His left hand couldn't hold him. As he fell, his feet hit something that jackknifed him away from the wall. His back slammed into a sharp object, and he came to the floor with his left leg twisted up under his right thigh.

* * *

Steve came through the same window that he and Mark Bimonte had come through the previous year. It was locked. He broke it with his Swiss Army knife, opened it and crawled into the bathroom. He shouted out for help as soon as he was in the building. His ankle was killing him, but he had ignored it and had moved through the grove as fast as his ankle allowed.

He burst into the conference room that he and Mark had entered during the last initiation. It was again filled with folding tables and chairs. Steve smashed into the tables and chairs throwing them out of his way, calling for help as he bulldozed his way toward the door.

"Hold on, Jeremy, I'll be there in a few minutes." Steve entered the hallway.

The exit sign was still the only light at the bottom of the stairs. Steve limped up the stairs, shouting for help. It had taken him too long to get here. *If those bastards did anything to you, Jeremy...* He pulled himself up the steps. Father Francis was the first to respond to Steve's calls for help.

"Steve, what are you doing here?"

"Quick, Father, the basement. They're after him."

"Who's after who, Steve?"

"There's no time to explain right now, Father. We've got to get to the basement to help Jeremy. Please, go. I'll catch up."

But Father Francis came down the stairs and placed a hand on Steve's shoulder. "Steve, you're hurt. What's wrong?"

Steve flashed angry and exasperated but at the same time pleading eyes at Father Francis. "Father, it's nothing. I'm okay. Please, go to the basement. Jeremy is stuck down there by himself."

Steve's eyes and face told Father Francis that this was serious. "Okay, Steve. You take it slow and easy, and I'll get to Jeremy right now."

Father Francis raced up the stairs and into the sacristy of the old church. He grabbed the keys to the basement from a drawer in the vestry stand. As he ran from the sacristy into the hallway, he found Kevin Greene and George Wright standing there. Both were pale and frightened.

"Father Francis," George shouted, "Jeremy Wilcamp fell into the basement. I think he's hurt pretty bad."

Father Francis gazed into the faces of Kevin and George with astonishment. *What in the name of God is going on here? What are these kids doing here?* He scanned the faces of Kevin and George again, and then returned to Steve struggling up the steps.

"God help us."

Father Joseph and several priests and novices had assembled in the hallway.

"Call an ambulance," Father Francis ordered, and he raced for the basement.

"Oh, God, no, no," Steve yelled.

He limped up the rest of the stairs and followed Father Francis into the basement. Father Francis unlocked a grey metal box at the top of the staircase and flipped on several switches. He hurried down the stairs and onto the walkway. He saw four boys leaning over the railing.

Father Francis fumbled with the keys and then opened the chain link gate. He went down the stairs and moved as quickly as he could through the items stored on the basement floor to where the boys above were standing.

Steve got to the stairs leading down into the basement and called out for Jeremy. "Please, don't be hurt."

* * *

As he lay on the floor of the basement, Jeremy opened his eyes. They were filled with tears, but he wasn't crying. In the darkness of the basement, he saw a small window near the top of the wall in front of him, the faintest moonlight shining through. He blinked his eyes and looked again. It wasn't clear. It was as if he were seeing a hundred, maybe a thousand, tiny sparkling lights in the window. He searched for the window again, but he now couldn't discern the window. He could only see thousands of lights shining at him in a black sky.

Jeremy closed his eyes and tried to concentrate. *This room will stop spinning if I think about it hard enough.* He knew that his left leg was bent up under him, but it didn't hurt. He supposed that it had to be broken. His heart pulsed rapidly, but it seemed to him that his heart was working too fast for right then. He wasn't afraid.

Why is my heart beating so fast?

His breathing wasn't right either, but none of it hurt him. He heard the voices of the boys above on the walkway, but he didn't understand what they were saying. *Steve, it's okay. I'm going to be all right.*

He heard Father Francis's voice calling to him, but he wasn't sure of where it came from.

His lips weakly formed one word, "Stevie."

Father Francis was talking to someone, but somewhere in the background, Jeremy heard Stevie calling him. It was distant, but Jeremy recognized Stevie's voice. He wanted to answer, but there wasn't enough air in his lungs. Still, he kept forming Steve's name on his lips.

And then, Jeremy sensed him. Stevie was close. He peered through all the lights flashing in his eyes. Stevie knelt next to him and was talking to him.

"Please, don't try to do anything. Please, Jeremy, hold on. We're getting help. Stay with me, okay. Please, stay with me. We're getting help right now."

He was sure that Stevie was holding his right hand. Jeremy wanted to squeeze Steve's hand and tell him that he was okay, but he couldn't squeeze Steve's hand, and he couldn't feel Steve's hand, but he knew that Stevie was holding it.

Jeremy closed his eyelids. They were heavy. They didn't want to open. He forced them open. *Stevie, it's all right. I'm okay.*

Steve leaned over Jeremy and whispered in his ear, "Jeremy, hold on. Please, hold on."

Jeremy felt Steve's warm tears on his face.

No, no, Stevie, don't you cry. Steve, we're the best friends ever. Jeremy wanted to give the words life on his lips, but he couldn't. *I'll have to think it to you. Open your mind. Let me come in there. We will always be the best friends.* He wanted to speak, but all he could manage was a practically inaudible, "Stevie."

I'm hurt bad. Why can't I feel it? His heart was beating faster and faster, but it also seemed weaker. The lights flashing in his eyes were getting dim and faint. Jeremy kept trying to see Steve, but he was now nothing more than a shadow. Jeremy became afraid. *I'm dying. I must be dying. Oh, God, Stevie, I don't mean to. Stevie, don't you ever blame yourself. There is no blame between best friends.* He wanted so much to reach his hand up to Stevie and tell him. But nothing moved. *I'll think it to him.* S.t.e.v.e………...S...t...e...v...i...e………...S....t...e....v...i...e...... …………………………………………………………….Mom.

* * *

Jeremy's eyes closed. Steve knelt on the floor next to Jeremy holding his right hand, rubbing it between his hands.

"Jeremy."

Father Francis leaned over Jeremy and put his face next to Jeremy's. He felt no breath. Then he placed his ear over Jeremy's heart and listened. He heard no heartbeats. Father Francis sat up. The priest knew that nothing could be done. Jeremy Wilcamp was dead. He thought of administering last rites to Jeremy, but he would not do that in front of Stevie.

Tears streamed down Stevie's face. "Jeremy. Don't do this."

Ever so slowly and gently, Stevie Stockton placed his hands behind Jeremy's shoulders and lifted his best friend up from the basement floor and brought his chest and head next to his.

"We're getting help, Jeremy." Steve felt a warm, wet sensation on his hands as he held Jeremy. He raised his hand and saw Jeremy's blood. He closed his eyes and held Jeremy tightly in his arms.

"Father," Steve said softy, "please, see if the ambulance is coming." "Please try."

"Yes, Stevie, I am going to try right now."

Father Francis faced the boys and novices and the other priests, who now crowded the basement. He indicated that they were to go back upstairs and leave he and Steve alone.

When Father Francis was busy clearing the basement, Steve reached into his pants pocket, got out his Swiss Army knife and opened it behind Jeremy's back. Steve made a gash into his left hand and pressed it tightly onto Jeremy's back.

"Jeremy, let our bloods mix. You in me and me in you. You're not going to die. You're going to live on with me."

Steve did not want to let go of Jeremy, and he held onto Jeremy's back in as close an embrace as two humans could be. How was it possible for his friend to be so limp and lifeless? There was no strength in Jeremy. No muscle tone...nothing. Struggle as he might to deny it, the feel of death was profound. Jeremy's head and chest slumped onto Steve's shoulders.

Oh, God, Jeremy. Why can't you be faking this? Maybe you're thinking something to me. Maybe your mind is still working. Go ahead, Jeremy. I'm listening. I'm listening like I never listened for anything in my whole life. Go ahead. It will come to me.

Steve was aware of things going on around him, but he didn't identify with any of it. Someone had unbuttoned the sleeve of his jacket and was rolling the sleeve up. He felt a sting in his arm. He rocked back and forth on the floor of the Monastery basement holding Jeremy snuggly next to himself. Steve fell into a sleeplike trance. He wasn't exactly asleep, but he could not resist. Instead of taking Jeremy to the hospital, the ambulance took Steve.

Chapter 12
Daddy

Never in his career had such a sorrowful task as this befallen Father Francis. How could he find words to tell the Wilcamps what had happened to their son? He wanted to console them, but his mind was as stunned as theirs, and there was no comprehending this act.

My God, he repeated to himself as he drove the church car to the Wilcamp's home after the ambulance had taken Steve to the hospital, how can this be? *What is so wrong that children would mastermind such a deadly plot?* If only it had been a car accident or some other unforeseen, unpreventable catastrophe. Perhaps the priest could tell the Wilcamps that it was God's will that this beautiful child pass quickly and not suffer, and that it was somehow good that it happened unexpectedly, even though it hurt all who remained behind so deeply.

But not this. He was certain that Jeremy Wilcamp had suffered unnecessary and inhuman acts in his last hours, all inflicted upon him by his own peers.

Try as hard as he might, he was unable to concoct an explanation that even began to satisfy himself, let alone the family of a child so wronged. Not in the house of God. The weary, sad priest did not know with whom to be angry. *How is it possible that God wanted or allowed this death to occur in such a holy place?*

An altar boy. My, God!

Surely someone was beseeching the Lord Almighty to not allow this event to culminate with this senseless tragedy. Why were those prayers not answered?

When he arrived at the Wilcamps' home, he did not have to say much. His face said most of it better than the words he spoke. The only consolation that he could offer the Wilcamps when he left was that he and the priests and novices of the Monastery were going to prepare a beautiful and holy ceremony for the beautiful child and son that Jeremy had been.

* * *

Two days later, Steve lay in bed at home. His mother sat in a chair next to his bed holding another sleeping pill and a glass of orange juice. It was time for the next dose, but she didn't want to give it to him.

A mother's eyes roamed over her son's face. *Steve is maturing.* The boyish features had yielded to adolescence. The lines in his face were growing deeper and taking on more definition. His voice had changed. *He has so many of his father's features. He has my lips, but he has his daddy's face and frame. He's got John's thick eyebrows and long eyelashes.* She noticed the faintest suggestion of a mustache on his upper lip and a few whiskers growing on his chin. *We'll have to get him his first razor for Christmas.*

The rise and fall of Steve's chest as he breathed, brought warmth to Mrs. Stockton. She was so thankful that her son was alive. Steve's eyes were roving around under his eyelids. *He must be dreaming.*

Stevie, dear, don't be having nightmares. She fondly moved a wisp of his hair from his forehead. *Please, wake up and talk to me. Tell me that you feel better.*

Steve opened his eyes from an uneasy sleep. Something bothered him. Something was wrong. Steve raised himself up on his elbows and peered into his mother's eyes. A sensation of profound weakness overtook him, and the room spun, blurring his vision. He fell back onto his bed. He rubbed his eyes and again raised himself up on his elbows.

"Mom, is Jeremy all right?"

Mrs. Stockton shuddered. She told herself she had to be strong. "Stevie, here now, you have to take this medicine."

Steve saw the pill. Then he understood. Sleeping pills. Steve focused his eyes and tried to clear up the blur and stop the spinning.

"Mom, it's you, isn't it?"

Mrs. Stockton put both the pill and the orange juice on the night table next to Steve's bed. She wrapped her arms around her son and hugged him.

"Yes, Stevie, it's me. I'm here." Tears filled her eyes.

"Mom, why are you crying? Mom, tell me, is Jeremy okay?"

Mrs. Stockton leaned forward and held Steve's face in her hands.

"Stevie, Jeremy is going to be buried tomorrow."

Steve lay frozen on his bed, his eyes fixed on his mother's eyes. Events were falling into place in his mind. He was awakening.

"Mom, can I lay here for a few minutes?"

"Of course, Stevie. Do you want to try to go back to sleep?"

"No, I need to think." He laid back on his bed and stared at the ceiling. Nothing was said. Minutes passed with agony.

Mrs. Stockton prayed to God that she had done the right thing. *But why didn't he remember? It must be all the medicines that he has had since the ambulance crew got to him and took him to the hospital.*

"Mom, I don't want any more of those pills, okay?"

She again moved a wisp of Steve's hair from over his eyes. "Yes, Stevie, it's okay."

"Where is he going to be buried, Mom?"

"Oh, Stevie, you shouldn't worry about that for now. The doctor wants you to get a lot of rest and not worry about things until you get your strength back."

"No, Mom. Tell me. I've got to know. Where is he going to be buried?"

Mrs. Stockton sighed. "He's going to be buried in Lorraine Park Cemetery."

"Are we going to the funeral?"

She wiped her eyes with the pink flowered handkerchief that she held.

"Stevie, we don't know what to do. I feel so badly about calling and asking the Wilcamps if we can come. Daddy went to the funeral parlor last night, and he said it was unbelievably sad and intense. No one hardly even talked. Daddy said the Wilcamps sat there like stone.

"They are in an awful shock, Steve. I don't think they can believe that any of this has happened, and I guess they must be blaming everybody. Father Francis told Daddy that the Wilcamps do not want any of the school children or altar boys at the funeral. I know that you two are best friends, but I don't know what to do." She took Stevie's right hand into hers and caressed it. "Maybe Daddy will come up with a solution later."

"Mom, help me up, will you, please. I feel weak, but I have to get up."

"Stevie, you don't have to get up. The most important thing you've got to do is rest so that you heal and get better. How about I bring you up a nice bowl of hot soup?"

"I'm okay, Mom. Let me get up and go downstairs and I'll eat the soup in the kitchen."

"Oh, Stevie, are you sure? You're so weak yet, and you're going to be that way for a while."

It was as if his mother hadn't spoken. Steve forced himself to sit up in bed.

He saw the bandage around his left hand. "What happened to my hand?"

Mrs. Stockton struggled to keep herself calm. Steve's lack of memory flummoxed her. "Well, you cut yourself, didn't you?"

He flexed his fingers around the dressing. "Yeah, I remember now. Where's my knife?"

Mrs. Stockton's heart throbbed. What was she going to do? *Why is he thinking of all these things so quickly?*

"Daddy put it away for a while, I guess."

"Mom, I want my knife. I want it right now, please."

"Stevie, wait until Daddy gets home, and we'll talk about it then."

"No, Mom, I've got to know that I have it."

"Stevie, I don't want to give it to you now. You might hurt yourself again." Mrs. Stockton spun her wedding ring around her finger in alarm.

"Mom, I wasn't trying to hurt myself. I wanted Jeremy's blood to mix with my blood in my body. I wanted some part of him to stay alive in me."

Mrs. Stockton gazed at her son with absolute sadness. The desperation of her son to do such a thing to himself and believe that it could happen, was heartrending to his mother. *Stevie needs to believe that Jeremy is still alive. Oh, my son.*

She groaned inwardly. "But suppose you feel differently later, Stevie, and no one is here to help you?"

"Mom, if it had happened to me and Jeremy was sitting at home like this, do you think I would want him to feel like it was his fault?

Mom, best friends don't blame each other. He's up there in heaven telling me that he will hurt and hurt if I don't get myself together. I know Jeremy is telling me that. I can feel it. Best friends don't feel guilty about anything between them."

Steve's words amazed and frightened his mother. She could not believe what Steve was saying. *How can he have processed what happened so quickly, and yet believe that Jeremy's blood is alive within him? The medicines must still be affecting him.*

"Yes, Stevie, I know what you mean, and I know Jeremy is not blaming you. He would never do that."

Steve pulled back the covers from his bed and saw his left foot wrapped in an ace bandage. "Boy, I took it all on the left side, didn't I?"

He lifted his legs over the side of the bed and tried his left foot. "It still hurts, Mom, but it feels a lot better than it did."

"Mom, we never hurt each other here, do we?"

"No, of course not."

"Then, please, give me my knife. I can't keep talking about it. It's too painful to think that you don't trust me. It isn't like it's my knife anymore. It belongs to both me and Jeremy."

She sighed, wanting to tell him no. But at this moment, she couldn't say no to Stevie about anything. "Yes, Stevie. Sit here on the side of the bed, and I'll get it for you."

His mother left the room, and Steve sat on the side of the bed feeling his left ankle. It was better, but he feared that it might slow him down. His mother came back into the bedroom and handed Stevie his knife.

"Thanks, Mom. Don't worry. I'm okay."

She kissed his forehead and went to his clothes closet. She brought back his bathrobe and gave it to him. Steve laid it on the bed.

"No, Mom, I want to get dressed, and then we'll have that soup."

Mrs. Stockton was in a state of turmoil. Nothing made sense at this point. She knew that Steve was a strong-willed child, and she had always let him be that way. Neither she nor her husband regretted allowing Steve so much freedom as a child. *That's why he has matured so much sooner than other children his age.*

But she could not convince herself that Steve had adjusted to Jeremy's death so easily. "Stevie are you sure?"

"Yeah, Mom, I've got to get up. I can't stand lying here in bed for the rest of the day."

"Okay, Stevie. Call me if you have any problem dressing or getting downstairs. I'll make some soup for us. Be careful with your hand. There's about twenty stitches in it."

"Wow, that many?"

"Yes. The doctor warned us that you have lost blood and are going to be weak and tired. It's going to take a while to recover from that."

"I guess I will feel better after I have some soup."

When Steve slurped down a second bowel of soup, Mrs. Stockton began thinking that her son was going to be all right.

"Boy, Mom, you mean I slept through almost two days of school?"

"That's what it has been. The doctor wanted to keep you in the hospital, but Daddy was not having any of that. He wanted you to be here at home. He insisted that he had heard too many stories of what happens to people in hospitals who have suffered any kind of emotional trauma. He said that the doctors and nurses wrap restraints around any patient who is the least bit out of control. They tie the patient down in bed and stick needles into them and inject sedatives. Daddy believed that you had plenty of reasons to be disturbed, and he would never allow anyone to restrain you."

"Mom, I am so glad Dad did that."

"Daddy stayed in your bedroom with you all the rest of that night and all the next day and last night too. The only reason he went to work today was because you slept all night and most of the day. The sleeping pills were doing their job. I was about to give you another pill when you woke up. Somebody did call Daddy from work and tell him that they needed him, but he would have never left you if you were having any trouble."

"I'm okay, Mom. You can see. Dad didn't have to stay with me."

"I know, Stevie, but we weren't taking any chances."

"Why did the doctor want me to sleep?"

"Your Daddy and the doctor almost had an argument over that. The doctor didn't know it, but he trod a fine line with your Father. Daddy was losing patience. He was adamant about not leaving you in the hospital, but the doctor kept demanding that you stay because you needed rest and he wanted to observe you. When the doctor produced papers for Daddy to sign to take you out of the hospital against medical advice, something about Daddy made him stop. I don't know what it was, but the doctor agreed that we would take care of you and bring you back if anything was wrong. He finally understood that it was much better for you to wake up with people who knew you and loved you than in a hospital where you didn't know anybody.

"The doctor instructed us to give you one sleeping pill twice a day for the next two days and get at least a glass of orange juice in you every four to six hours along with almost anything simple that you wanted to eat, even if it was just candy, and you would be fine. The sleeping pills were only strong enough to make you inclined to stay in bed without overwhelming you, and the orange juice was supposed to keep you hydrated and give you some sugar if you didn't eat a whole lot.

"That way, your hand and foot were getting rest, and the doctor felt that you might deal with everything better. When you go back to get the stiches out, the doctors are going to see what kind of help you need with the hand and...and everything."

Mrs. Stockton did not want to tell Stevie that the doctor had recommended a psychiatric evaluation at some point in the future and suggested that Stevie might need therapy. She and her husband had decided to wait on that until they took Stevie back to the doctor to examine his hand and remove the stitches.

"And," she went on, "that is exactly what happened. You slept like a baby. But I wanted you to wake up. It didn't feel right to keep giving you sleeping pills. Daddy's probably going to be upset with me when he gets home. I couldn't stand not being able to talk to you anymore. I hope Daddy understands."

"He will, Mom, and I wouldn't have wanted you to give me any more pills. I don't want to sleep all day. You know what, Mom. Maybe we can call Dad after lunch. I'll tell him that I am up and doing fine and that we had some good soup for lunch. We'll catch him by surprise, and he'll be happy when he gets home."

Mrs. Stockton's face lit up. *Now that's my Stevie.*

"That's an excellent idea, Stevie."

Steve puttered with the spoon, and he finished the last of the soup more slowly as he mulled over what he would say to his father. The more he thought about it, the more he suspected that calling his Dad was a bad idea. *As soon as he finds out that I'm up, he'll come home no matter what I say.*

Steve set his soup spoon on the table. "Mom, it's probably a bad idea to call Dad. He'll be worried and rush home, and then people might get mad at him at work because they did call and ask him to come in. He'll be home in a few hours anyway. I'll go back to bed soon, and we won't even have to tell him I was up. After all, it's only lunch."

"But what about your knife?"

"We can tell him about it tonight, but it's no big deal. Mom, I've had that knife since my twelfth birthday, and Dad gave it to me. You know he doesn't mean for me to not have it. He put it away to keep it safe for me. That's all. It's going to be hard for him to talk over the phone while he's at work. But Dad isn't going to be upset. He never gets mad."

"I know, Stevie, but this is something different." Mrs. Stockton collected the dirty dishes and piled them in the sink.

"I do feel tired, Mom, and I'm not going to stay up for long. I want to go downstairs and organize my books, so I can catch up on my homework once I get over those sleeping pills."

"Stevie, you shouldn't worry about homework right now. You don't have to go back to school until..." She didn't know what to say. "Well, you're excused from all that for now. You're not responsible for homework assignments, and the days you miss are not going to be counted as absent days."

"That's great, but I better do some anyway. I don't want to get too far behind."

His mother protested more, but Steve insisted that he was only going to work for a short while and then go back to bed.

He took his time navigating the basement steps, not wanting to push his ankle too much. He opened a book and stacked two more to the side on his desk and sat in his chair listening to his mother upstairs.

He had no doubt that she would find some reason to come down and check on him. Ten minutes later she came downstairs with a load of laundry. She placed the load of laundry into the washer and turned it on.

Then she came to her son's side. "Are you sure you want to study, Steve? It's not necessary."

"Mom, it's so hard to catch up when you fall behind. Don't you remember that pneumonia I had in the fifth grade that kept me out of school for so long?"

"Oh, goodness, yes. You were so afraid that you were going to fail and be required to repeat the grade or go to summer school. But you didn't. You passed with very good grades."

"Yeah. I am going pass now too, Mom. I am going to do it for me and Jeremy. I'll pass for both of us. I can't let myself fail the eighth grade. No way I am going to repeat this year. I don't want to think about something like that."

Mrs. Stockton marveled at her son. *How can he think about school at a time like this? Maybe it's a defense mechanism or perhaps he is in denial. What if he believes that the only way to survive is to throw himself into school work and pretend that Jeremy is still sitting next to him, working right along with him?* She shuddered knowing that such a delusion would not comfort her son for long.

"Okay, Stevie, but don't do too much. You know that you're one of the best students in your class. You won't fail if you miss a few days. And Sister Verona likes you so much. She told Daddy and I that you are an excellent student when we met her. She kissed his forehead. I'll be upstairs. Call me if you need me."

"I will, Mom. Thanks."

When he heard his mother bustling around in the kitchen, Steve scuttled to the storeroom where several boxes of his childhood toys were stored. *Somewhere in here is my water gun. Man, what a break that Mom turned the washer on. She'll never hear me doing this.* But he still searched through the toys as quietly as he could. *Here it is.*

It looks like it's in decent shape. The water gun brought memories of the water battles that he and Jeremy used to have.

They played hide and seek, and when they found each other, the water guns raged. It was unfair because Jeremy's parents never bought him an expensive, quality gun. Steve's gun was bigger and better. But once Steve realized that he always soaked Jeremy, he suggested that they swap guns every other time.

"Jeremy, what a great friend you are."

When Jeremy used Steve's gun, he still refused to soak Steve. It didn't take Steve long to understand that Jeremy felt so bad about doing anything that resembled fighting that he wanted no part of it. *You were so afraid that if we fought, even only in play, we would get mad at each other and lose each other, weren't you? We would never have let that happen, Jeremy.* When Steve told Jeremy one day that he had forgotten his water gun and said they were dumb and insisted that they stop using them, Jeremy had been exhilarated. He had jumped up and thrown his water gun into the woods.

Steve sat on the floor by the toy box holding the gun. *Jeremy, you know what. I didn't like soaking you either. The only reason we ever got into those battles is because our parents bought the guns for us. Everybody and his brother had a water gun at the time. It was the latest rage for kids, and our parents got us one. It was fun playing hide and seek, though, wasn't it? We had forgotten that baby game existed until the water guns showed up.*

Who would ever believe what I am going to do with this water gun now?

Steve peeked up the stairs. There were no noises coming from the kitchen. Steve went to the laundry room and picked up the bottle of sudsy ammonia from beneath the sink. He stood over the sink and filled the gun doing his best not to spill any, lest his mother smell the ammonia. He went to his desk and hid the water gun in his bookbag.

As he sat in his desk chair, he examined his left hand and the dressing wrapped around the wound. He felt no pain when he flexed his fingers over the dressing. *It's healing nicely, Jeremy.*

"Boy, Jeremy, I hope a whole lot of your blood went into me. I'm going to need all of you." He raised his left leg up, crossed it over his right knee, and massaged the ankle. "It feels good. It's going to be okay, Jeremy. I'll make it. You'll see. A whole lot of your blood must have gone into me; otherwise, I wouldn't be this ready. I know it must have."

Steve sighed. He pushed his chair away from the desk. *I am tired. May as well go back to bed.* But his eyes roamed around the basement and fell on his and Jeremy's delta kites, rolled up in bundles, leaning against the wall at the far end of the basement. Steve got up and went to the kites. He took Jeremy's kite into his hands and sat down in the middle of the basement floor and unrolled it.

Steve eased his back to the floor and raised the six-foot-wide delta kite up into the air. Steve got teary-eyed as he raised and lowered the kite with enough force to make the leaflets flutter. The bright, beautiful colors blurred in his tears.

The room seemed to spin ever so slightly, and all Steve saw was the colors of the kite, as if he was peering into a kaleidoscope. And that easily, he and Jeremy were out on Lincoln Field flying kites for the first time. Steve and his dad stood together seeing the excitement on Jeremy's face and watching his legs running so fast that day.

When the wind was right, Jeremy and Stevie loved kiting more than anything else, even bike riding, and Jeremy had instigated all of it.

"You're the best kiter I'll ever know, Jeremy."

They had been ten years old and Steve's parents had talked the Wilcamps into letting them take Jeremy to the Maryland State Fair. None of them had even known that kite flying events were going to take place at the fair. It was a first for the state fair that year. Fifty or more people were flying kites on Lincoln Field next to the fairgrounds with lots of onlookers enjoying the scene and cheering the kiters on. Vendors selling a wide variety of spectacularly colored kites, crowded the periphery of Lincoln Field.

Mr. Stockton had caught the excitement in Jeremy's face as Jeremy fastened his eyes on the kites dancing in the sky.

They had seen all the livestock and observed some of the animal competitions and wandered through halls filled with craft exhibits and 4H projects, stuffing themselves with various homemade dinner and dessert concoctions. But Jeremy's eyes kept wandering over at the kiters flying their kites. Jeremy didn't say anything for the longest time because he knew that everybody else wanted to see all the events and demonstrations, and he didn't want to cause any problem, but as it got later into the afternoon, the kiters tantalized Jeremy beyond restraint. He wanted to go over to Lincoln Field and join in the festivities before they ended.

Jeremy bumped Steve's shoulder while they were standing in line waiting to buy tickets for a ride and asked Steve if his parents might take them to see the kiters. As Steve reminisced about it now, he was sure that Jeremy had only asked when he thought that his dad wasn't paying attention. *Dad never missed anything when it came to you and me, Jeremy.* Nope, Mr. Stockton was unbelievably observant.

Mr. Stockton had spotted Jeremy questioning Steve. He pulled them out of line and said, "What do you say, fellas, how about we go over and check out those kites."

Steve lowered the kite and laid it on the floor with part of it covering his chest. He grinned as he recalled that he hadn't been too sure about buying those kites because none of them had ever flown a kite before, and he couldn't imagine what made Jeremy think they would succeed at getting one up even if his father did buy one. But seeing the excitement in Jeremy's eyes and the perk in his footsteps had made Stevie want to try it also. Mrs. Stockton remained in the exhibition hall admiring the crafts and 4H projects.

Mr. Stockton had asked one of the salesmen which kite would be the easiest for the two boys to fly so that they had a good chance of getting it up. The man produced two cellophane thin dragon kites with ten-foot-long tails, Steve and Jeremy's first kites. Who knew that a kite that long would be the easiest to get up?

Jeremy had been ecstatic holding his beautifully-colored kite, wanting to open it and try it. A beginner might have thought that getting a kite up was about as easy as launching a rocket with a rubber band, but the salesman assured them that if they got the front of the kite up into even a slight breeze and ran along letting the string out, it would take off. The secret was in the lightness of the kite and the long tail.

Dad, you're so great to do things like that. Not many fathers would have laid out that much money for something they had never tried before, especially when half of it was going to someone else's kid. But you did it. Bought me and Jeremy a kite and a roller of string, knowing full well that we might never get it up.

You did it because Jeremy wanted to try it so much. Dad, thanks for doing that. I'll never forget it.

But Jeremy didn't just do it. He excelled at it. He launched the kite on his first try. *Wow, Jeremy, you must have had a premonition that you could do it.*

Steve and his Dad had been trying to get Steve's kite up, but they both had to stop when they saw Jeremy's going up. A smile brightened Steve's face. Steve pictured Jeremy backpedaling on Lincoln Field and stringing that kite out. What a beautiful feeling to have that kite pulling in your hands and teasing you from maybe two or three hundred feet out. Jeremy was almost as high as the kite, he was so excited.

Once Jeremy had his kite up, he had given it to Steve. Steve closed his eyes and lay there on the floor smiling through his tears. With Jeremy's kite in his hands, he knew what Jeremy was feeling. It was amazing. Mr. Stockton and Jeremy had then gotten Steve's kite up while Steve ran back and forth on the field pulling Jeremy's kite along in the wind.

Steve and Jeremy had attempted to make the kites hit each other in the sky, but they couldn't get them close enough. They kept running into each other on the ground, stumbling over each other, and bursting out laughing every time they did it.

Finally, they decided to race each other to see who could get their kite down first. Jeremy did that as well. Steve had been ahead, but the string slipped out of his hand, and the kite soared back up.

Almost lost it, didn't I. Man, Jeremy, you were going to stop and let me catch up. But Dad told you to keep hauling it in because you might do the same thing and fall behind. Dad loved the whole thing. You sure beat the heck out of me getting your kite down. What a perfect day. Perfect, that is, until we got home.

Jeremy didn't know what to do when they got home. Mr. Stockton had not known what to do either. Mr. Stockton appreciated that Jeremy wanted to take his kite home and tell his parents about it. But he had no doubt that Jeremy feared how his mother would react when she saw that Mr. Stockton had spent all that money so that Jeremy could fly a kite. Mr. Stockton read Jeremy's mind, but he didn't have the heart to suggest that he leave his kite with Steve and say nothing about it.

They had toyed with the idea of telling her that they had won the kites at a game, but Mr. Stockton knew that was too unbelievable. They don't give prizes like that at those games. At last, Mr. Stockton said that he would tell Jeremy's parents that he had seen how the kids on the field were having so much fun and that experts were on hand helping kids learn how to do it, and it was he who insisted that the boys try it. And, Mr. Stockton had claimed, that's the truth. He had wanted them to try it.

Mrs. Wilcamp was mad, nevertheless, and they all felt it. It was that expression on her face. As Mr. Stockton talked, they saw her getting angrier and angrier as she stared at the long dragon kite with its beautiful colors and the roller of string. No matter how Mr. Stockton tried to smooth it over, Mrs. Wilcamp counted the dollars in her head wondering how Jeremy had dared to let Steve's dad buy that kite.

She didn't say a word about it then, but not one week went by before she caught Jeremy doing something wrong. For his punishment, she wrenched the kite in her hands, broke it in two in front of him, carried it out into the backyard, and stuffed it into the trash can. Jeremy had to wait until the next Christmas to get another kite, and he insisted that it was the only thing he wanted. Even at that, it was his father who bought the kite for him.

Jeremy, I know they're your parents, and you love them and all, but, I swear, they ought to be punished. Why did they have to be so mean to you? Why didn't they, just once, go out and watch you fly a kite and see how happy it made you and how good you were at it? Let you hand them the kite to hold and fly it. Feel what you were feeling. Share something with you.

At that moment, Steve was so angry with Mrs. Wilcamp. *I ought to take your kite over to your mother right now. She'd never believe that we saved up our money from cutting lawns and bought these beauties. Then she'd have to think about how she broke your kite like that. I wonder how she'd feel if she knew that her own son had to hide his kite over here so that his mother wouldn't find it and break it into a million pieces.*

Steve raised the kite in the air once more and brought it back down. *Don't worry, Jeremy, your kite is staying here next to mine where it belongs. Jeremy, who am I ever going to want to fly kites with again? Steve could not hold back the tears. He bunched the kite up and hugged it to his chest.*

"Why this?" He wanted to let it all go but managed to hold himself in check. His mother was calling him from the kitchen. *I can't let Mom see me crying.*

"Don't bother coming down, Mom. I'm on my way up." He heard his mother's footsteps at the top of the stairs. "I'm gathering my books, and I'll be up as soon as I get my bookbag packed. I'm doing all right."

"Are you sure you don't need some help, Steve?"

"No, Mom, my bookbag is packed, and I am on my way right now. I'm moving slowly because of this ankle, but I'm getting there. I'm thirsty, Mom. Is there any orange juice left?"

"Of course, there is. Come on, I'll get you a glass."

Steve stopped on the stairs, wiped his eyes, and tried to make himself look as though he had not been crying. *I knew you would get the orange juice when I told you I was thirsty, Mom. You'd do anything for me, and I know that, but you can't help me with this, and I can't tell you how much it hurts.*

Steve sat down at the kitchen table and rotated the chair toward the window. He saw that his mother had been crying as well. *It's funny. She's trying to hide it too. Wonder if she can spot it as easily in me.*

"Here, Stevie." She set a large glass of juice in front of him. "We've practically got tons of it. When the doctor told Daddy to give you orange juice, he went out and bought three gallons of it."

"Yeah, that's Dad, Mom."

Steve stared out the window and held back a sudden urge to bawl his heart out as it came to mind how much his father would have done anything to prevent what had happened.

"Mom, I am tired." Steve downed the last of the orange juice. "Bed seems like a good place for me. I'll lie there for a while and try to read. That'll put me to sleep for sure. I don't think that last pill has worn off yet."

"Good, Steve. Sleep is the best thing for you now. You know what? I am going to lie down on the sofa and take a nap before Daddy gets home."

Steve hugged his mother, tossed his bookbag over his shoulder, and headed for the second floor. When he got to his bedroom, he pulled his sleeping bag down from the top shelf of his closet and unrolled it on his bed. He grabbed his leather gloves out of the bottom drawer of his dresser, placed them and the water gun in the sleeping bag, rolled it up and slipped it under his bed. After spreading a few books on the floor next to his bed, he shed his clothes and flopped into bed. He nestled up under the blankets, buried his head in the pillow, and fell asleep.

* * *

He had fallen asleep at 2:00 in the afternoon. At 5:30, he awoke from a deep, pleasant sleep at the sound of his father's car pulling into their driveway. Steve sat up on the side of his bed. Across the room, he faced himself in the mirror. His eyes did not leave the mirror as he got up and walked toward his dresser.

He leaned across the dresser and rested his forehead on the mirror. *This is so heavy. I can't give in. I've got to be strong. Dad's got to believe I'm okay.* He wiped his face with the undershirt he wore, went back to his bed, and put on his socks.

"Stevie," his father called.

"I'm up, Dad."

Mr. Stockton sat on the bed next to Steve. He put his arm around Steve's shoulders and gently brought his son's head next to his and held him there.

"Are you taking it okay? Stevie."

Steve started crying as his father held him. "Dad, I'm trying. I really am."

Mr. Stockton ran his hand through Steve's hair. "Stevie, don't you try so hard. You let it go. It's not weakness, son. It's love, Stevie, it's love."

Steve cried like a baby in his father's arms.

"Stevie," his father whispered, "you two were such great friends." "You will hurt the whole rest of your life every time you think of Jeremy. Your Mom and I will too. I am so sorry that you have to learn about death this way, when you're so young. It shouldn't be that way. Kids shouldn't know."

His father held Steve as he let go of so much that he was trying to hold in. When he thought his son was coming together, Mr. Stockton held him tighter and kissed his forehead and whispered, "Stevie, your Daddy and your Mommy love you so much. You are everything to us. You're our entire world."

Mr. Stockton rocked back and forth ever so slightly on the bed, clinging to his son. "I want you to take your time and get over this as much as you can. You will never be the same person after this but find ways to go forward carrying Jeremy with you. Keep him alive in your mind and in your heart. Whenever you think of Jeremy, remember all the good times you two had together. Think of how much Jeremy wants you to keep being you and the happy, friendly person you are. He's there with you every day sharing things and doing things with you. Jeremy Wilcamp will never be buried. We will keep him alive here in our home and in our hearts."

"Daddy, why did it have to happen?" "I tried so hard to protect him," Steve sobbed. "Daddy, why couldn't it have been me instead of him?"

Mr. Stockton wrapped his arms around Stevie and hugged him. "No, Stevie, no, don't say that. It isn't meant to be that way. You can't blame yourself. Stevie, we are not God. A power much greater than any of us called this. It was not you. We must accept it and move on. Sometimes we cannot explain why things happen. Fourteen is so few years, so few pieces of life. You can never understand this. I can't understand it.

"Why this happened to a great kid like Jeremy is something none of us can comprehend. It's the harshest fate, Stevie. It's destiny. No human has control over it. Steve, all of history is filled with things that make no sense. Don't you try to take it on yourself. You've got to know that Jeremy would never want that. And you, Stevie, would never want Jeremy to ask why couldn't it have been him if it had happened to you? You would only want him to remember you and carry you along with him wherever he went."

They held onto each other for a while longer. Mr. Stockton let go of Stevie when he stopped crying. Steve wiped his eyes with his undershirt.

Mr. Stockton rubbed Stevie's back and kissed his head. They sat in silence for a few moments.

"Do you think you can eat some dinner tonight, Stevie?"

"I can eat a little, Dad."

"Okay, take your time. Mommy's making a light meal for us."
Mr. Stockton looked at Stevie again.

Their eyes connected, and Steve smiled.

Mr. Stockton walked toward the door and stopped. "Call me if
you have any trouble getting downstairs."

"Yeah, Dad, okay."

Dinner passed slowly and a little painfully but the atmosphere
in the kitchen of the Stockton's was all right that night. The feeling
of relief among them was palpable, as they were all together.

After dinner, Mr. Stockton relaxed in his recliner in the living
room, opened his canister of pipe tobacco, and filled his pipe for a
smoke as he had done on most of the days of his married life. He sat
back and smoked his pipe, but he did not turn the television on as
usual. He thought about his son and Jeremy.

Steve went down into the basement, sat at his desk, and wrote a
note to his father. *Dad, you've got to understand.* Steve read his note
for a third time. *I know you will.* When he got to the living room,
Steve went first to his mother, who was sitting on the sofa making
believe that she was reading a book. He kissed her and then he went
to his father and kissed him.

"You might not believe this, but I think I can sleep. I feel tired,
so I'm going to go back to bed."

"It's good, Steve," his father said. "Sleep is one of the most
powerful medicines. You sleep as late as you want in the morning
and don't worry about school for now. I've taken care of all that."

"Okay, Dad."

"Stevie," his mother laid her book in her lap, "if you need
anything during the night, you come and get me."

"Sure, Mom, but I think I'll be fine."

Steve sat on his bed and read his note again. Then he folded it
and put it under his bed next to the sleeping bag. He crossed his left

leg over his right knee and felt his ankle. It was feeling a lot better. He decided to unwrap the ace bandage and check his ankle. It was bruised but the swelling was entirely gone.

"Sons-of-bitches," he muttered.

The bandage wrapped around Steve's left palm was making it impossible for him to re-wrap the ace bandage on his foot. "Man, why did I unwrap it?"

"Steve," his father called.

Steve looked up from the ankle as his father entered the bedroom.

"I wanted to tell you something before you go to sleep."

"Yeah, Dad."

"What're you doing?"

"I wanted to see if my ankle is getting better, but now I can't get it wrapped up. It seems like it's healing nicely."

"Here, let me do it for you." Mr. Stockton stooped down and wrapped the ankle. "Remember how I used to tickle your feet when I put your shoes on you when you were a kid?"

"Yeah. Boy, that made me laugh. Remember that time when we were playing something, and you took my shoe off and tickled my foot, and then you put my sock and shoe back on and that fast, you grabbed the other foot and ripped that shoe and sock off and tickled that foot. I didn't think I was ever going to stop laughing."

"You were mad about something. I can't remember what it was, but once I got you laughing, you forgot about it. It's a good trick to use if you ever have an unhappy kid, and you want him to get over it. Tickling beats punishing every time."

"Is that why you did stuff like that?"

"Definitely. I used to get a kick out of seeing you laugh too. I never liked punishing you, but sometimes you were doing something that had to be stopped and that was a rewarding way to do it."

"Yeah, I know."

Mr. Stockton sat down on the bed next to Steve. "This isn't going to be easy, but I am sure you want to know. I guess you learned a long time ago that the Wilcamps are strange about some things. I don't know what they're thinking, but they don't want any of the school kids at the funeral. Maybe they're so hurt that they want to go through this with only a few family and close friends. Anyway, I didn't feel right about pushing things at the funeral parlor. I talked to Mr. Wilcamp, and he said that Mrs. Wilcamp does not want any kids at the funeral, even altar boys. I can't do anything about it."

"I'm not surprised at all, Dad. It makes sense when you think about how Mrs. Wilcamp is. She never seemed to want me and Jeremy to be close friends. It was as if she didn't want Jeremy to have any friends. I never felt welcome in their house. She didn't say anything like that to me, but I always had this feeling that I wasn't wanted. Jeremy and I never stuck around his house for long. We always came here or went playing somewhere."

"You know, Steve, I can't explain this, but at the funeral parlor, I got the distinct impression that she was mad. Not as much at the kids who were responsible as she was at Jeremy. I'm probably wrong. People are affected by something like this in all kinds of strange ways that defy explanation, and good friends must be tolerant and accept it.

"But, here's what I'm thinking. I plan to come home from work at noon tomorrow, and maybe you and I and Mom can go out to the cemetery, if you want, and we'll say our own prayers for Jeremy. We don't have to go to the cemetery. We can go to the church and pray there and go to the cemetery some other time when things heal up. But we don't have to go to the church either. We can stay home, or perhaps we can go for a walk and remember Jeremy and talk about some of the things you two did. What if we went to some place where you and Jeremy had an exciting time, like Lincoln Park?"

"You know what, Stevie? We might even find a way to sneak into that grove you're always telling me about. What do you think?"

Steve stared dumbly at his dad and then the wall. It was obvious to him that his dad was trying to find some way to do anything that he wanted to have a service for Jeremy since Mrs. Wilcamp had dumped this final insult on her son of not letting any of his friends attend his funeral. If she had allowed it, the entire student body would have been present in church for Jeremy's funeral.

"I would like to go to the cemetery, Dad. I think Jeremy would like that too."

"Okay, Steve. That's where we'll go."

Mr. Stockton wasn't sure of what to do. It amazed him that Steve seemed to be holding himself together so well, and he didn't know whether to leave the room or stay longer.

He put a hand on his son's shoulder and kissed his head. "Try to sleep. Call us if you need anything. Even if you just want to talk. Come on into our room or call me. I will hear."

"I will Dad."

"Do you think you might want to take one of those sleeping pills?"

"No, Dad, I don't want to."

"Okay, kiddo. Nighty night."

"Nighty night, Dad."

CHAPTER 13
MY PARENTS NEVER DID THAT TO ME

Steve awoke from an uneasy sleep at 1:00 in the morning. He sat up in bed and listened. He heard his father snoring. Steve crept to his bedroom door and closed it. Then he tiptoed to his bed, took the pillow case off his pillow, draped it over the lamp on his night table and turned it on. He stepped softly to his closet.

Where are my green pants? What if Mom put them in the laundry? "Ah, here we go." *Somewhere in here is my green plaid shirt. Yep, here it is, and I'll wear my black jacket, but I'll take it off when I'm ready.*

It worried him that the plaid shirt might be detected. *It's mostly green, Jeremy. But it's the best shirt I have for what we need, so it'll have to do.* Steve put the clothes under his bed and pulled the sleeping bag out. The water gun and gloves were still in place, and the gun was fully loaded.

Good, Jeremy, no leaks. What a neat gun this is. Too bad your parents never saw this baby. Then they would have known what a real water gun is. Steve aimed the gun at one of the bed posts. *Could you ever conceive of me using this gun again?* It was tough to resist the urge to squeeze the trigger. *This is one battle where you and I are going to fire this gun like it's never been fired before.*

Steve toyed with the gun for a few moments. *I wonder why parents always want to save their kid's toys, Jeremy? It must be an*

202

almost magical moment to go to a toy box in the basement or the attic after your kids have grown up and gone, and hold the toys they played with, and relive the things they did. Yeah, I can see parents doing that, especially my mom.

Jeremy, your mom probably broke up so many of your toys and threw them away that she doesn't have any to hold now. No parent has the right to punish their kids by taking their toys away from them. The toys belong to the kids, and that's it. Parents do things wrong, and no one takes their stuff away. It's spiteful. How's a kid supposed to learn anything good if his parents do that to him? He'll think he doesn't own anything because his parents are going to take it away from him. My parents never did that to me.

Steve returned the gun and his gloves to the sleeping bag, rolled it up, and carried it to his bedroom window. He opened the window, trying to not make any noise.

Steve leaned out the window and tossed the sleeping bag to the ground so that it came to rest behind a spreading yew bush beside the house. The bag had been placed so that the branches cushioned its landing and concealed it at the same time.

Perfect! Dad will never see it when he leaves for work in the morning. Steve closed the window and climbed back into bed.

I wonder how it is going to be? Steve pulled the covers up to his waist and leaned his back against the headboard. *Brad's got to be going to school. He'll be trying to convince everyone that he's innocent, blaming his high school buddies. It was a prank. They were only playing, and Jeremy Wilcamp refused to play along. He panicked.* "I can hear you talking now, Brad. You're queer, Brad, and Jeremy knew it. And Jeremy's not queer. Jeremy knew what you were really after."

Visions of Brad twisting the tale to protect himself burned through Steve's brain. His face reddened with anger.

And then he'll tell the school kids how maimed you were. How your legs were broken like pretzels and the floor was covered with your blood. Well, you go ahead Brad, run your mouth. Jeremy outsmarted you, and you're too dumb to know it. He showed you what it is to be brave. You can always say no and not give in. And Jeremy told you and your gang of mighty football players, no. That's what it's all about.

We'll fix you. Stevie Wilcamp is coming for you. We're blood brothers now, Jeremy. Your blood and my blood are still together. There's something of you alive in me, and we'll get him. Brad might be big, but he doesn't know anything about being brave. Steve's chest rose as he took a deep breath.

Sleep was far from Steve's mind. He went to the bookcase in a corner of his bedroom and pulled out his scrap book, filled with pictures of Jeremy and himself and his mother and father.

"Thank goodness Mom is so excited about taking pictures. Dad isn't into it quite that much," Steve spoke as if Jeremy was sitting next to him, "but he never complained about her taking so many pictures. Guess the pictures are like the toys, huh, Jeremy? They're even better. I'm glad I've got them."

An hour flew by as if it were a minute. Steve viewed the pictures, recalling everything that he and Jeremy had been doing in each picture. He closed the scrapbook, pressed it against his chest, and held it there.

Jeremy's face flitted in front of him, smiling, talking, laughing, beckoning Steve to join him.

"Oh, God," Stevie sighed.

He opened the book again and took out a picture of him and Jeremy at Ocean City that past summer. They appeared so beautifully natural and full of happiness and excitement in the picture. His mother had gotten a blowup of the picture because she liked it so much.

Mrs. Stockton had been trying to get them to look at the camera, but they had been so giddy that afternoon because they had rented circus bicycles with a large front wheel and midget back wheels and were having such fun trying to ride them. They couldn't keep a straight face long enough for a picture, and his mother had snapped the camera when she thought they were ready and caught this picture.

Instead of being focused on the camera, they were looking at each other. Steve and Jeremy had an arm across each other's shoulders with smiles on their faces against a background of the azure sky and the aquamarine ocean meeting across the center of the picture as if the sky and ocean were holding each other in an embrace. Steve focused his eyes on the sky and ocean and then on himself and Jeremy.

Steve swallowed. He kissed the picture. *This is a powerful picture.* A warm feeling passed through him and, as if by enchantment, he was transported to Ocean City with Jeremy.

Mr. and Mrs. Wilcamp had been so tough to deal with. Steve's Mom and Dad had been imploring them to allow Jeremy to go to the ocean with them every summer since the third grade, after they discovered what great friends he and Steve had become. Steve's parents had always worried about Steve being lonely because Steve was their only child. The move to Baltimore when Steve was six years old had taken Steve away from his prior friends. His parents were so thankful that Steve and Jeremy had found each other.

The Stocktons had no doubt that Steve and Jeremy were special friends, but it took the Wilcamps forever to figure it out. They didn't, or wouldn't, realize that a kid might have one friend closer than any other. A person for whom the term, best friend, did not begin to describe the depth of the friendship.

Jeremy had been 11 years old before his parents let him stay overnight with Steve for the first time. Kids at school were always staying at each other's houses over weekends and having sleepover parties. But not Jeremy. A whole new world had opened for Jeremy. He had never watched television so late on Saturday night as Steve's parents allowed, and he was astonished that Mrs. Stockton served them coke and pretzels or potato chips and topped that off with a cake or ice cream snack before they went to bed.

Mr. and Mrs. Stockton and Steve and Jeremy sat at the kitchen table and talked and laughed about whatever they had done that day. Sometimes, Steve's parents took them to the movies. Jeremy had hardly ever been to the movies before he started going over to Steve's house on Saturdays when his parents permitted it. But, of course, Jeremy never told his parents that they went to the movies.

"We learned our lesson over that kite, didn't we, Jeremy. We weren't going to give your mother something else to ruin. You liked it here, didn't you? I was so happy when your parents started letting you come over on weekends. We used to sit up and talk and giggle half the night away, and Mom and Dad never said a word about it."

Steve ran his fingers over the edges of the picture. After years of asking, the Wilcamps had agreed to let Jeremy go to the ocean with the Stocktons for a five-day weekend vacation.

Jeremy had been so nervous at first. He didn't want to take anything that the Stocktons offered him and said very little. *I'll never understand your mother, Jeremy. Why would she want you to be so afraid of everything, all the time?*

In the middle of their second night, Steve's father had come into their bedroom, awoken Steve, and taken him into the kitchen of their apartment. His father had inquired about what was wrong with

Jeremy and why he wasn't having fun and what could they do for him. *Jeremy, I didn't know what to tell Dad. I didn't understand it either. You were like a different person.*

Mr. Stockton had decided to let the boys rent bicycles the next day and go riding, and Steve was going to try to find out what was wrong. Steve and Jeremy went riding up Coastal Highway toward Delaware which is not far from Ocean City, Maryland. They had been a couple of miles above Ocean City when they stopped to rest on a sand mound that looked out over the Atlantic Ocean. It had taken Steve almost twenty minutes before he understood.

Jeremy feared that Steve's mother might happen to tell his mother everything that they had done, what they had eaten, where they had gone, and everything they had bought for him. Jeremy knew that his mother was going to be mad at him because he had taken all those things. His mother had instructed him to order the cheapest things on the menu if they dined in restaurants, to stay out of everyone's way, and to say as little as possible so that he didn't cause any problems. And if he did cause a problem, he was going to get the beating of his life when he got home.

Tears had pooled in Jeremy's eyes, and he withdrew a twenty-dollar bill out of his pocket and told Steve that he was supposed to buy his own meals or be sure to give the money to Steve's parents when the time was right, as his mother had described it. Jeremy didn't know how to do it because he was certain that Steve's parents didn't want money from him, and they might feel hurt if he tried to give it to them.

Steve grinned as he envisioned it now, but back then when Jeremy had explained his predicament, he had cried along with him. They had decided that it was a big problem because Steve's parents were going overboard trying to make them happy so that Jeremy would want to come to the ocean with them again.

What a lousy thing to do to a kid. Why didn't she herself give the money to Mom and Dad if it was so important? Why would she want to ruin the whole trip for you? What fun is there in worrying about all that? She made you miserable, Jeremy. Buy the cheapest things, don't accept anything, keep out of everyone's way. What crap. How's a kid supposed to know when it's the proper time to give money to adults? You knew that it might be insulting to proffer money to my parents, but your mother couldn't see that. Who invites someone's kid somewhere and expects the kid to pay his own way? Nobody.

Your mother had to know that my parents were inviting you because they wanted me to have a friend along. Your parents were doing us a favor by letting you come. She can't possibly not have understood that. Someone ought to give her the beating of her life. But they need to tell her a week ahead of time, so she has to think about it all week.

"Oh, man, Jeremy, what if Dad hadn't seen that something was wrong?"

Dad worked it out nicely, didn't he?

That afternoon, Mr. Stockton had taken Jeremy and Steve to an ice cream parlor. Steve had been excited because he had known his father was up to something, and he was anxious to see what. Of course, Jeremy had wanted a popsicle, but both Steve and his father knew why he wanted a popsicle. It was the cheapest thing one could buy, and even at that, Jeremy had wanted to split it with Steve. Nope, no popsicle.

Mr. Stockton had strolled back and forth checking out all the flavors. Then he suggested Chocolate Ripple. It was a brand-new container that had been opened recently, and the ice cream was slightly softer as those new containers usually are when first opened.

He had ordered two triple decker cones. Both Steve and Jeremy's eyes looked like they might pop out as they watched Mr. Stockton take those two huge cones into his hands. His dad held the cones, making conversation with the clerk. By the time Steve's dad sat him and Jeremy on one side of a table, and himself on the other and had given the cones to the boys, the cones were already dripping ice cream.

Then Dad said, hurry up and eat, fellas, otherwise, it will be dripping all over you.

"Man, Dad, triple decker cones."

Steve remembered every detail. Once he and Jeremy were busy feasting on the cones, Mr. Stockton had started talking. Steve figured it out immediately. No way could either he or Jeremy cry or say anything with those cones melting in their hands. They had to sit, lick and listen.

His dad had told them that he understood the problem. They were going to the amusement park that night, and Jeremy would buy Steve's ticket as well as pay for his own, and they would tell the Wilcamps that Jeremy had insisted on paying his and Steve's way.

So, you see that, Jeremy, Mr. Stockton had said. You figured out the right time to give us the money and the right way to do it. Very ingenious. And then, Mr. Stockton had said, we will buy a big sea shell, and Jeremy can say that he bought it as a gift for us for taking him to the beach.

Steve recalled that he had thought it was a great idea because Mrs. Wilcamp would be thinking she had to pay them back somehow, and here, Jeremy had already done it. Jeremy loved Mr. Stockton's ideas.

"And, to sweeten the deal," Mr. Stockton had said, as he swept his hands across the table in a grand gesture, "we'll tell your parents that you had enough money left over to buy them a box of Turkish toffee, and you can give that to them."

Mr. Stockton had promised Jeremy that no one would tell his parents any of the things that they had done. "We'll tell your parents that we spent the whole weekend swimming, beachcombing, and camping out, roasting marshmallows, and eating hot dogs and baked beans. We won't tell Jeremy's parents anything about what we did in the afternoons or evenings or about the crabs, the shrimp, and the lobster."

Jeremy, that was the first time you ever ate lobster. Wow, Dad, you even let us sip your beer. Bitter stuff.

Then his father had taken a twenty-dollar bill out of his wallet, folded it up, and put it in Steve's shirt pocket. "No more worrying about anything you two. I want you guys to go into that amusement part tonight and ride on every ride you want as many times as you want."

"That's what Dad said. Do you remember, Jeremy?"

What a time they had had. Jeremy had never been to anything like the amusement park at Ocean City before. He fell in love with the roller coaster. Steve's parents had sat on a park bench feeling so proud and happy as Steve and Jeremy screamed with delight on each ride.

When we got back to the apartment, I bet we spent an hour talking about that haunted house, where those kids with summer jobs played being ghosts and axe murderers. What a riot. They were good. Oh, yeah, how about the bumper cars. Remember them?

"Jeremy...I so wish we could do it again, even if for only one more time. You'll never know how much I wish that."

It had been even better this summer. They had vacationed in Ocean City for a whole week. Steve's Dad had rented the best ten-speed bicycles available for himself, Stevie and Jeremy. The three of them had ridden into Delaware and camped out in a camp ground overnight and ridden back into Maryland the next morning. They had laughed and talked late into the night next to their campfire. They stared up at the stars and listened to the roar of the ocean waves hitting the beach.

Mr. Stockton had shocked both Steve and Jeremy when he suggested they rent bikes and camp out overnight. Steve had never seen his father ride a bike before.

"Yeah, Dad, you knew how much Jeremy and I loved riding bikes. And camping out overnight! Wow! Jeremy couldn't believe it. I'll never forget it, Dad."

Steve paused.

I wonder what your parents would say if they had known we did that, Jeremy. Did your father ever spend time with you like that? Jeremy, we would have done it again next summer.

Steve focused on himself and Jeremy in the picture. He closed the scrapbook, shoved it under his bed and put the pillow case back on his pillow. He slid the picture under his pillow, turned the light off, snuggled up in bed, and fell asleep.

CHAPTER 14
OH, NO. I CAN'T DO THAT

The noises his father made while getting up and dressed for work awakened Steve. He heard his father coming toward his room. Steve rolled over and sat up as his father opened the door.

"Why'd you close the door, Steve?"

"I woke up in the middle of the night, and I didn't want to wake you and Mom. I did go to bed pretty early last night."

"It hurts, doesn't it, Stevie? I'm so sorry." Mr. Stockton sat on the bed next to Stevie.

"Yeah, Dad, but I wasn't up for long. I feel tired, though, like all I want to do is sleep."

"Sleep is one of the best medicines. That's what most wild animals do when they're sick. They cuddle up in their nests or whatever their home is and sleep until they feel better, and the sickness usually passes.

"Stevie, do you want to drive to the church with me, and we'll sit in the car during Jeremy's funeral mass? At least we can be close."

Oh, no. I can't do that. What am I going to say? Think fast.

"Dad, I can't take it. I don't want to see the Wilcamps. They were too mean to Jeremy too many times. But if you come home early from work, like you said, and we go to the cemetery, that would be fine with me."

"Okay, Steve. Are you sure you're feeling all right?"

"Yeah, Dad, I think so. I just want to be here in my bedroom if it's okay."

That was understandable, but Mr. Stockton wasn't sure. A troubled father looked long and hard at his son. He ran his hand through Steve's hair.

"Good enough, Stevie, I'll be home by noon." Mr. Stockton headed for the door.

"Dad."

"Yeah, Stevie."

"I love you and Mom too. Please, don't worry so much. That hurts too. I'm going to make this. That's what Jeremy would want me to do and that's what I am going to do."

Mr. Stockton came back to his son's bed and kissed him. "Okay, kiddo." He waved and left the room.

Steve sighed with relief when he heard his dad start his car. "You've got to admit it, Wilcamp. I must be a borderline genius to pull that off." *That was close. Dad's worrying himself sick, trying to figure out what to do. He wants to cuddle me like a baby, but he knows I'm not a baby anymore, and he's trying his best to not treat me like one. Don't fret, Jeremy, we'll show all of them what to do before this day is over.*

Steve was half dressed before his dad had backed the car out of the driveway. He shoved his Swiss Army knife into his pants pocket, unbuttoned his shirt and placed the picture behind that, and grabbed his jacket. When he got to the bottom of the stairs, he saw his mother washing breakfast dishes. Steve tiptoed across the living room floor and placed his note inside his father's tobacco cannister.

Steve shocked his mother when he entered the kitchen.

"Steve, what are you doing up and dressed?"

"Got to go to school, Mom."

"No, son, no. You can't go back to school yet. Your ankle and hand need time to heal. You've lost blood. You need more time to get over things."

"Mom, I've got to go. I can't stay in bed anymore. I can't mope around here. I've got to get back into things. You have to see that."

"I do see that, Steve, but you have to visit the doctor first and have the stitches removed, and, believe me, no matter how much you are trying to hold it in, you are hurt inside."

"Mom, I'm hurt, but I'll go crazy if I keep sitting here. I don't want to hide. I can't do that. I can't do that for both myself and Jeremy. He would never hide. What am I supposed to do all day? I have to be doing something."

"Steve, I know you don't want to hide, and I don't want you to either, but you are so much weaker than you think you are. Now, listen, go upstairs and I'll bring you breakfast, and we can have breakfast in bed. Then we can watch TV if you want."

"Mom, I'm going to school. Can't we have some breakfast together before I go. Do you want me to leave without anything to eat?"

"Oh, Stevie," she hugged him. "Don't talk to your mother like that. You're my son. I'm your mother."

"Mom, I've got to go to school. I just can't lie here. I've got to do things."

"How is your mother supposed to sit here all day and not worry herself sick about you?"

"Mom, the same way I'm going to go to school. Because we will all go insane worrying about it if we don't just do it. It won't be any better next week, and it won't be any easier. We've got to move on and get it over with."

"Oh, Stevie." Mrs. Stockton was almost at her wits end. "You've never deliberately disobeyed me. I'm your mother."

"Mom, you've always understood me and known what was important to me and never told me I couldn't do something that mattered this much. You can't do that now. This is more important than anything, ever."

"Stevie, you tricked your father. You know you did. Do you have any idea of how much this will hurt him?"

"Mom, I'm not tricking Dad. All I want to do is go to school. You and Dad are going to try to protect me forever from this. But you can't do that. We can't change what happened. We've got to deal with it. That's how you and Dad raised me. You never taught me to run and hide.

"Once I get up and start living again, we'll get back to being normal. Come on, Mom. Please, I can do it. Don't make me feel guilty. I'm going to mess it up if I am thinking that my mother is angry and disappointed with me because I can't sit around here doing nothing."

Steve's eyes filled with tears, but he sniffed them back and opened the refrigerator. "Come on, Mom, please, let's have some breakfast together."

Mrs. Stockton slumped into a kitchen chair. The common sense of what Steve said was obvious, but she felt it belied his injuries, and she was uncertain of what he was thinking. Steve wiped his eyes and took one of the gallon jugs of orange juice and a loaf of bread and some butter out of the refrigerator. He poured a glass of juice for his mother and one for himself and put two pieces of bread in the toaster.

"Mom, it's going to get harder on all of us the longer you and Dad try to protect me." He buttered the toast and put a piece on a saucer in front of his mother. "Mom, I had to get myself up to do this, so let's go with it, okay."

"Stevie, Daddy will never understand this."

"Sure, he will, Mom. He'll know it's the best thing to do. He went to work yesterday and today, didn't he? It's not a big deal, Mom. I'm only going to school like every other day. I'll be fine."

"Steve, it's only been three days since it happened. Jeremy isn't buried yet. Daddy believes that you need to go through some of this in your own time and in your own way and to get it together in your mind. But he is ready to come home here the minute I tell him you need anything."

"Mom, I know what Dad is doing. He knows I need to figure out how to deal with this, and he's giving me room to do it. He's not going to feel like I tricked him. He's going to know that I am trying. He knows he can't go to school for me. He'll understand.

"If the Wilcamps were allowing Jeremy's friends to come to the funeral, it would be different. All of Jeremy's friends are in school except me. I want to be there too. You and Dad can't do this for me. It's on me to step up and break out of this. I'm going to ride my bike. It will be a lot easier on my ankle. I can put it into one of those high gears, and it's next thing to nothing to push the bike."

Steve's comment about Jeremy's friends being in school and him not being there, stunned her. She had not thought about that. *Perhaps we should let Steve be in class with his and Jeremy's friends. And, no doubt, Sister Verona will have the class say some prayers and she will say something nice about Jeremy. But why didn't Stevie tell his father? He would have taken him to school.*

"Stevie, have you thought all of this out. Are you sure you can manage?"

"If I have any trouble, Mom, I'll come home. The sisters all like me. They'll understand and let me go.

"Mom, please, don't make a fuss at school. I know I can do this. I've got to go."

"But it's too early to go to school, isn't it?"

"A little, but I figure I'll go slow, so I don't hurt my ankle. It's feeling pretty good."

He gave his mother a kiss and went to the back door and then the garage. Mrs. Stockton wanted to say something, but her lips wouldn't move.

CHAPTER 15

LORRAINE PARK

Steve hopped onto his bicycle, fetched his sleeping bag from behind the yew bush, and pedaled down the driveway onto the street. He kept his sleeping bag in front of him so that his mother couldn't notice it if she was watching him from a window.

Lorraine Park Cemetery was only three miles away, and Steve reckoned that he had plenty of time. The funeral would probably be at 9:00 and certainly no later than 10:00. As soon as he was out of sight of the house, he stopped his bike, took his gloves out of the sleeping bag, and put on the left-hand glove to protect his hand.

He worked the picture into one of the folds of the sleeping bag, slung it over his shoulders, fastened it across his chest and set off for Lorraine Park.

No one paid him any attention. The red ten-speed Schwinn bicycle amazed Steve and Jeremy. It was the latest thing in bicycles. Steve was sure that no one else in his class had one. His parents had always gotten him the best of anything Steve asked for. The red Schwinn had captivated him the moment he and his dad stepped into the bike shop. They had come to buy an inner tube for his bike. But Steve couldn't take is eyes or hands off the Schwinn. The hand brakes and the multiple hand gears had mesmerized him.

Initially, Mr. Stockton had thought it would make the best Christmas gift possible. But he could not ignore his son's excitement. What if he couldn't find one at Christmas time? No, he had told himself, the bike is standing in front of me right now. This is what he wants. He had bought the bike for Stevie that day.

So many times, Stevie had gotten Jeremy to sit on the bike frame in front of him, and they had raced as fast as Steve could pedal the bike. Steve had insisted that Jeremy get on the bike with him so that he could appreciate the speed the bike achieved. When he had first gotten the bike, Jeremy used to swear that Steve was crazy. *Jeremy, you were a real sport about it. You were afraid in the beginning, but you never refused to hop on.*

After Jeremy discovered that Steve had become the master of the ten-speed bike, Jeremy didn't want to ride his own bike. It was a secondhand bike, much older and heavier than Steve's new bike. No matter how hard he tried, Jeremy's hand-me-down bike couldn't keep up with Steve's new Schwinn. They took turns pedaling, Jeremy on flat land and Stevie on hills.

Steve could practically smell Jeremy's hair and feel it blowing back in the wind, hitting him in the face as it usually did when they raced down a hill. He felt Jeremy's arms touching his as they both held onto the handle bars. His right thigh felt Jeremy's right leg with each stroke of the pedals.

After a while, the two of them had grown to love flying down hills. Steve stopped the bike at the top of a steep hill that he and Jeremy had taken on many times.

"Jeremy, where are you? Why are you gone? This couldn't have been meant to be." Steve was close to breaking, but he would not yield. He gritted his teeth and clenched the handbrakes. "Parents or no parents, I'll be there."

His feet pedaled faster than he intended, but his left ankle was not bothering him as he passed through the stone pillars and high wrought iron gates of the entrance to Lorraine Park Cemetery. It was a well-maintained cemetery. Steve got off his bike and walked it to the top of a hill. His eyes roamed around the cemetery. He hid his bike beside a crypt and sat in a spot where he was out of sight but from where he had a clear view of the entrance.

It was a bright, beautiful day. A few clouds drifted in an otherwise perfectly blue sky, and a soft breeze glided aimlessly over the cemetery.

It must be well after 9:00 by now. What can the Wilcamps be thinking with their son lying in a casket. It must be awful in that church. No one ever feels sorry for hurting other people unless they die or something like that happens. What good does it do to be sorry then? What does Mr. Wilcamp feel like after smacking Jeremy across his mouth on his last night alive? And then you tell him you think he is a good boy. I wonder if Mrs. Wilcamp hasn't gone out of her mind by now?

You were such a good kid, Jeremy. Why didn't they see that? I guess that I will never know what you went through because I didn't have a brother or sister for my parents to compare me to. But even if I did, I can't believe that my parents would have been any different. Steve picked up a stone and threw it into the distance.

"God, Jeremy, if only we were out here playing ball instead of…this." *No, this is not the time to cry. I've got to be strong.*

The minutes passed. A pickup truck and a work crew on a faraway hillside attracted his attention. The sight brought chills to his body, but he couldn't take his eyes off the crew. Suddenly, he felt sick to his stomach. He got up and went around the other side of the crypt and vomited.

"God, you've screwed up enough things this week, haven't you? How about giving me a break."

The hearse driving through the entrance of the cemetery stopped Steve. He felt frightened. His friend was surely gone. How was he going to face the future?

Steve dropped to the ground and watched the procession. The hearse, eight cars and a bus. *Did the Wilcamps allow some of the school kids to attend anyway?* He watched the bus from his hiding place. The priests and novices of Saint Michael's Monastery rode in the bus. His heart jumped when his eyes returned to the hearse. Jeremy's casket was in the lead car.

"Come on, Stevie Stockton, you've got to follow them."

He pushed the bicycle along, staying back far enough so that the bus was barely visible. The procession approached a stone building and veered off to the right. *The building must be for the caretakers.* Steve headed the bike off the road and into the cemetery plots to avoid the building.

He pedaled up a hill between the graves hoping that none of the caretakers would see him. When he got to the top of the hill, he saw the school bus. He raced the bike down a hill through the graves.

"I can't lose them."

He could not see the grave marker nearly covered with grass in his path as fast as he was moving. When he hit it, Steve shot over the handle bars as the bicycle flipped through the air. He landed on the ground and rolled to a stop in front of a tombstone marked Evelyn Delutsche.

"Shit." Steve jumped up, grabbed the bike and took off for the bus, but he paid more attention to the ground. He came back onto the drive when he figured that the caretakers' building was out of view and picked up speed.

At the top of the next hill, Steve slammed on the hand brakes and spun the bike around and brought it to a stop. He pedaled it with all his strength back over the hilltop that he had just crossed. The procession had come to a stop about a hundred feet ahead on the cemetery drive.

Jeremy, I hope they didn't see me. Steve rode the bike between the graves and hid it behind a large monument. He knelt on the ground next to his bike. *Jeremy, I'm about the last person in the world who wants to make this any harder on your family than it already is. I know you love them. If they saw me come over that hill and hate me for being here, I am so sorry. I didn't mean to do that. The world is full of it, isn't it? So many I-didn't-mean-its. I hope it's not that way in heaven.*

Steve got to his feet and inched up the hill hidden by a tombstone. The funeral procession had gathered together in front of Jeremy's tombstone on a knoll next to two shrubs. Steve settled to his knees. His eyes fell on Jeremy's casket. It was blue-grey, sitting somberly above the grave site on its supports. Steve was oblivious to whatever the people were doing. His eyes were frozen on Jeremy's casket.

Jeremy, are you really in there? This can't be true. Please, let this be a dream. God in heaven, please, wake me up. Wake my best friend up. God, there is no other friend for me.

Steve felt weak. He observed the proceedings from his hiding place. He didn't know how many minutes went by, but he bolted up in the air. Jeremy's casket was being lowered into the grave. Every part of Steve's body wanted to run up to that casket, but he held back.

If I come to you, Jeremy, all those people at your burial will think that I've gone out of my mind and want to take me home. I can't let that happen.

Steve remained hidden and listened as the noises of the departing cars and the bus grew weaker and faded into the distance. When he was sure they were gone, he stood up and faced the gravesite.

"Oh, no," he sobbed. The caretakers were throwing dirt on top of Jeremy in his casket.

Steve returned to his bicycle, curled up on the ground, propping his head on his sleeping bag. His mind was blank. He had nothing more to give of himself. He cried himself to sleep.

CHAPTER 16
WE CAN DO ANYTHING TOGETHER

Birds chirping awakened Steve. He sat up and surveyed the cemetery. Nothing stirred.

I wonder what time it is, Jeremy? It's got to be after 1:00, but it can't be after 3:00 yet, can it? The shadows aren't long enough. No way I have slept all that time. Not on this ground. It's hard as a rock.

He extended his legs and flexed his shoulders, trying to loosen his muscles. He rose to his feet, his heart heavy, as he looked upon Jeremy's grave. The freshly dug earth overlying his best friend drained every bit of energy out of Stevie. He didn't want to do anything. *Can I really do this? I've got to. It has to be done.*

Jeremy, you aren't dead. Your blood is still floating in me, right along with mine. We've got to be together this one last time. Let's go.

He strapped his sleeping bag on, leapt onto his bike, rode it onto the cemetery drive, and pedaled toward the entrance.

May as well go by the caretakers' building. It doesn't matter if they see us now. The stone building came into view as he topped a hill. He sped down the hill, but then he saw two Doberman Pinschers charging at him from behind the building.

Oh, no! Hang on, Jeremy. I'm going to outrun them. Come on, Stockton, you can do it.

Jeremy, I can't do it. They're going to get me.

"I'll kick your asses," and he swung his right leg out into the air attempting to threaten them. But as the Dobermans hurled themselves at Steve with their growling mouths dripping saliva, the chains holding them yanked them out of midair and dragged them onto their haunches.

"Jesus, Jeremy!" He scowled at the dogs who were still yelping and howling even though one of the caretakers was running up to the dogs trying to calm them.

"You sons-of-bitches," Steve swore. *That was close.*

When his heart stopped racing, Steve turned his attention back to the driveway. He pedaled the bike out of the cemetery and rocketed forward toward the grove of Saint Michael's Monastery.

The breeze flapped his jacket around his chest and danced through his hair so that it tapped his face and ears. His hair was longer than usual. He hadn't gotten around to getting a haircut for a while. The sun's warmth felt good, and he squinted his eyelids as he hunched his chest and head down over the handlebars trying to make time. Mild pangs of pain shot through his left ankle, but he ignored them.

It's great to be out riding isn't it, Jeremy? We've got to do this more often. We can't let school interfere with our real lives, can we? "That's it, Stevie, come on," he shouted, as he propelled the fire-engine red Schwinn over a hilltop and crouched in closer to the handlebars, racing it down the hill.

Steve and Jeremy hunched together when they raced down hills, Steve bringing his head close to Jeremy and Jeremy curling his back into Steve's chest. They huddled together as much like one person as possible to gain speed.

As the bike sped through the trough of the hill Stevie raised his head and sang out, "Yahoo," as he and Jeremy had done. Then he switched to a higher gear and pushed the bike up the next hill.

I bet that's as fast as I have ever taken that hill, Jeremy. Had you scared, didn't I? You can't fool me. Someday, you've got to ride this baby downhill. You're fine on flat land, but you've got to take the hills too. I know you can do it. You can handle this bike the same way you can fly a kite. We won't get hurt. I've told you about good luck, Jeremy. Some people have it, and most don't. You and me together, we've got it.

He arrived at the Monastery. *No kids so far. That's a good sign, Jeremy. Soon, we'll see the church clock.* No sooner had he thought it then there it was. *We're going to have plenty of time.*

Steve stopped the bike beside the curb at the top of Monastery Avenue at Montclair Street. He lifted the Schwinn onto the sidewalk.

Oh, man, Jeremy, why do those two old ladies have to be waddling up to the church now? They're moving so slowly. They might take all day getting there. "Please, ladies, hurry up."

Steve propped a leg up on the knee-high fence that encircled the Monastery lawns and sat on the bicycle seat, monitoring the ladies slow progress. With exasperation, he glanced up at the clock in the Monastery tower. Precious minutes were ticking by.

We can't let those ladies see us going into the grove, Jeremy, but if they don't mosey into the church soon, and if someone else comes by, I am going to have to go for it regardless.

Steve rejoiced with a soft howl when the ladies opened the church doors. He pedaled the bike to the hedges on the east side of the church walkway and hoisted the bike over the fence onto the church lawn. He guided the bike across the lawn to the spot where he and Jeremy had gone into the grove three days earlier on Monday morning after the 8:00 mass. He laid the bike down behind some bushes where no one would find it and threw his sleeping bag over the fence.

"Jeremy, you've got to give me a boost." Steve struggled to get over the fence. He used his left hand like a claw, putting his fingertips through the holes in the chain link fence, supporting himself without stretching his palm. It was enough support to balance him as he pulled with his right hand and pushed with his right leg and foot. He dropped to the ground in the grove without sustaining any new injury.

Okay, Jeremy, I've got it all planned. You're going to like this one. Wait until you see how smart I can be if I put my mind to it.

Steve ambled through the grove concealed by the pine trees. When he came alongside the fire hydrant on Montclair Street, he retrieved his water gun from the sleeping bag and dropped the gun over the fence. He left his sleeping bag and jacket in the grove.

"Give me a push, Jeremy, that left ankle is hurting me."

Steve plunged to the ground on the other side of the grove, sweat pouring off his forehead and his hands sweating. He rubbed his right hand over his pant leg to dry it. He mopped his forehead with his shirt sleeve and removed the glove from his left hand. The bandage was damp with perspiration and blood tinged the edges of the dressing. *A bit of oozing, Jeremy. It's not bad. It'll be okay.* He put the glove back on his hand.

Brad's going to come up Montclair Street, Jeremy. He always does, and he is usually alone. The only guys in our class who hang out with him live in Abingdon, and no one else wants to walk with him. For good and sure, no one wants to be with him today.

Now listen, Jeremy, you grab him around the legs. I'll get him from the top. Yeah, kick, scratch, even bite ass, but don't panic. Stay focused. We can do this together. I've got the real weapon here in my hand. Steve shook the water gun, loaded with sudsy ammonia, in his right hand. *That's what's going to get him, and he'll find out what a tiger Stevie Wilcamp is. We're blood brothers and best friends. What could be stronger?*

Steve eyed Montclair Street through the pine trees. He surveyed every inch of his hiding place. He knew precisely where he was going to position himself, but he checked it all over anyway.

What a perfect spot for an ambush, huh, Jeremy. John Wayne couldn't have planned it any better than this. Bet John Wayne would love to be here. I mean to observe us. He wouldn't have to help us. We don't need him. Now, Brad, he's a different story. He'll be wishing that he had John Wayne to help him. But John Wayne isn't the kind of guy who wants anything to do with someone like Brad. John Wayne shoots people like Brad, just like we're going to shoot him.

Steve pointed the gun at a mailbox across the street. "Bang, you're dead!" *He'll be sorry he ever messed with Stevie Stockton and Jeremy Wilcamp before this day is over.*

Steve sat down on the ground. The Monastery bell had not yet rung three o'clock.

Holy shit, Jeremy, Brad is walking up the street now, by himself. Nobody wants to be near him. Everyone in our class must hate him now more than ever. They're giving him plenty of room.   I wonder if Sister Verona let the class out early. The sisters might have planned to let 8B out early to prevent all the gossiping.

No, it can't be that. No other students are coming yet. Maybe Brad made up some excuse for why he had to leave early, and Sister Verona let him go. Maybe he didn't want to have to talk to anybody about it. Well, whatever, this is good for us, Jeremy, if it holds up for a few more minutes.

It must have been an incredible nightmare in school today. Yeah, that's Brad. I couldn't miss him anywhere. Imagine what he's been dealing with today, sitting there pretending he had nothing to do with the death of a classmate, while he knows you're lying up in the Monastery with the priests throwing holy water and blessed dirt and incense all over you and praying for you.

"You, guilty shit, Brad."

He's getting close, Jeremy. We've got to get ready. Look at him hanging his head. He's probably been retching his guts all day. He wanted to get out of that class and go hide somewhere.

Steve stood behind the trunk of a pine tree, held the water gun in his right hand, and stretched his arm out along the length of a pine branch making him invisible in the pine trees.

"Come on, Brad. Come to Stevie." Steve stood motionless in the cover of the trees with his eyes fixed on Brad as he approached.

When Brad came abreast of him, Steve shouted, "Brad."

Brad pivoted toward Steve, and Steve squeezed the trigger hard and fast. Two of the three shots Steve fired splashed into Brad's face before he could duck his head. Brad dropped his bookbag and bent over coughing violently, rubbing his face. Steve transferred the gun to his left hand, leaped through the pine branches, grasped Brad by the hair and wrenched him into the pine trees. Brad tried to scream and gasp for air, but the ammonia was like fire on his face.

Brad flailed his arms wildly, attempting to fend Steve off. Steve yanked Brad's head up with his right hand, but he couldn't pull the trigger because of the glove. Steve kicked Brad in the stomach with his right foot. The force of the kick was not as great as Steve hoped for because Brad was so close to him, but it still made Brad fall to his knees. He kept swinging his arms wildly, trying to hold Steve off, gasping for air at the same time.

Steve had moved the water gun to his right hand.

From his position on his knees, Brad was lined up against Steve like a football lineman. Even in his frenzy, he realized his advantage, and he charged Steve smashing him into the trunk of the pine tree behind him. Brad had Steve pinned, and he burrowed his shoulder into Steve's abdomen, trying to squeeze him to death.

Steve tried to bring his knee up into Brad's abdomen, but Brad was so big and so close to him that the maneuver was futile. Steve recognized that Brad was recovering from the initial shock of the ammonia and getting his wind back.

The gun, Stevie! The gun! Use it! You've got to get him with it. He placed the gun alongside Brad's head and fired. Even though Brad had his head down and buried into Steve's abdomen, the soapy ammonia solution still trickled down the side of his face toward his mouth and nose. Brad tried to twist his head farther away from Steve and drive him harder into the tree trunk, but his right foot slipped causing him to lose his balance. The sudden loss of footing exposed the left side of Brad's face, and Steve pelted him squarely in the eyes and nose.

Brad made screeching noises and was audibly wheezing. He rubbed his face with his hands and tried to crawl away from Steve, screaming violently. Steve stopped everything when Brad was forced to release his hold on him because of the second barrage of sudsy ammonia. Steve leaned against the tree trunk catching his breath.

Jeremy, help me. We started this. We've got to finish it. Steve jumped onto Brad's back and pummeled him to the ground. Brad coughed and hacked violently, shielding his face with his hands. He rolled onto his back and kicked his legs in every direction hoping to hurt Steve and stop his onslaught.

Steve stood and fired another salvo of sudsy ammonia at Brad. Brad roared furiously, threw his hands aside and tried to catapult himself onto Stevie. Steve shot him straight in the mouth. Brad fell onto the ground. Steve plunged onto Brad's chest ramming the gun into Brad's mouth, pulling the trigger time after time until he saw sudsy ammonia flowing from Brad's mouth.

Brad turned blue. His eyes were swollen and filled with blue blood vessels.

Steve jumped to his feet, mystified, as Brad's body convulsed. He had never witnessed anything like it. He stepped back. The ammonia was getting to him. He leaned against a pine tree feeling weak and fearing that he might faint. He looked up and down Montclair Street. Three boys were crossing Montclair Street near the school, and others were coming farther behind, but no one was close enough to have seen anything.

Steve yanked Brad's bookbag into the pine trees. He got to his knees and threw handfuls of pine needles and dirt over Brad and his bookbag. As the school kids approached, he stopped everything and lay motionless on the ground.

Many of the kids crossed the street. No one noticed anything. When there was a break in the school kids coming, Steve piled more loose dirt, pine needles and pine cones onto Brad. Then, he tossed the water gun over the fence and climbed over himself. He knelt by the fence and watched another group of kids coming up Montclair Street.

Jeremy, we're okay for now at least. No one noticed anything and if anyone from those houses across the street had seen anything, they would have done something about it by now. Everything looks as peaceful as it did when we got here. Let's get out of here.

Stevie shoved his water gun into the sleeping bag, snatched it up in his right hand and sauntered toward the west side of the grove where he left his bike.

Chapter 17
You Stand Guard, Okay?

After a few steps, Steve paused and gaped forlornly in the direction of his favorite place in the grove. *Jeremy, do we dare go there for a few moments? Some of your blood must still be in me. I can feel it. You must want to go there one more time, don't you? It's the last time we'll ever be able to do it together.*

Steve sat down in the same spot where he had been on Monday after school, directly across from where Jeremy had sat. He felt a burning sensation in his left hand, and he removed the glove.

"It bled. Keep your blood away from my hand, Jeremy. I don't want to lose any of your blood."

Steve pulled the glove back on and picked up a fist-sized rock. He placed it in the palm of the injured hand and gently squeezed the rock. *I'll keep pressure on it. It'll stop bleeding.*

Steve took the picture of him and Jeremy out of the sleeping bag. *We did it. I knew we would. Oh, God, why did this ever have to happen? I never dreamed that something so freakish, so out of this world, had the power to tear us apart like this, Jeremy, and make us into whatever we are now. But I vowed to not let Brad get away with what he did. He'll never bully anyone again.*

At that moment, Steve didn't care if he ever got up, but the sound of a siren breaking the quiet afternoon brought him to action.

"Have the police found him already?" Steve bolted up. "Jeremy, I forgot my jacket." The siren got louder, but it hurtled past the grove.

Wow, I don't need this right now. He replaced the picture in the sleeping bag and headed back to get his jacket.

Stevie knelt on the ground beside his jacket and glowered at the pile of pine needles, pine cones, and dirt, covering Brad. Four girls were belatedly coming up Montclair Street. Steve assumed that they had remained after school to help one of the nuns. Some of the girls did that frequently. The girls gave no indication that they had noticed anything unusual.

So far, so good, Jeremy. What a reputation the grove will have if Brad's body is ever discovered. Everyone will swear that God struck Brad down for trying to come into the grove. He's dead, but there's not a mark on his body. They'll never figure out what happened. The ammonia will evaporate. Yeah, People might make a horror story out of it. How God stuck Brad down. The grove will be all ours then. No one will have balls enough to come in here.

He put on his jacket, grabbed his gear and hustled toward his bike. The bike seemed so heavy and hard to push as Steve drove it onto the sidewalk that wrapped around the Monastery lawns and gardens. He stopped at the hedge near the entrance to the altar boys' room. Exhausted, Stevie lifted the bike over the fence and hedge, and maneuvered it up the hill to the altar boys' room entrance. He laid the Schwinn on the ground and went in to check the room.

The room was empty. The basement door was unlocked as it had been every other time he had tried it, and the light above the staircase was on.

He carried the bicycle down the stairs and into the altar boys' room. His left ankle ached with each step, but nothing like he had endured when the sprain had occurred. Sweat dripped off his forehead and he suspected that he had a fever. Steve stood the bike on its kickstand, opened the door to the basement and stared at the staircase.

Can I risk leaving the bike in the altar boys' room? No, I can't take that chance. If anyone found my bike in here, they would call my parents. Everybody knows the Schwinn is mine.

Steve dreaded the thought of lugging the bike down the stairs and onto the walkway, but he saw no other way. *It won't be that bad going down. All I've got to do is guide the bike and hang onto it. The stairs will do the rest.*

Steve was right. It wasn't too bad. The steps supported the weight of the bike, and all he had to do was hold on. But it was awkward and tiresome, and sweat poured off Steve when he reached the walkway. *Whew, Jeremy, that was tough.*

Steve climbed the stairs to the altar boys' room and plodded to the bathroom. The cold-water felt refreshing as he drank from the faucet. He ran the water over his right hand and splashed water over his face. He stood over the toilet and pissed. His mind refused to contemplate anything as his exhausted body carried out each task. He took a second drink and returned to the altar boys' room.

The room appeared untouched from Monday night's meeting. *That's strange. Usually the chairs are folded up and put away and the blackboard cleaned by the next day after an altar boys' meeting. Father Francis is probably so stressed out that he hasn't thought about it. Or maybe the priests had a meeting in here to discuss what they wanted to do at Jeremy's funeral. Who knows?*

Steve felt faint as he fixed his eyes on the chairs that he and Jeremy had sat in during the meeting on Monday night. *Jeremy, I wish we were sitting there now. I've got to get out of here before somebody comes by.*

When he got to the walkway, he muttered, "Ugh, I've got to turn the bike around." He rolled it over to about midway on the walkway, picked the bike up into the air above the railing and rotated so that the bike faced the stairs.

Steve's arms felt like lead. *If the bike weighed one more ounce, I don't think I could have done it.*

"I feel so cold and weak, Jeremy." *Get into the sleeping bag. That's why you brought it. You're freezing.* He snatched the picture and the water gun from the sleeping bag and crawled into it.

No sooner had he zipped it up than he had to unzip it. The urge to vomit was overwhelming, and he slithered to the edge of the walkway and leaned over it in time. It was only water and dry heaves. Finally, the heaving stopped, but now he felt even weaker. The bag was comforting as he nestled into it and pulled the zipper up. The basement was cold and damp, and he was glad to have it.

A light-headed feeling scared him, but it passed as he rested. *Our plan worked, Jeremy. Things went pretty much as they came to my mind when I held you on the basement floor and asked you to think something to me. If you hadn't hollered at me to use the gun when you did, I might have lost it. Thanks, man.*

Steve rolled onto his side and peered into the basement. He noticed a red light in the distance.

"Jeremy, did you sit here and look at that red light? You must have."

Steve shivered inside the sleeping bag. He zipped his jacket all the way up and wiggled around trying to get warm. His eyes fell onto the red light again. His eyelids were heavy, and sleep was overtaking him.

Don't you worry, Jeremy. I'll wake up in plenty of time to take care of everything. I promise you. You stand guard, okay?

CHAPTER 18
STEVIE, WHAT ARE YOU DOING?

Mrs. Stockton sat at the kitchen table pondering what to do. She debated whether to call the school or to call her husband. But her husband would not be at work yet, and the school would not have opened. In the meantime, Steve was gone.

She scrubbed the remaining breakfast dishes more forcefully than necessary. She was angry with herself and wondered why Steve had not obeyed her. Her anger passed as she stared out the kitchen window at their backyard. Stevie meant everything to her and her husband.

Their marriage had been good until Stevie was born. Then, it became so filled with life and energy and purpose that neither had dreamed it was possible to feel such joy. They had been married for eight years before Steve came along. They had been to several doctors and had tests, but none of the doctors had discovered a reason for why she couldn't get pregnant. Sure enough, when her husband had returned home after his second tour of duty in the Army during World War II, she had gotten pregnant. There wasn't anything they would not do for Stevie.

She sat down at the kitchen table. *God, why do this to Stevie? Why did you let this happen? Why?* Her anger grew. *Why did you put this burden in our son's life? He's never seen or known anyone who has died. How could you let it be his best friend? He feels responsible. I know he does.*

Her eyes drifted up to the clock over the kitchen sink. The hands had barely moved. *How is it possible for time to move so slowly and yet be so relentless?*

John, please, get to work early, will you. She picked up the receiver off the wall phone in the kitchen and began to call work, but she stopped before she dialed the second number. *It's too soon.*

Stevie, why did you have to do this? Why wouldn't you listen to me? The clock seemed frozen and lifeless, as if time refused to move forward. Not even a minute had passed. Nevertheless, Mrs. Stockton smiled.

Stevie had given them the clock two years earlier, after they had redecorated the kitchen. She and Steve and Mr. Stockton had had a wild time sloshing around in the kitchen tearing off the old wallpaper. Steve shot every square inch of the wall paper with his water gun, loosening it up, and his dad scraped it off the wall. Every now and then, Stevie would shoot his dad. His father would throw his scraper down, grab Stevie and tickle him and then shoot Stevie with his own water gun. The two of them had laughed away the entire time.

What a mess it had been, but her husband had said that they were going to do the kitchen over from top to bottom, and they were going to have fun doing it. Then he had shown Steve how to hang wallpaper. Mrs. Stockton believed that there wasn't a child anywhere Steve's age who knew how to hang wallpaper.

They had painted the ceiling and woodwork and put in wood paneling around the lower half of the kitchen walls and then installed a new floor. Mr. Stockton had taken Steve down into the basement and shown him how to turn off the electricity when they were ready to hang a new kitchen ceiling light. He had spent an hour showing

Steve where the electric lines came into the house and traveled to the electric meter and then to the fuse box and from there through cables all over the house.

He even produced some gas and electric bills, showing Stevie how his parents paid for the service. Stevie knew that his parents had to pay to put gas in the car, but he had no idea that they were paying for the gas and electric in the house. Mrs. Stockton loved how her husband made so many things around the house adventures for Steve.

As her husband hung the new wallpaper, Steve asked if he could try it. Her husband taught Stevie how to hang wall paper and stood next to him, holding the ladder the entire time that Steve experimented with the new wall paper.

When the job was finished, Mr. Stockton had hung the knickknack shelf on the wall by the table, where it had been.

Steve had frowned at the knickknack self. "Dad," he had said, "don't you think the wall looks better without the shelf?"

Stevie, what made you think of that?

Her husband had dropped his arms to his sides, listening in amazement as Steve declared that the kitchen seemed roomier without the shelf.

Mrs. Stockton had tried to save the day by telling Steve how neat some of the trinkets were and how they had gotten them from the many places where they had vacationed. Steve had picked up one of the tarnished silver spoons and pointed out the dust and grease that had accumulated on it. There was no escaping it.

They had had such an enjoyable time redecorating the kitchen, and Steve had learned so many things that his dad was not going to allow a knickknack shelf to interfere. He removed the shelf leaving four holes in the new wallpaper. If Steve had known how much work his suggestion was going to make, he would never have persisted with it.

But his father had not complained. He had agreed with Steve that the kitchen did look roomier without the shelf. Of course, that piece of wall paper had to come down, and the holes had to be filled in if the job was going to be done correctly. Steve did not realize that his father would have to buy more wallpaper to replace the piece that they were taking down.

Steve soon saw what a problem he had created, but his father never let him feel badly about it. He had insisted that Steve's idea was better and that his mother would be glad that she didn't have to clean the shelf anymore and that it was a smart idea to have extra wallpaper in case the wall got damaged later.

Two weeks after they had finished the kitchen, Steve had come home from school late one day, wearing a smile on his face. At dinner, he took the clock out of his bookbag and gave it to his parents. It was the perfect clock for the kitchen. It had a wooden border that matched the new wood paneling and a white porcelain face with rose-colored flowers that matched the new ceiling light.

Stevie had no idea of how much he had warmed his father's heart that day. Mr. Stockton had intuited that his son was trying to say thanks to them for being such a great Mom and Dad.

Later that night, after Steve had gone to bed, Mr. Stockton had confided to his wife that he would never regret replacing that piece of wallpaper. He had said that he had seen people ruin so many beautiful events over some simple thing like that. Anger and arguments had supplanted love and sharing, and he was not going to allow that to happen in his home.

He also told her that of all the things that he had planned to teach Stevie while they worked on the kitchen, Steve had learned more because of that knickknack shelf than anything else. He understood that he had caused a lot more work at the precise moment that they had finished the job, but his parents did it, regardless. Saying thanks to his parents had become important to him. Steve's clock was the best thank you they had ever received.

Mrs. Stockton's eyes returned to the hands of the clock. *John will be at work in ten or fifteen more minutes. I'll go up to Steve's bedroom and sit there. The time will go faster.*

Her mind didn't want to dwell on anything as she made Steve's bed. She stopped when her foot hit something under the bed. She got to her knees and slid the object out.

Oh, my God. She sighed, as she lifted Steve's scrapbook into her arms.

Her heart thumped loudly within her chest. She sat on the bed and held the book in her lap. Her face was sadder than it had ever been in her life. Nothing had ever hurt her before as much as finding Steve's scrapbook under his bed. She raised the scrapbook in her arms and pressed it against her chest.

Stevie, you're in such pain, aren't you? It's not your fault. Dear God, please, let him come home to me.

She stood and paced around the bedroom in a circle. *Stevie, you're blaming yourself. I know you are. You're making yourself sick over this. How could I have ever let you leave? Why didn't I see it? You're driving yourself insane.*

Mrs. Stockton stood still in the middle of the room clinging to the scrapbook. She wanted to scream. She wanted to cry. She wanted to fight. She wanted Stevie. But she couldn't do anything. She stood there spellbound, hopeless, not knowing what to do. Her eyes focused on the mirror of Stevie's dresser. *Something happened. What was it? The telephone.*

"The telephone. It's ringing."

She placed the scrapbook on the bed and raced across the hall to her and her husband's bedroom and snatched the receiver from the phone.

"Kate," she heard her husband say. "Kate, what's wrong? You're crying, Katie," he shouted. "Is Stevie all right?"

"Oh, John!"

"Kate, tell me what's wrong."

"John, he's gone. He refused to listen to me. He insisted that he had to go to school. He said that he was going to go crazy if he sat here for another day, and he took his bicycle and went off. I couldn't reason with him. He kept saying that if he got up and went to school, it would be over. He said he was going to school like every other day.

"That child stood here telling me that we couldn't do it for him. He had to step up and do it himself. John, what got to me was when he said that all of Jeremy's friends are in school except him, and he wanted to be there with them. How could I refute that? I feel so badly for him, John. Stevie must be feeling so alone without Jeremy. We've got to do something. It's too early to call the school. Everybody goes to the 8:00 mass."

Silence emanated from the phone as Mr. Stockton listened to the impossible.

"Please, John, talk to me."

"Kate, listen to me. It's okay. He probably isn't at school. That's not Stevie. He's hiding somewhere waiting for the funeral. He wants to be there for Jeremy. That must be what he wants. We'll only cause trouble for ourselves if we call the school. The sisters will know that we don't have control of him. I can't believe he wants to go through it. I asked him this morning to go to the funeral with me. I told him that we could sit outside in the car so that we were at least nearby.

He told me that he couldn't take seeing the Wilcamps. They were too mean to Jeremy too many times."

"John, what if Mrs. Wilcamp loses control of herself if she sees Stevie? What if she gets hysterical and yells at him and blames him for everything? What kind of reaction would Stevie have?"

Mr. Stockton sensed the panic that was about to erupt in his wife as her voice skipped, and her words came faster and more tearfully over the phone.

"Katie, you've got to believe me, that isn't going to happen. I am certain that Mrs. Wilcamp blames Jeremy, the same way that she blamed everything on that kid his whole life. Kate, sometimes I get the feeling that she hates Jeremy. Maybe not all the time, but sometimes... Well, it's too much to even think about.

"Kate, you've got to get control of yourself. I've got to go look for Stevie, and I can't worry myself sick about what's happening to you at the same time. Katie, I love you with all my heart, but this is our son. We've got to stick together. You've got to be there for me no matter how much it hurts. You've got to do it now and tell me you're going to be there in one piece for us when we get home. Can you do that?"

"John, I will be here for you. I promise you. Don't worry about me. I will be every bit the mother Stevie needs. I'm going to sit in his bedroom and hold onto everything, but I am so frightened. Do you think Stevie might be going crazy? I was making his bed, and I found his scrapbook underneath it. He must have sat up all night looking at those pictures and remembering so many things. The determination in his face scared me, John. He begged me to not abandon him now in something that was so important to him. He's going to do something, John. I can feel it."

Mr. Stockton's mind was firing away. *I've got to calm her, but I've got to find Stevie, fast.* "It's the most natural thing in the world for him to look at that scrapbook, Kate. That's what people do when something like this happens. Lots of people put pictures of their loved ones up in funeral parlors when they pass. You want to let all that hurt and love out somehow and that's what Stevie is trying to do. Find some way to express it to Jeremy. He'll go to either the funeral or the cemetery, and I'll be there to hold onto him and help him with both of our loves Katie."

"We are going to have to work to get him out of this, but one thing is certain. He knows how much we love him and how much he means to us. To him, we are not the enemy. We've got to keep that foremost in our minds, hope and hold on, so we can help him when he comes home. Stevie trusts us. He will come to us, Kate. I know he will. Why don't you lie down and take a nap? You've hardly slept since this started."

Mr. Stockton was about to hang up, but he spoke once more. "Katie, don't forget, I love you too."

"I know, John. And I love you. Stop worrying about me, I'll be okay."

"All right, honey."

Mrs. Stockton heard the phone click. She held onto the receiver. Her body felt feeble and her mind uncertain as if she had been mangled in a beating or been in a car crash or an explosion. The loud, high frequency beeping, signaling a receiver off the hook, startled her, and she replaced the receiver. She went back to Stevie's bedroom, picked up the scrapbook, and sat on Stevie's bed.

John has an uncanny ability to size up a person or a situation. But could he be right about Mrs. Wilcamp? Could she have felt hate for Jeremy?

Maybe the Wilcamps had a much harder time in their marriage than we did. They are at least eight to ten years younger than we are, they were younger than John and I were when they married, and they had Brian and Jeremy so early in their marriage. Jeremy's arrival might not have been planned. Perhaps he made it difficult for the Wilcamps. Jeremy's dad does not have a job nearly as good as John's.

Mrs. Stockton rose from the bed and made a full turn around the room, taking in everything of her son's, clasping Stevie's scrapbook.

No, it's not a good enough reason. It might not have always been easy, but I would have loved every child I had, and it would not have mattered how well off we were. If you ever felt hate for Jeremy, Mrs. Wilcamp, I feel sorry for you, because there must be no forgiveness for that.

* * *

Mr. Stockton left work immediately. He sped off in one of the company cars, thinking that Steve might try to elude him if he spotted his car. He drove to the church and then the school searching for Steve. His wife's words haunted him all the while he drove.

He's going to do something, John. I can feel it.

Her words burned through his brain. His fists clutched the steering wheel, threatening to smash it in his hands. *If I screwed this thing up... I was so sure that I was doing the right thing. I was sure that he needed to be by himself, at least for a while, and I was going to give him the time and space, but...damn... We could have gone to the funeral or to the cemetery..., whatever he wanted... We...* "Am I losing my son or something?"

When he didn't find Steve or see his bike at either the church or the school, he drove to the funeral home and parked the car in a place where it was unlikely to be noticed. Loosening his hold on the steering wheel, he slumped back in the seat allowing his muscles to relax. He raised his right leg up onto the hump over the transmission, rested his elbow on his thigh and his chin in his hand and fixed his eyes on the funeral home.

Mr. Stockton's mind focused on his wife. Her tears and the love and panic in her words ravaged his mind.

Katie, I hope I wasn't too harsh on you. You've been such a great wife and fantastic mother. You've always done it my way. You deserve more credit. We've been such a team when it comes to Stevie. You see and feel things the same way I do, and there is so much love among us. Poor Jeremy, what a mother.

Mr. Stockton's eyes flashed, and his muscles tensed anew. "If Steve is in there and that bitch utters one word to him, I'll... I swear, woman, you better not mess with my son's head." He didn't dare blurt out what he was thinking. He might attract attention.

There was a chance that his powerful hands might have broken the steering wheel this time, but some movement by the entrance to the funeral home captured his attention. Whatever it was, it stopped.

No. Any tirade from Mrs. Wilcamp would be thrown back at her so fast that she wouldn't know what hit her. Stevie is quite capable of cutting her down.

Yeah, Stevie will let you know what blame is about, Mrs. Wilcamp, and you'll soon find out what a lousy mother you've been. When that boy has something to say, he'll say it, and you'll hear it. And he could tell you a world of things about your son that you didn't know and didn't care about.

Mr. Stockton and his wife had tried to make Stevie an intelligent kid with a creative imagination who had real values, who knew what was important and had the courage to act. All the things that he had taught Steve, worried him now. *Stevie, your mind is fixed on the same thing my mind would be if we could change places. Jeremy your best friend lying dead in a casket. Those two were together all the time. How is a fourteen-year-old kid ever supposed to deal with that?*

"Stevie, what are you doing?"

The front door of the funeral home opened. Mr. Stockton watched as a group of pallbearers, whom he did not recognize, carried Jeremy's casket out and placed it in the hearse. From a safe distance, he followed the procession of only eight cars as they drove toward the Monastery church. *Eight cars. How could Mrs. Wilcamp not want Jeremy's friends to be at his funeral?* Stevie was not to be seen.

Mr. Stockton parked the car in an obscure place under a tree and gazed at the procession as it entered the church for Jeremy's funeral mass. Oddly enough, he scrutinized himself. So many heartrending things had happened to him that he had become hardened to all of it. His brain had built defense mechanisms of iron to protect him from hurting and feeling. His psyche had been impregnable. The defense mechanisms had enabled him to survive the destruction and devastation of everything and everyone around him and empowered him to destroy and kill in return.

After two tours of duty in World War II, he had stopped believing in anything good when he and his wife were denied children. But then, they had Steve. Just when he was sure that he would have seen and known only the worst things that life had to offer, this baby had been born to them. The defense mechanisms had been shattered. A son and father had been born in the same moment, and this Daddy was determined to see that his son would have a beautiful life and damned be anyone who hurt his son.

But he felt pitiful sitting behind the steering wheel of the company car. He was such a powerful man who had mastered things by himself that dozens of men around him together had failed. But no man had put this hurt on his son. It was as if all of mankind, all the evil that he had seen so many times over in his earlier years, had invaded his life again and thrust this horror of death at him yet another time.

Mr. Stockton had convinced himself that he had handled the progression of events wisely so far. But now, doubt plagued him. He anticipated a day by day, maybe even an hour by hour journey, but he felt prepared for it. He intended to change his plans and his actions as he saw any change in Steve. But now, fear gripped him. Steve was nowhere to be seen.

He couldn't know what Stevie was thinking. He didn't know what Stevie was doing. It had been a long time since he had known fear, but he had always been able to overcome it. This calamity bewildered him. At age fourteen, right here in his own neighborhood where Stevie lived, went to school, and played, Mr. Stockton feared that his son's life might be in danger, and he could do nothing about it.

This situation was incomprehensible. How did it happen? An awful realization dawned on him as he observed the mourners escorting Jeremy's casket into the church. Stevie had always seemed to Mr. Stockton to be a part of himself. They were not two. Somehow, they were one. Up until now, he had never envisioned the child venturing into danger without the father. But today, for the first time, he was acutely and painfully aware that his son was another person. Stevie was more than John Stockton's son. He was Stevie Stockton, too. What would Stevie do?

Stevie had not yet revealed himself. When Mr. Stockton felt confident that the funeral mass was well underway, he slinked into the church and lingered out of sight in shadows. He surveyed the entire church, searching for Stevie. He was not there.

After the mass ended, he followed the procession to Lorraine Park. He stopped the car high up on the west side hill above the cemetery entrance and watched for Steve. *Steve's got to be here somewhere, waiting for the burial party to arrive.* But as his eyes roved up and down the street and all over as much of the cemetery as was visible, he saw no sign of his son.

Lorraine Park Cemetery was one of the most distinguished cemeteries in Baltimore, noted for its rolling hills and attractively placed trees, shrubbery and flowers. The landscaping was just enough to make the cemetery a beautiful and peaceful place of final rest, rather than a desert of tombstones. All the hills of the cemetery now disturbed Mr. Stockton. Hiding places were innumerable. Stevie could be anywhere.

"Stevie, I know you're here. You've got to be. Come on, show yourself."

The funeral procession had passed through the gates and disappeared into the rambling hills of Lorraine Park ten minutes earlier, but he saw no sign of Steve trailing the procession.

That settles it. If he's not following the funeral procession, he's got to be inside the cemetery waiting. He'll recognize me if I go in there, and if he is not ready for me, he'll hide. Mr. Stockton weighed the options and decided that he had better wait for the funeral procession to leave and then go into the cemetery. It might be an unpredictable and even explosive confrontation if he ran into the Wilcamps with Stevie hanging around watching the whole thing.

Stevie will go to the grave when the mourners are gone. Then I will find him. He maintained his watch with a sick feeling in his stomach.

Forty minutes later, the last of the vehicles left the cemetery, and Mr. Stockton rode the company car into the cemetery and asked the caretakers where Jeremy had been buried. There were two burials that morning, and the caretakers directed him to the wrong site. He felt like telling them that there was going to be another burial in a big hurry if they gave him the wrong directions again, but they set him on the correct path the second time.

He had driven the car by his sleeping son and gone to the gravesite. *How did the Wilcamps come up with that tombstone so fast? The inscription is already on it. Someone in their family must have had that plot prepared for themselves or some loved one and given it to the Wilcamps for Jeremy. Of course, that must be it. It was probably his grandfather. Jeremy loved his grandfather. I know that. The Wilcamps could probably not have afforded to put Jeremy in here any other way. Well, that was certainly a nice thing for his grandfather or whoever, to have done for Jeremy.*

The longest and saddest hour of Mr. Stockton's life passed with him waiting for his son in vain. He sat on the ground beside Jeremy's gravesite disbelieving that this child whom he had seen just four days earlier and who had spent so much time in his home with his son, was now dead. *This is where Stevie should be. Why isn't he here? Even if he is hiding out there somewhere, he would come to me now. What am I missing?*

A somber and disappointed father went back over the church and school properties. Then he called his wife from a phone at Montclair Market and told her that he was going into the grove. But it seemed to him impossible for even Steve to get his bike into the grove.

Mr. Stockton marveled at how well Steve had described the grove. It was as mysterious and estranged from the world around it as Steve had suggested. He roamed through the pines and noted that weeds and vines had infiltrated the grove especially along some of the fences. *That was what Stevie had said made it so easy for him to hide in here.* No one could see him.

Mr. Stockton wanted to feel good, since he had at last found his way into this haven that Steve has claimed as his own some time ago. But the stark realization that he had failed to find Stevie was too overwhelming to allow him even a moment's respite. He had not found his son when he was certain that he would. He did not know where Steve was or what he was up to. It was an unbelievable strain on him. One more drive around the church and school properties did nothing to help him. Finally, he went home.

Mrs. Stockton felt her husband's sense of defeat as he described all the places that he had been to over and over and still not found Stevie. She hid her fears and controlled her emotions wanting to not make him feel worse.

Timidly, she asked, "Do you think we should call the police?"

She hoped that her question would not anger him. She wanted her husband to realize that other help was available, instead of him trying to be everywhere by himself, all at the same time.

The question stopped Mr. Stockton cold. Some twisting, sinister feeling wrenched his heart and chills broke out over his neck and arms. He put his hands on her shoulders and said softly, "No, Katie. It's not a good idea. Not right now. Maybe later." He released her shoulders and hugged her.

"I can't even think about the police right now, Kate. He hasn't run away from us. He is trying to find answers that we can't provide. Let's give ourselves more time, okay. Somehow, I know that he is going to come through this thing, whatever it is.

"Kate, I am going to go up and lie down and try to take a nap. When school lets out, I'll be there looking for him. And if I don't find him, I'll go out after dark and search for him. Perhaps darkness will make him less sly than he has been so far.

"But, Kate, I feel certain he is going to contact us, and if the police are involved, it might make a lot of problems for both Stevie and us. At least this way, we will have a chance to help him without interference."

Mr. Stockton turned wearily toward the stairs and trudged for the bedroom. He fell into an uneasy sleep lying across the bed.

Mrs. Stockton sat on the sofa trying to contain her emotions. She did not want her husband to see her crying. She perceived that her husband blamed himself, yet she did not understand why. This was a terrible, terrible, tragedy.

No one can understand an encounter with fate like this, and he shouldn't blame himself.

"John," she whispered, "you should not be blaming yourself." She curled up on the sofa and drifted to sleep.

CHAPTER 19
PARENTS LIKE YOU AND MOM

At 2:15, they both stood on the front porch of their home wishing that Stevie might magically appear. Both knew that it was too much to hope for.

"Kate, later, could you make us something for dinner. Something light, maybe soup and some rolls. He probably isn't going to want to eat a heavy meal. Whatever you make, if he is with me, it'll be perfect." They kissed, and he departed.

He went to all the same places he had gone earlier but saw no sign of Stevie. At last, he parked the car on Saint Michael's Street and faced the school. He watched the school children leave, but Stevie was not among them.

I've got to know if you were in school today, Steve, but I can't give a thing away. I have no idea of what you are up to, but I better not let that nun know that I don't know where you are. If she's not in school, I am going to have to go to the convent to see her, and that might really arouse some suspicions. "Umm," he hummed.

He got out of the car and hesitated, but he noted on his watch that it was close to 4:00. He had to hurry if he was going to find Sister Verona in the classroom. He went into the west side entrance that Steve and Jeremy always used.

He paused at the top of the stairs and gave thought to what went on inside this building. So many kids of different ages growing up and learning together. Older kids being forced to recognize their own metamorphosis, from a six-year-old to a teenager, every time they gazed upon the first-graders playing on the playground or sitting in their tiny seats at their tiny desks. The teenager had once occupied those desks. Weird feelings crowded the teenagers' minds when they encountered their own first or second grade teacher, knowing that they had advanced so far beyond the ABCs and 1+1 that those teachers taught. Mr. Stockton smiled as he wondered if Stevie ever felt awe at how much he had changed since he stepped through the front door of this place where he had spent almost eight years of his life. *This building holds a mountain of memories.*

Mr. Stockton turned to his right and saw the door of 8B. He opened the door quietly. Sister Verona was sitting at her desk with a stack of papers in front of her, but she held her head in her hands.

"Excuse me, Sister," Mr. Stockton stepped into the classroom. He had surprised Sister Verona. She wiped her eyes and adjusted her glasses.

"Please, come in, Mr. Stockton. It is so good of you to have come. I've been so worried about Steve. We all have." Sister Verona stood up from her desk. "Is he doing all right? Do you think that he is going to...to ever get back to being himself? I do wish I could see him if that's possible. If there is any way I can be of help, please tell me."

Mr. Stockton sighed. She had told him what he wanted to know without him having to ask her a single question. It was the first thing that had been easy.

"Thank you, Sister. It's been difficult, but we are a close family, and we are holding our own so far."

He did not want to say much to this nun, but Steve had liked her better than any of his previous teachers. Mr. Stockton approached her desk and reached his hand out. They held hands for a moment.

"Thank you for offering to help, Sister."

He glanced at the papers on her desk and saw that she was correcting a test. Jeremy's test lay on top.

"It's been very hard on you too, hasn't it, Sister?"

Sister Verona slumped into her chair. "Mr. Stockton, you have no idea of how much a teacher fears this sort of thing. I've known a lot of teachers in my years of teaching, and I have never understood how a teacher can be too hard on a student. They are so easily hurt, and some of them have miserable lives at home. You never know what they are going to do, or what's going to happen. I have always tried to be a kind and understanding teacher because I didn't want to live with this kind of tragedy.

"Some of the sisters are mean to their students." Sister Verona spoke to the back of the classroom as if she were not aware of Mr. Stockton's presence.

"I would never strike a child or stand a child up in front of the class and embarrass or humiliate him. Some sisters do those things. I don't understand why. We aren't taught to do that, but maybe some of them think that that's what parents do to train their children, and so they do it. Maybe that's how they were raised." She stopped talking and stared at the coatroom doorway.

Uniforms, Mr. Stockton wanted to say, but didn't. Uniforms. Put them on people and they become something other than what they are. It gives them power, and they feel that the uniform enables them to use it.

"Why did this ever have to happen in my class?" Sister Verona bemoaned sadly.

Mr. Stockton appreciated that Sister Verona was conversing with herself, but she surely needed someone to talk to.

Abruptly, she stood. "I'm sorry, Mr. Stockton. I don't know why I said that. It's something that has been bothering me since this happened. Please, tell me what I can do that might be of any help."

Mr. Stockton was speechless. *What disciplined lives these religious people live.* She appeared to be embarrassed because she had revealed the tiniest speck of her inner self in a setting of profound tragedy.

He peered out into the classroom. "Where does Stevie sit, Sister?"

Mr. Stockton felt her sigh of relief as he changed the topic.

"Here." She walked down the third aisle and put her hand on the desktop of the sixth seat in the fourth row.

"This is Steve's desk."

Mr. Stockton lifted the desktop. He found a pack of loose leaf paper, a few notes, some pencils, a couple of spit balls and a few rubber bands. He smiled as he guessed that Steve shot off an occasional spit ball to brighten up a dull school day, probably straight at Jeremy.

"Where did Jeremy sit, Sister?"

Sister Verona's face drooped, and she pointed to Jeremy's desk across the aisle from Steve's in the third row. Mr. Stockton picked up Jeremy's desktop. It contained pretty much the same stuff as Steve's, but there were two wads of paper rolled up sitting in a back corner. Again, Mr. Stockton smiled. *Jeremy had to have blasted Steve on the head with those wads of paper.* Mr. Stockton squeezed himself into Steve's seat.

"How did they manage to sit across from each other, Sister? Students were always seated in alphabetical order when I went to school."

Sister Verona let herself rest on the desktop of the desk behind Jeremy's, and a smile lightened her face as she ran a hand across the back rest of Jeremy's seat.

"You know, Mr. Stockton, that's quite a story. It was the first time I understood that Steve and Jeremy were exceptional students and close friends. It was my first encounter with them, and the first day of school. We were doing exactly as you said, seating the kids in alphabetical order. The kids were crammed into the first and last aisles and the back of the classroom, waiting to be assigned a seat, when Steve raised his hand.

"I acknowledged him. He suggested that it might be pretty good if the class didn't have to sit in alphabetical order because they were eighth-graders this year, and eighth-graders ought to be treated differently from the lower grades.

"That comment had the whole class buzzing, and I had to raise my voice to get them to stop. I told him that I didn't think that that was a smart idea because friends would choose to sit next to friends and be tempted to fool around instead of paying attention. Steve came back and declared that this class was not that way. He claimed that 8B was a good class, and everybody worked hard and didn't fool around.

"I told him no, that a good teacher cannot place the students where the temptation to talk to their friend confronts them every day, all the time, and it was unreasonable to expect school children to resist communicating with their friends when they are sitting next to each other.

"Steve had an answer for that too. He claimed that being eighth-graders ought to mean something more than that they had gone through seven grades, and here they were. It had to mean that they had matured and learned about being responsible, and even if there was some clowning around, they would stop as soon as I said anything. By that time, I recognized that this student was a class leader, and meant everything he was saying.

"It's never wise to brush off a child who is being serious about something. Especially in this case where Steve had appointed himself a spokesman for the entire class. I had no doubt that this was not a spur of the moment idea. Steve had planned it out before the first day ever started, and he had his mind set on going for it.

"I wanted to be fair with Steve. I told him that I had to be responsible too, and there might be a lot of students who preferred to be assigned alphabetically. Some students might not be sure of who their friend is and prefer being assigned a seat.

"As you might guess, my comment about kids preferring to be seated alphabetically prompted Steve to suggest that we put it to a vote. Steve is very quick-witted, Mr. Stockton. Everyone in the class raved over Steve's suggestion, and most of them wanted to vote, but to me, Steve had lost the argument. A classroom is not a democracy. What counts is what the teacher decides.

"I was about to inform Steve of that when Jeremy raised his hand. I decided to let this fellow have his say, and then put an end to the discussion."

Sister Verona paused and tried to collect her thoughts. It hurt her to remember this.

"Jeremy had a serious look on his face, and he started slowly, almost reluctantly, but he forced himself to speak. He said that he didn't think it would be bad for a teacher to let friends sit next to each other. It might make learning a lot more fun if friends were close to their friends.

"What Jeremy said next was a real shocker. He said that there might be kids who want to be friends with somebody else in the class, but they've never had the chance to get close enough because of being seated alphabetically in every class and having to do everything in single file and being forced to be silent all the time. And as if to throw salt in the wound, Jeremy then said that there might be some students who wanted to get away from the person whom they had been forced to sit next to for seven years. That statement was really a bombshell.

"Jeremy's face had gotten as red as a beet by then, and his voice was getting shaky because he recognized that all noise in the class had ceased, and everybody had their eyes focused on him.

"What he had said was brazen. When Jeremy said that maybe kids couldn't be friends with other kids because they were always being seated alphabetically, or being made to do everything in single file, or forced to be silent all the time, he had attacked the entire system of discipline that we have here, whether he intended to or not. Everyone in the class knew that he had escalated the matter into something much deeper than a discussion about seating.

That statement alone was enough for more than one or two sisters here to slap Jeremy upside the head. His comments sounded disrespectful of our discipline, as if he knew some better way of doing things. But the second statement. That was fire. Most teachers would not tolerate that. Jeremy was accusing our system of forcing students who didn't like each other to sit next to each other. For seven years! Jeremy wasn't just begging to be put in his place; he was daring to be put in his place. And he would have been.

"But I did not see it that way. I wasn't angry with him. Jeremy had sensed that I was not allowing a vote, and he was trying to find a way to pitch in and save the thing for Steve. What he said was what popped into his mind. I understood that. And, like it or not, I saw some truth in what he said. I knew that he meant no harm. Nevertheless, he had taken a straight and hard shot at how we keep control in our classrooms. All the kids were quiet, wondering what was going to happen next."

"Yeah," Mr. Stockton agreed, "it sounds as though Jeremy meant that kids can't be friends with other kids because they go to this school, and that is a pretty harsh message even if it is a partial truth."

"I can guarantee you, Mr. Stockton, that by the time a student reaches the eighth grade in this school, he or she has seen more than one nun take off on a student for a lot less than what Jeremy had implied, and Jeremy had to have recognized the risk he had taken.

"I felt nervous, because I feared that Jeremy might cry. It amazed me that such a simple thing had blown up into a confrontation so easily. To me, it is dangerous and defeating for an adolescent to be shamed or humiliated in front of his peers. A teenager will carry that memory for a long time. That is a hurtful thing for a teacher to allow to happen to an adolescent. Peer pressure can be so intense at that age.

"The expression on Jeremy's face was incredible. There were so many things he wanted to say to me, without saying a word. He was trying to say, please, I didn't mean anything disrespectful. Please, do it because Steve is my best friend, and he wants to do it so badly. And his face pleaded with me not to hit him or embarrass him because he didn't want to take that.

"And yet, on top of all of that was an element of himself. A determination. In boys Jeremy's age, their masculinity is emerging. They are growing and becoming men. It means something that they don't understand, but they know that it is important. They don't want to be weak even though so much of the child is still in them.

"Jeremy had stepped onto a tightrope between boyhood and manhood. It was written all over his face. It was a quality of expression that only an adolescent could have produced. It would have been so easy to hurt him."

Mr. Stockton looked at Sister Verona with admiration and surprise. Her understanding of the male adolescent seemed exceptional to him. No wonder Steve liked Sister Verona. It made sense to him that she was teaching the eighth grade.

"I had not made a move toward Jeremy or said a word. He had astonished me as much as the rest of the class. Jeremy is just as quick-witted as Steve, Mr. Stockton, and he took advantage of my silence, and dared to speak up again. He said that if we tried it this one time, teaching and learning might be better than ever in our class, and they might try to be the best students they could be because they liked being with their friends and were happy that their teacher let them try it. He claimed that if it didn't work, the class would understand and go back to alphabetical order, but if we didn't give it a chance, we might miss this opportunity to be an outstanding class.

"Mr. Stockton, the class went completely quiet. The silence hung there. And, the next thing you know, Steve broke the silence. He started clapping his hands and then the whole class joined in. I was proud of Steve for clapping. He was telling me that if I was going to slap Jeremy because of what he had said, I'd have to slap him too.

"And that's how it happened. How could I refute what Jeremy had said without making myself out to be an awful bully by imposing my will on them. It all went smoothly and, I guess, everybody sat near their closest friend. When I saw Jeremy and Steve sit across from each other in these two seats here, I knew they were great friends."

Mr. Stockton worked himself out of Steve's seat. "Steve told me the story, Sister. Certainly not with your perspective. I know much more about it now than I did from what Stevie told me. I must say Sister that your understanding of a male adolescent is remarkable. I wanted to hear the story from you. I hoped it might help you to remember them together."

Mr. Stockton opened Jeremy's desktop again. He picked up the two wads of paper, a half-used pencil, and a notebook that Jeremy had written in.

"Do you suppose I could have these, Sister?"

"Certainly, Mr. Stockton. I was going to leave them there for Steve, but I am sure you will give them to him. I was planning on keeping Jeremy's test, unless you think I shouldn't."

"Sister Verona, there are few other things that could make Jeremy happier than to know that you wanted to keep a remembrance of him. I have heard Steve and Jeremy talking about you on several occasions, and, always, it has been something good. They admire you greatly. Jeremy told Steve that he was doing the best he had ever done in school because you are such a good teacher, and he was sure that you liked him. No, Sister, I had not thought of asking for his test. It is best kept with you."

Sister Verona smiled and struggled to maintain composure.

"Thank you, Mr. Stockton. Thank you, so much. Your words are very kind."

They walked slowly up the aisle toward he door.

"Sister, the reason I came here is that I am not sure of when Steve is going to be able to come back to school, but it's important to him that he finish the year. For him to have to repeat this year after having lost Jeremy, would be more heartbreaking than what he is going through now."

"Don't say another word, Mr. Stockton. I spoke to Sister Sullpicia about it, and she will allow me to work out some special classes with Steve after school so that he can catch up. He is a bright student. If he has any trouble with tests, I will give him oral tests that will be so easy that he cannot fail. I will give him the answer before I ask the question. Steve has already done better than every other student in this class. I promise you, Mr. Stockton, he will not fail this class."

"Thank you, Sister Verona. That's very generous of you and the school. You have taken a tremendous burden off my and Stevie's mother's shoulders at a time when we really need help." Neither said another word and they parted company.

* * *

Mr. Stockton made one more trip around the school and church properties and then drove to the cemetery. He sat in the car and watched the sun set in the western sky over Jeremy's grave. Finally, he drove home.

What a long day this has been.

The October daylight faded, and still he did not know where his son was. He and his wife simply looked at the dinner she had prepared. They decided to wait until Stevie got home.

Mr. Stockton went to the front door. His eyes roved up and down the street. No sign of Stevie. He turned the porch light on. Then he went to the back door and turned the light on in the backyard. At last, he sat down in his easy chair and reached for his tobacco canister. When he saw the note inside, he bolted up in the chair.

> Dad,
> You know how much I love you and Mom. You
> know I don't ever mean to hurt you or disobey
> you. But you can understand this. Mom can't.
> Maybe you can tell her somehow, so she understands.
> I've got to get Brad. He killed Jeremy, Dad.
> I've got no choice. I don't want a choice. I
> want him. I've got to get him this day. Stevie
> Stockton will not go to sleep tonight, until he

takes care of Brad. Don't try to come for me, Dad. I
must do this on my own. It's the only way.
Please, Dad, don't call the police. I am sure
you know what I mean. I don't know why I
am sure, but I am.
Dad, no matter what happens, there hasn't
ever been a kid who had parents like you and Mom,
who loved him so much, and gave him so much, and
who felt every pain he felt, and suffered
through everything with him, the way you and
Mom have. I love you both.

Stevie

"Oh, Stevie. What have you done? Where are you? You're only
fourteen years old. Oh, no, nooo." After a few minutes, Mr. Stockton
sat back in his chair.

*Yes, I understand, but how could Stevie understand? How could
he know? I have never mentioned the war to him. I have never
spoken once about the army. It's like that boy knows I have killed.
Killed hundreds of men. No, more like thousands of men died
because I was a good soldier.*

He folded the note and held it in his hand.

*Yes, Stevie. I understand. Killing one more of the enemy doesn't
matter when you have killed as many as I have. But you're my son.*

CHAPTER 20
IF THOSE QUESTIONS BROKE THROUGH

Hours later, Steve awakened in a cold sweat. *Boy, Jeremy, it's dark down here. I didn't think it ever got this dark.*

Steve lay there not wanting to move. He needed to think things out, but his mind had constructed a merciful block. With an inexplicable chemistry and electricity, the neurons of a central nervous system struggling for meaning, still served a master that was more than the sum of the parts. They refused to allow the disorder that raged in so much of his mind to tear him apart. They did not allow him to conceive of what his parents might be feeling, or how worried they might be, or how they would cope with what he had done. His mind did not ask why he had denied his parents the chance to sway him or why he persisted in going it alone. If those questions broke through, perhaps he would not be able to go on.

Steve turned onto his right side facing the red light. *I wonder what time it is, Jeremy? Bet you got to be friends with that red light, didn't you?*

He unzipped the sleeping bag and crawled out, keeping his eyes fastened on the light. The damp coldness of the basement cut through him, and he zipped his jacket up to his neck. He grasped the handrail.

Jeremy, I can feel you. Part of you is still in here. Oh, God, it should have been so simple. How did Brad and his punk friends figure it out? Why couldn't I get back here in time? I was moving as fast as my ankle allowed.

I have no answers. I swear, I've been missing for hours now, sleeping here and not even a mouse bothered me. I put you in here, and they find you. One of those high school bastards had to have remembered the basement.

You really fought them, didn't you? You weren't going to give in. You were going to drop down into the basement and dare them to come after you. You knew they didn't have the guts to do it. Making fun of you and mocking you and calling you dirty names could not erase what you had accomplished.

They were outsmarted and empty-handed. Six big, brave bullies failed to lay one finger on you. You challenged them. If you're so mighty, let's see you come down off that walkway and get me. Each one of them had to do it on their own. They had to pick their wimpy asses up and climb over that railing and drop down into the basement all by themselves, not knowing what they were falling into and not being able to see a thing. You knew they didn't have the guts to do it.

This basement wasn't like some poor kid somewhere with six other kids, bigger than he is, beating up on him. It was a gigantic monster, cloaked in darkness, that you had conquered. Those pathetic cowards weren't going to take this monster on. Six of them ganging up on one guy in a place like this didn't faze them. They couldn't put themselves in your place and ask why? Why do this to someone? Why force someone into a position where having the courage to fight back could kill them?

Why didn't they back off and just go when they realized how dark and dangerous this place was, and you were in here alone? They couldn't fathom you challenging them. You, calling them out as cowards and daring them to be brave. You were supposed to get on your knees, beg, cry, crawl, and let them tear your clothes off you, and kick the shit out of you. A real bully's party.

Steve was angry. He clenched his teeth and peered up into the darkness with bitter eyes.

"Why, God?" he spoke with a subdued fury. "Why didn't you let Jeremy have that moment? Why didn't you protect him? What kind of God are you? Why did he have to land where he did?"

God, a broken printing press for the Sunday church bulletins. Why? Why did somebody put it on the floor where Jeremy was going to land? The useless piece of junk should have been thrown away years ago. A couple of inches, God. That's all. A couple of inches, and Jeremy would have survived. Couldn't you have given him that? No. You broke his back and let him bleed to death. God, how could you let that happen to Jeremy?

Steve slumped to his knees and cried bitterly.

When the emotion subsided, he rose to his feet. *Don't worry yourself about me, God. I don't want your protection. Not now.*

"Jeremy, if only it had been me and not you. I'd give anything to do it over and let it be me down here instead of you."

The darkness of the basement played with Steve's mind. A chill broke out over his body, and he focused his eyes on the red light. M O N S T E R. He said it himself. It had been his own imagery, but now it haunted him.

In the next moment, Steve would have jumped out of his skin if that had been possible. The loud ringing of the Monastery bell breaking the silence of an early fall night added some new, more frightening element of misery to his loneliness. Still, he concentrated enough to count the tolling until it stopped at ten.

Jeremy let's get out of here. I don't understand why I wanted to explore this place. Come on, man. For all I know, someone might check in here at night.

This is a perfect time to leave. Brad's parents must be used to him getting home after 10:00 or 11:00, and they probably don't care what time he gets home. There's a good chance that no one suspects anything yet except my dad.

Dad. The word stopped him.

"Dad, I'm so sorry." *How could all of this have happened? Now I am forced into the same kind of position that Jeremy was in.*

Stevie stood, jostling the sleeping bag on his shoulders to balance it. He glanced at the red light for a final time and rolled the bike across the walkway to the stairs.

At the bottom of the staircase, Steve drew in a deep breath and shuddered as he eyed the stairs. His whole body felt weak. Every muscle ached. Leaning against the wall contemplating where he would find the strength to get up the stairs, he became aware of the only part of his body that felt good. Something had stimulated him. He had almost forgotten that part of his body existed.

Man, Jeremy, imagine having something that feels so good on your body all the time. No way God could be all bad if he had anything to do with inventing dicks. Steve pressed the growing erection into his thigh.

Maybe he had had a few erections in his sleep since Jeremy's death, but this was the first time that he was aware of one since that moment. He smiled. Then he laughed, gently at first, but the laughter quickly grew, and Steve roared away at the bottom of the staircase.

Some torrent of playfulness and happiness and just plain boyishness, that were so much a part of Stevie Stockton, that had been crushed under an avalanche of tragedy, erupted from their shackles, and Stevie laughed for the first time since his best friend had left him.

Jeremy, what would they think if some watchman, or maybe one of the priests, like maybe Father Brendan...Oh, God, he laughed even harder, *Father Brendan…opened the door and caught me holding my bike in one hand wearing a leather glove and holding my dick in the other hand, giggling away like some weirdo? They would swear I am the craziest pervert ever.*

And then, it stopped. The laughter ceased. The smile faded. The erection retreated, and the sadness returned. It reached into his heart and mind, and the boyishness vanished.

"J e r e m y."

The fleeting stimulation that had infused strength into him for a few moments, like some miracle medicine, slipped off into the darkness.

All right, Jeremy, let's do it. He picked the bicycle up and lumbered up the stairs. At first, he tried to raise the bike frame under his left forearm, but the handlebar fought him, swinging from one side to the other, banging into the railing and then the wall.

I'm going to have to hold the handlebar with my hand no matter how much it hurts. "Oh, shit," Steve moaned, as the pain pierced deeper and deeper into his hand with each step.

It got to be more and more difficult to raise the front wheel and hold onto the rear of the bicycle so that it didn't roll backwards. Sweat poured off him, and he now felt hot. Stevie paused and tried to loosen his jacket, but his gloved fingers were unable to grasp the zipper, and it was impossible to contort the injured hand into the proper maneuver.

He tried to hold the bicycle with his injured hand and unzip the jacket with his right hand. Sharp, burning pains exploded within his cut palm and radiated up his arm when he released his hold on the rear of the bicycle.

This is supposed to be the lightest bike you can buy, but, I swear, it feels like a ton of bricks. The red Schwinn almost slipped out of his grasp before he regained his hold on the seat with his right hand.

He rested against the wall and mopped his brow on the sleeve of his jacket and thought about Jeremy.

Jeremy, don't you ever think it. I cut the hand for a reason, and it's the only thing keeping me going. I'll never be sorry I cut it. Okay.

There was no rest on the staircase. The bike only got heavier, and Steve knew that he had to keep moving, or he might drop the thing and possibly fall down the stairs.

Come on, Stockton, get up there before you die down here. Jeez, what a thing to think.

With his next step, he saw the light bulb and the platform at the top of the stairs.

Keep moving, Stevie, you're almost there. At last he got to the platform. Sweat poured off him, but the relief of having gotten there was immeasurable.

Wow, Jeremy, that was bad, but not so bad that we couldn't do it.

Steve opened the door to the altar boys' room a crack, but darkness awaited him. He closed it. *I've got to unscrew the light bulb and adjust to the darkness. Who might be outside to see this puny light, I don't know, but why take the chance?*

He closed his eyes, unscrewed the bulb and stood there letting his eyes adjust to the darkness.

Oh, Jeremy, you were standing here three nights ago. What must have gone through your mind? Go down the stairs, stand here and wait. Try to find me. Help me. But you did it, Jeremy, didn't you? You did exactly what I told you. I am so, so sorry.

I made you promise me.

Steve impulsively thrust the door open, as if he wanted someone to be there. He guided the bike into the room. Steve refused to give into his frenzied thoughts. But his eyes could not be stopped. They traveled to the two chairs that he and Jeremy had sat in during

Monday's altar boys' meeting. An unstoppable urge to sit in Jeremy's chair jabbed at his mind.

Steve grimaced, frowned at the floor and rolled the Schwinn across the room to the hallway. He couldn't walk by. He leaned the bike against the wall and sat in Jeremy's seat.

"Jeremy, I miss you so much. Where are you? I'd give anything for you to be sitting here."

After a few moments, he rolled the bicycle to the bathroom and went in for a drink of water. The cold-water sated his thirst. He splashed some of the water onto his face with his right hand and ran his hand through his hair.

Steve managed to get the bike out of the altar boys' room, up the outside stairs, and onto Monastery avenue without too much trouble, but his hand ached, and the glove felt warm and wet.

My hand is bleeding. I know it is.

He laid the bike on the ground, pulled the right-hand glove out of his sleeping bag and cut the palm of the glove out with his Swiss Army knife. Steve rolled it into a ball and pushed it down into the glove over the bandage, hoping that the extra pressure might stop the bleeding.

Jeremy, please, I need you now more than you could believe. Don't let your blood go near my hand.

He closed the knife, put it in his pocket, and headed up Monastery Avenue. The moon was almost full, and the night air was cool and refreshing. At the intersection of Monastery Avenue and Montclair Street, he held up and peered down Montclair Street.

Nothing is happening, Jeremy. If Brad had been found, cops would be swarming all over the place. We're still safe. We put it to him, didn't we? I hope his last thoughts were that he was dying because of what he did to you, and I was killing him. Brad Maddox, what an incredible low life you were.

The sound of the tires treading over the blacktop road distracted Steve's mind as he pedaled the bike. His spirit lightened, and he reveled in the feel of the wind across his face.

Jeremy, the night is different. It's exciting, mysterious. You can't see what's ahead of you or know if someone is lurking out there, waiting to jump you.

The bike ride up Coastal Highway and camping out in Delaware was the first time that he and Jeremy had been out overnight. The Wilcamps always wanted Jeremy home by dark. But Steve had been concocting ways for them to investigate the night. They planned to try out for the freshman basketball team in high school next year and that made a perfect excuse for getting home late.

You know what else they have in high school, Jeremy? The school sponsors mixers. They're dances for the freshmen where you don't have to have a date. You're supposed to go and meet girls from a girls' high school. The brothers stand by and make sure it's all pure and holy. Good Catholic mothers and fathers like that for their sons and daughters. Everything is supervised and nice and normal.

We could have told your parents that we were going to a mixer and then clowned around until late. We show up at the dance and when nobody is paying attention, we're out of there. Perfect.

Steve was intent on star gazing when a car came onto the road half a mile ahead of him. The light on the roof brought him to action.

"The police."

Steve wheeled the bike in between two parked cars and laid the bike on the ground behind the foremost car and then got himself on the ground. Two policemen were out on patrol.

Please, Jeremy, don't let them have seen me. What if they're hunting for a murdering fourteen-year-old eighth-grader from Saint Michael's Monastery Grammar School?

Steve's heart pounded as he lay on the ground. A bulletin flashed over the radio as the police car passed. *I'll stay here until I'm sure they're gone.* When he no longer heard the police cruiser, he hefted the bike onto the road, hopped on, and pedaled faster.

Whew, that might have been close. I've got to stop fooling around and make tracks. I don't know what I've been thinking. Maybe I've been trying not to think. I guess I've been favoring my left foot. Man, it hurts.

As he came over the first hilltop on his journey and picked up speed, he squeezed the hand brakes and slowed the bike. Downhill had always been race time for him and Jeremy.

Jeremy, if you think that this is scary during the day, you've got to try it at night. It's a scream. I can hardly see. All I need to do is run into a pack of wild dogs or ride into a pothole. I'd be on my ass in an instant and bang up my foot and hand even more. I know you won't believe this, but I can't fly down this hill.

It was getting harder to pedal the bike, and Steve let his legs fly out in the air and drifted the bike as much as possible to spare his ankle. At last, he saw his destination. Lorraine Park Cemetery.

CHAPTER 21

STEVIE STOCKTON AND JEREMY WILCAMP

The locked gates to the cemetery were nestled in the trough of two long sloping hills, one on the western side of the gate and the other on the eastern side. A large cast iron sign, bearing the name, hung above the cast iron gates. Iron supports holding the sign were attached to stone pillars on each side of the entrance. A cast iron fence extended from the stone pillars up each hill and around the periphery of the cemetery.

Steve stopped his bike on the crest of the east side hill and stared at the entrance. All the senses of his body were sharpened as he sat on the bike seat, wondering what the dogs were up to. *They must be unchained at night to roam the cemetery, chasing intruders like you and me away, Jeremy.* A light breeze wafted in from the south. Steve guessed that it had to be close to 11:00.

If the wind keeps coming from the south, the dogs will always be downwind of us. If we stay upwind of the caretakers' building, I can travel in a big arc around the building and the dogs and get over to you on the west side without them ever getting a whiff of us. The dogs should stick around the building at night. They must have a place there where they sleep, and any animal is going to hang out where it gets fed, right? They're just dogs, Jeremy. Dobermans or not, they're only dogs. Steve was determined, but the dogs were preying on his mind before he had even entered the cemetery.

Steve pedaled the bike across the street. *This must be as safe as any other place up here. We're a hundred feet or more from the entrance.* He held the bike and stood before the glossy black cast iron fence. He guessed that the balusters had to be eight feet high.

Eight feet, that's going to be tough with this hand. He leaned the bike against the fence, took off the sleeping bag, and examined the water gun. Some sudsy ammonia remained in the handle. *I've got five, maybe ten* shots *left.* But Steve knew he was exaggerating. *Well, I've got at least three shots. If the dogs find us, I'll wait until they're almost on top of us and then let the bitches have it. Dogs have sensitive smellers, Jeremy, and if they get any ammonia on their faces, they'll hightail it away from us.*

Steve shoved the gun into the sleeping bag and tossed it over the fence. He pulled his Swiss Army knife out of his pocket. His father had wanted him to have it, but his mother had not liked the idea. Mr. Stockton had insisted that Steve was old enough and smart enough to use it for what it was intended.

Wow, Dad, did you have a premonition that I might need this knife to defend myself someday and that's why you wanted me to have it? That's too freaky, Stockton.

Maybe it's not. Dad seems to know things. I hope you're okay with what I did, Dad. How else could I have stopped Brad from coming over that fence? Dad, I would have been lost without my knife. He shoved the knife into his pocket.

Steve fixed his eyes on the fence. All he could think about was Jeremy climbing over the fence at the grove. He fell to his knees cupping his hands in his lap and fought back tears. He felt Jeremy's foot in his cupped hands. He saw himself boosting Jeremy up and over the fence at the grove. He could feel himself falling on top of Jeremy and see them lying on the ground, kidding with each other.

Steve jerked his head up. *No, no. I can't give in. I've got to do this.*

Steve rose to his feet, jumped up, and grabbed the top cross rail of the fence. Intense burning pain in his left-hand forced him to let go. He fell back to the ground curling up, cradling his left hand to his stomach.

"Oh, my God. This is unbelievable." He rolled onto his back grasping his left palm with his right hand, massaging the wound.

"How am going to do this? Jeremy. I don't remember anything hurting me like this." When the pain was tolerable, he positioned the bicycle up against the fence and straightened the front wheel. It seemed stable when he tested it with his weight. Steve placed his right foot on the bike frame, grabbed a baluster with his right hand, and hoisted himself up onto the frame. The bike held as Steve stood on the frame.

It's going to hurt if I come down on my left foot or hand. I can't let that happen.

Supporting himself with his right foot on the bike frame, Steve lifted his left leg up and maneuvered it between two of the balusters until he was almost able to flex his knee over the top cross rail connecting the balusters.

He checked the bicycle once more. "Here goes."

With a push from his right leg and a pull from his right hand, Steve heaved himself onto the top of the fence finding himself pinned between two of the balusters, squeezing the hell out of his balls.

"Oh, shit!" He pushed himself up from the cross rail and lifted his right leg over the fence in one rolling motion.

When his right leg was over the fence, Steve let go of it and plummeted down the eight feet into the cemetery holding his left foot and left hand in the air.

This unlikely, youthful interloper sat up and gave the cemetery a quick once-over. Nothing moved. "Other than me having blue balls, Jeremy, that went okay," and Steve had a weak laugh.

Now this is what we're going to do. We're going to pick out a tall tombstone with a cross or a statue on top of it, something that we can grab onto and climb, about every twenty feet or so. If the dogs detect us, we're going to race to the tombstone and climb up on it before they get to us. We'll shoot them smack in their faces when they're trying to bite us. We'll get them in the mouth if we can.

If we don't have time to climb the thing, we'll get our backs to it, so the dogs can only attack us from the front or sides. But dogs will come at us from the front. They go for your face. I can kick my feet at them until I get a good shot. If you've got to fight, get your back to the wall. That way your back is protected. It's a basic principal of war called protecting your rear. You and I need to protect our rear big time in this place.

We'll make that arc to the north around the dogs and the caretakers' building like I said. Steve gathered his gear and armed himself with his gun in his left hand and his knife in his right hand.

Steve chose a tombstone and set forth toward it. His feet felt like lead as he plodded along, checking his surroundings with every step. After only a few steps, the headlights of a car appeared coming over the hilltop on the western side of the cemetery. Steve stood frozen. The car didn't seem to be moving fast enough to be just anybody. It had to be somebody up to something, maybe hunting for him.

It wasn't a police car, and Steve didn't recognize it. The car slowed as it approached the entrance.

Goose bumps broke out over his skin when the two Doberman Pinschers charged down the cemetery driveway and raced up to the gate barking and growling, two crazed, insane monsters as fierce as anything Steve had ever seen in any movie. Steve couldn't move. Someone threw something from the car at the dogs. The smashing of glass made Steve think it was a beer bottle.

"Oh, no. It's a bunch of clowns messing with the dogs."

The dogs were in an unbelievable rage. They first tried to squeeze their bodies through the fence, and then they jumped up in the air, attempting to leap over the fence, all the while barking ferociously. The people in the car antagonized the dogs, yelling at them, throwing things at them, and teasing them by sticking their hands out as close to the snapping muzzles as they could without getting bitten. The incensed dogs followed the car, repeatedly charging the fence and ramming their heads between the iron bars, flashing their teeth trying to bite the taunting hands.

"They're coming this way. My God, those fools will bring the dogs right here."

Steve wanted to move, but the scene unfolding before him mesmerized him. *I could be halfway to Jeremy's grave while the dogs are here, barking their heads off.* But he remained rooted to the spot.

The dogs advanced up the eastern slope along with the car, nearing Steve's position. Steve saw a series of mini blasts scud over the fence toward the dogs. Five or six fire crackers strung together exploded over the dogs. The dogs vaulted backwards making strange howling noises, whirled around, and raced down the hill with their cropped tails between their legs.

They stopped at the bottom of the hill by the gate and resumed barking and growling, but the car had sped off. Steve heard joking and snickering coming from the car as it roared away. He surmised that it had been kids from Saint Michael's High School. Steve's heart pounded, and he felt as though he might collapse, but he stood there petrified until the dogs retreated from the gate and faded into the darkness.

Steve let himself sink to the ground feeling weak. *How is it that I didn't move? What is wrong with me? Was I that scared? I didn't even get my water gun in my right hand. I could never have pulled the trigger with that glove on my hand. I'd have been minced meat if the dogs had spotted me.*

Maybe, if I had moved, the dogs would have sensed it and detected me. They've got such sharp senses. What if my mind knew that any movement would alert the dogs, and that's why I didn't move. My mind wouldn't let me.

I don't know what it was, Jeremy. I couldn't take my eyes off what was happening. Steve's shoulders drooped, and he stared at the ground.

Jeremy, you've left me, haven't you? I can feel it. Every blood cell and every fragment of whatever cells were left. They're all gone. All your blood is gone, isn't it?

The thought of escape churned in his mind. His brain and heart shouted at him to get out. Go. Run away. It's enough. You've done what you can. He doesn't want more.

But Steve stood and picked out another monument.

I'm not letting you down, Jeremy. I'm coming. Stevie Stockton trudged along among the graves in the moonlight, holding his water gun in his right hand and his Swiss Army knife in his left hand.

It bothered him that he progressed so slowly, but he could not force himself to move faster. After a while, each monument he chose seemed to be more grotesque than the last. They morphed into monsters that he dragged himself to like a lamb to slaughter.

The breeze had gotten stronger, and now, occasional gusts blew in, but it still came from the south, carrying his scent away from the dogs. When he got to the top of the next hill, he saw another car traveling on Montclair Street. Steve stopped.

"My bike. I left it leaning against the fence as big as life. Suppose someone sees it?" He rested against a tombstone and mulled it over. *You're not supposed to be so dumb, Stockton. I'm not going back for it now, and besides, all I could do would be to knock it over onto the ground where it won't be so obvious. I can't climb the fence again. That's for sure.*

Steve shivered. He heard Jeremy talking to him. *You told me about good luck, Stevie. Remember? We've got it. Don't worry about the bike.*

Stevie flexed his shoulders around inside his jacket, shaking off the chill and stared at the stars. *Okay, Jeremy, okay.*

He chose another tombstone and marched forth again on his trek through the cemetery. A sudden gust of wind blasted across the cemetery. An imperceptible movement to his left caught Steve's eyes, and he sensed that something was coming for him. He screamed and raced for a tall tombstone with a cross on its top. The knife fell out of his hand, and he dropped the water gun as he hurled himself into the air, grabbing the cross with his right hand. He glanced behind himself while he pushed himself up the tombstone. Nothing. Steve ceased clambering up the tombstone and let himself slide to the ground as his eyes searched the surrounding area.

There's nothing. What was it? What scared me? He scanned the area again, but all he saw were the grave markers and their shadows. *I don't even see a piece of trash blowing around. What is happening to me?*

Minutes dragged by, but Steve resisted moving from the spot. It unnerved him to comprehend that he had been so frightened by a breeze.

Jeremy, we are so alone in here. I've got to get to you. I feel like I am coming unglued. I am trying my best to make this. He located his knife and water gun and set out anew.

The strongest urge to run for the fence and flee, twisted his mind even more. Steve halted. *You would never understand, would you, if I don't do this?*

"Listen to me, Jeremy, I am going to get there. Believe me, I am going to make it."

He arrived at a knoll overlooking the cemetery drive. *If I can cross the driveway here and get behind the hill on the other side of the driveway, I'll almost be there and hidden from the dogs. I won't be coming toward them, and they won't be able to catch my scent.*

I'd be safer if I went farther to the north and made a wider arc. If I cross the road here, the dogs might happen to look my way and see me. I know I wouldn't be visible to them for more than a few seconds, but if they sense me, they're going to come after me.

"What to do?"

Steve sniffed the ammonia, fiddled with the trigger of his gun and stepped forward toward the road. He inspected the ground carefully with each step, trying to avoid stepping on a twig and making a noise.

If you dogs want me, come and get me. I guarantee you, I'll shoot you in your faces before you get me.

When he reached the driveway, the caretakers' building came into view. A dim light on the front wall of the building illuminated one of the dogs sitting on its haunches, staring at the moon. The other dog was not in sight. It must be there somewhere, Steve reckoned. *You know what, that dog hasn't budged from gaping at the moon, and the other dog must be sleeping. I'm going to stay on the driveway.* He quickened his pace away from the building. In a few minutes, the caretakers' building was no longer in view, and he was standing a hundred feet or so away from his best friend's grave.

It's so desolate in here, Jeremy. You're in here all alone. His heart felt heavier and heavier as he got closer. Steve sank to his knees on top of Jeremy's grave, his eyes fixed on his tombstone.

"Oh, Jeremy."

The knife fell from his left hand. He dropped the water gun to the ground and took off the glove. Stevie placed his hands on the cold stone and read the inscription:

JEREMY WILCAMP
AUGUST 20, 1944–OCTOBER 2, 1958

Steve wrapped his arms around the tombstone as far as they could reach and hugged it. He put his face against it and kissed it.

"Why? Why?" Steve ran his fingertips over Jeremy's name and the dates. Minutes passed, but time did not matter to Stevie anymore. After a long while, he removed the sleeping bag and sat on Jeremy's grave, leaning his back against the stone.

"Let my warmth go in there to you, Jeremy. Feel my body here next to you." Steve leaned his head back and rested it on the tombstone. "If only I could bring you back."

Jeremy, you won't believe this, but getting here was the toughest thing I ever did in my life. I've never been so afraid. You know why? Because you weren't with me. You were gone. I knew it when I saw the dogs. I've never been so alone as when I watched them coming up that hill.

You know something, maybe the reason I was never afraid when I roped you into doing something that might be dangerous was that I knew I had to protect you. I couldn't let myself be afraid.

Jeremy, did I scare you the same way this cemetery scared me? Did I make you go through things that you were afraid of, but you did them because of me? Were you frightened all the time because I got you into things you would never do on your own? I didn't mean for it to be that way. If I put you through the same kind of horror that I just went through, I would feel so bad. Please, tell me somehow.

Tell me that you knew we were playing. You knew we were having fun. Tell me it was okay. Jeremy, I can't stand this. I see everything we ever did. Did you hate me? Were you afraid of me? No, no, you couldn't have been? I can sense things like that, especially in you.

Steve got to his feet and stared somberly at Jeremy's grave. He fell to his knees in front of the tombstone.

Then why did I let this happen to you? I was so sure that you were safe in that basement. If only I could have been there with you. I should have known.

Steve was overwhelmed. The pain in his heart and mind was crippling. He laid down on Jeremy's grave and rested his head on his folded forearms facing Jeremy's tombstone.

"Jeremy, I was afraid that if we went out of the altar boys' room and Brad and his goons came after us, I wouldn't be able to protect us. I didn't think I was big enough or strong enough to do it, even with my knife. We had to use our brains and not our bodies to outsmart those guys. If they ever got to you, or if they got my knife away from me and had both of us, I don't know what I could have done.

"I couldn't stand for that. I would never allow us to be caught and held helpless by a bunch of bullies. We're free birds. We can't be caught."

Steve wondered if Jeremy could possibly be listening to him from heaven or wherever he was. *Yes, somehow, you know I'm here, don't you Jeremy?*

You must have wondered why I thought I could get Carl and Mickey out, but not you. They wanted you. They thought you were afraid of them, and they wanted to play with that. Brad hated our friendship. I had no idea of it until he attacked you in the bathroom. If I had known, I would have beat the shit out of him a long time ago. It's so ugly. So stupid. So unnecessary. Why did any of this ever have to happen?

"I was wrong, Jeremy. I felt it when I saw you on the basement floor. You were as free a spirit as I am. You weren't going to be caught either."

We should have stayed together. We would have fought and bit and scratched and clawed. Whatever it took. You as much as told me before we went into the meeting. You were ready to go for them. Why didn't I see it that way? I thought it was me who was going to get mauled, Jeremy, but I had my knife. My whole plan was to lead them away from you.

You should have been safe. God, the least you could have done was let it be me.

Steve lay silent on the grave for a long time. Finally, he lifted his face up from his forearms and focused on the tombstone.

Why am I asking you this stuff, Jeremy? Of course, we were the best friends. I can hear you laughing and see your face lighting up with a smile every time we got together. You weren't afraid. We loved doing things together.

But being alone. Not having you. That's so hard. It's impossible. It hurts like you can't imagine. I miss you. How am I ever supposed to make it without you?

Time passed, and the moon and stars traveled in their nightly course over Lorraine Park Cemetery. Steve unfurled his sleeping bag on top of Jeremy's grave and crawled into it. He put the picture on the ground next to him and lay on top of Jeremy's grave.

He reached out and picked up his Swiss Army knife and held it in his hands over his chest. He opened the longest blade of his knife. He rolled the knife with his fingertips and fixed his eyes on the steel blade as it glistened in the moonlight.

"Jeremy, I'm going to think it to you. If you're in heaven, open your mind to me. I am going to think it like I never thought anything else in my life. I am so sorry. We were the best friends, and we always will be."

Steve unzipped his jacket and unbuttoned his shirt over his chest. He held the knife in his left hand and ran the fingertips of his right hand over his chest seeking a spot where his heart beat the strongest. He placed the tip of the longest blade over that spot. He held the knife firmly in his fists over his heart.

"Jeremy," he whispered, as he felt his heart beating under the knife blade, "please, be listening." "Please, hear me. Hear me, if you can. I never meant anything more than this in my entire life. If I could change places with you, if it could have been me, if I could bring you back, I would do all of it."

He clasped the knife tighter in his fists and closed his eyes. The sharp tip of the blade was biting into the skin of his chest as it rose with a deep breath and the muscles of his hands and arms tensed. But he stopped. He heard a noise. He opened his eyes and raised himself up on his elbows. Someone was riding down the drive on a bicycle.

"It's got to be Dad. It's Dad. He found my bicycle."

Then he heard his father calling him. Steve dropped his knife, opened the sleeping bag, sprung to his feet, and raced toward his father.

"Dad."

His father flung the bike down and ran toward him. Father and son met and held each other as tightly as ever two people could hold one another.

Mr. Stockton took Stevie's face into his hands.

"Stevie, are you all right?"

"Oh, Daddy," Stevie cried, "I don't know what to do. I've got to do it. I've got to do something. Jeremy can't be gone for no reason. Just for nothing. Oh, Daddy," Steve buried his face in his father's shoulder. "Daddy, it's my fault. I know it is. It doesn't even matter about fault. I've got to go with him."

Mr. Stockton brought Stevie's face next to his and whispered in his ear, "I know, Stevie. I know."

He lifted Stevie up into his arms and walked towards Jeremy's grave, carrying his son.

Steve put his right arm around his father and rested his head on his father's arm. He stopped crying. It was what his father had said. It rumbled around inside Steve's head. *I know, Stevie, I know. That's what Dad said. He knows that I have to kill myself.*

Steve repeated it in his mind. *That doesn't make sense.* That was not what he thought his father might say. *Wouldn't he be telling me no? No, I don't have to kill myself?*

"I can walk, Dad. You don't have to carry me."

"It's okay, Stevie. I can still do it. I want to hold onto you right now."

He sat Stevie down and gently leaned his back against the tombstone. Mr. Stockton took off his jacket and wrapped it around Stevie's shoulders. He brushed Steve's light brown hair out of his face and peered into his deep blue eyes that tears had made sparkle in the moonlight. Father and son sat in silence on top of Jeremy's grave.

Mr. Stockton saw Steve's shirt unbuttoned and the Swiss Army knife laying on the ground with the longest blade opened. He then looked at Steve, who leaned against the tombstone staring back at him. He saw the blood-soaked bandage wrapped around Steve's hand and noted the peculiar way Steve held the hand, but he said nothing, even though he knew that the hand hurt.

Steve noticed mud and pine needles on his father's shoes. The scratch marks on his father's face and hands that had to have come from the branches of mighty pine trees slapping his father, jolted Steve. *You've been all over the grove searching for me, haven't you, Dad?* Steve fought back an urge to burst out crying.

He wanted to tell his father something, but he wasn't sure of what it was. Maybe it was a lot of things, but Steve did not have the energy or the words.

The silence was becoming overwhelming to Mr. Stockton. He wanted his son to talk, to cry, to let it go, but Steve resisted. A terrifying feeling took hold of Mr. Stockton. An intense fear shook his insides. The spot of blood on Steve's shirt, over his heart, seized Mr. Stockton's mind. How unbelievably close it had been.

Stevie wasn't questioning or debating taking his life. He was in the act of doing it. What if I had been a few minutes later? He felt weak but straightened his back and shook it off.

Mr. Stockton's eyes traveled from the spot of blood to the open knife blade on the ground and then back to his son's eyes. The calm that shone on his son's face, belied the inner confusion.

It was maddening. *Stevie has spoken. He has said all that he has to say. He's exhausted, and he has no more to give. That's why he is here. That's why the knife is the way it is. And now, he wants me to look and see and accept. I can't let him discover how scared to death I am. I've got to find strength and give it to him.*

Mr. Stockton picked up the knife and placed it in Steve's right hand with the blade still open. He closed Steve's fingers around the knife handle, raised his hand to his lips, and kissed it.

"Stevie, I didn't come here to stop you from what you were planning to do. If you are going to do this, I am going to do it right along with you."

Steve's eyes sparkled, and he bolted upright from the tombstone, wanting to speak.

But his father's hand went up. "No, no, Stevie. Don't. Don't, because, you see, I don't know any more than you do what's the best thing to do. I know, more than you will ever believe, how much this hurts. I know, Stevie."

The jet darkness of the night, the lonely, eerie cemetery surrounding them, the stars shining above, Jeremy, so young, lying in the ground beneath them, so many things cut through the years that separated these two. They were no longer only father and son. In that moment, they were something more. Perhaps they were best friends, or perhaps, Mr. Stockton wanted to be Stevie's best friend, if his son would allow him.

"Stevie," Mr. Stockton spoke with tenderness, "somehow, you know I can feel it, don't you? I always intended to keep it hidden from you, but you sensed it all, didn't you? You perceived that something deep and wrong hurts me and lives with me. You must have. I never kept one thing, not one picture, not one record, nothing from the army. I never wanted you to know.

"When I finished my time in the army, I took everything that I had of the war and the army and threw it away. If there had ever been another war and the government wanted you in their army, we would have left the country. I vowed to never let you go where I had been forced to go.

"When I came home after being in the Army, I told your mother to never talk about it or even ask me about it. I told her the same thing only one other time in our married life. That was when I held you, my baby boy, in my arms for the first time. I couldn't take my eyes off your little face or put you down. I never wanted to let you go, and I swore you were never going into their wars.

"Stevie, how could this ever have happened? You've been through as bad a battle in the last three days as any I ever fought." Mr. Stockton reached across the grave, wrapped his arms around his son and hugged him.

After a few moments, he let go of Stevie.

"Stevie, do you want to know how long it takes to be a best friend in the army? One look. One look between you and another soldier just before the battle or anytime during the battle. In that moment, when you feel death and battle and destruction all around you, and it's all so senseless, but you're there with some other guy or bunch of fellows, there is a friendship and a kinsmanship like no other.

"It doesn't matter where they came from or how far apart you've been all your lives. You're best friends. That look goes through all of them. It doesn't know time or place. Help me. Protect me. Don't leave me. Because I am here with you. I am not going to leave you. There is no army now. There is no government now. There is no God now. It's us and the battle.

"Stevie, so many times they died next to me. Sometimes, in my arms. I could do nothing. I tried, Stevie. But there was no way to change it. Their body took the bullet I missed. I never got nicked. There's not one bullet hole in my body to help with that hurt. Nothing helps that pain, Stevie. Not God. Not country. Not religion.

Nothing. I came to believe that soldiers on the battle front where I was, fought hardest to keep each other alive.

"I watched the Wilcamps this morning at church. It was so barren, so empty. It was too late to have feelings. Too late to care. No matter what those priests said or did on the altar, the Wilcamps will never be forgiven. They had fourteen years with a beautiful son, and they couldn't love him."

Mr. Stockton paused, looked down at the ground and then back to his son.

"And so, you see, Stevie, I can't sit here and tell you to accept it, because God wanted it that way and that it's a part of some divine plan where everything is right, no matter how wrong. I don't know what God and religion are about, but they don't help the hurt. They can never take away the pain I saw on all those faces surrounding me in battle, any more than you will ever forget Jeremy. Nothing can explain why. Why we were there. Why it had to happen. The same way that nothing will ever explain why this had to happen to you and Jeremy.

"Stevie, I wanted to die. I prayed that the bullet or bomb would come and end it all. I didn't think that I could do it anymore. But it didn't happen, and I had to go on. Finally, I came home."

Steve listened to his father in silence.

"The sole reason for why I am here, is that I didn't die. It didn't happen to me. I lived. I don't know why. Maybe I was smarter, or stronger, or just plain lucky.

"Killing myself wasn't the right answer. Somebody should remember those guys. They mustn't die in vain. Their deaths must come to mean something to someone. To give purpose and direction to those who survived. There was so much in all of them that didn't want to die. They all wanted to live. They all had dreams. They were filled with hope and desire.

"In the middle of all that hell was something so beautiful. Something so worthwhile. Some excellence that only humans have, Stevie. Something that's got nothing to do with God or government or whatever the war was about. It was friendship, Stevie. It was love. It was best friends like you and Jeremy."

Mr. Stockton took his son into his arms and whispered, "Stevie, if best friends die this way, something so beautiful is lost. The human being is gone."

"Stevie, listen to me now. I can't tell you that it's a worthwhile thing for you to go on and try life again. That is something for you to work out. Maybe you and Jeremy don't belong in a world where there must be a war before people can be best friends.

"It stuns me Steve. Here we are putting you kids into a place where we think you will be protected, and sheltered, and never find out what really happens until you are old enough to understand—a Catholic grammar school. Those nuns would never have allowed this to happen if they could have seen it coming. Kids your age shouldn't have to know. You should never have experienced what you have been through. How can you possibly understand? I want so much for you to believe that you should go on, Stevie. You should carry Jeremy with you. Let his life be in you. Keep that love within you. It will grow, and it will do good, and it will make you smile again.

"I went on, Stevie, and you were born. You're the best kid a dad ever had. But, Stevie, you're you, and you have as much of life in you as I have. The best reason I can give you for getting up from here and trying again is that you lived through this thing. You're alive, and so, you must go on." Mr. Stockton took Stevie's hand in his.

"If it's not enough reason for you, I'll understand. I am going to leave you now, and I am going back to the entrance of the cemetery and wait until daybreak."

Mr. Stockton wanted to grab his son, hug him and kiss him, take him up in his arms, and run home as fast as possible. But he held it all back. He leaned over and gave Stevie the softest kiss on his lips and ran a hand through Stevie's hair. Mr. Stockton stood up. He reached down and put a hand on Stevie's shoulder as he was about to get up also.

"No, Steve. You stay here. This is your decision. You think it out as best you can. Take as much time as you want. Whatever you do, I'll always love you, and you can never do anything wrong as far as your Daddy is concerned. I'll be waiting on the other side. If you don't come, I will know what it means, and I'll come back. And the three of us, you, me and Jeremy, will all meet again."

Mr. Stockton started toward the cemetery driveway.

"Dad, there's two Doberman Pinschers down there."

"Don't you worry about those Dobermans anymore, Stevie. They're howling to a different master now."

It was the hardest thing Mr. Stockton had ever done to hold himself in control, say that to his son, smile once more, and then disappear into the darkness, leaving his son behind. The only thing which allowed him to put one foot in front of the other was the thought that if his son killed himself, he was going to do it also with the same knife in his own heart with his son's blood on it. *Maybe, if he does it, his last thought will be that he is going to meet up with his best friend, and his dad will soon join them.*

* * *

Steve held the opened knife in his hand, watching his father walk out into the night. He closed the blade and got to his knees, facing Jeremy's tombstone.

"Jeremy, I can't do this now. Not like this. You understand, don't you? I can't hurt Dad like this. I'll try real hard for as long as I can. You're going with me, Jeremy. You're going with me everywhere, all the time, like Dad said. I hope that wherever you are, something of me goes along with you. It would be so great if only we could share it, wouldn't it? I'm going to try, Jeremy. I hope you can do it too."

Steve placed his right hand on the edge of Jeremy's tombstone and gently moved it back and forth across the edge. He leaned over and kissed Jeremy's name.

"Listen, I'll be back tomorrow. I'll bring my homework, and we can do it together. See you then."

Steve rolled up the sleeping bag. He put his knife in his pocket, shoved the water gun and picture into the sleeping bag and fastened it across his shoulders. He put on his glove and raced up to his bike. At the top of the hill, he paused and gazed back toward the grave once more, but the darkness hid it from view. Steve kissed his fingertips and blew the kiss toward the grave and pedaled off down the drive.

His father sat in the driveway on the other side of the hill. Steve got off the bike, let it fall to the ground, and ran for his father. He leaped into his father's waiting arms. They held each other in a tight embrace.

"Stevie, thank you so much. There's no way I can ever put into words how much you mean to your mother and me." He hugged his son tightly and kissed him. They walked back to the bike with Steve's dad wrapping an arm around his son's shoulders.

Mr. Stockton got on the bike seat and had Steve sit on the frame in front of him. As he headed the bike down the drive, he asked Stevie, "How fast should I take it?"

Steve smiled. "As fast as you can, Dad."

"Okay."

"Dad stop."

They stopped, and Mr. Stockton asked Steve what was wrong.

"Look on top of the gate. What is that, Dad?"

"That, Steve, is a Doberman Pinscher."

"How did you do that?"

"Tricks of the trade, Stevie." The dog had been impaled on one of the bars of the gate.

"Where's the other one?"

"He managed to crawl under the rear porch of the building before I could finish him off. It's doubtful that he'll be chasing anybody for quite a while if he survives, but even if he could, he won't be coming near me. No way I was going to let those dogs get to you once I saw them. I didn't want to do something like that, but when it comes to a couple of cemetery hound dogs or my son, it's good-bye dogs.

"I was afraid they had gotten to you, but I knew my son was smarter than a couple of dogs. It didn't do any good to think otherwise."

Steve grinned at his Dad.

Mr. Stockton climbed up on the stone pillar on the right side of the entrance. He hoisted the bike over first, and then he lifted Stevie up to the top of the pillar. They both sat there.

"Steve, what did you do with Brad?"

Steve's shoulders slumped, his head drooped, and he felt as if he was going to burst out into tears. His dad had to know. Steve understood. This was not the time to cry. It was his father's call for responsibility. With as much courage as he could muster, he answered his father.

"You know where that fire hydrant is on Montclair Street by the grove?"

"Yeah, I know where it is."

"He's across from the fire hydrant. I covered him up with leaves and pine cones and pine needles and whatever loose dirt I could scrape up."

Mr. Stockton immediately decided that he had to get Steve home and go back and give Brad a burial somewhere in the grove where nobody would ever find him, or even look for him.

He stared at Steve quizzically. "Stevie, isn't Brad the kid who ran away from home last year?"

"Yeah, Dad," Steve nodded in agreement and wondered if that had some importance. "As a matter of fact, that's how he got to be in Jeremy's and my class. Brad missed three weeks from school because of that caper, and Sister Sullpicia refused to allow him to graduate. Brad had to repeat the eighth grade, and he ended up in our class. Guess how the cops found him?"

"I have no idea Steve."

"The story I heard was that he went to Ocean City with a couple of high school kids who had a car and, apparently, there is some way you can jam a soda machine by pouring ocean water into the coin slot. When you do that, the machine will keep giving you a soda every time you pull a lever.

"Brad and those guys got caught robbing a soda machine. Supposedly, they had the trunk of the car filled with soda bottles. One of those guys was Denny Schermer. He dropped out of high school sometime after they got caught."

"Well, you know what, Stevie, after all that has happened, there's a strong possibility that everybody might believe Brad ran away again, especially since he had all those high school guys helping him. Any one of them with a car could have gotten him to Ocean City again. It might be a long time before anybody seriously considers anything else."

Mr. Stockton detected a degree of relief and relaxation in his son as Stevie considered the possibility that people might believe that Brad ran away.

"Yeah, Dad. You know what, I was thinking about the same thing earlier today when Brad came walking up Montclair Street after school. Not the way you're thinking about it. I thought he wished he was somewhere else."

"Stevie, it wouldn't surprise me if Brad's parents aren't the first ones to suggest that Brad ran away. They might even be hoping he ran away."

"Do you think anyone suspects anything, Dad?"

"There wasn't a word about any of this on the evening news. Nobody from school or the police have questioned us."

"Could someone have seen you, Stevie?"

"No, Dad. You can be sure that no one saw us."

Steve's remark puzzled his father. "How can you be so sure?"

"Dad, you know about good luck, don't you? Jeremy and I, we've got it. That's how I know nobody saw us."

Steve and his Dad's eyes met with solemn faces. Mr. Stockton nodded to his son. He hopped down off the stone pillar and reached his arms up to Stevie. Stevie leaned forward, and Mr. Stockton put his hands under Steve's arms and lowered him to the ground. He wrapped his arms around Steve's shoulders, put his right hand behind Steve's head and brought his son's head to his chest, kissing him.

Almost instinctively, they both faced the cemetery one final time. Neither said a word, but both were thinking that they couldn't believe they had to leave Jeremy behind. They went home.

CHAPTER 22
THOSE TWO WERE TOGETHER
ALL THE TIME

Three days later, Steve was awakened in the middle of the night by a dream. His nightshirt was damp with perspiration, and he felt hot. He sat up in bed letting his eyes adjust to the darkness. All he could remember from the dream was that he heard Jeremy's voice calling him. His voice seemed hollow, empty. There was no emotion, no feeling. Stevie could not tell if Jeremy was happy or sad, if he was afraid or in trouble and needed help…nothing. The sound disturbed him. He didn't know what to make of the dream.

Stevie, he told himself, *it's only a dream. It's not Jeremy. After all that has happened, you've got to expect to have dreams and nightmares. So, face up to it and get used to it. It's probably not going to stop for a long time. And if it is Jeremy, be glad that you're hearing something that sounds like him.*

"Oh, my God, Jeremy. I'm so sorry. I can't believe you're gone." *I don't want to wake up and know we're not going to get together and do something. You're not here. I've got nothing. Nobody, other than Mom and Dad. They can't go to school with me and do any of the stuff that you and I do. Dad says I should carry you along with me, and remember you, and that will make me happy and make me smile again.*

"I love you, Dad. I love you so much, but it isn't happening." *I feel sad all the time. All I want to do is sit here and cry. I miss Jeremy. I don't know what to do. I don't want to do anything. Dad, that therapist you and Mom sent me to isn't going to help me. I know what he's going to say. I'll sit there in his office and make believe I'm all happy and cured so he leaves me alone. He wants to give me some pill that makes me feel like a zombie. Some medicine that messes with my mind so I can't remember and can't feel what I felt when I was with Jeremy. I'm not taking that medicine.*

"Dad, you and Mom are desperate to help me. Please, believe me. I know what you are trying to do, and I love you for it and for everything you have done for me." *But I don't want to forget. I don't want to move on and start over, especially when it means taking pills.*

Steve grabbed a pair of socks out of his dresser and sat on his bed. The sounds of his father snoring, coming from his parents' bedroom, reassured him.

"Dad," Stevie whispered, "please, don't wake up now. You and Mom haven't had a good nights' sleep in a long time. You keep waking up and checking on me."

Mr. Stockton had taken a leave of absence from work, and he and Stevie's mother had been with Stevie every moment of every day since Mr. Stockton had brought Stevie home from the cemetery.

I understand everything you are telling me, Dad, and I believe it. And I know how much you and Mom love me, but it's my fault. What those guys did to Jeremy can never forgive me for my part in what happened. My whole plan was to lead them away from Jeremy, and I didn't do that. I put Jeremy in the basement. I made him promise to wait for me there. He trusted me, Dad. He believed in me, and I failed him.

I used Jeremy's and my friendship to force him to stay in that basement instead of letting him use his own judgement. I should have told him that if it got late and I hadn't shown up, he should get out of the basement and go into the grove. But I was so sure that he would be safe in the basement. If I hadn't made him promise me, Dad, he would have gotten out of that basement. I know he would have come looking for me. There's no way I can ever forgive myself for doing that to Jeremy.

Stevie tried to see himself in the mirror on his dresser, but his bedroom was too dark. He was so close to breaking.

No, Dad, there's no way out. I don't want a way out. I didn't protect the best friend anybody could ever have wanted. My best friend. The best friend I will ever have. This is the only way. So, please, Dad, stay sleeping. Don't wake up. I miss Jeremy so much. I've got to be with him, Dad.

Despite the darkness, Steve dressed quickly, put on his jacket, and grabbed his Swiss army knife from the top of his dresser. In the hall outside his bedroom, he stopped and stared into is parents' bedroom. He wanted to scream. He wanted to cry out for help, but nothing had helped so far. Nothing could replace Jeremy. No one could sense the immense hole in Stevie's existence, unless they had suffered through what Stevie had suffered, and their best friend had been violently torn away from them and sacrificed, and they were fourteen years old. Stevie listened to his father snoring.

"Oh, Dad."

He kissed his fingertips, blew the kiss toward his parents' bedroom, tiptoed down the stairs, and went to the back door. Once he was outside the house, he closed the door enough to hold it in place without allowing the latch to snap shut. Steve got his bike out of the garage and pedaled toward Lorraine Park Cemetery.

Steve pedaled furiously, not allowing himself to think or question. He had been over it too many times. His dad had stopped him the first time. Steve did not plan on that happening on this night.

"I am not crying tonight, Jeremy. I'm coming. Nothing is going to stop me."

When he arrived at the cemetery, he placed his bike against the fence, stood on the bike frame, climbed the fence, and plummeted into the cemetery. *No problem this time, Jeremy.* He rose to his feet, got out his Swiss Army knife, opened the longest blade, and searched the darkness. Nothing moved. The stillness of the cemetery was eerie. Steve zipped his jacket up to his neck and flexed his shoulders trying to chase the chill away.

"If whoever owns this place has gotten any new dogs in here, they should've sniffed me by now, Jeremy. The wind is coming from my back. Dogs should have picked up my scent."

What is it with people running cemeteries? Gates locked, no lights, wild dogs roaming around at night scaring people. Don't they know you don't stop caring just because it's nighttime? I can't be the first person who had to come back.

"If more dogs are out there, Jeremy, I'll kill them, like my Dad did."

Steve ran for Jeremy's grave. He raced by the caretakers' building without checking to see if there were any new dogs. At the top of the next hill beyond the caretakers' building, he stopped to catch his breath.

Without speaking a word, or thinking a thought, he walked the rest of the way to Jeremy's grave. Steve knelt in front of Jeremy's tombstone. He rubbed his right hand along an edge of Jeremy's tombstone as he had before, leaned forward, and kissed his name.

In silence, he lay on top of his best friend's freshly dug grave. It was a beautifully clear night. Thousands of stars were visible. He unzipped his jacket and unbuttoned his shirt. He grasped the knife handle of his Swiss Army knife. After a few moments, he put the knife down and scooched back to Jeremy's tombstone and leaned his back against the stone.

"Mom…Dad…It isn't like I love Jeremy more than I love you. I love all three of you with everything I've got. Dad, do you remember how you told me that I am everything to you and Mom? Well, you and Mom and Jeremy are everything to me. If I can't have all of you, then I just can't be. I don't want to be.

"I don't want to hurt you, but you two will still have each other. I'm lost without Jeremy. We did everything together. I feel like I've got nothing. It's tearing me apart. I must find him. If there really is a heaven, Jeremy will be there. I'm sure of it. And I'll find him there.

"I believe in God the way you do, Dad. God isn't going to send me to hell for loving Jeremy. And if God does do that, I don't care. That means that someday you and I will be together in hell.

"Mom and Dad, I don't know what else to do. I can't go on without Jeremy. I just can't. Dad, in the cemetery, you said you were going to kill yourself if I killed myself. Please, don't kill yourself over this. You must take care of Mom. You two are so happy together. I'll be in heaven and there must be ways in which I can be with you and Mom from there. I will do that Dad. I promise. I will."

Stevie lay on top of Jeremy's grave again. He picked up his Swiss Army knife. Stevie found the same spot on his chest where his heart beat the strongest and placed the longest blade on that spot as he had done three nights earlier.

"Jeremy, I'm coming. Please, be waiting for me when I get there. Please, be there."

Stevie plunged the knife into his heart with all his strength.

"Oh, my God. This hurts. Oh, my God…"

Stevie writhed around on top of Jeremy's gravesite before coming to rest. He was aware of the pain subsiding and of his hands falling limply off the knife handle.

He stared up at the stars, searching for Jeremy.

Made in United States
North Haven, CT
14 July 2022

21254286R00189